The Awakener

Amanda Strong

Clean Teen Publishing

Mattie
We loved coming to
your school today!
Always believe in yourself
and your "Captain"!
Miracles can happen!

Amanda E Strong

Content Disclosure

For more information about our content disclosure, please utilize the QR code above with your smart phone or visit us at
www.cleanteenpublishing.com.

For my husband, Josh,
You caught the vision of this book
And helped me run with it!

Chapter One

A locker clanged behind Eden just as someone shoved her elbow, knocking the folder from the crook of her arm. Papers flew from the pockets, fluttering to the ground, and then kicked along by the sea of teenagers.

"Oh geez, sorry," a boy said over his shoulder. He was gone before she could even tell what color his hair was. She stooped, retrieving her class schedule, school map, emergency contact sheet, and other forms from the office for her parents to sign and return. Straightening up, she glanced one last time at her schedule before tucking it in her jeans pocket. *First trig- and then Biology.* On second thought, she pushed the map into her pocket too. *Just in case. Bon Air High's a lot bigger than Portsmouth.*

"Hey, watch it, man," a boy crowed. Two boys began scuffling and, anxious to avoid having her belongings knocked to the floor again, she quickened her pace. As much as she wanted to blend in, standing inches above those around her made it difficult. Avoiding eye contact, she maneuvered through the crowd, determined to reach her destination. She couldn't help but notice how plain her white Keds were compared to the fuzzy, knee-length boots on the two girls in front of her. The giggling girls reached their lockers, and the view in front of Eden temporarily cleared.

She bit the inside of her cheek, the instinct to duck behind the two girls intense. Spine tingling with adrenaline, she pushed her glasses up. Down the corridor, sandwiched between two girls and a guy, was her childhood best friend, Micah. Though no longer a lanky boy, she still recognized his light blue eyes. The mop of black hair he had as a kid was now short, a little longer than a buzz. Eden was drawn to his smile, even if it was meant for the blonde girl at his side. A good foot shorter than him, the girl craned her neck up as she wrapped an arm around his waist. *Has to be his girlfriend.* A stocky, jock-type boy with chestnut-brown hair and a tan girl with jet-black hair stood next to them. The jock slugged Micah's shoulder as his bellowing laugh made its way down the hall to Eden.

Then the scene was gone as jeans and a myriad of different colored t-shirts blocked her view. She sucked in a deep breath, her lungs burning from holding it too long. Sweat was beading at the top of her forehead as she prayed she could pass Micah's entourage unnoticed. *If I can't see him, he can't see me either, right?* She hoped.

The staircase loomed nearer. *I'm going to make it,* she thought, wishing the kids in front of her would move faster.

"No way, dude. Coach always gives you the ball, Micah," a male voice boomed.

Eden glanced over. Micah's group was directly left of her now.

He hasn't noticed me, just keep moving, she told herself.

Face ducked down, she lifted her leg up, only to have her foot land sideways and to the left. Her weight uneven, she feared toppling over, but a pressure on her left side held her up. Confused, she again attempted to move away, only this time, her body made a ninety-degree turn, bringing her a foot away from the blonde girl.

Horrified, Eden's legs stepped one in front of the other, heading straight towards Micah. Within seconds, she stood dead center, stopping his small group of friends short. Sky-blue eyes swam in front of her vision before she was lunging forward, throwing her arms around his neck, hugging him.

Funny the things you notice in a moment of sheer humiliation, she thought, as time dropped into neutral, prolonging her torture.

There was a hiss-like sound from the short blonde. *Yep, definitely his girlfriend.*

A male was chuckling. *Not Micah. Must be the jock.*

Arms wrapped around her, hugging her back. *Oh my gosh!*

She shifted her weight back, trying to detangle herself from Micah's arms. Pulling her face away from his neck, the memory of his scent automatically tucked away in her mind, she met Micah's raised brow line, wide eyes, and even wider grin.

"Eden? Is that you?" he asked, as they separated further.

Aware his hands still held her forearms, she was forced to remain and maintain eye contact. She nodded, terrified to speak.

"Wow! How the heck are you? It's been forever!" Though *his* face appeared delighted, she couldn't help but notice how *un-delighted* his girlfriend was, as her amber eyes glared up at her.

Unfazed, Micah continued, "My dad told me your dad got hired on at his firm. That's awesome! So, did you guys move back then?"

Again she nodded, hoping Micah would realize he was still holding onto her. *What's wrong with me? Running up and hugging him!*

"What's it been four, five years?" he asked.

Deciding his friends might think her a mute, she answered, "Five." Her mouth was so dry her upper lip got caught on one of her braces as she spoke. She licked her lips, pulling her mouth shut.

Micah didn't seem to notice but the tan girl did and smirked.

"Yo, Micah, are you going to introduce us or what?" the big guy asked.

"Oh, yeah, sorry guys. This is Eden. We grew up next door to each other, best friends our whole lives." Micah's eyes danced with pleasure. He gestured to the jock. "This here's Chase, his girl Willow, and Megan," there was the slightest hesitation, "my girlfriend."

At the word *girlfriend*, Micah's blue eyes registered something and he released Eden's arms.

She gratefully let them drop to her sides. "Nice to meet you."

Willow cocked an eyebrow at her, her icy-blue eyes sweeping up and down Eden's frame as she twirled a lock of her black hair between two fingers. "Where'd you move from?" she asked.

Eden tried to answer under Willow's icy stare, but her voice cracked.

Micah jumped in. "Portsmouth, wasn't it? That's where your dad got work after—" he stopped, searched her face, and then glanced at his friends.

Oh gosh, he's embarrassed by me!

"I, I have to go, get to class," she said, sidestepping, tugging at her backpack.

Micah frowned. "Do you need any help? Know where you're going?"

Her eyes were stinging. *Not now, please not now.* She hated her overactive water works. She waved, saying, "Yeah, I'm good, thanks," and shuffled away.

"It's sweet you're back," Micah called out.

She peeked back. Megan was scowling at her from behind Micah.

"Yeah, see ya." She slipped into the throng of almost-tardy kids. She had barely ascended the steps and darted into the classroom when the bell shrilled.

Spying the only free seat on the opposite side of the room, she hurried across, aware of gawking eyes. In the second to last row, three seats back, she sank down into the chair, sliding her backpack to the floor.

"Mr. Giles's not going to like you, you know," a boy to her left leaned over and whispered.

She wanted to ignore him, but his emerald-green eyes were startling bright and so close.

"Whatever, Andrew," the redheaded girl to her right whispered.

"Ah-hum," the teacher coughed.

Eden snapped to attention.

"Are you a transfer student?" Mr. Giles asked, holding the roll in hand, his bald head reflecting the overhead lights.

"Yeah, from Portsmouth High."

"I need your *name*," Mr. Giles said, apparently not caring where she'd come from.

"Oh, sorry, Eden McCarthy."

"Ok, I assume you were given the right textbooks at the office. We're now halfway into the school year. You missed the final before Christmas break." There were a few grunts of 'so not fair' and 'lucky you'. Mr. Giles's stare silenced them. "I'll get you a syllabus at the end of class to get you up to speed."

She nodded, anxious for everyone's eyes to be elsewhere. Mr. Giles walked away, methodically taking roll.

"He's the worst teacher ever," the redheaded girl muttered.

Eden's face flushed, afraid the teacher might overhear.

"I'm Jessie, by the way," the girl said, offering a hand. "So, from Portsmouth, huh? Navy brat or something?"

"No, my dad switched jobs." She shook the proffered hand as inconspicuously as she could.

"So, where's your family's mansion?" Jessie asked.

"I, we don't live in one. I live in Sturbridge."

"A townhome baby like me." Jessie smiled. "We're neighbors."

She smiled back. "Really? Cool."

"I can tell I'm going to like you," Jessie announced, receiving a stern *shh* from Mr. Giles and snickers from other students.

Eden sunk deep into her seat, ready to be buried in her comfort zone of solving math equations.

Chapter Two

"So, what was up with you and that girl today?" Megan asked, hands on hips.

By the way she stood in front of the couch glaring down at him, Micah had one guess why he'd gotten the silent treatment the entire drive to his house after school. *She's upset about Eden still.* He sighed. "I already told you—she's my best friend. Or was," he added, seeing his girlfriend flinch. "Why are you being like this anyway? What's the big deal?"

Megan let out a short blast of air from her mouth, making a face at him. He hated when she did that; it really wasn't attractive.

"*What's the big deal?* Micah, you're leaving me in like two weeks!" Her voice hitched up in a hysterical sob.

Great, now everything's my fault because she's crying. He cringed..

"Sorry, Meg. I know you're upset I'm going," he soothed. He patted the seat cushion next to him. "Come here."

Pouting, she sank down beside him. She sniffed and then leaned her head against his chest. "Why do you have to leave? Just stay here with me." She sniffed again.

Irritated, he rehearsed the same lines over again. "My parents already paid for the semester. My cousin gets here next week. I'm only going to be gone three months."

"And you're probably going to flirt with every girl in Rome too, right?"

"Meg, don't you trust me at all?" Now he didn't hide his irritation.

"No, not after how you acted today with that Eden girl!"

Ironically, what was irking her was the same thing bothering him too. He'd been happy to discover the tall blonde bowling him over was Eden. His parents told him the McCarthy's were moving back to Bon Air and he'd been hoping he'd get to see his old friend again before leaving. What he hadn't counted on was how rude his friends would act.

"Yeah, about that. What was up with you guys today?" he asked.

Megan stared at him.

"You all acted like jerks," he reminded her.

Her eyes bulged. "I can't believe you're making this all about *her*. You're totally dodging it."

"Dodging what?"

"You were holding her arms like forever! I saw the way you looked at her. Don't even try to deny it!"

Micah threw up his hands. "Meg, really? Are you *that* jealous of Eden?"

"Yes, well, no... I don't know! So you swear you don't *like her* like her?"

"No more than Chase or any other of my friends. She's just a friend to me, I swear."

She smiled and then giggled. "Ok." She laid her cheek against his upper arm, too short to reach his shoulder. "Guess I just want you all to myself until you leave."

He moved his hand to the top of her head, brushing her hair back. Normally, he'd kiss her forehead or utter some reassuring nonsense, but not today. Since Megan was engrossed in the TV show, he let his eyes wander the living room. *Hard to believe I'm actually leaving.* With football done for the season, he didn't mind being gone the last half of his junior year. Megan minded.

Knowing his parents were out to dinner with friends, a movement in the front entry caught his eye. Rotating to get a better look, he disturbed Megan. She peered up at him.

"Sorry, I thought I saw—" He froze, staring.

Poised in the entryway, a woman appeared out of nowhere. Her pearly white skin contrasted with the form-fitted crimson gown she wore. Her face was beautiful: a straight nose, red full lips, and riveting, onyx eyes. Black hair reached the leather belt at her waist.

Megan spun around, searching the room. "Micah, saw what?"

His eyes flickered to Megan and then back to the woman in red. *She's breathtaking.* His jaw went slack, his mouth gaping open.

"What is it? Why won't you answer me?" There was panic in Megan's voice now, but he felt transfixed. The woman's lips slowly parted, opening. His breath caught, waiting for her to speak. Instead, her head inclined, her body bowing, and then she was gone. Disappearing into the nothingness she'd come from.

"Sorry," he said, exhaling, his shoulders slumping forward.

Megan was either going to cry or scream, he wasn't quite sure yet. "I thought I saw something," he explained.

"What? What'd you see?"

"Uh, nothing, really." It sounded lame. *I'm a terrible liar.*

"Nothing? You're totally freaking me out! That wasn't *nothing.*"

"Sorry," he repeated. He didn't know what else to say. *Man, I feel like I just did football drills.* He noted Megan's scowl. *I'm not sure I can handle her hysterics. I just saw a freaking ghost!* Somehow, he knew Megan would *not* be able to handle *that* truth.

"Sorry? You're sorry! I swear, Micah—"

"Megan, please. I just can't do this with you right now."

Her mouth snapped shut, her eyes narrowing.

When he remained quiet, she stood in a huff. "Fine, be that way. I'm going home."

He forced himself to his feet, but she was already storming from the room. *Do I even want to follow?*

"Meg, wait," he called, stepping after her.

"First the flirting and now this… I just can't take anymore." They were by the front door now. She whirled around, facing him. "Go to Rome and forget all about me." She jabbed a finger at his chest. "We're through, Micah!" She threw the door open and slammed it behind her, leaving Micah speechless.

Wow, didn't see that coming... Chase wasn't kidding about her being the jealous type. Feeling guilty, yet relieved she was gone, he returned to the couch, sinking down into its cushions. He kneaded his eyes with his knuckles before staring back at the entryway.

Who was that woman? he wondered. *Will she come back?*

Chapter Three

"Lacey Hawkins invited us over for dinner tomorrow night," her mom announced just as Eden threw popcorn into her mouth. Startled, she clamped down on a hard kernel. It lodged into her gums. *Ow...*

"That's great," her dad said, passing her mom the popcorn bowl.

Losing her appetite, Eden set her popcorn aside, only to have her younger brother, Brendon, take it. After the movie ended, she ran up to her bedroom and changed into her favorite boxer shorts and t-shirt before climbing into bed with a fantasy novel in hand. There was a soft knock at the door.

"Come in," she called. She already knew it was her mom. Brendon was thirteen and would never knock that softly, or even knock at all.

Beth McCarthy came into the room and sat at the end of the bed, wearing a fuzzy nightgown. One Eden was sure she'd prefer for her daughter to wear as well. Stretching her legs down into her covers, Eden knew she'd hate being twisted up in that during the night.

She set her book aside and waited.

"Sweetie, how are you doing? With the move and all?" her mom asked, her hazel eyes penetrating.

Eden knew what her mom really wanted to ask. *Are the kids teasing you again? Are you finding friends this time?*

When her dad's engineering firm went bankrupt, their family downsized, leaving their home next to the Hawkins to move into a small apartment two hours south. Her dad had found work as a water treatment engineer in the naval shipyards. Eden had been ten at the time and had never given any thought to popular verses unpopular. She'd only known Micah, her best friend. Hitting a growth spurt that left her lanky, and needing glasses as well as braces, changed everything. Receiving the brunt of jokes, she turned inward, escaping in books and academics.

"I'm fine."

"Are you sure? You haven't said much about your first week of school." Her mom tilted her head to the side, her dark brown curls framing her chin. Eden wished she'd gotten some of her mom's natural curls, but Brendon inherited that gene. Already taller than her mom and sharing the same blue-gray eyes as her dad, the only one thing she'd gotten from her mom was a wide smile.

"It's been great," she lied. Since running into Micah, she'd yet to see him the rest of the week at school, though she'd seen Megan one too many times, each time receiving a fake smile. She saw Willow and Chase less frequently, but it was equally uncomfortable. Being a sophomore, her locker was upstairs, along with most of her classes, but to get to trig, she had to cross the junior hall, the longest walk of her life. The only highlight so far was her new friendship with Jessie, who was indeed her neighbor, living two doors down.

Her mom continued to gaze at her. "Just know you can tell me anything and I mean anything, ok? I moved a lot as a kid and I know it's tough."

"Ok, thanks, Mom."

Her mom kissed the top of her head. "Good night, sweetheart."

"Night, Mom."

She left, closing the door behind her, and Eden stared at her bulletin board, counting the number of pushpins on it. She slid off her bed and began pacing back and forth.

I'm faking sick. There's no way I'm going tomorrow night. I'm almost sixteen, old enough to stay home by myself.

The ride over to the Hawkins was quiet as Eden pressed her face against the glass. *So much for faking sick.* Since she rarely was ill, she knew it'd look suspicious if she tried, and probably raise questions of why she wouldn't want to see Micah.

Surrounded by tall, arching trees, the highway was more like a tunnel of thick foliage pressing down on them. The sun was setting, dripping down from the sky like a magical paintbrush, smearing its hues across the trees. Then, as the sun sank beyond the horizon, the vibrant colors were gone, leaving the forest dark and ominous.

Eden shifted away from the window, goose bumps crawling down her arms. She saw the Ram's Gate sign as her dad slowed the car. This was the Hawkins's neighborhood, her old neighborhood. Memories flooded in her mind as lights pierced through the trees' silhouettes, the shadows of the night hiding the southern mansions tucked deep in the woods. They passed the Johnson's, the Moody's, the Myers—homes she knew well and had targeted with Micah for toilet papering on more than one occasion.

As the SUV veered right, her pulse quickened. The circular drive leading to the colonial estate with white wicker furniture on an oversized porch was all too familiar.

I cried so many times to come back here as a kid, she thought. *But Micah's not my partner in crime anymore. He's a stranger to me. His social life's a polar opposite to mine.* Obviously handsome and popular, he was ashamed of his nerdy friend's return.

The car stopped and she sighed, yanking the door handle back. *Guess I have no choice but to get this over with.*

Chapter Four

Micah knew it would end, it always did, at least so far, but it still terrified him. The black, scurrying bodies, hiding in the shadows with red, beady eyes glaring back at him. It was happening so frequently now that he could hardly sleep or eat. Loss of appetite and exhaustion had his mom keeping him home from school the past week, which was fine with him. He didn't know when the 'visions' would begin or end. The first time it'd occurred, his dad had been mid-sentence about a scout's interest in Micah for a possible football scholarship. One minute his dad was there, the next, Micah was running for his life in the forest, countless black creatures chasing after him.

It'd taken his dad shaking his shoulder to snap him back to their living room. Micah had tried to explain what'd happened but his dad had asked if he was using drugs. Stunned, he decided to keep his supernatural senses to himself after that. He knew his dad meant well. He had been the partying type in high school and had warned Micah as a kid to stay clean, which he had.

Relief flooded him. *The monsters are gone.* He was back in his dad's study. Heart thumping, he typed the word *demon*.

It was the only logical thing he could think of. What else could they be? As the computer page filled with definitions, classifications, and history of, the room brightened and warmed.

He glanced up, inhaling sharply. *She's back!*

Leaning over the desk, her black hair tumbled forward as her hand reached toward him. Eyes wide, he waited to see what she'd do. After seeing the dark creatures, he no longer feared her. In fact, he was almost happy she was there.

There was a tap-tap at the door, drawing Micah's eyes away long enough. The woman was gone, vanishing like she'd never been there.

Frustrated, Micah expected his dad or mom to enter, but it was Eden. Her eyes darted around and then landed on him.

"Your mom said to come get you." Her tone sounded apologetic.

"Oh hey," Micah said, still trying to compose himself. He found each vision left him physically drained. She hesitated in the doorway. "You can come in. I was just doing some," he paused, "research."

She stepped in, her expression hard to make out. Realizing the lights were off, and the natural light from the window was gone with the sunset over, he flicked on the floor lamp next to him. The light cast long shadows on the walnut bookshelves.

She chose one of the high-back leather chairs across from him, keeping her face pointed down at her intertwined fingers.

Micah considered her a moment, and then deleted his browsing history before his dad saw it. He turned off his laptop, shutting the few books he'd found referring to heaven and hell, and closing the leather-bound Bible he'd discovered on a bookshelf.

"So are you glad you're back?" he asked, rising to his feet and collapsing in the chair next to her. He wasn't sure why, but he hung onto the Bible.

She lifted her eyes briefly to his, before shifting them back to the floor. "Yeah, I guess. It's different."

"Different? So in other words, you hate it?"

She smiled, it was small, but he was glad to see it. "No," she answered. She peeked over. "Is it a good book?"

"Huh? Oh yeah this." He peered down at what was in his hands. He hadn't realized he'd been rubbing the spine with his palm. "As a matter-a-fact, it's The Good Book." When she didn't say anything, he explained, "You know, the Bible."

"Oh." Her eyebrows shot up.

"Guess you didn't peg me for the Bible-thumping type, huh?"

She giggled a little.

Guess not, he thought, smiling. Something about her quiet way made him open up. "Eden, have you ever wondered what it's all about?"

"What do you mean?"

"Life, religion, what's really out there." He spread one hand out, like he was feeling the air in the room.

"Yeah, I suppose I have. Why?"

He was tempted to tell her everything, hoping she'd believe him, but instead he said, "It's funny, my parents have always taught me to be good, you know, make good decisions and stuff, but now that I'm," he paused, not sure how to say it, "searching for my own truth, they're worried about me."

"They are? Why do you think?"

He snorted. "I don't know, maybe 'cause I'm not sleeping."

"That explains it."

"What?"

"The dark rings under your eyes. You didn't have them before, I mean, when I saw you at school..." Her words trailed off, her face growing pink.

"Oh yeah, hey about that, I'm sorry."

She shot him a glance. "Why are you sorry?" Her words were barely audible.

Man, she feels really bad, doesn't she?

"'Cause my friends were total jerks to you." He was glad to get it off his chest.

Her glasses slid down her nose, landing in her lap, and she fumbled to replace them. Without them, she reminded him of the girl he'd once known.

She slid them back on. "No, they weren't. They were fine."

"Whatever, now you're lying for the worthless sacks." He grinned, hoping to see another smile.

She giggled again, her blonde hair blocking her face from his view.

He noticed. "Your hair's gotten long."

"I know. My mom's dying for me to chop it off."

"What? No way, it's really pretty."

"Thanks." There was an awkward pause. "Oh, shoot. Your mom told me to get you for dinner. Wonder if they're already eating."

Always worried about obeying. Micah grinned. "All right, want to go?"

She nodded and he followed her, noticing for the first time how long and lean her legs were. It felt odd to realize her body was attractive. He cleared his throat. "How tall are you?"

She turned, pausing in the doorway. "Uh, five eight, maybe nine, I don't know, why?"

"It's not a bad thing; don't look so offended."

"I'm not." Her tone said otherwise.

Wonder why that struck a nerve? "It's nice not staring at the top of your head," he said honestly.

She cocked an eyebrow at him. "Huh?"

"Oh, never mind." He steered her by the shoulders. "Let's go get some dinner before Caleb eats it all."

Chapter Five

Sitting around the oblong dining table, the roll of laughter ebbed. Micah's parents hadn't aged a day to Eden. Lacey was still slender with short, blonde hair, Jared was tall, muscular, with the thickest black hair she'd ever seen. Caleb, Micah's brother, now a junior at UVA, was home for the weekend. Micah leaned over, informing her Caleb was into body building and that he swore up and down he wasn't on steroids.

Eden wasn't so sure; he was a giant. After eating, the two families retired to the living room to visit. Without a word to anyone, Micah slipped from the room. Feeling more confident since his apology, she followed. Crossing the front entry, she found him in the formal sitting room. He stood with feet shoulder-width apart, and hands clasped behind his back. She hesitated. *Maybe he doesn't want to be disturbed. I don't think he knows I'm here yet. Maybe I'll just slip out...*

His body stiffened, a groan escaping, like he'd been punched in the gut.

"Micah, are you ok?" she asked, moving closer. She was surprised to see his eyes were shut. She watched as his brows furrowed deeper, creasing his forehead.

Is that sweat above his lip? It's like he's having a nightmare... standing up.

"Micah." She touched his shoulder.

His eyes flew open and searched the room. Finally, his gaze landed on her. She dropped her hand.

"Eden?" he panted.

"Are you ok?"

"Yeah. Was I... were you in here long?"

"No, just came in."

He swiped his forehead. "Oh."

Trying to act like nothing had happened, she turned, saying, "I still love it."

"What?" His breathing was ragged.

"That." She pointed at the painting behind the couch.

Impressionistic strokes depicted a downtown street in Paris caught in a torrent of rain. Her favorite part was the café, the round tables in the courtyard empty because of the inclement weather. Inside the windows, she could see people gathered in the warm, glowing restaurant. She remembered each little scene at the white tables visible through the windows. The young couple holding hands at one table, the single woman shaking her umbrella out at another, the man holding his newspaper up with one hand while drinking from a coffee mug, the waiter displaying a bottle of wine to another table, and the little girl with her face plastered against one of the windows with the look of yearning to play in rain, while her parents chatted behind her. The painting was on canvas, there was no glass, but she could have sworn in that moment she saw something, like a glimmer of light.

Eden gasped. It was like the painting became a mirror. The reflection of a woman with long, black hair was staring back at them. Her dark red dress clung to her body, and the skin on her face and chest had a pearly glow. The woman's gaze shifted from Micah to her. Her inky black eyes widened, her lips spreading into a bewitching smile as she raised an arm, extending one slender finger toward Eden.

She's pointing at me! Terrified, Eden opened her mouth to scream, but Micah muffled it with his chest as he pulled her to him.

A warm hand landed under her jaw, lifting her chin up to him. "Eden, what did you see?"

Being in his arms, his blue eyes studying her, their faces inches apart, she realized there might be another reason why her heart was thumping now.

She didn't have time to answer because Brendon barged into the room. He stopped short. "Ah, Mom wanted me to get you for dessert."

By the time Brendon finished relaying his message, Micah had released her, and they had stepped apart.

"Ok, thanks, be there in a sec," Micah said.

How's Micah so calm? she thought as Brendon left. She peeked back at the picture. The woman was gone.

"Did you see her?" Micah's tone was eager.

She met his probing eyes. "I... I'm not sure what just happened, but there was a lady in a red dress."

He ran his hands through his hair. He stepped closer, "Did you see anything else," he paused, "when you came into the room?"

"No." Her knees felt weak, her ears ringing.

Micah's face was close again as he gently took her arm. "You look kind of pale, maybe we should sit down."

"No, I'm fine," she said, but her body was shaking. He guided her to a couch, thankfully not the one in front of the painting.

They were both quiet. She glanced over.

"So yeah, I see ghosts. That's what you wanted to ask right?" he asked.

"No, that's not what I was going to ask. But that means I see ghosts too then, right?"

"I suppose so." He seemed thoughtful.

"Who is she?"

"I don't know. I've only seen *her* a few times." The way he emphasized *her* led Eden to believe he'd seen others. She wasn't sure she wanted to know more—it scared her.

"I guess I know why you're reading the Bible now." She had said it in all seriousness, but Micah started laughing.

Confused, she stared back at him.

"Oh, Eden." He threw his arm around her shoulder, pulling her close. "I can't tell you how glad I am you're here."

Startled, she felt him squeeze her shoulder. She was at a loss for words. Boys never acted like this around her. *But this isn't just any boy, this is Micah. We're friends, so this is normal*, she reminded herself.

She relaxed a bit and smiled. "I'm not, should've stayed in Portsmouth, no ghosts there."

He chuckled, his smile lingering. And then she wasn't so comfortable anymore. *He's so close. Why isn't he laughing anymore? Why's he still staring at me like that? Why isn't he saying something?*

She looked away, breaking the weird moment. "I haven't seen you at school lately," she admitted.

He sighed, bringing his arm back around as he lowered his body, resting his elbows on his knees.

"Yeah, well, I sort of see things *a lot*. Like almost all the time. Kind of makes it hard to be anywhere public."

"Oh." Comprehension dawned on her. "Like when I walked in and you were—"

"Yeah," he interrupted. "Just like that."

"What are you going to do then, homeschool?"

He sat back. "No, I'm, oh, I guess you don't know. I'm leaving for Rome in a few days. I'm going to be a foreign exchange student."

Eden's mouth opened, but nothing came out. *He's leaving? Just when I feel like we're friends again and he's gone?* The pain shooting through her heart was too much, and her eyes began welling.

I am not *going to make a fool of myself crying!* She jumped to her feet, forcing out the words, "That's awesome, Micah. That'll be fun."

He rose, standing behind her. "Thanks?" It came out like a question.

She accidentally sniffed. *Crud!* She scurried from the room, but he was right behind her, keeping up.

"Eden?" His hand first touched her arm, and then secured it in his grasp, making her halt. "Wait, are you crying?"

"No," she croaked.

Now he was in front of her, his eyes sweeping her face. "What's wrong?"

"Nothing." She directed her stare to the carpet.

He raised her face to his, their eyes finally meeting. There was a hitch in his voice as he said, "I'm going to miss you too."

She was dumbstruck. *Can he possibly feel the same way?*

This time her mom walked in, interrupting what might have been a moment, but he didn't let go of her arm.

"Oh sorry, I just wanted to tell you we're getting ready to go, Eden," her mom announced.

Eden tried to place her mom's tone. Then her mom smiled brightly at Micah. "I'm so glad you two are getting close again."

Thanks, Mom, for making this even more awkward!

But Micah grinned back. "Me too, I've missed my best friend."

Chapter Six

*M*icah's gaze remained fixed on the painting long after the McCarthy's had left. *I can't believe Eden saw the woman.* With his dad helping his mom with the dinner dishes and Caleb talking on his cell phone, no one noticed him slip back into his dad's study. He wasn't entirely sure what he wanted, he just felt a need—an insatiable hunger. Scanning the desk, he realized he was searching for something specific. *Not here.* He turned and spied it lying on the chair where he'd left it earlier that night, the leather Bible.

Anxious to open it, he decided he might have more privacy in his bedroom. He was at the base of the staircase when his mom came into the front entry.

"That was a fun night. Looks like you and Eden really hit it off." Her eyes spied the book in his hands. "Did you have a nice time?"

"Yeah." He felt bad leaving her standing there, but the need for answers was overwhelming. "Good night, Mom," he called, jogging up the stairs, feeling her eyes on him the whole way.

Shutting the door to his room, he sank into his recliner, turning on the floor lamp next to him. His hands seemed to have mind of their own, his fingers rifling through the book. The pages stopped turning and he tilted it toward the light. It was the Old Testament, in the book of Samuel.

And Samuel answered Saul, and said, I am the seer: go up before me unto the high place; for ye shall eat with me today, and tomorrow I will let thee go, and will tell thee all that is in thine heart.

Micah typed one word into his laptop's search engine bar. The room brightened at the same time he felt her presence. He glanced up to see her standing over him, the hem of her red dress almost touching his feet.

He was exuberant. *She's back.*

She leaned over and pointed at the page.

"What? You like what I read?" he asked.

She nodded, smiling.

"So, what's it mean?" he asked.

Her eyes flicked to his computer screen, where the search results for *Seer* had popped up.

Micah followed her gaze and read aloud, "A person who sees, an observer, a person who prophesies of future events, a prophet, a person who has special powers of divination, a crystal gazer, or palmist." He stared at her, "Is that why I see you? I'm sort of a seer?"

Her lips puckered and then her finger rested on the page in the Bible.

He re-read the four words she was pointing at. "I am the seer."

She nodded once. With her so near, he had to fight the temptation to touch her. *She looks so real, tangible...*

Then his bedroom was gone, replaced with a tunnel-like room with marble floors and walls lined with statues. *This is new, no black monsters,* he thought, relieved. He saw himself in vision staring at a statue: a Roman or Greek bust of a man. A guy with a stocky frame walked up and Micah immediately recognized it to be his cousin Trent; the brown hair spiked with hair gel in every direction was a dead giveaway. The room disappeared, replaced with St. Peter's Cathedral looming before him, lit up, glowing orange against the black night. Though he had never been there, he recognized it from his parents' vacation pictures. Then it was all gone, his bedroom returning.

He inhaled sharply, trying to reorient himself. He gazed up at the woman. "So you want me to go to Italy still?"

She nodded, her black hair bobbing with her movement.

"Micah?" his mom's voice called at the same time there was a knock at his door. "Can we come in?"

The woman was gone before his mom had finished talking.

"Yeah, sure," he said, disappointed. It'd been the first time they'd actually conversed.

His mom and dad walked in as Micah stood up. His mom announced, "Micah, we need to talk."

"Ok." He dreaded the conversation they were about to have. His parents sat on the bench at the foot of his bed, so he opted for his recliner again. His mom's eyes glanced at the Bible on the desk next to him.

"We've been worried about you lately," she paused, "We're thrilled you want to learn about religion but..." She hesitated.

His dad jumped in. "It's not healthy the way you're going about it. You're not sleeping. You're hardly eating. You aren't acting like yourself. When was the last time you went outside and played ball?"

Micah waited, not sure what to say. He sort of doubted saying, *But Dad, I'm the Seer*, would improve their opinion on the matter.

"Micah, hon, we don't think you should go anymore," his mom said quietly.

He stared at his parents. "What do you mean, to Rome?"

His parents exchanged a glance. His dad responded, "It's not a good idea, son. We've made an appointment with Dr. Childs—"

"No way, I'm good. I don't need a doctor. I *need* to go to Rome." He didn't mean to bark his words. His mom's brow knitted together as his dad crossed his arms.

Micah took a deep breath in. *I need to calm down*. "I'm not trying to worry you. I think what I'm going through is normal." *Total lie, seeing ghosts isn't normal*, he thought. "Dad, you can't tell me you didn't try to figure out the world when you were seventeen. At least I'm reading the Bible and not," he stopped, opting for better words, "doing other things."

His dad must have understood his meaning and sighed. "You're probably right."

"Jared," his mom sputtered.

His dad turned to his mom. "Lacey, he's got a point. He's a good kid. There's nothing wrong with wanting to know about God and religion." His gaze returned to Micah. "But you've got to promise us you'll take care of yourself. Don't read all the time. Get outside."

Micah nodded. "I promise. Thanks, Dad."

His parents didn't stay long after that. Lying in his bed that night, Micah's mind replayed the verse he'd read over and over.

I am the seer: go up before me unto the high place; for ye shall eat with me today, and tomorrow I will let thee go...

For some reason, the last phrase made him think of Eden. *Funny, we did eat dinner together and now I'm leaving.*

And tomorrow I will let thee go...

Chapter Seven

"I'm serious, Eden. Andrew digs you," Jessie said again. When Eden remained silent, she added, "Hello, earth to Eden."

"Huh, what?" she answered, her eyes focusing on her friend, who was sprawled across her bed, lying on her stomach.

Jessie shoved her math book aside as she sat up. "Did you even hear what I said?"

Eden eyed the book, now teetering at the edge of the mattress. "Y-e-s."

"Liar, you've got no idea what I've been saying for the past ten minutes, do you? Why aren't you excited? Andrew's way cute."

She considered her friend's words before it registered. "Wait, you think Andrew likes me? Jessie, you're crazy."

"No way, he stares at you like the whole time during trig. He's always talking to you too."

"He's teasing me, making fun of me. I'm pretty sure that means he does *not* like me."

"Whatever, I know what I see—"

Jessie's words were cut off by Eden's mom hollering. "Eden, phone's for you."

Eden jumped up off the floor, her own math book falling from her lap, and ran to the door. Her mom met her in the hall, handing her the cordless phone.

"Hello," she said, returning to her bedroom, where Jessie was off the bed, peering at herself in the mirror, fiddling with her red curls.

"Hey, what's up?"

Eden instantly knew the voice; it was one she longed to hear almost daily now.

"Nothing. How 'bout you?" she answered, trying to ignore Jessie mouthing the words *who is it* over and over.

"Not much. Just getting everything ready, you know."

"Yeah, bet you're excited, right?"

Micah sighed. "I guess. Hey, can you come over?"

She swallowed. "Sure."

"I'm leaving pretty early in the morning, and... well, I'd like to say good-bye."

She struggled to keep her voice even with the lump lodged in her throat. "Ok, yeah, me too."

Jessie was now throwing her hands up. "Eden, who the heck is it—?"

"I can come get you if you want," Micah offered.

Eden waved her hand at her friend to be quiet as she said, "Ok, thanks."

"See you in ten." He hung up and Eden stared at the receiver.

Jessie's hands were on her hips. "So?"

"It was Micah. Guess it's time to say good-bye."

"Oh well, good riddance if you ask me."

"Jessie, Micah's my—"

"Best friend, yeah, I know. But the dude's popular and cocky."

"Micah's *not* cocky."

"Ok, well, maybe he's not, but all his friends are stuck up. And don't even get me started on his girlfriend, ugh, gag me."

Eden smiled, agreeing full-heartedly with Jessie on that point.

"I just don't want you to get hurt, Eden," Jessie sighed. "Micah's not like us. And I know how you feel about him." Jessie cut off Eden's protests, "Don't even try to deny it, I can totally tell you like him. Just remember, Micah thinks of you as a friend, nothing more. He's got a girlfriend, Megan, the biggest—"

"Trust me, I know where I stand with Micah. And we *are* just friends, anyway."

"Ok." Jessie grinned, raising an eyebrow. "Now Andrew, on the other hand…"

Chapter Eight

Eden was not happy to be home alone waiting. Jessie left soon after the phone call, her dad was working late, and her mom had taken Brendon and his friends bowling. Since seeing the woman at Micah's house, she jumped at shadows, turned on lights in every room, peeked under beds, behind shower curtains, and in closets just to make sure.

What was strange to her was how easily she fell asleep at night. It was like a calming blanket wrapped around her, leaving her feeling safe and relaxed. She'd never felt anything like it before.

The living room darkened as the sun went behind the clouds. She hurried to the light switch, flipping it on.

There, that's better.

Spying a novel she'd left on the end table, she moved to grab it, and heard a resounding thump upstairs. She froze. *Is it another ghost?*

Eyes searching the room, she remained planted, terrified to move. The blood pounded in her ears, making it hard to hear.

Just the house settling, nothing's going to happen, she reassured herself.

There was a firm knock and she sprinted for the front door, throwing it open.

Micah filled the doorframe. "Hey, ready to go?"

"Yep." She practically shoved him out of the way, trying to escape.

He stepped back. "Well, ok then."

Once inside his Ford F-350, she finally felt safe. She ignored the nagging fact she'd only seen the supernatural while with Micah. *Seeing a ghost without him would be way worse.*

He threw the truck into reverse, pulling out of the parking lot. He was quiet as they drove.

She peeked over. He turned, their eyes meeting briefly. She glanced away.

"So you leave tomorrow?"

"Yeah."

"You don't sound excited."

He made a sound, somewhere between a grunt and a hum, then said, "I know I need to go, so I guess that's enough for me."

She stared at him. His eyes were focused on the road, one hand on the steering wheel, the other arm resting on the cushion between them.

"You *need* to go to Rome?" she probed.

He glanced over and smiled. "Saw another vision." He laughed. "Man, I sound nuts."

"No," she asserted, realizing she believed him. "You don't actually."

He glanced over again, but said nothing.

Micah's mom was chatting to Eden as they chopped carrots and potatoes together. Micah sat on the bar stool watching; it was a comforting sight. How many times had he sat at these stools as a kid with Eden, staring wide-eyed and hungry as his mom prepared snacks for them? He smiled to himself. Now, Eden stood taller than his mom did, which wasn't hard since Lacey was probably 5'4". Micah had passed her up years ago.

"Micah, your dad's going to be back soon from the airport with Trent. Are you sure you packed everything?" his mom asked.

"Yes." He wanted to add, *You've only asked me a hundred times…* but he didn't want to spoil the moment.

He gazed at Eden; her lips were pulled together, a crease between her brows. He knew she was concentrating her efforts on slicing the carrots evenly. It was the face she'd made since they were kids, only now her lips were fuller, and the effect it had on him was… different.

"Hey Mom, care if I show Eden something?" he asked, rising to his feet.

His mom didn't look up from the potatoes she was shoveling into a pot of boiling water, "Sure hon, that's fine."

Eden glanced up from her task, her brows remaining bent. *Funny how I can still read her. Now she's curious.*

He grinned at her. "Come on, it's out back."

Eden's feet sloshed through the damp grass, which got longer the further back they wandered. Snow in January was rare in Richmond and its suburbs, but cold, drizzly rain was not. The trees were getting closer together as they trudged on, the fading light of day harder to see. She stayed close behind Micah, preferring to follow his path through the woods.

When he paused abruptly, she collided into his backside.

"Sorry."

He turned around partway and she saw why he'd stopped. "The tree house!" she gasped.

"Remember all the good times we had in there?" he asked, grinning.

"Yeah." His smile was infectious and she beamed back at him.

She stepped forward, resisting the urge to fly up the ladder. The square fort nestled in an old oak had been there as long as she could remember. When she and Micah were about three and four, their dad's had built it together. Being engineers, they crafted a two-bedroom tree house with a pitched roof, four windows, a ladder ascending into the middle of the larger main room, and a fireman pole and tire swing off the sides.

She gazed up at the rusted telescope poking through one of the many spy holes.

"And I remember you made *me* play the dragon every time too. I never got to be the princess or damsel in distress—"

"What?" he cut in, "A knight needs something to fight! Besides, you hated princess crap anyway. Don't lie," he stated, when she scoffed at him. "You loved being the dragon because you got to kill me."

"You're right. I did like killing you *over* and *over* again."

"Hey, as I recall I wasn't *that* bad." He gave her a crooked smile that left her insides feeling like jelly.

"Think it's safe?" she asked, touching the ladder.

"Only one way to find out." Micah was bounding up the steps with her right on his heels.

Something magical about this place, she thought as she playfully pushed him out of the way once they climbed inside. When he shoved her back with a mischievous grin, she corrected herself, *No, there's something magical about Micah.*

He peered through the telescope. "Pretty dirty, but still works."

"See any monsters?" She moved behind him.

He turned unexpectedly, bringing his face close to hers.

His eyebrows knit together. "Eden, can I tell you something?"

"Sure."

He exhaled and she waited.

"I do see monsters." She surveyed their surroundings and he added, "Not now. I mean, I see them in my sleep, in visions. I guess that's what I'm calling them."

"You do?" Her skin crawled.

"Yeah. It's kind of freaky." His eyes searched hers.

"Totally freaky. What are they?"

His shoulders hitched up as his brows relaxed. "Don't know. They look black, sort of human. They have arms and legs. All I can ever make out is their red eyes though and," he frowned, "they're always chasing me."

She stared back at him, his expression almost pleading. *He needs to tell someone*, she realized. *Wonder why not Megan?*

"That's creepy. What does it mean?"

"I don't know. That woman told me I'm the Seer, so maybe that's why."

"Seer?"

"I think it means I'm sort of a prophet. I see dreams, visions of what's going to happen. I've seen Trent and me in Rome, so maybe I'll learn more there."

As much as she hated him leaving, she understood and nodded.

She was surprised when he said, "Thanks."

"For what?"

"Believing me."

She gazed back at him, afraid to say anything. *Another stupid lump in my throat.*

"Man, I'm going to miss," he hesitated, "it here."

She was confused by his closeness, so she deflected with humor. "Mm, Bon Air High or the Coliseum? It's a pretty tough decision. I can see why you're torn."

He scratched his forehead, smiling, "I know, right?" Then his gaze was intense. "But you won't be there."

"Like you'll miss me!"

"I will," he insisted.

Not as bad as I'm going to miss you. She shook her head, determined not to take him seriously. "There's so much to see and do there. You're going to have the time of your life...." Her words faded as he took a step toward her.

"I wish you were coming with me." His eyes were focused on her.

Objectivity was getting harder. *Friends don't act like this, do they?*

"Your cousin's going to keep you company. I'm sure you'll make lots of friends."

"Yeah, you're probably right." His eyes searched her face. "I'm glad you're here. You make me feel," he paused, "normal again."

That she could understand. He was seeing monsters and ghosts now. It was probably comforting to have a friend to tell.

She grinned back at him. "Normal's my thing."

She didn't see him move, until his arms were already around her, hugging her. Her heartbeat became erratic.

I don't think I'm breathing anymore.

His hand brushed the hair from her face, his fingers warm against her skin. It felt so natural, like they'd done this a thousand times before. *But we never did this as kids...*

The euphoria shattered with a loud bang from below. "Time to stop making out, Micah," a masculine voice called out in a fake, high-pitched, singsong voice.

The spell broken, they stepped apart.

Through the hole in the floor, a boy emerged. His spiky, brown hair came first, followed by a lean frame.

"Trent!" Micah slugged his cousin in the shoulder, who stood inches below him.

Eden met Trent once before, when they were kids. All she remembered was a boy two years older than she was, who teased her mercilessly. He looked the same, except bigger, built like a wrestler.

Trent punched Micah back in the arm and then stared at her.

Her mind was still spinning from Micah's hug. *Great, I probably look like a deer caught in headlights.*

"Oh, you were really getting it on. Didn't know you were with your girlfriend. I can come back later." He chuckled and walked closer to her. "Hello, gorgeous."

His statement dripped of sarcasm, and she braced herself for the mockery.

"Hi Trent."

"Look at you, you're really growing up. Holy big bird, you're tall." He gaped at her.

"Jealous, Trent?" Micah asked when she remained speechless.

"Jealous? Who me? I'm the perfect specimen. Tell me, pretty boy, when was the last time you got lucky, huh? Me, on the other hand, I have to beat the girls off with a stick." He paused and emphasized again, "With a *stick.*"

"The girls in Italy have no idea Romeo's on his way," Micah countered.

"You better believe it, short stack. Now let's stop playing house, or whatever you two were doing up here, and go eat. Airplane food totally sucks." Trent disappeared through the hole in the floor.

Micah glanced over at her and shrugged his shoulders. "I know I saw him there but..." Then he was sliding down the fire pole, hollering, "Come on, Eden, slide down!"

Micah's mom cleared the plates, saying to Trent, "I'm so glad you're doing this together. It's going to be such a neat experience for both of you."

"We're going to have an *experience*, that's for sure," Trent responded, straight faced.

Yes, we will, Micah mused, *but probably not the type you're thinking, Mom, or what you're hoping for, Trent.*

Dinner was over and they all moved to the living room. Micah couldn't help but notice how quiet Eden had become since Trent showed up. She watched Trent like a nervous cat.

It was getting late and he knew he should take her home, but he didn't want to. Being around her settled him. He'd been dead serious when he'd told her he wished she were coming with him. *She doesn't understand what it's like when she's not here.*

Still, he knew he had to get up early. Eden seemed to jump at the chance to go when he asked her if she was ready.

"Thanks for dinner, Mrs. Hawkins," she said as they left the room.

"Sure, hon. Anytime," Micah's mom called back.

Trent followed behind them. "Hey Micah, your dad said there's a photo album somewhere in here?"

Micah turned toward the formal entry room and pointed. "Yeah, on the bookshelf behind the piano. Be back in a minute, taking Eden home."

Trent grinned, giving him a wink. "S-u-r-e."

Micah ignored him. It wasn't like *that* with her.

Eden, who was quiet next to him, stopped walking. Micah glanced over, wondering why. He was shocked to see her step over to Trent and throw her arms around him.

Trent snorted and then slowly patted her back. "Whoa Tiger, I know you're going to miss me. I'll miss you too."

Micah gaped at her as she flew back, her face beet red as she bee-lined for the front door. Her actions had caught everyone off guard, but it seemed her most of all. It amused him but, if he was honest, there was small part of him bothered by it too.

Once they were both in his truck, he glanced over. She was still flushed.

"Ok, got to ask, what's with hugging Trent? I didn't think you really liked him all that much."

"I don't know why I did that," she mumbled, not looking up from her fingers in her lap.

"Well, you made Trent's day."

"I doubt that."

"No really, a cute girl like you hugging him, his head was already too big to begin with. You just made him unbearable to be around."

"If anything, I deflated his self-image."

He tried to disagree with her, but she gazed out her passenger window. It was quiet for a few minutes, nothing but the roar of the truck's engine.

"You'll have to write me sometime, k?" Her voice quavered, "Maybe email me."

"I will, I promise."

"I bet calls are super expensive. Probably should just do that with your parents and," she hesitated, "Megan."

Now it was his turn to snort. "I won't be calling Megan."

She peeked over.

He grinned and said, "She dumped me."

"Oh." Her brow tucked together, "You sound happy about it."

"I am actually, she was a…" He stopped short and finished with, "Well, let's just say, it's a good thing."

He was surprised to hear her giggle. He waited for her to look his way.

"Sorry, I shouldn't laugh," she said, licking her lips.

"No, you should. She was a mess. She was definitely nothing like you." The words filled him with an unfamiliar longing. It was silent again between them.

Eden weaved her fingers together in her lap and stared at her thumbs. They were almost there now. He was tempted to turn down a random road, make the ride last longer, but he didn't. He pulled into the small parking lot and slotted his truck in front of the McCarthy's town home. His chest felt heavy.

He let his truck idle in park; the heater was warm, and the night was cold. He wasn't anxious to leave the cab just yet to walk her up. He needed something and wasn't entirely sure what it was.

Eden's hand rested on the door handle and then returned to her lap. Their eyes met, hers were watering. The tip of her nose was slightly pink.

"I hate saying good-bye," he admitted. "Feels like we just got back together and the funny thing is," he hesitated, "it sucks just as bad now as when you first moved away."

She nodded, her eyes turning into reservoirs. Her bottom lip trembled.

"Come here," he whispered, surprised by how hard it was to breathe at the moment.

She scooted over and he wrapped his arm around her shoulders, pulling her close. He felt her body shake and heard her sniffle. He just held her tighter.

"No matter what happens from here on out, you'll always be my best friend," he reassured. She nestled her face into his chest, inhaling deeply. He buried his lips into her hair, kissing the top of her head. "Just promise me you'll be safe while I'm gone."

Chapter Nine

Micah stifled a yawn as he listened to Trent converse in Italian with their host family, Gustavo and Caterina Gennaro. Sitting in the back seat of the Fiat Sedici, the European equivalent to the American SUV, he gazed out his window. Driving on the left side of the road added to the novelty as they passed miles of fields, rolling green pastures, old barns, and wooden fences. Exhausted from the long flight over, Micah was relieved when buildings began emerging. They were coming into the city now. Trent informed him many of these buildings dated back to the Renaissance. Crowds of people were passing between cafés, open-air piazzas, shops, and ancient ruins. From studying maps, Micah knew their host family lived northwest of St. Stephen's High School, and a few miles from the Vatican.

I can't believe I'm here, he thought, stretching.

Glancing up, he met Gustavo's mud-brown eyes in the rearview mirror. Micah guessed the Gennaros were both in their seventies. He liked how they resembled one another; Gustavo was stockier, but they shared the same long nose, olive skin, and gray hair.

Caterina was speaking. "Domani essendo domenica, andiamo a visitare la piazza di San Pietro e la Basilica. Tutte e due sono davvero belle."

He glanced at Trent. Since Micah's dad spent a few summers in Italy growing up, he grew up hearing sporadic Italian in his home. Even with taking Italian his freshman and sophomore years, Micah hadn't picked up on the language at all.

Trent rolled his eyes at him. "They want to take us sightseeing tomorrow, see St. Peter's Square, the Basilica." Trent gave him an appraising look. "You're going to choke at school, aren't you?"

"Probably."

Gustavo cleared his throat. "And what do you think of our city, Micah?"

"It's amazing. So you speak English?"

"Of course," Caterina said. "We wanted to hear your Italian. The program wants us to speak to you in our native tongue, but we have found many students come understanding very little of what we are saying. I am very impressed with you, Trent."

"Well, since Italian's the language of love, I studied hard," Trent said with all seriousness. Both Gustavo and Caterina chuckled.

"If you are looking for love, Trent, you have come to the right place. This is the city of romance." Caterina gestured out the window as they passed another outdoor café.

Doubt I'm here for love, Micah thought.

"We are getting close now," Gustavo said as they turned down a small road.

"Have you been a host family before?" Micah asked.

"Oh yes," Caterina answered. "We have been doing this for what, thirty years now, is it?"

"Yes, thirty years I believe," Gustavo confirmed.

"Long time," Trent murmured.

Caterina and Gustavo exchanged a glance.

"Yes, it is," Caterina answered. Micah caught Gustavo's eyes peering at him again.

"That is the Piazza Mazzini," Caterina said, pointing out her window. They were passing an open courtyard with a large fountain spraying water in several different directions. "We live in the Prati district and here's our apartment building."

The 19th century building had been restored, Caterina informed them, as they parked in the parking garage. They gathered their suitcases and followed the couple into the main lobby. Marble floors, pale yellow walls with white trim and baseboards, and electric candles gave the building an antique feel. They entered a black cage and rode up the elevator.

On the third floor, they stopped. Gustavo fished his keys out of his pocket. "Here we are."

The tour didn't last long and Micah was grateful to be directed to his room. It shared a Jack and Jill bathroom with Trent's. He collapsed on the queen-sized bed, not bothering to kick off his shoes. He stared at the bright blue paint on the wall, the white trim standing out. Turning onto his side, he scanned the room: a wooden desk, empty bookshelf, and an over-stuffed chaise with bright yellow pillows thrown on it. No woman in red.

"Are you hungry?" Caterina asked, poking her head in the open door.

"Yeah," Micah said, feeling his stomach complain.

Since it was their first meal together, Caterina wanted to eat in the dining room. Micah had a feeling most other meals would be eaten in the kitchen breakfast nook.

"Che buono," Trent said, stuffing a spoonful of manicotti into his mouth.

"*Grazie,*" Caterina replied.

Micah assumed Trent had told her the food was good and she had said thank you. Starting school on Monday did not appeal to him anymore.

He glanced up halfway through the meal to see Caterina studying him with a thoughtful expression. He thought maybe he was imagining it until he caught her twice more gazing at him, with a look of concentration. Gustavo kept shooting Caterina questioning glances, at which Caterina shrugged her shoulders, shaking her head slightly. Trent was oblivious and left the room for more food.

"Micah," Caterina said slowly, "you are very familiar to me. Has any of your family been to Rome before?"

So that's it, he decided, relieved to know the reason behind all the staring. "My dad's come to Rome before. I look a lot like him, maybe you met him somehow," he offered.

"No," she paused, "I do not think so. I doubt I would have remembered his face for that long. Maybe you look like one of our students from before. That must be it," she said, answering her own question.

"Yeah, maybe," he agreed. Trent returned and the conversation shifted into Italian, leaving him lost.

Returning to their rooms later, Micah said to Trent, "You've got the Italian thing down."

"Heck, yeah. Oh Micah, you have so much to learn about the opposite sex," Trent said with mock exasperation. "What do you think these fine young Italian girls will find irresistible? I know you think it's my body, and I know it's fine, or maybe you think it's my hair, which I admit is appealing, too, but no, when they see this fine-looking American stud come to school and speak their language, they will be on me like white on rice." Trent flicked his wrist, making his fingers snap together.

"I should've known it had to do with girls."

"Everything has to do with girls, Micah! When are you going to realize that? Girls are what make my world go round. Why else would I get out of bed? My parents think I'm here for the language and the experience. Well, I am—the experience of making out with hot Italian chicks. And you should be, too," Trent said, poking his finger in Micah's direction, accentuating his words like a parent reprimanding a child.

Micah snorted back at him.

Hoping the woman in red would appear to him, Micah was sorely disappointed that night. Although he enjoyed seeing St. Peter's Square and the Basilica the next day, he was partially listening to Caterina saying the church was over five-hundred years old, with many famous artists contributing to its beauty. She pointed out Fontana's fountains in the square, Bernini's colonnade, and Michelangelo's Pieta. Gazing up at the sculpture of Mary and her slain son, Micah couldn't shake the feeling he was missing something.

Staring at the gigantic baldachin, a bronze canopy that stood high above them, resting on four ornate pillars, Micah's eyes were drawn to the four angels resting on the corners. *Is the woman in red an angel like these?* he wondered. He was again disappointed when she did not appear that night.

I can't believe over a week has passed and she hasn't come once, Micah fumed. The school week hadn't gone *bad* exactly, Trent had already made friends for the both of them, but Micah wasn't feeling very social. With St. Stephen's being a boarding school with many of the students living on campus, they rode the city bus in, since the metro didn't have a stop near the school. The campus was old and beautiful, with a large courtyard in the middle and classrooms forming a square around it.

Trent had already met a pretty brunette named Gianna, and like a good cousin, had tried to set Micah up with her friend, Viola. It wasn't that Viola was *unattractive.* She was actually quite beautiful with light brown hair and blue-green eyes. It was just Micah was too distracted by his vision-less night.

Funny, I would've killed to stop seeing things back home but now…

Trent was whistling as he waltzed into the bathroom, and then seeing Micah sitting on the chaise, stepped into the room.

"I couldn't help but notice your new shade of lipstick. Nice," Micah remarked, knowing exactly what Trent had been doing at the school dance he'd dragged Micah to earlier that night.

"Hey, at least I got a new shade. Don't hate me because you were too lame to get some yourself. Viola was practically begging for a little smooch goodnight. What's wrong with you?"

"Nothing. I just like to take my time." *Yeah, like longer than five days.*

"Naw, I think you're still moping over Megan," Trent said, walking back into their shared bathroom, retrieving his toothbrush.

"No way, dude."

Trent turned, "Ok, then Eden. I know she's got the hots for you."

Micah didn't answer, but stood up instead. For some reason hearing Eden's name made him feel homesick.

Entering the bathroom, he picked up his toothbrush. "You're off your rocker; we're just friends."

Trent snorted. "I think she's hot. I love her glasses and braces. Ow!" he howled, rubbing his arm where Micah punched him. "Dude! I'm just teasing. She really *is* hot though."

Seeing Micah's face, Trent shrugged. "Ok, ok, mister touchy. I didn't know you were such a girl."

Micah turned his electric toothbrush on, drowning out his cousin. Secretly, he wondered why he got upset. *Because I care about her and Trent's making fun, that's why.*

It was late and he was exhausted. Lying on his back, hands tucked behind his head, he closed his eyes. The image of Eden tearing up when they parted flashed through his mind. He was surprised it made his chest constrict again. The wave of heat touched him before the light penetrated the back of his eyelids. He bolted up.

She's here; she's finally here.

Micah knew the woman in red was close and that should bring him some comfort, but he didn't feel it. All of his senses were overloaded by the devastation before him. The smell of charred houses mingled with burnt flesh, all of his surroundings devoid of life and color, nothing but black ash left behind. The air was stagnant, no breeze to cool the heat from the midday sun or remove the stench. His footsteps sounded hollow crunching through the rubble. He felt desperate to find someone, anyone. He had to know something had survived, but there was nothing, not even rats to gnaw through the debris. He'd lost count of how many neighborhoods he'd sprinted through, now his pace was slow and labored. His foot caught on something, and he threw his arms out to steady himself. The idea of falling into the wreckage filled him with horror. He turned, spying what snagged him. Crouching down, he slowly lifted it up. Sadness flooded him. Brushing away the ash, he peered down at the small baby doll's face. *This had been a*

child's toy, probably a little girl. A girl that's gone. Buried in this...

Like being pulled from the bottom of a pool, the woman placed her hand on Micah's shoulder, and the scene disappeared before him. He was panting now, bent over with his hands on his knees, clamping his jaw shut to keep the nausea in check, as well as his emotions. It didn't help—his head was still spinning.

"What was that?" he gasped between breaths. She didn't say anything. Slowly, he straightened, gazing at her. Pain etched the lines around her eyes, her lips turned down.

"Why did I see that?" He hoped there was a reason for that nightmare.

Her head tilted to the side and her mouth opened. He eagerly awaited her words, but as her lips formed them, no sound came out.

"I can't hear you," he blurted.

She nodded and continued speaking nonetheless.

He stepped closer. "I still can't understand—"

"Micah!" Trent's voice boomed out from the other side of the bathroom door. Micah jumped and spun around. *Trent's up? It's probably three am.*

"What the banana balls are you doing in there?" Trent growled through the wood. The woman disappeared.

Frustrated by her short visit, Micah threw the door open and Trent barged in. Trent surveyed the room and then stared at him. "Who were you talking to?"

"No one," he responded, surprised Trent could've heard him through the closed bathroom doors. He hadn't spoken loudly, or that much, and he knew his cousin was a pretty sound sleeper.

"Whatever. I heard you talking to a girl. Were you talking online with someone or something?"

Micah's body stiffened. "How did you know I was talking to a *girl*?"

"Ha! I knew it! Who is she? Megan?" Trent grinned.

"How'd you know, Trent?" He took a step towards his cousin, who was now checking out his closet. *Does he think I hid someone in there?*

Trent turned around and snickered. "Dude, what were you doing online? Do I need to talk to your parents?"

"Trent, I wasn't on my computer. Tell me how you knew it was a girl!" Micah shouted, annoyed his cousin was ignoring his question.

Trent cocked an eyebrow at Micah and then shrugged. "I heard her, ok, loud and clear. So loud I'm beginning to wonder if you somehow snuck Viola in here." Trent dropped down and peered under Micah's bed, calling, "Viola, are you in there?"

If it had been any other time, Micah would've laughed at him, but his mind was buzzing. *Trent heard her?*

"What did she say?" he demanded, but Trent was peeling his covers down saying, "Viola, come out, come out, wherever you are."

"Trent." Micah's tone was firm. His cousin stopped chuckling and stared at him. "I need to know what you heard. What did the girl say?"

"Am I on crazy pills here or are you going to tell me what's going on here? Who is *she?*" Trent retorted.

He struggled to respond. He supposed it was as good of a time as any to tell Trent he saw ghosts or angels, or whatever the woman in red was.

Trent huffed impatiently. "Fine, I'm too tired for this. She said something like you did the right thing coming here, and he'll hear me," he paused, Micah hanging on his every word, "and it's time to study. You're supposed to live with the Gennaros. They'll show you what to study." Trent stopped talking and threw his hands on his hips, waiting.

So the Gennaros are why I'm here, Micah thought. *I need to talk to them. But I guess it'll have to wait until morning.*

"Che cavolo," Trent muttered, bringing Micah back to present.

"Thanks, Trent," Micah breathed out, his shoulders relaxing.

Trent eyed him suspiciously. "If this happens again, you're going to talk, got it? I can't have you turning into a nutcase while we're here. You will freak out the ladies. Now I, for one, am going back into my room to think about Gianna's soft lips on mine." Trent left, mumbling, "Poor kid's losing it. I hope it's not contagious."

Chapter Ten

Micah was grateful Trent acted like nothing had happened the night before, announcing he was going sightseeing with Gianna since it was Saturday. Anxious to talk to the Gennaros, Micah was upset to learn, by the small note Caterina stuck to the fridge, they'd gone early to the markets to shop for fresh produce. Micah peeled the yellow stick-it off, crumpling it and tossing it into the trash can.

Now what? I might as well browse Gustavo's library. Maybe I can figure out what I'm supposed to learn. The apartment was quiet as he made his way to the den. One solid wall was devoted to books with a built-in white bookcase and a white, wooden ladder leaning against it. Scanning, he was slightly disappointed to see they were all in Italian. Looking higher up, he was happy to discover old copies of Tom Sawyer and Huckleberry Finn, both in English. Up higher still, there was a whole row of Jane Austin books and the complete works of William Shakespeare in English.

They must have gotten them through all the years of housing American kids.

Curious as to what was on the top shelf, he ascended the ladder. Again, most of the titles were in Italian, but he gathered from the covers that they were books on philosophy, architecture, and world history. One large, cloth book was titled *Bibbia*.

Looks like the Bible. Cocking his head, he surveyed the volumes next to it, surprised they were in English. Drawn to the old, leather binding on one hefty-looking book, he pulled it out, reading the title, *The Apocryphical*

Book of Enoch.

> *Huh, wonder what this is about?*

Tucking the book under his arm, he climbed down. *Hope Gustavo doesn't mind if I borrow this.* He settled on the chaise and carefully opened it. It landed somewhere in the middle.

He read aloud:

"And I saw there something horrible; I saw neither a heaven above nor a firmly founded earth, but a place chaotic and horrible. And there I saw seven stars of the heaven bound together in it, like great mountains and burning with fire."

He paused. *Fire?*

"'For what sin are they bound, and on what account have they been cast in hither?' Then said Uriel, one of the holy angels, who was with me, and was chief over them and said: 'Enoch, why dost thou ask, and why art thou eager for the truth? These are the number of the stars of heaven, which have transgressed the commandment of the Lord, and are bound here till ten thousand years, the time entailed by their sins, are consummated.'"

He jumped ahead a bit. *"...and I saw a horrible thing: a great fire there which burnt and blazed, and the place was cleft as far as the abyss, being full of great descending columns of fire: neither its extent or magnitude could I see, nor could I conjecture."*

He stopped reading. *Is this what I saw in my vision? I saw a fire, or at least I saw the aftermath of a huge fire.*

The front door opened and the Gennaros entered, Caterina coming in first. Micah wanted to ask if it was all right if he borrowed the book, but Caterina's eyes were darting between his face and the book in his hand. She dropped her grocery bag, her hand flying to her mouth.

"Caspita! Is it really you?" she gasped.

Dumbfounded, he stared back at her.

Gustavo was grumbling something as Caterina whirled around, clutching his arm. "Gustavo, I think he is *the one!*"

Gustavo's eyes peered up at Caterina and then wordlessly squinted in Micah's direction. A large smile cracked under his long nose. "I think you are right, Caterina! He is finally here!"

Micah set the book aside, rising to his feet. "What do you mean, *the one?*" he asked.

Caterina bustled into the room, grabbing Micah's hands. "We have so much to discuss. How about some tea first?"

Micah followed them into the small kitchen. He sat down at the square table in the bay window as Caterina put the kettle on to boil. Gustavo settled into the chair across from him, folding his wrinkled hands. After she had set out the cups and tea bags, Caterina brushed her hands on the apron she'd hastily tied on, and moved to stand next to Micah.

"Many, many years ago, Micah, I had a dream," she began. "In my dream, I saw destruction. I saw the world in chaos and misery. It was terrifying. Everything was burned. I found myself wandering through the ruins, crying at the horrible loss, asking why this could not have been prevented."

Micah gasped slightly, and both sets of eyes riveted on him. "I sort of had the same dream," he explained, feeling bad about interrupting.

Caterina's eyes widened. "I knew it. I knew you would come." Micah waited and she continued, "My dream shifted to a new place. I saw a young man with dark hair, leaning over a book, reading. He was a very special young man. I could tell in my dream because I saw angels around him as he read. It was like they were protecting him, watching him."

Micah's skin crawled with goose bumps.

"In my dream," she continued, "I knew the boy was American. He was speaking English to me. He was telling me he had a mission to save mankind from complete destruction. At the time of my dream, I spoke very little English. I remember I woke up and told Gustavo the words I had heard. He translated it into Italian for me." Caterina glanced at Gustavo.

Gustavo cleared his throat as Caterina got up to pour the boiling water into the teacups.

"I knew this dream she had was important. We were still raising our children at home, but we both felt that we were supposed to do something.

We decided to start hosting foreign exchange students. We have been doing it for over thirty years, waiting for the time when we would meet the young American from Caterina's dream." Gustavo gaped at Micah. "And now you have come."

"How do you know it's me?"

Gustavo and Caterina exchanged stares as she set the teacup in front of Micah.

"We know because of what you were reading," Gustavo answered, taking his tea from Caterina.

"The Book of Enoch?"

Gustavo smiled. "Yes, my boy! That is your destiny!"

Trying to grapple with what their words meant, Micah swallowed the hot tea, searing his tongue and throat. He gasped and sputtered, until Gustavo gave him a resounding thump on the back.

"I'm okay, thanks," Micah coughed, hoping to avoid having the air knocked out of him again. *Gustavo's stronger than he looks.*

Caterina sat down, her eyes full of empathy. "I am sure this is very confusing to you, my dear." She sighed. "In my dream, I saw the book the boy read. It was a book about the City of Enoch. I told this to Gustavo. He has made it his life's mission to learn everything there is about Enoch and his great city. And now you have come to learn from him."

Though unfamiliar with Enoch and the city they spoke of, Micah knew they were right. The woman in red said he was to study with the Gennaros; this must be what he was to learn about. Gazing at the elderly couple, he realized how incredible it was that this was lined up thirty years ago, long before he'd even been born.

"All right," Micah replied. "I want to learn everything you can teach me."

And, he thought grimly, *about how I'm going to save everyone from that fire.*

Chapter Eleven

"I wish you had Biology with me," Eden sighed to her friend on Monday.

Jessie leaned back in her seat and, in a not-so-quiet voice, said, "Why? You love that stuff. I hate science."

"I like the class. I just wish it wasn't so... awkward," she admitted.

"Huh, awkward?" Jessie asked, hefting her trig book out of her backpack.

"What are you two banshee's whispering about?" a male voice whispered. Eden turned, already knowing it was Andrew.

I don't know why he likes teasing us so much.

She was surprised his face was close, emerald eyes staring back at her.

"Hey, you got your braces off!" His eyes widened further.

She felt herself flush. Yesterday, her mom had taken her to her new orthodontist for a check-up. She'd been thrilled when he decided it was time for the braces to come off. All night she had rubbed her tongue across her teeth.

Even now, she couldn't resist feeling how smooth it felt. It was almost slimy. "Yeah, got them off yesterday."

"Nice." He grinned back at her. He didn't hide the fact he was gawking now. She turned away, meeting Jessie's wide grin.

She couldn't help but be aware of Andrew's quick glances throughout class though. Unfortunately for her, Jessie noticed too, and kept shooting her winks. Jessie had many qualities Eden loved, but subtlety was not one of them. Shorter than her, Jessie was as outspoken as her bright red, curly hair.

Eden peeked in Andrew's direction. As always, he was dressed in expensive clothes with his dark blond hair having that messy look she was sure he'd spent a long time creating.

"Eden," Mr. Giles voice asked impatiently. She snapped her eyes to the front, terrified she'd been caught unaware.

"Yes?"

"Do you know the cosign of $\varpi/4$?"

"Ah... square root of 2 over 2," she answered.

She glanced over; Andrew was gazing at her. Embarrassed, she looked away.

Thankfully, class ended and Jessie moaned about the homework load. "Mr. Giles's a tyrant."

Something brushed her arm as Andrew muttered, "I'm totally not getting this."

She glanced down, gaping at his hand near her arm. *Did he touch me?*

"Hey, you get it, don't you? Do you want to help me out?" he asked, grinning.

She eyed him. *Wonder if he means copy my homework.* "Sure."

"Great! Can you study after school some time?" He slung his backpack on his shoulder.

Wait... study together? That hadn't been what she was thinking.

"Um, yeah." She threw her backpack on her shoulder too. "Just let me know when you want to." *Like never.*

"My dad's got me working after school all this week; how about Friday?"

"Ah," she stammered. *I'm in the twilight zone.* "Ok."

She shuffled away, with Jessie following behind her, mouthing the words, *I told you so!*

Eden hurried to her next class, Biology, not wanting to acknowledge that maybe Jessie was right. It was a study date, not a *date* date. She flopped down in her seat and pulled her textbook out.

Glancing up, she saw the reason she dreaded Biology walk down their aisle to take the seat behind her—Damon.

At least he always smells like clean soap.

Damon's jeans hung low, revealing blue boxers today. He wore black t-shirts most days and skater DC shoes. His fingernails were painted black and he had hand-drawn tattoos on his arms of snakes and dragons. His black hair hung over his ears and into his face. She knew he belonged to the skater crowd and assumed he did drugs because of the dark bags under his eyes, but those weren't the reasons she dreaded sitting by him. It was the memory of 3rd grade, when he sat next to her all day long, every day.

And he threw spit wads in my hair, pulled my seat out from underneath me, and scribbled on my homework assignments.

She knew it was a long time ago, and she should forget it ever happened. She wished she could. Logically, she knew he wouldn't throw spit wads anymore, but she still felt uneasy being so close to him.

Chapter Twelve

Eden half-hoped Andrew wouldn't be in class on Friday—the week had been a long one—but he came in right after her and Jessie. Eden caught his scent as they all sat down.

Geez, he not only looks goods today but smells good too.

"So, still good with studying?" he asked, leaning back in his chair.

"Sure. Where'd you want to meet?"

"How about the football bleachers?"

"Ok," she replied as the teacher flipped on the overhead projector. Eden tried to concentrate on the lesson, knowing she was going to have to try to explain it to Andrew later. She felt pretty confident she knew the stuff.

After class, Andrew got up, saying, "See you later."

Once he was gone, Jessie turned to Eden. "Meeting you on the bleachers! I was so right, admit it."

"Whatever. It's not like that."

"Eden, I don't think you realize you're a pretty girl and—" Jessie began.

"Jessie, please don't give me the *'you're a pretty girl speech'*! I know what I am, and pretty isn't how I'd describe myself. But thanks for being nice," she added with a smile.

Jessie shook her head. "You're hopeless."

"Sorry, I'm late," Andrew called as he jogged up the bleachers. He tossed his backpack down next to her, and sank down on the bench.

Spying her trig book open on her lap, he asked, "Were you waiting long? Chase was yapping at me."

"No, just got here," she lied. She didn't want to admit she'd been waiting ten minutes. *Did he say Chase?*

"Is Chase your friend?"

"Yeah, you know him?"

"No, not really, just met him once." She zipped her jacket up. *Who studies outside in February?*

He noticed. "Guess it's kind of cold, huh? Are you ok? We could go inside. Maybe the library's open."

"No, I'm fine. We should get started." It wasn't just the chill making her uncomfortable. Boys were not familiar territory for her.

"Sure." He pulled his book out. "But I'm warning you, I'm not as smart as I look." He winked at her. Forty minutes later, they were done.

"What a relief," Andrew sighed. "No homework for the weekend."

She glanced over at him. He was leaning against the bench behind them, with both hands behind his head.

"You know, I don't think you really needed my help." She cringed inwardly. *Why did I just speak my thoughts?*

He chuckled. "Ah, busted. You really are too smart for your own good, you know."

She stared back at him, lost.

He sat up, his green eyes dancing. "You're right. I didn't really *need* your help. But I wanted it."

She pulled her legs to her chest, wrapping her arms around her knees, trying to get warm. She resisted the urge to push her glasses up; it was a nervous habit.

"I don't understand."

He stared down at the football field, cleared his throat, and then glanced her way.

"Chase is throwing Willow a surprise birthday party next weekend."

Chase and Willow, both names filled her with dread.

"Oh."

"And, I sort of wanted to know…" He hesitated and she realized he was just as nervous as she was. "If you wanted to go with me, you know, like a date."

She swallowed hard to keep from gasping. She could only imagine how loud Jessie would crow about being right if she'd been here.

"Sure," she said finally. She could feel the heat coming off her face.

Andrew's eyes lit up and he grinned. "Awesome."

Gathering their belongings felt awkward. She was reeling that he was actually interested in her. All the teasing, the looks her way, had meant something after all.

I'm not good at reading body language. Maybe I had better listen to Jessie more. She's in drama—maybe they teach that stuff there.

"Do you need a ride?" Andrew asked as they bound down the steps.

"No, my mom's coming. How about you?"

They'd reached the field. He held up his keys and grinned. "Got my license in October. When's your birthday?"

The question seemed casual, but she couldn't help but notice his direct gaze.

"March 10th. So no keys for me."

He grunted. "I know the feeling. My friends are all older than I am, so last year didn't suck too bad 'cause I just rode with them. But my dad and I started restoring my Bronco." He glanced at her. "It's a '69, blue, chrome trim, all-leather bikini top, nice rims, all-terrain tires."

He stopped and she decided he thought she should be impressed. "Sounds nice." *No idea what he just said.*

"So I was chomping at the bit for my license this year. I've got a sweet ride now."

Again, he peeked at her.

"Cool," she confirmed.

He grinned. They were passing the tennis courts now. She could see across the front lawn that her mom's SUV was idling in the bus loop, waiting to pick her up. Glancing at the students parking to the left, she spied a blue, jeep-looking thing. *Must be his Bronco.*

They'd come to a parting of ways.

Andrew spied her mom's car too. "Thanks for the help."

"No problem." She wanted to flee before he might bring up their date.

"So, see you Monday?" he asked slowly.

"Yep, see ya." She was turning on her heel, ready to bolt, when her body lunged forward instead. In one step, she was face to face with him.

His emerald eyes opened wide and then she was hugging him, almost knocking him backwards.

What the heck! She detangled herself, backpedaling as fast as she could. *What's wrong with me?*

He grinned widely, masking his surprise. He gave her a wink. "See ya, Eden."

Then he jogged away, leaving her smoldering in shame.

It's like my body has a mind of its own, hugging everyone and their dog.

Chapter Thirteen

icah knew Trent was worried so he took a break from his research. After all, it *was* Friday night, Trent reminded him. It'd been a week since the woman in red had relayed her message. Micah wished she'd return; he never thought he'd miss her so much.

They were meandering through the salas of the Museo Pio-Clementino, just one of the many museums within the Vatican. Trent had been anxious to see the Sistine Chapel, the most famous gallery of the museum. The tour group they joined had stopped at a single statue; the tour guide was rattling off an explanation in Italian. Micah glanced at Trent.

He whispered, "She's telling how the sculpture of Laocoon was the first purchase they made five-hundred years ago—it was the start of the museum. Pope Julius II had Michelangelo and Guiliano da Sangallo go and buy it in the vineyard of," he paused, "do you want to know all the details?"

Micah shook his head no. He had enough names, dates, and facts running through his head with reading the Book of Enoch. Trent shrugged and began listening to the tour guide again. Micah knew his cousin secretly loved the history lesson that came with each tour. He happily followed the group as they moved on.

"We're in the gallery of statues now," Trent informed him, as they entered a tunnel-like hall with statues lining both sides of the walls. There were frescos painted on the walls, mosaic tiles patterning the floors, and several marble figures filling the hall. The guide was pointing to a marble bust of a man, probably giving the story behind it. When she moved on, her short heels clicking on the tiles, Micah stepped closer to admire the sculpture. He was drawn to the man's face, the long, straight nose, semi-parted lips, wavy hair, and unseeing eyes all carved out of marble.

"The guide said he was a Greek Dramatist born in 342 BC. He wrote hundreds of comedies. She said they used to think this was Marius, but now they think it's really Menander. Poor Marius got the shaft," Trent said, startling Micah. He had walked up behind him. Something was so familiar about this moment… the sensation of déjà vu prickled the hairs on Micah's arms.

This is my vision! This was what I'd been staring at when Trent walked up. So, now what?

"Who was Marius?" he asked, hoping to glean the reason behind seeing this.

Trent stared at him. "You've never heard of Marius? You need to get out more, or at least listen in World History class more. Marius was a stallion! He completely reformed the Roman military. He went about everything on his own terms, didn't care for all the bureaucratic crap. Before he came along, you had to own land to be in the army. Marius formed his own army with anyone who wanted a job, a paycheck, and the promise of land once their service was over. And he was unbeatable. Those that didn't like him tried to replace him, but when the Barbarians took over northern Rome, they called him back. And he saved Rome, again. His army was loyal to him. He was the beginning of 'He who controls the army controls Rome'. He is legendary to Romans."

"I'm impressed. I had no idea you were so into this stuff."

Trent shrugged. "I don't know why, but I love Italy. I've been studying the culture, language, and history for a while. So I guess," Trent said slowly, "I can understand your obsession with the City of Enoch, in a way."

Startled, Micah replied, "I didn't know you knew what we're reading about."

"Micah, I see things you don't see. I hear things you don't hear," he joked. His last words left them both silent.

"Trent," Micah began. *This is what I've been dreading—how to tell*

Trent the truth? He was afraid if he told Trent about the Gennaros part in it, he would tell Micah's parents and he'd be on the next flight to Virginia. The last thing his parents wanted was for their already-kooky son to be around two kooky old people.

"About the other night, you did hear something that I didn't hear," Micah finished.

Trent was sober. "I know. I've been stressing that I'm catching your Looney Tunes stuff."

Micah took a deep breath. *Here goes nothing!*

The words tumbled out. "I have visions… dreams, at night, and sometimes during the day. I saw you and me here, in Rome, in this very room actually. There's a reason I'm here. I need to learn from the Gennaros. I don't expect you to believe me."

Trent listened and then asked, "What do you dream about?"

The group they were with had begun walking to the next *sala*, and they followed, lagging behind.

"I've seen one thing over and over." *And Caterina's saw it too*, he thought, but didn't say. "It's a fire that consumes everything. No one survives it."

Trent said nothing for a moment. "What else do you see?"

This dream was much more pleasant to Micah, filling his mind for the past two nights.

"I keep seeing a building. Well, more like a fortress. It's huge, its brilliant, and it looks like it's made out of gold or something. In my dream, I want to go in. I need to go in and there are tons of people entering large, tall doors. The line of people goes on and on. I don't go in though. I hang back, although I'm not sure why. I feel like I'm searching for someone."

Expecting a smirk, or punch in the arm, Micah waited. Trent was staring at the ground.

He glanced up and, with unfocused eyes, stated, "And you've been studying the City of Enoch." He paused. "There *is* going to be a fire, like the one you saw, and it'll cover everything, I mean *everything*, the whole world.

But some people *will* survive. It'll be those who are inside the city you saw, the golden city, the new City of Enoch. It's sort of like the ark with Noah. Only those inside the ark were safe from the flood." He locked eyes with Micah. "You have a part to play in building these cities, these modern arks."

Micah gawked at him, dumbstruck.

Trent's under some sort of spell; he never talks like this. He said cities, not city. I didn't tell him I saw more than one. The hairs on the back of his neck stood up.

Trent cleared his throat, shaking his head. "Man, you've been studying some heavy stuff, not sure I want to know anymore."

Micah grunted. "Tell me about it."

Trent's cell phone chimed. Micah watched him dig it out of his jeans, shoot off a text, and then tuck it in his back pocket. "So... we probably can't do too much more tonight, right?"

Micah cocked an eyebrow at him.

"Well, now that I single handedly solved the world's problems, we have a little time for a date, right?"

There was much Micah wanted to discuss with Trent, but he knew Trent had one thing on his mind now and it wasn't visions of fire. It was a brunette with a tight, white T-shirt and brown leather jacket on, standing next to Viola, waiting for them in front of the cafe. Micah glanced at Trent, astonished he could brush such a serious discovery under the rug, like it was no big deal.

It's just the end of the world.

Gianna smiled up at Trent, her lips a startling shade of red.

I guess with Trent, sometimes hormones win out.

He, on the other hand, was still dwelling on what he needed to do, as they were directed to a free table in the corner. The café was packed with couples, enjoying the mist from the gurgling fountain in the middle of the room, and the serenading violins playing in the background.

I should try to have fun, Micah thought, glancing over at Viola. Her eyes sparkled back at him in the dimly lit room. But he couldn't forget Trent's previous statement. *I don't know about construction—how am I going to do this?* Micah knew summers spent dry walling hardly qualified him to build a golden, fireproof city. He became aware of Viola's eyes, staring at him. *Did I just tune her out again? I'm a terrible date.*

Chapter Fourteen

Micah blinked. *Oh no, not now!* But the vision remained.

The woman in red was perched precariously on top of the Fiat as it darted through streets, passing crowds of people, all of them unaware of her presence.

Micah watched her stand up straight, perfectly balanced on the moving vehicle. She threw her arms out, spreading them like she was about to take flight, her black hair whipping behind her. Her inky eyes scoured the streets as the buildings were replaced by trees. She hissed at the forests whipping past. He was enthralled by her, almost feeling the boiling rage within her. He wondered what was making her so upset, when flames burst across her body. The fire flamed out in all directions, licking her face, arms, and back. He'd never seen anything like it. She was consumed, but not consumed at the same time.

"Micah?" Someone jostled his arm. He wanted to swat them away; it was distracting, making the woman in red hard to see. Then he realized it was Viola's voice.

Micah closed his eyes, trying to disguise how hard he was panting.

"Are you okay?" she asked, her tone worried, her hand still touching his arm.

He glanced at her. "Yeah, sorry, guess I'm sleep deprived." He wasn't sure what he'd been doing or looked like during his vision.

She raised one eyebrow. "Do you want to get out too?"

Huh? Oh, the car's stopped. The front seats were empty, Gianna and

Trent already gone. Staring out his back window, he saw nothing but trees.

"Where are we?"

"A villa," Viola explained as they climbed out of the car. Micah caught sight of Trent and Gianna disappearing from view into the trees. *Bet he doesn't want to be followed. Great, this should be fun,* he thought, unenthused.

Viola shivered and he glanced over. "Are you warm enough?"

Her teeth chattered. "I am all right."

"It's pretty cold out here," Micah observed, as they began ambling through the large ilex trees. With so many trees close together, it formed a canopy overhead.

Viola pulled her jacket tighter.

An icy gust sent the trees shaking, rattling their gray brown branches, bouncing the holly leaves, and sending small acorns falling down on them. They crunched underfoot as they continued to walk aimlessly, his uneasiness growing with each step.

Something's not right. The air feels damp. He stopped short and faced Viola. *I need to get her out of here.* "Why don't we go back to the car? It's really cold and I know you're freezing."

She started to protest but he grabbed her hand, redirecting their steps. She seemed to brighten at her hand in his. Once at the car, Micah opened the back door for her. She climbed in and gazed up, probably expecting him to follow in after her.

Her smile faded when he leaned in and said, "I'll be right back. Stay here and keep warm."

He shut the door before she could respond. His heart was thumping wildly as he sprinted back. Not caring about the grief Trent was going to give him, he yelled their names as he searched in the direction they'd walked off in.

Panic flooded him. *What if I can't find them in time?*

Finally, he heard a growled, "Someone better be dying!"

Relieved, Micah spied them emerging from the shadows, Gianna's hair tousled, and Trent's annoyance clearly written on his face.

"Trent, we've got to go," Micah said firmly.

Gianna glanced at Micah's expression. "What is wrong? Is Viola ok?"

Another blast of wind hit them. This time Micah smelled something foul in the air.

"Viola's fine, she's in the car," Micah responded. "Let's go."

Trent didn't move as Gianna scurried away. Once she was no longer visible, he muttered, "Micah, what the *cavolo*—" but his voice died as his face contorted with terror.

In that split second, Micah was sent hurtling down, smacking the ground with his chest. Gasping for air, he struggled to right himself, but there was no time. Something cold seized his calves, the pressure of the grip so severe, he gasped, inhaling dirt. Lying on his stomach, he tried to twist and kick free, but the captor's hold felt like steel. Then they were flying across the ground, every branch, rock, and bump abusing Micah's body as he was drug along. He felt like a ragdoll tied behind a horse—the speed felt inhuman. Straining to see behind him, Micah watched Trent grow smaller and smaller, sprinting after them.

Micah tried to grab on to the ground, leaving both of his palms bleeding and raw. Realizing it was futile, Micah tried to shield his face from the rough terrain he was slicing through.

His body ached, his skin burned, and he could hardly feel his legs anymore. *I need a plan now!* Straining to look over his shoulder, he caught a glimpse of his captor as they passed under a small clearing in the woods. Horror shot through him.

The moonlight bounced off naked, black, scaly skin. The figure was lanky, hunched over, with a bony spine pushing against dry, leathery skin. The arms were long, ape-like, and twisted backwards to hold Micah's legs. The torso of the thing was still facing forward as its massive legs propelled them deeper in to the woods. It turned its ugly head and glared at Micah. In the blackness, all he could make out were two beady, red eyes. He shuddered as the thing roared a wet, vicious laugh.

"You are mine, Seer," it spat out, abruptly stopping and shoving its ugly face into his. The words resonated from deep within its chest. Its breathing rattled and purred, like there was liquid in its lungs. Its blood-red eyes bore down on him, glowing ominously.

"Semjaza's praise and glory be mine," the beast growled.

Micah's mumbled an incoherent prayer. "The Lord is my Shepherd, I shall not want. I will fear no evil—"

A light pierced through the darkness, blinding him.

The iron hands released him.

Micah pulled his legs back, scrambling to his feet. Disoriented, he attempted to run, but found himself on the ground again.

I can't feel my legs!

There was a crackle and a hiss as a wave of heat hit his body.

"Run, Micah!" a female voice commanded.

He jumped up again, relieved he could feel his feet beneath him. He wanted to see who had saved him, but he obeyed as he half-ran, half-stumbled.

The female cried out, "How dare you cross the line! You shall pay for this! You and all the others in these woods!"

The creature wailed as the heat behind him escalated, searing Micah's backside. The cries turned to shrieks and Micah smelled a horrible stench of sulfur and rotten flesh. He pushed his legs harder, his muscles burning with exertion. He was no longer numb. The wave of heat was suffocating, leaving him feeling like he was literally on fire. Desperate to move faster, he didn't see the rock jutting out of the ground and tripped, landing hard on his right knee. Unsure if he could stand, two hands reached under his arms and pulled him up.

It was Trent. He threw Micah's arm over his shoulder and they began sprinting back, with Trent swearing the whole way. Micah could see dirt and tear tracks down his face.

They were almost out of the trees. That thing had carried him far. The heat from behind had subsided and they stopped for a moment to catch their breath. They bent over, wheezing.

"Thanks," Micah said between gulps of air.

"What the *cavolo* was that thing?" Trent gasped, both hands on his knees.

"I don't know, but let's get out of here." Micah straightened. His knee throbbed, but the adrenaline was still surging.

As they ran, Trent yelled, "How'd you get away?"

They almost ran into his answer. She appeared out of nowhere, his lady in red. Standing directly in front of them, she put out her hand to stop them. Smoke curled off her dress and hair.

"Holy Zena Warrior Princess," Trent gasped.

"I can't stay long. You must leave this place—*never* return here. Get to your apartment quickly. You'll be safe there. I'm going to make sure I destroyed all of them and then come to you tonight." Her voice was melodic. The woman's eyes darted back to the trees. "Go now!" she commanded.

Micah and Trent didn't need to be told twice and sprinted back. Throwing open the car doors, they jumped in.

"Gianna, my love, why don't we get out of here?" Trent said as the girls gaped at them with wide eyes. Viola brushed Micah's cheek and he winced. Something warm dripped off his jaw; he wiped it away. Seeing his red fingers, Viola promptly handed him a tissue from her purse.

"Thanks," he mumbled, tapping the front seat with his fingers. "Let's get out of here, Trent."

Trent gave Gianna a reassuring smile and she threw the car into reverse.

Once back on the main road, both girls asked, "What happened?"

Micah glanced at Trent, who was covered in sweat and dirt. He realized he was a mess too, when Viola reached over and pulled some leaves from his hair.

"Micah was mugged," Trent said, not missing a beat.

"Caspita! We should call the polizia!" Gianna gasped.

"Are you okay?" Viola asked.

"I'm fine. We should probably head home though, sorry." Micah was desperate to obey the woman in red's directions.

"What happened?" Gianna asked again as she brushed twigs out of Trent's hair.

"Well, after you left, this dude comes out of nowhere and hits Micah with a bat. Micah goes down and the guy starts wailing on him. I jumped in, grabbed him from behind, and threw him to the ground. The guy starts crying about how he needs the money for his kid's surgery, blah, blah, blah... and I'm like, *No one beats the crap out of my cousin but me, idiot!*"

Micah bit the inside of his cheek to keep from cracking up. *I can't believe they're buying it. But I guess it's more believable than what actually happened.*

Chapter Fifteen

"Okay, Micah, you better start talking. What kind of crap have you stepped in? I saw things tonight I didn't know existed except in messed-up movie producers' heads. And please tell me who that," Trent paused with a look of longing, "Greek goddess was."

They were standing in Micah's bedroom now. The girls had dropped them off and Trent had locked every door behind them.

Micah didn't hold back and told Trent everything.

Trent's hands were on his hips when he'd finished. "So she comes to you at night? Why are *you* so lucky?" he demanded.

"Trent. Focus. I've never even talked to her. That night you heard her, she was in my room mouthing words I couldn't hear and then you barge in telling me what she said. I still don't know how that worked, but the message was important. She told me to learn from the Gennaros."

"About the City of Enoch, yes, I know," Trent said, keeping up. "She was there that night? I was right; you did have a girl in here."

Micah shook his head. "Trent, it's not like that, and you know it. This is serious."

"What? I am being serious. I almost wet myself tonight. You don't need to tell me this is serious!"

The room brightened and warmed at the same time. *She's here.* They stared at her simultaneously.

She checked them both over. "You're both all right."

Micah didn't know how long she would stay. "Who are you?" he blurted.

"Other than the girl of my dreams," Trent added wistfully.

The woman smiled. Her features were breathtaking. "I'm Sage, your guardian."

"Like guardian angel?" Micah asked.

"Yes, something like that," she replied.

"Do I have a guardian like you?" Trent piped in.

"Your guardian was there fighting too, Trent."

"What was that thing?" Micah asked.

At the same time, Trent asked, "My guardian was there?"

Sage looked first at Trent. "Your guardian fought bravely." To Micah, she added, "That was a demon, one that shouldn't have been able to touch you." Her black eyes narrowed.

"That's what I thought," Micah murmured.

"Demon?" Trent croaked.

Sage clasped her hands together, her long, white fingers intertwined. "There's a line, a barrier between my world and yours. Tonight, it was breached. You need to know some places will be off limits to both of you now, unless we want a repeat of tonight. You'll be protected while here. The Gennaros were selected long ago because they're good people. Their home's safe. Your school's named after the martyred apostle, Stephen, and it's on holy ground. Rome was chosen because much of the land's holy, where it's harder for demons to break through... usually. Do *not* wander in parks or forests, especially at night. You should plan on being home by sundown."

Trent's eyes were wide as saucers. "Home by sundown?"

Micah grunted. *That's the worse news he's heard all night.*

Sage's voice was soft, "I'm always with you, Micah, even when you can't see me. Don't be unduly concerned with the demons—I'll stop them. You need to focus on your purpose as the Seer."

"What do I need to do?"

"You'll need to learn that for yourself. My visits with you are limited. Angels can't appear whenever they want, we must be told to, but I needed to warn you. You both need to stay safe."

"What do *I* have to do with all this?" Trent asked, eyebrows shooting up.

Sage's gaze moved to Trent. "You're very important to Micah's mission. You'll need to be there for him. You're his Interpreter."

"Interpreter? You want me to help him with his Italian? It's pretty bad, I admit, but I don't know how that'll be useful against demons from Hell," he replied, half-jokingly.

"An Interpreter's much more than that. Remember the night you heard my voice?" Trent nodded. "That was me calling you. You'd been awakened but had yet to experience anything. You have a gift. You'll be able to help Micah understand his visions, his dreams, and his thoughts. Without you, he'd go mad."

"You see, Micah, even this beautiful angel agrees with me. You're a total nut job without me," Trent chuckled.

Only you could find humor in all this, Trent. Micah remembered the night at the museum and how Trent had easily deciphered his dreams' meanings.

"What do you mean, he has a gift?" Micah asked, determined to not waste any time with Sage.

"Everyone has gifts. They're spiritual gifts from the King. They're to be used for good. Some gifts, like kindness and patience, come naturally. But some are a little more unique and special. They're gifts from the Captain and he decides who gets them. These gifts need an Awakener."

"What's an Awakener?"

"I can't tell you more, Micah. You need the journey of learning it on your own."

I really hate that answer. He decided on another question. "Were you on fire tonight?"

"Say what?" Trent asked.

Sage's eyes widened.

Micah continued, "I saw you on top of the car, on fire."

"You do see everything, don't you?" She separated her fingers, letting her hands fall to her sides. "I'm Seraphim. We light on fire."

"Oh, well that explains it," Trent muttered.

Sage stared at Trent and then Micah. "You haven't read Isaiah, have you." It was a statement.

They both glanced at each other, Micah feeling slightly guilty. "No."

"That's a negatory," Trent answered.

She sighed. "Isaiah wrote about us. We are fiery beings that surround the King's court. We usually don't leave." She paused.

"So why did *you*?" Trent asked.

Sage's lips twisted to the side. "I wanted to be involved in the Captain's plan. Be a part of it." She gazed at Micah. "I wanted to be a guardian."

It was such a new concept to him, angels choosing to guard mortals. Micah stared back at her in awe. *She chose me.*

Like she'd perceived his thoughts, she said, "The Captain chose me to guard you, Micah. It's an honor for me."

"Who did he chose for me? Is she hot?" Trent asked, grinning.

"Trent," Micah warned.

"Sorry, is she *attractive*?" Trent asked again. "Please, tell me she's a redhead."

A musical, warm sound flowed from Sage, filling Micah with peace. She was laughing and he didn't want it to end.

Her face radiated. "Trent, you'll be happy to know that your guardian does have red hair."

"When will she come to me at night?" he asked, looking like he might pass out at the thought.

"Most guardians don't make appearances, but maybe one day, you'll see yours, Trent." Her smile widened further.

"I live for the day," Trent sighed.

A new thought occurred to Micah. "You said you don't appear unless told to. I get why Trent and I saw you, but why Eden?"

Trent stared at Micah.

"Ah," Sage said. "Now you're on the right path."

"Path? What path?" Trent asked.

So, Eden has a part in this too. "Wait, does she have a guardian like us?" Micah hoped she wasn't in danger.

Sage nodded, her eyes softening. "She's in very good hands. Don't worry, Micah."

"But she could be attacked too, right? Demons might want her too?" Micah persisted.

Sage shook her head. "It's difficult for demons to physically manifest themselves. It takes very old, dark magic."

"But one did tonight," Micah reminded her.

For a split second, Micah saw the panic in her eyes, and then it was gone. "I know and it wasn't alone either. I'm going to discuss it with the guardian council."

"It spoke to me," Micah murmured.

In one fluid movement, Sage was right before him. "What did it say *exactly?*"

"Ah," Micah stuttered, surprised by her sudden closeness. "You are mine, Seer. Semjaza's praise and glory are mine. At least that's what I remember."

Sage's black eyes stared past them. Her lips turned down. Under her breath, she mumbled, "Old magic indeed."

"What does it mean? Who's Semjaza?" Micah asked.

She focused on him again. "I must leave. This must be taken to the council immediately. Study from the Book of Enoch, Micah. Read about the Watchers. You will find your answers there."

And she was gone.

Chapter Sixteen

Eden assumed she'd have good dreams; she had been asked on her first date today, after all, but she was wrong. A dam of nightmares had broken, leaving her tossing and turning. She dreamt of someone in her room, hiding in the dark corner, waiting... watching.

It was so vivid and real, that when the furnace clicked on, she bolted upright in bed, panting and covered in sweat. She took a deep breath and scanned her surroundings. Everything seemed normal. Still, the lingering dream made her uneasy. She reached for her glasses on the nightstand, but knocked them to the floor instead.

"Crap," she muttered, not wanting to get out of her warm bed to retrieve them. *Why is it so cold in here?* she wondered. *I can hear the heater blowing.*

She sat back and pulled her blankets higher, trying to settle her nerves. She heard a few creaks, and the scratching of branches hitting her window.

Those are familiar sounds, she told herself. *Nothing to be jumpy about.*

Something felt off.

She figured it was just being in that half-asleep, half-awake state, where senses are in overdrive. She strained to see better, still not wanting to uncover herself to retrieve her glasses.

Why's it reek in here? I'm going to kill Brendon, leaving another rotten sandwich in my room. But it smells like eggs. He hates eggs...

The sulfur-like smell grew stronger. Tugging her blanket over her nose, she felt something bump her bed. She froze.

Straining to hear anything in the profound silence, she was completely paralyzed by fear, seeing only smeary, black shadows. *Don't panic; don't panic.*

Her bed rocked as something pushed on her mattress from below. She screamed hysterically but, to her horror, no one came bursting through her door.

Is Brendon playing some kind of sick practical joke?

Gritting her teeth, she threw the covers aside, forcing her legs off the side of the bed, determined to jump down.

An icy breath hissed on her bare skin from below.

Shrieking, she pulled her legs in, burying herself in the blankets. Someone was in her room, under her bed, and just like her dream, that person was going to hurt her. She bit her quilt as tears splattered down on her arms.

It was silent.

This doesn't make any sense. Am I still dreaming? This is just a nightmare. I'm just imagining things, she consoled herself. *It's cold in my room; the mattress's springs are probably popping . . .* She stopped short.

Something dragged across her carpet, at the same time her bed shook. A low, unmistakable growl came from underneath her, a wet, gurgling sound. She screeched so hard her throat felt raw.

A black silhouette rose beside her bed.

Horrified, she launched herself back, smacking the headboard. The shadow grew until it hovered over her, rattling and sucking with each inhale, and spewing white, cold smoke with its exhales.

She wailed, though she knew it was useless. *No one's coming; I'm going to die!*

The black thing leaned over the bed. Its dank breath only inches from her face.

She scrambled back and, not caring where she was going, fell off the side, landing backwards with a thud.

It crawled onto her bed and was instantly above her, glaring over the side, panting. Trying to crawl back and regain her footing, she scraped her back on the dresser behind her. Sandwiched between the bed and the dresser, she gasped. *I'm trapped!*

She threw her hands out, hitting cold, damp flesh. She thrashed against its slippery hide, as its red, beady eyes bore down on her. Her attacks were futile. Something wet landed on her cheek; it slid down her skin like slime. Convulsions rocked her body as it drooled on her.

Frantically, she scoured the floor for anything to fight with, coming up with nothing. Hopelessness engulfed her.

The red, menacing eyes drew closer. Then she saw nothing but a blinding, white light. Squinting, she tried to make sense of the dancing, swirling light. Hit by a wave of heat, she realized it was fire blazing across her room like a fire dancer.

The black shadow shrieked and recoiled off the bed. Crippled by terror, she watched the fire chase the creature. There were scuffling sounds, and then a high-pitched screeching.

Overcome with curiosity, she climbed to the side of the bed and peeked over. The black shadow was gone. The fire was no longer moving, and she saw it was held like a weapon. Dancing in the dark, the flames lit up the holder.

Looks like a man. He stooped down, grabbing something, and then moved toward her.

She dropped back against the dresser, pulling her knees in, begging, "Please don't hurt me!"

The man paused and then held something out to her. She flinched away, until she saw it was her glasses. Tentatively, she snatched them from his outstretched hand. Slipping them on, she gaped up at him, relieved to see he was human, not a monster.

Blond, wavy hair reached just past his ears, with dark blond stubble covering his chin and jaw. Startling blue eyes gazed back at her, his features the perfect mixture of ruggedness and soft angles. A black shirt stretched over his muscular build. *He seems normal, except for the fact he carries a sword of fire. And he appeared out of nowhere...*

He finished scanning the room, and then locked eyes on her. "Are you hurt?"

She was surprised his voice sounded so real, with even a hint of an accent, which she couldn't place.

"No." She continued to hug her knees.

His eyes studied her. He appeared to be debating something in his mind; his eyebrows furrowed and then relaxed.

Extending a hand to her, he said, "Come on."

She slowly placed her hand in his and he pulled her up effortlessly. *His hand's tangible, not a ghost.* He released her hand.

"Who are you?" she asked again, when he pointed to her bed.

When he didn't answer, she didn't move.

The man sighed heavily and sheathed his fiery weapon. Instantly, smoke curled around his legs. The room remained bright, even without the fire. The light seemed to be coming from the man himself.

"Climb back in bed," he instructed. "You're safe now."

Not taking her eyes off him, she reluctantly obeyed. Coming around her bed, she stopped at the pile of ash on the floor.

Is that all that's left of that thing? she wondered, as the man bent over, scooped it up into a small container, and tucked it into one of the pouches hanging from his belt. Hoping that meant the creature was finally gone, she clambered back into bed.

She stared at the man—the whiteness of his skin and the perfection in his features reminded her of someone else who suddenly appeared. "Are you like the woman I saw at Micah's?"

He didn't respond, his eyes again scouring the room.

"Look, a monster just crawled out from under my bed, and you appeared out of thin air with a fire sword. I know you can talk. Please, I need some answers." Her last words came out in a whisper.

The man seemed to consider her and then sat at the bottom of the bed.

"I'm not supposed to stay and talk. But that *thing* was not supposed to be in here either, so I suppose it's a night for exceptions. I'm your guardian."

"Like a guardian angel?"

"Yeah, I protect you from demons."

"That was a demon?" She tried not to hyperventilate.

"You're safe now. It won't happen again." His jaw muscles tightened. "I was called to a council. That won't happen again either," he muttered, more to himself than to her.

"What council? What do you mean?"

"Don't worry. I'll send someone to take notes for me next time."

Sensing his brooding mood, she changed the subject. "The woman I saw, is she Micah's guardian angel?"

"Yeah," he hesitated, "Eden, I can't stay, but you need to know I'm still here, even when you can't see me." His tone softened as he continued, "I'll protect you."

She knew his words should make her feel safe, but when he stood up, she panicked, "Wait! Don't go! Please don't leave!"

"I'm not leaving. You just won't be able to see me," he explained again.

"Even if that's true, I want to see you. Can you stay until I fall asleep?"

He grunted, and then sat back down. She supposed it should've been an awkward moment, both of them looking at each other in silence, but she was too drained to care.

"How come I've never seen you before?" she asked.

"I'm not supposed to be seen by you. It could," he paused, "mess things up."

She wanted to ask what he meant by that, but she somehow knew he wouldn't answer.

She rubbed her arms. "That demon would've hurt me?"

His eyes clouded as he gave one curt nod.

She shivered, pondering the fact that demons were real. Continuing on that line of logic, she concluded something else as well.

She sat up. "So if there are demons and angels, there's a God too, right?"

The man smiled. "Remember that, Eden. That's important."

She supposed it was his way of saying yes, and as she thought this, she felt something warm spread over her. A sweet peace settled in her chest, and the fear dissipated. She lay back down in her bed, feeling very tired.

"Are you doing that?" she asked. It felt almost like a drug, a pleasant numbness spreading over her entire body.

"Mm?" he hummed, his gaze intense.

"I feel totally…relaxed. You're the one I've been feeling at night. You've been helping me sleep, haven't you?"

"Glad to see my comforting abilities are working. I'm pretty lousy at it usually."

She was curious as to what he meant, but instead said, "Thanks."

He nodded.

Her eyelids drooped. She slurred her words, "Wait, if I'm in danger—how do I call you?"

"I'll know you're in trouble before you do. Now go to sleep."

Her body obeyed, and she fell into a deep, dreamless sleep.

Chapter Seventeen

Trent waltzed into Micah's room the morning after the attack, announcing, "Hey, so what do we need to study, 'cause I'm pretty important to this whole shindig."

Micah finished pulling his t-shirt down. "Did your hot guardian come to you last night?"

"No, man, so not cool," Trent replied, throwing himself down on the chaise.

"Well, at least you didn't get manhandled by a demon." Micah rubbed his knee. "I've got bruises everywhere."

"All worth it—you have Sage," Trent stated, as if that made it even.

"And you have Gianna. Don't you think you should tell her about your new redhead?"

"I think that would be best kept between you and me. I wouldn't want to scare her with demon stuff, you know." Trent grinned, standing up.

Micah grunted back at him.

Entering the kitchen, it didn't take long for Caterina to know something had happened the night before. The large, jagged scrape on Micah's face gave it away. With a glance at each other, they told her everything, with her gasping at their words.

"Wait, Gustavo needs to hear this too," she interrupted, poking her head into the hall and hollering his name. Gustavo came in and they relayed the story over again, while Caterina fussed over Micah's cut. She unscrewed a small vile and, dabbing some on her finger, she rubbed earthy-smelling liquid on his skin.

"What's that?" he asked, as his cut smarted.

"Frankincense oil. It'll keep that gash from scarring your handsome face."

"Thanks." The ache subsided, the oil soothing it.

Gustavo cleared his throat. "I think everyone would agree we need to get back to our reading."

Micah said, "Yeah, we need to read about the Watchers."

Gustavo stared at Micah.

"The demon said the name Semjaza. I want to know who he is," Micah said firmly.

Gustavo sighed and then nodded.

"Wait," Trent interceded. "I haven't been privy to all this because *someone*," he shot an accusing look at Micah, "didn't invite me. So you better get me up to speed first."

"You're right," Gustavo said. "Let's start from the beginning."

Gathering at the breakfast nook, Gustavo pulled out their research—papers, volumes of old, heavy books, various maps, and even pamphlets and brochures, sprawled across the wooden table, while Caterina put the kettle on.

"There is much to learn of Enoch," Gustavo deep voice began. "There are many different writings about who he was and what he did. I have studied in the Vatican from the Book of Enoch itself. As you know, it is considered to be pseudoepigraphal, which is a big word for a work that claims to be written by a character in the Bible. In your Bible, you probably don't see a Book of Enoch. He is barely mentioned in Genesis. There are many interesting things in the Apocryphal Book of Enoch, though."

Trent listened, uncharacteristically quiet.

"According to Masonic Lore, and other sources, Enoch was the inventor of writing and books. He was a God-fearing man, teaching people to worship God, pray, fast, and pay alms and tithes. He was also a builder, teaching men, and his son Methuselah, the art of building cities."

"Like the city Micah saw?" Trent asked.

"Perhaps, just like that. Enoch knew there was going to be a flood, so he built within his city an underground Temple, a vault." Gustavo paused, Trent wide-eyed and waiting. "Let me back up a little. According to some Sumerian legends, there used to be seven wise men, or Sages. Each of these wise men had sacred knowledge on different subjects. On a tablet of the Assyrian oath incantations, it lists Enoch as the seventh wise man."

"What did he know? What was his sacred knowledge about?" Trent asked, engrossed.

"Depends on what version you believe. Some writings say he discovered the Zodiac and knew the course of the planets. In the Book of Enoch, it says he saw the heavens and the stars. The Masons pass the tradition that he knew the secrets of building. Whatever his secret knowledge was, he buried it deep in his vaults. He knew the great flood was coming so, as I said before, he built an underground temple in his city. This temple was a series of vaults stacked one on top of another. In the deepest level, the ninth vault, he buried the secret he feared losing the most in the flood.

"Some say it is the Grand Secret, engraved on a white, oriental stone. Others say it is written on a triangular tablet made of pure gold, called a delta. Another account says Enoch made two golden deltas, the larger one he placed on a white altar in the lowest level, and the other he gave to his son, Methuselah. Methuselah did work on the brick chambers of the temple. Then there is the legend of Enoch's columns, made of granite and bronze. The bronze is a symbol of the mysteries. The Masons believe these columns hold philosophical and religious truths, unknown to the rest of the world, passed down through the years in tradition, allegories, symbols, and emblems."

All of this Micah already knew, but it was new to Trent. Everyone's eyes were directed to him.

"So we don't know for sure what's buried in vault nine," Trent processed slowly, "but we know it was so important to Enoch, he built this underground temple before Noah to keep it from being flushed away in the flood. So we just have to find the underground vault, so we can see who's right and what it was."

"Easier said than done." Gustavo smiled. "But yes, that is exactly what we need to do."

"We think we need what's in vault nine to build the golden city I've seen," Micah added.

Trent rubbed his hands together. "Sweet, now all I need's a wicked leather jacket and a whip."

Both Gustavo and Caterina exchanged confused looks.

Trent grinned. "I'd make an over-the-top Indiana Jones, don't you think?"

The couple smiled and Micah cleared his throat. "So, Semjaza?"

Gustavo nodded. "Yes, let me tell you a little story first. Enoch's father, Jared, was a prophet. During his life, a group of angels decided they wanted to leave heaven to be with mortal women. This was forbidden, of course, and these angels knew it. They did it anyway, signing an oath with their leader, an evil pact. These angels were known as the Watchers and their leader was Semjaza."

Micah felt the hairs on his arms raise.

"Before they fell, the Watchers had been given sacred knowledge as well, when they were still good, not corrupted. They knew the mysteries of the clouds, sun, moon, stars, astrology, enchantments… you get the idea. When the angels fell from grace, they came to earth with that knowledge, but they used their sacred gifts for evil. Semjaza knew the mysteries of enchantments and root cutting. The Watchers taught man half-truths, powers, and for lack of a better word, magic."

"Like the old black magic Sage talked about," Micah said, feeling uneasy.

Gustavo answered, "Exactly that. Semjaza had a right hand man, Azazel. Azazel taught the art of war, how to form and use weapons, tempting man with the desire to kill."

Micah nodded his head slowly. "So, somehow Semjaza taught the demons how to break through the barrier and physically attack me, probably using enchantments."

"Yes, it appears so," Caterina agreed.

"This is very grave news," Gustavo stated. "More serious than you realize."

"Why?" Trent asked.

"You see, the Watchers were rounded up, bound, and buried, deep in the earth, long ago. They've remained imprisoned for thousands of years. The fact that they are somehow breaking through their own binding is very—"

"Freaky," Trent cut in.

"Yes, Trent. Very freaky indeed," Caterina confirmed.

Chapter Eighteen

Eden woke to loud banging on her door. Disoriented, she popped up, her eyes darting back and forth. Sunlight peeked through her blinds, leaving sun lines on her carpet.

"Wake up, Eden!" Brendon's voice hollered.

She shoved the covers off, slid her glasses on, and peered over the side of her bed. Examining the carpet for any trace of ash, she saw nothing. *Was it all a horrible dream?* Continuing to scan her room however, she spied the items on her dresser knocked over. Remembering how hard she had hit, she gingerly touched her back and winced.

Not leaving her bed, she called, "I'm up."

She was happy Brendon barged in, because now she felt safe getting out of bed. No claws reached out and snatched her legs. She remembered her guardian saying he'd always be with her and, taking a deep breath, stood up. Thinking of him, she realized there were no burn marks anywhere, no sign anything had happened last night, other than her room was a mess, which was common.

"So?" Brendon asked, staring at her. "Want to go rollerblading or something?"

"Uh, sure. What time is it?"

"Like eleven, you never sleep this late." Brendon looked around the room. "Man, Eden, you're a slob."

"Thanks, Brendon, I know. I'm going to get dressed now so..."

"Say no more, I'm leaving."

After he'd gone, Eden surveyed the clothes on the floor, reached down, and picked up whatever was on top. She began pulling her t-shirt off but stopped. Last night, the idea of a big, muscular man always being with her, had been comforting, but now...

Is he watching right now?

She grabbed her clothes and entered the hall bathroom. Glimpsing in the mirror, she gasped. Apparently, leaving her makeup on last night had been a big mistake. With all the crying she'd done, black streaks ran down her face. She'd thought Brendon meant her room made her a slob, now she knew he meant *she* was the slob. She tugged the shower curtain back and stepped in, still fully dressed.

She whispered, "Ok, I'm getting in the shower now. And you can stay on that side of the curtain. I'll let you know if something attacks me in here. Ok?"

I'm talking out loud to an invisible person. I'm certifiable.

Still, she stripped down and threw her clothes over the shower curtain, just to be safe. After she shut the water off, she dried and dressed in the shower.

Climbing out, she mumbled, "Sorry, I know you've seen it all before, but it's still creepy."

Jogging down to breakfast, she realized something. *Darn, I didn't even find out his name.*

Eden spent the rest of the day hashing and rehashing the entire study date for Jessie. Once Jessie heard Andrew had asked her out, it was all Jessie wanted to talk about, she'd even dialed up Caitlyn. By the end of the day, all Eden could think about was Andrew. She wondered what her guardian did all day.

I must be the most boring person to guard.

After dinner, she decided it was time to email Micah. She needed to tell him what had happened. She figured of anybody, he'd understand.

That night, she purposely left the lamp on in her room before climbing into bed. She didn't think she'd be sleeping in the dark for a while. She carefully set her glasses down on her nightstand, making sure they were reachable, just in case.

She peered around. "Are you here right now? How do I know if I can't see you?"

She knew she shouldn't feel disappointed when she saw nothing, but she was. Then she felt a warm, comforting feeling washing over her.

So you are here. She smiled.

She laid her head down and whispered, "Good night, Guardian."

Sunday night, Eden opened her nightstand drawer, pulling out books, stationary, and other random things. She stopped digging and sat back on her heels.

She'd found her Bible; it was a gift from her grandma in Arizona.

She shoved all the stuff back into her drawer, and then climbed on her bed. She stared at the book for a minute, without opening it.

"When Micah started seeing things, he read the Bible. So, I'm thinking maybe I should read too," she said as she leaned against her headboard.

Flipping through the book, she stopped a few times, scanning the pages. Sighing, she shut the book. "What am I supposed to read?"

She decided just to let the book open up. She peered down. It was in Isaiah.

"Awake, awake; put on thy strength, O Zion; put on thy beautiful garments, O Jerusalem, the holy city." She looked up. "What the heck does that mean?"

Her fingers began turning pages again. She watched, fascinated. It was like they weren't her hands anymore. Feeling how involuntary it was, made her realize something else.

The book fell open but she glanced around. "It was you, wasn't it? You were the one throwing me into people, making me hug them."

She didn't feel anything, but she knew she was right.

"Why'd you do that? It was really embarrassing."

She felt a flicker inside. She knew he was listening. *Probably laughing.*

It made no sense to her either way. *Why does he want me hugging everyone?*

She looked down; this time it was in Corinthians, in the New Testament.

"Though I speak with the tongues of men and of angels, and have not charity, I am become as sounding brass ... and though I have the gift of prophecy, and understand all mysteries ... and though I have all faith, so that I could remove mountains, and have not charity, I am nothing." She paused. "When I was a child, I spake as a child, I thought as a child: but when I became a man, I put away childish things. For now we see through a glass, darkly; but then face to face: now I know in part; but then shall I know even as also I am known. And now abideth faith, hope, charity, these three; but the greatest of these is charity."

She stared at the page, willing the words to make sense.

"*For now we see through a glass, darkly; but then face to face,*" she re-read. "That's how it is, isn't it? There's some kind of barrier between your world and mine. Like dark glass. And then I saw you last night."

She felt the good feeling.

"*Now I know in part; but then shall I know even as also I am known.* You know me, don't you? Probably better than I know myself. I know so little right now. As it said, it's like I'm a child, still thinking as a child. It's time for me to think like an adult. It is time for me to awake to what's truly happening."

The good feeling engulfed her. She smiled.

"It calls them spiritual gifts in the next chapter. The gift of prophecy, of tongues, of faith, of knowledge, but says without charity, they would all be nothing. That charity's the greatest of them all. What am I to learn from that?" She waited.

Nothing.

"Well, I think charity's important. Maybe that's what I need to focus on right now," she said decisively.

Shutting the book, she stood, stretching her arms above her head. "Well, I guess I better get back to my family and homework. Nice talking with you."

Chapter Nineteen

*E*den stopped at her locker, cranking the dial a few times, and then methodically selected the lock's combination. The metal door swung open.

"So?" Caitlyn asked over Eden's shoulder.

Eden jumped.

"Sorry," Caitlyn said. "I didn't mean to scare you."

"No, you're fine; I'm just a little..." She let her words trail. *Skittish, freaked out, scared of demons? Somehow, I don't think she'll understand that.*

Eden was kicking herself for the umpteenth time for not asking what her guardian's name was. *With how much I've talked to him all week, it'd sure be nice to have a name.*

Caitlyn's hazel eyes were watching her, puzzled. Unlike Jessie, Caitlyn waited patiently; she didn't push for details. Since they were both reserved by nature, it had taken them a few days to connect in the English class they shared. Now Eden was thrilled to have another good friend.

Caitlyn was slender, standing only a few inches shorter than Eden did. Her light brown hair was naturally highlighted and her hazel eyes were framed with thick, black eyelashes.

"Eden," Jessie's voice cut in. She had come up behind them. "Are you so excited? Tonight's the night!"

Eden groaned inwardly. She was *not* excited; she was dreading it. As if to nail in her reservations further, Willow stalked past them, nose held high, refusing to acknowledge their presence.

"Ok, maybe you're not excited about *that*," Jessie sniffed as Willow disappeared in the crowded locker hall. "But Andrew's worth it. He just needs to dump his friends, and then he's totally cool."

Caitlyn smiled, wrinkling her nose.

"I kind of doubt that's going happen, Jessie," Eden said, trying to smile, but it came out a grimace. *What was I thinking agreeing to this?* "Andrew has no idea he's about to commit social suicide tonight with me as his date."

Jessie barged into Eden's room later that night, carrying an oversized makeup bag. Eden cringed.

She likes theater makeup. I hope I don't end up looking like I'm playing a part in Hamlet.

"We've got to figure out what you're going to wear, because it's obvious you haven't got a clue," Jessie announced. "And I brought my makeup because someone has to show you there's more to makeup than eyeliner and mascara." Jessie held up her enormous bag to make her point. "It's a shame you can't borrow some of my things. But you are tall and thin and I'm short and fat, so that's not going to work," Jessie stated matter-of-factly.

Eden half-laughed, half-gasped. "That's not true!"

"Oh stop it, it is true. I'd like to see you in my pants; they'd be capris on you. And you'd swim in my shirts. So let's move forward. You do have a few shirts I really like. I just hope they're clean."

Eden bit the inside of her cheek to keep from laughing. "Jessie, you're not fat."

"Ok, fine, I'm not fat, just really curvy."

"Wish I was curvy." She glanced at Jessie. "You know, boys like curves."

"Well, no one has liked mine," Jessie huffed, "but we're wasting time. Come on, we've got work to do." For an hour, Jessie fussed over Eden's hair, face, clothes, and eyebrows.

"Honestly Eden, didn't you know girls pluck?" Jessie mercilessly took a pair of tweezers to her eyebrows while Eden did her best not to cry.

For some reason, the thought of her guardian having to sit through all this with her made her smile. *He doesn't strike me the type to be caught dead in a beauty salon. Poor guy's probably begging to trade places with another guardian.*

Andrew does have a nice laugh, Eden thought during dinner. They were alone, waiting on Chase and Willow, who were supposed to meet up with them forty minutes ago. Andrew didn't seem to mind and they'd ordered food.

Bet they don't even show. Poor Andrew, he's going to lose all of his friends because of me.

"I loved how red your face got when Mr. Giles caught you talking to me today." Andrew gave her a crooked grin.

"Ah," she croaked. "You got me in trouble on purpose! That's terrible." She remembered Mr. Giles glare.

He leaned forward, his face inches from hers, and grinned sheepishly. "Sorry, busted, you got me."

Oh gosh, I think he's going to hear my heart beating.

She opened her mouth, with only, "Uh..." coming out.

He moved back into his chair. Noting his tousled hair, his clothes having the thrown together, but coordinated, look of a beach worshipper, she was stunned they were on a date.

"Yo-yo-yo watz-up," Chase's voice boomed.

Eden's neck jerked up; Chase and Willow stood next to the table. Willow's long, black hair was swept up in a clip, bearing one huge, white flower. She was attractive with her tan skin, bright blue eyes, and glossy makeup.

Chase's honey-brown eyes were staring back at them. Andrew stood up to smack hands with him, and Eden rose to her feet, unsure what she was supposed to do.

She was shocked when Chase pulled her into a bear hug. With all the hugging she'd been doing, she immediately knew this time was different. Her body wasn't tumbling into him. If anything, she felt a resistance pulling her back.

"Hey Eden-bo-beedan. I know you're a hugger, saw how you bowled Micah over," Chase crowed.

Eden moved back quickly. Andrew was staring at her, his mouth half-open. Willow was taking turns glaring at her and Chase.

It was the last thing she'd expected Chase to do, and she was lost on what to say.

Chase was chuckling though, and she realized he saw it all as a big joke. She decided to play along.

"Yeah, I hadn't seen Micah since we were kids. I guess I sort of surprised him," she said, trying to make light. Her tone sounded weird.

Willow pulled her lips to the side, squinting at her.

She really likes to dish out the glares, doesn't she?

"Hey, hope you don't mind we ordered. You guys were late and we were starved," Andrew said as they all sat back down. Eden was happy Andrew sat next to her instead of across. She feared Willow might stab her with a fork under the table if she were near enough.

Willow sulked through dinner, her brows bent, lips pouting. Chase and Andrew talked sports a lot of the time, Andrew peeking her way whenever Chase would stop to shovel food in.

His smile is so endearing, almost boyish. It made the night bearable.

Knowing they were getting ready to leave, Eden tried to quietly inform Andrew she needed to use the restroom.

"I'll go with you, Eden," Willow stated, making Eden feel terribly cliché.

Willow's high heels smacked the wooden floor as they made their way to the back of the restaurant. Eden hustled into a stall, mostly to avoid

Willow's glares.

"I could just kill Chase," Willow announced.

Was I supposed to hear that?

"Why?"

There was no response. Eden finished quickly and walked to the sink, where Willow was reapplying lip-gloss.

"Sometimes boys can be," Willow stared at her, "clueless."

Ok?

Eden turned the sink off, hands dripping.

Great, the towel dispenser's behind her.

She moved towards it, but Willow continued to gaze into the mirror, pulling out her powder.

My jeans will do.

"Eden, have any of your boyfriends ever forgotten your birthday?" Willow blurted, snapping her powder shut.

She's joking, right? Surely she knows I've never had a boyfriend.

But Willow's eyes were conflicted. It dawned on her why Willow was ticked off. *She doesn't know about her surprise party yet.*

"Is today your birthday?" Eden asked, playing dumb.

"Yes! And I really thought he was planning something special tonight." Willow's eyes filled with pain. "I didn't think we were really going out with *you* and Andrew, not that I didn't want to go out with you," she added.

Eden could tell by her tone her last statement was forced, but at least she wasn't scowling now.

"Well, maybe he didn't forget. Maybe he does have something fun planned still."

Willow shrugged her shoulders and then sounded urgent, "Don't say anything, ok? I know I'm being dumb to even care, but you'd think he'd remember with Megan putting birthday stuff all over my locker." Again, the annoyance crept back into her voice.

"I won't, don't worry."

Willow appeared relieved and, for the first time, smiled genuinely at

Eden. It was amazing how much prettier she became with a softer expression.

Eden felt something then—a need—like she wanted to... hug Willow.

Oh no, not her! Come on, Guardian, you have to be kidding me.

She didn't know if he could read her thoughts or not. Perhaps he did, because she found her body moving, and in one movement, she was embracing Willow.

Willow stiffened, sucking air in. Eden backed away quickly.

"Sorry, just thought you could use a hug," she said lamely.

You're not going to hear the end from me, Guardian!

To her complete shock, Willow replied, "Thanks, I guess I sort of did."

Chapter Twenty

They followed Chase's black FJ Cruiser back to his house, where the party was waiting. Andrew's Bronco was warm and smelled wonderful, a combination of musky cologne and leather upholstery. With the stereo thumping alternative rock, she mused, *A month ago, I'd never dream of doing this.*

Andrew was surprisingly easy to talk to. She was giggling over his last joke when they turned into Rams Gate. Her pulse quickened.

For one moment, she hoped Micah was back, home early from Rome. Swallowing hard, she tried to ignore the pang of longing in her chest.

"This was your old neighborhood, right?" Andrew asked, glancing over.

"Yeah."

"You grew up by Micah then?"

She nodded. She hated the lump forming in her throat. *Why is it when someone even says his name, I about burst into tears? I'm so pathetic.*

"When did Chase move here?" she asked, blinking back the moisture.

"Uh, three years ago, I think." Andrew hesitated, and then glanced over. "So you probably miss Micah, right?"

She stared at him. "Yeah, we were good friends, a long time ago."

He cocked his head to the side. "That's not what I heard."

"What?"

"Rumor is you're the reason Micah broke up with Megan." Andrew peeked in her direction, and then turned down Chase's driveway.

"What? That's not true," she sputtered.

"Really? That's what Megan told Willow, who told Chase, who told... well, you get the idea. Got to love gossip. So you and Micah—"

No wonder Megan and Willow hate me!

"No, Micah and I aren't anything. Megan lied. Micah told me *she* broke up with *him*." Eden was enraged. *Sort of wish it were true though...*

"All he said, she said." Andrew grinned, shutting off the engine.

Eden had to smile back at him; he'd been nothing but nice to her all night. They climbed out of the Bronco and heard Chase calling, "Come on, babe," over his shoulder as he stepped out of his Cruiser. She didn't hear Willow's response, just Chase's. "Oh come on, Willow, you don't want to sit outside by yourself."

They all heard the door slam as Willow got out; she shot daggers at Chase's back up the driveway. The house was dark, not even an outside porch light on. Eden was anticipating the 'surprise' when Andrew grabbed her hand. Distracted by his soft skin touching hers, she hardly noticed Chase open the door and Willow stomp inside.

The lights shot on and voices yelled, "Surprise!"

Eden jumped and Andrew chuckled. "You knew it was coming."

"Yeah, I know," she said, reeling that he didn't let her hand go as they pushed through the teenagers thronging the entrance.

A boy with blond, spiky hair appeared, slugging Andrew in the shoulder. "Dude!"

Andrew turned to her. "Hey Eden, this is Jake."

Eden nodded at him, feeling completely out of place, Andrew's hand the only thing anchoring her to the floor.

Willow threw her arms around Chase's neck, kissing him. "And here I was pouting all night because I thought you'd forgotten!"

There was laughter. Blonde hair pushed past, running up to Willow. *Megan.*

"How did you keep this from me?" Willow asked her friend.

Megan gasped dramatically. "Trust me, it wasn't easy!"

Willow's eyes flicked to Eden, and Megan immediately followed her gaze. Knowing the lie Megan was spreading, Eden no longer cared if she glared at her, which she did.

There was a table with food set up, a DJ blaring music in the great room, and teenagers everywhere. Andrew stayed by her side. She tried to act like she was having fun, but she really wanted to run and hide.

Feels like I'm crashing one of Micah's parties.

Andrew tugged on her hand to dance, and she stalled, asking for more food. *There's a reason I've never been to a school dance!* He complied, piling more food on her plate. *Probably thinks I'm a pig.*

When a popular song came on, and everyone was hitting the floor, whooping and hollering, Andrew raised an eyebrow at her. "How about it? Want to?"

She sighed. "Sure, but I have to warn you, I don't really know how."

Andrew grinned and tugged on her hands. "Come on, it'll be fun."

She tried to mimic him, praying she at least swayed to the right beat. Knowing she needed to let go of inhibitions only made her tense up more. Luckily, he didn't seem to notice. Jake appeared next to them with Megan, and she wanted to shrink away. Megan snickered at her.

I'm over-thinking this, just listen to the song. Ignore Megan; ignore everyone...

Andrew pulled her closer. She panicked; she had no choice but face him. He smiled back at her, his emerald eyes caressing her face.

Feeling disoriented, she realized, *I'm actually dancing. And it's on beat!* The song ended and a slower one began. Andrew didn't hesitate to grab her waist, securing her in his arms. Feeling his body moving with hers was intoxicating. She hated that while she felt such a rush of new feelings for Andrew, she simultaneously felt sad Micah had never felt this way about her.

That's stupid, of course he wouldn't. We're just friends.

She moved closer to Andrew. Being so near his neck, she resisted the urge to inhale his cologne.

"I hope you're having fun," he murmured into her ear.

"I am," she said honestly. *And it's all because of you*, she wanted to add.

"Will you go out with me again?"

Does he think I dance like this with everyone? Ok, inner thoughts aren't helping... "Sure."

He grinned, pulling her even closer, which she didn't think possible. *I give.* She nestled into his neck. *Oh, he smells so good!*

He dropped his face into her hair. She had no idea how good this would feel, being held by him, and she wished the song would never end. But it did, and so did the party.

Chapter Twenty-One

*E*den was nervous about how Andrew would act around her at school, but he established how he felt, sitting with her at lunch, walking with her in the halls, and grinning at her during trig. On Wednesday, he asked her out for Friday night. She thought the day couldn't get any better, but her mom surprised her after school with an appointment to get contacts.

Driving home, her mom apologized for not being able to do it sooner.

"Don't worry about it, Mom. I understand," Eden responded. She loved the sensation of nothing on her face. She still caught herself pushing at the air above her nose all night.

Bad habit, better break it.

Andrew peered over at her the next morning in trig and unabashedly stated, "Wow, you look really good."

"Thanks." She ducked her head, embarrassed by his ogling eyes.

At lunch, Jessie announced to Andrew, "So we're going to swim at the rec center after school today. You should come too."

Eden gaped at Jessie. *What are you thinking? No way am I wearing a swimming suit in front of him!*

Andrew glanced at Eden and stammered, "Ah... I can't tonight."

"That's ok," Eden reassured quickly.

"It's not that I don't want to go, but I'm," he paused, "volunteering at the hospital."

"I didn't know you did that," Eden said. *Is it my imagination, or does he look embarrassed?*

"I just started on Tuesday. I'm going to go Tuesday and Thursdays after school."

"That's cool," Jessie interjected.

"What do you do?" Caitlyn asked, breaking her sandwich into bite-size pieces before popping them in her mouth.

"I'm really just a candy striper. I help the nurses out. Help get meals, you know."

Eden gazed back at him. "That's really cool, Andrew. Do you want to be a doctor or something?"

His eyes shifted to his lunch tray, and he stirred the Hawaiian haystack around. "Yeah, something like that."

Friday night, Eden climbed into the back of the Cruiser, with Chase crowing, "What up, Eden!"

She wasn't thrilled that Andrew wanted to double with Chase and Willow again, but tried to make the best of it.

"Hey Chase. Hi Willow," she replied, tugging the seatbelt on.

When done, she caught eyes with Willow, who was turned around in the passenger seat. Willow's waxed brow flitted from scrunched to smooth. She smiled.

"It's good to see you again, Eden."

Confused by her odd tone, Eden smiled and glanced away. With the music playing and Andrew discussing the movie they were about to see, she was surprised to see Willow continue to peek back at them. There was no scowl, no temper flaring; it was more of a curiosity. It was a little unnerving. *Think I'm starting to miss the glares.*

Ten minutes later, while the boys got the popcorn at the theater, Willow pulled her to the side, murmuring, "You and Andrew have something special."

Eden stared at her, and then managed to say, "You think so?"

"Definitely." Again, no sarcasm, no evil faces.

"You and Chase are good together too," she said automatically.

"Chase is," she paused, glancing over at him. For a minute, it was as if she'd forgotten Eden was standing next to her. She cocked her head to the side, seeming to consider Chase for the first time. "Ok," she finished, as if that's what she'd decided at that precise moment. "But we don't have what you two have."

Eden was speechless. *Andrew's my first real relationship; I guess that's always special, right?*

Willow nodded back at her, as if she'd read her thoughts. "Maybe it's because you're both so," she hesitated, "unique."

It was said without any malice—it sounded genuine. *I'm stumped. Who is this girl and what did she do with Willow?*

There was a hint of a smile on Willow's mouth.

"The more I get to know Andrew, the more I agree with you. But I'm about as common as they get," Eden replied, befuddled by her behavior.

Willow's eyes widened. "Trust me, *you're* unique."

They made their way into the show, Eden relieved to end their conversation; it was more than a little strange. Once the previews started and the theater darkened, Andrew reached for her hand. She smiled as their fingers intertwined. She tried to pay attention to the movie, but she was distracted by his warm hand. It felt different tonight; the warmth of his fingers radiated into her whole body.

She glanced down at their hands, just as her vision went awry. She gingerly pressed her eyelids with her free hand.

Andrew noticed. "Are you ok?"

She blinked. "I think," she paused, "I lost my contacts."

"You did?" he whispered back.

"I don't know. Everything's blurry..." It was more than blurry... it was almost too focused—angular, sharp, and distorted. She stood up, bending over to not block the view of those behind them. He followed her out, and then guided her up the aisle to the exit.

"Thanks," she said, once they were in the bright hallway. She blinked again. "Feels like they're in."

"But you can't see?" He sounded worried.

"They're probably just dirty." *Like, really dirty.* "I have solution in my bag. I'll go clean them."

He nodded, eyebrows creased.

She hurried into the bathroom, digging in her purse for the saline solution. Her eyes were throbbing, a pressure headache creeping in. She separated her eyelids and swiped her thumb and forefinger across, pinching. The contact popped out, sending immediate relief. She was glad her mom insisted she bring a spare case and solution wherever she went. She repeated the motion with the left, placing both lenses in the case.

She gasped at her reflection.

"What in the world…" She stepped closer, examining her eyes. "Everything's clear." She turned around, taking the restroom in with wide eyes. *How's this possible? I'm blind as a bat.*

Tossing the spare contact case back into her purse, she whispered, "Guardian, did you do this?"

She heard and felt nothing. Not sure how long she'd been gone, and feeling bad Andrew was missing the movie, she hurried out.

He was waiting, arms crossed, eyes concerned. "Everything ok?"

"Uh… yeah, sorry." She wasn't sure what to say exactly.

He cocked one eyebrow, but said nothing. Returning to the theater, her mind was no longer on the movie. She couldn't stop gazing around. Even in the darkness, she could see clearly. *I see better now than I did with my contacts!*

She caught Andrew staring at her several times, and decided to at least pretend to watch the show. *Poor guy did pay a lot for the tickets. Guess he doesn't want me admiring the walls.*

That night, after Andrew had dropped her off, leaving her with a warm embrace, she sat cross-legged on her bed, laptop humming. She took a swig from her orange soda, debating.

Why not? She set her drink on her nightstand.

She exhaled. "Well, Guardian, I'm not sure why I'm doing this. I still haven't heard anything back from Micah from my last email. But I've got to tell someone, so might as well be him, right?" She laughed a little at herself.

At least he won't think I'm crazy.

Chapter Twenty-Two

It was hard to believe that two weeks had passed since the demon had attacked. Micah rubbed his hand across forehead; he felt restless.

Lying on his back in bed, he couldn't shake the feeling he was missing something. It was late, probably past midnight. Trent had insisted Viola and Gianna come over earlier, telling him he desperately needed a social life. He guessed it was Trent's way of worrying about him.

Knowing sleep eluded him, he sat up and rested his elbows on his knees. Tonight had been a turning point with Viola; he knew he didn't like her as more than a friend. He'd confided this to Trent an hour ago, after the girls had left. Trent had just muttered something in Italian and gone to bed.

Trying to put his finger on what it was that was bothering him, he got up and paced the floor. When Sage came to mind, Micah mulled over what she'd said two weeks ago, like he'd done a thousand times before.

Why did she say I was on the right path when I asked about Eden? And why do I keep seeing Eden in my mind all the time?

Sighing, he flopped back on his bed, throwing his arms above his head. Staring at the ceiling, his mind wandered back to their younger years. He and Eden had been joined at the hip since he could remember until she had moved away. He'd been twelve; she was almost eleven. He'd been depressed for a while, but then Chase had moved to the neighborhood, and they'd become friends. At that age, it was nice to have guy friends who were into sports like he was. The last few years, he had gained more friends and a girlfriend or two. They had a tight group and did everything together. He hated to admit to himself now; Eden had been pushed to the background.

Then, out of nowhere, she'd plowed him over in the locker hall. He grinned, remembering how red her face had been. *It was almost as if it wasn't in her control, as if she was being moved by some unseen force. As if she was supposed to hug Trent and me...*

He bolted up. *Of course! How did I not see it before?*

Realizing what this meant, he wondered who else she may have touched. *Has she figured out what she can do? Ironic, such an unassuming person can hold such a gift and not even know it.*

Contemplating her ability, he saw her stormy-blue eyes staring back at him. In his mind, there was a yearning in her expression. It startled him. He'd never seen that look on her face before.

Then he was following her in his mind, watching her sitting on the bleachers with Andrew, walking alongside them through the school lawn, and then seeing her abruptly hug him.

So Andrew too.

Then he was at a dinner table with Andrew and Eden. He was trying to pay attention to what they were saying, but their voices were muted, and there was an annoying pressure on his chest. He took a deep breath, trying to shake it, and realized Chase and Willow had joined the table. This time, Chase hugged Eden.

Micah's eyes widened. *Wonder what* that *means...*

But he didn't have time to wonder; the visions were flowing now. He was following the girls into the restroom, something he wasn't entirely thrilled about. He pressed on, knowing there was always a reason behind what he saw.

Eden hugged Willow.

Micah gazed at Willow, and in that moment, he could have sworn Willow stared right back at him. He did a double take, but Willow was saying, "Thanks, I guess I sort of did," to Eden.

Very interesting.

The vision didn't end though. In a déjà vu way, he saw his friends at

Chase's for a party, and there was Eden right in the middle of it all, looking lost.

And beautiful...

Her hair was down, framing her face and covering her back, looking full and silky. He had the unexplainable urge to reach out and touch it.

She smiled; the braces were gone. *She always did have a nice smile.*

Andrew led her to the dance floor and a new feeling flooded Micah—jealousy. He knew he had no right to feel it, but he did. Andrew's arms around her made him sick inside and, as she nestled her face into Andrew's neck, he groaned. He'd had enough, and was glad his dream shifted. He pushed aside the ache in his chest. He didn't have time for that now.

I need to pay attention.

Eden was hugging another guy, someone Micah didn't recognize. It was right in the middle of the classroom too. Her face was very red.

Then there was a girl. She was hurt, limping. Eden was putting her arm around her, supporting her. It was a sideways hug. Micah supposed it counted.

Trying to place the details of the room the girls were in, his eyes flew open. Grateful it was morning, Micah rolled out of bed, walking through the bathroom and rapping on Trent's closed door. He didn't know what time it was. *Trent won't be happy if it's earlier than eight, but this can't wait.*

When he heard no response, he hesitated before knocking once more, this time harder. There was a squeaking floorboard, and then the door flew open.

Trent's eyes squinted back at him. "There better be a fire or a demon in your room, because my internal clock says I shouldn't be awake right now."

"Neither, but I need to talk to you."

"Tell me Sage's there at least." Trent sighed heavily.

"Nope, but I figured something out last night. Something Sage said to us a few weeks ago." He surveyed his cousin's head slipping down the doorframe. "Are you awake?"

"What?" Trent's head snapped up. "Yeah, you were saying..."

"Trent, this is important."

"All right, all right, give me a minute. Nature calls."

A few minutes later, Trent shuffled into Micah's bedroom. Micah had purposely turned his alarm clock so Trent wouldn't read 6:35.

He flopped down on Micah's chaise, groaning, "Man, why does it feel like it's still two am?"

Micah cleared his throat. "I've been having more dreams."

His eyes popped open. "Did you see where the vaults are?"

"No," Micah exhaled. Trent's lips turned down, but he didn't say anything. "I wish I had, trust me. But I've been having dreams about Eden."

"Really?" One of Trent's eyebrows shot up.

Micah knew he'd have a hard time not teasing him, but dove in anyway. He had to tell him, everything, he decided.

When he'd finished, Trent stared at him. "Do you think it's because of something she did?"

"Yeah. And I've been seeing others that she's been touching at school."

"I knew that girl was special. I felt something warm and tingly when she hugged me."

He knew Trent was joking, but he couldn't get the image of Andrew holding Eden close while dancing out of his head.

"Sage said Eden was important and she's right; Eden's very important. She's the one needed to start the gifts. Sage had a name for it, but I can't remember. Can you?"

Trent scratched at his short sideburn with his thumbnail. "I remember every word out of the beautiful woman's mouth."

"So?"

"Just a sec, it's coming to me. She said some gifts are from the Captain and need a... an Awakener. I think that's it."

"Awakener, yeah you're right, that was it." Micah couldn't shake the void he felt. The excitement over his new discovery was fading.

Maybe I'm just tired.

"What is it?" Trent asked.

Micah stared back at him.

"You look like you just saw something. You got that out-of-focus glaze you get." Trent half-rose from his reclined position.

"No, I just... realized something."

Trent studied Micah's face. "And?"

Micah wasn't sure what to say, but knew Trent wouldn't let up, so he admitted the truth. "I can't get her out of my head."

Trent chuckled. "Who? Eden? Ha! I knew it! I called it before we even left Virginia. You like her, don't you?"

"No, no it's not that..." Micah's words trailed off. His heart was telling him something otherwise. *Why am I jealous of Andrew? He's my friend; she's my friend... I should be happy, right?*

The ache in his chest startled him. *Of all the times to realize my feelings, did I have to do it in front of Trent?*

Micah conceded. "Ok, maybe you're right, Trent, just this once."

Trent was laughing hard now. "I'm always right, Micah. Just accept the facts, baby."

"I didn't even realize it until she was dancing with Andrew, and I wanted to punch his smiling face."

"Wait, what?"

"Nothing, she was on a date with Andrew, one of my friends." Micah grew quiet. *That sort of complicates things.*

"Ok, I get it, I get it. You've got it bad for this one. She's fine and, let's face it, her touch is pretty special. So what's the problem? I know she feels the same way about you. I saw it all over her face when I busted in on you two in the tree house. Which, come to think of it, what were you two doing anyways?"

"It wasn't like that, then."

"Wasn't it?"

"I don't know, and it doesn't matter; she's with Andrew now."

"You saw them *dancing!* That doesn't mean she's in love with the guy! Plus, you don't even know if it's happened. Your visions are sometimes about the future too. Man, I thought you knew your way around the opposite sex. It's like talking to a ten year old. Just tell her!" Trent shook his head in mock exasperation.

"When did you become the expert on love anyway?"

"I'm the interpreter. Pretty sure it's part of my gift."

"Oh really? That's a stretch, even for you, Trent."

As he walked sluggishly out of the room, Trent muttered, "I'm going back to bed. I think there's a reason you turned your clock around. I don't even want to know what time it is." Micah decided not to remind him they weren't sure yet what Andrew's gift was, and if they'd need him around for what they had to do.

Chapter Twenty-Three

Once the door shut, Micah grabbed his laptop. He wasn't going to put it off any longer. *Trent's right; I should tell Eden how I feel.* As he waited for the screen to boot, his eyes went out of focus. Glancing around, he was now standing in front of large crowd, seated on white chairs, facing him.

They were dressed nice, women in dresses, men in tuxedos. There was a cool, misty breeze on his skin. Hearing his shoe squeak, he glanced down to see black, shiny loafers. Gazing to the left, he noticed they were on top of a grassy hill, which sloped down to meet white sand. Maybe two-hundred yards away, there was a beautiful beach. He could hear the ocean's surf rolling and crashing against the shore.

Micah stared back at the group before him; they were seated in two sections, a long aisle with red, velvet carpet running between them. The carpet was covered with white petals. He wasn't sure which flower; they were bright against the deep red aisle. Peering at his own black tuxedo, it dawned on him that he was at a wedding, perhaps even his own.

A single violin began to play a sweet melody. It was soon joined by a cello; they harmonized for a few chords, and then a whole orchestra joined in, playing melodic music. It reminded him of Pachelbel's Canon, although it wasn't quite the same. As Micah searched for the source of the music, the audience rose to their feet in unison.

At the end of the aisle, a young woman wearing a white, silk wedding gown began to slowly step towards him. The small crystals on her bodice sparkled in the sunlight as she moved gracefully. She was breathtaking.

Micah recognized the man guiding her down the aisle; it was David McCarthy. He knew who the young woman was; her hair was swept halfway up, leaving her shoulders covered in blonde curls. As she approached, he could see her face, smiling back at him through the veil. He felt himself shiver. *Is this our wedding?* Tears flooded his eyes, and each step she took echoed his heartbeat.

Her eyes remained on him until she stood directly in front, and in that moment, she glanced to the right. He did too and was surprised Andrew was standing next to him, also in a tuxedo. A sinking realization crept through him.

This may not be our day after all. I might just be the best man.

Andrew was older, but still retained his boyish facial features. Since both he and Andrew stood in the middle of the aisle, he searched for the minister. Perhaps whoever stood closer to him was the groom, but they were the only two there. Eden continued to smile at Andrew, while Micah panicked.

This isn't how it's supposed to go.

She bridged the gap, her dad graciously stepping away. Standing before both of them, her eyes remained glued on Andrew. Micah's lips twitched, tempted to plead for her to glance his way. Mercifully, her eyes shifted back to him, and her smile deepened. He couldn't help it; he took a step forward, reaching for her hand.

There was a strange beeping sound. Distracted, Micah flipped around to see his headboard. Confused, he whirled back, but Eden was gone, and in her place sat his laptop, blinking for him to log in. Feeling drained, he opened his email. There were two emails from her. He clicked on the oldest one first. It was from two weeks ago.

Hi Micah,

How are you? Are you liking Rome? I'm sure it's been pretty incredible. And I'm sure Trent has kept you busy, or at least your lips busy, haha! How are your classes? Do you understand the Italian? I'd love to travel one day. There are tons of places in Europe I'd love to see. Rome is definitely one of them!

Things have been interesting here too. So, I'm not really sure how to say this, so I'm going to jump right in. Last night, a demon tried to attack me in my bedroom! It was the scariest thing ever. I think those black monsters you are seeing are real; actually, I know they are. The demon was black with red eyes, just like you said. It jumped on my bed and everything!

But, luckily for me, I have a guardian angel like you (your woman in red). He came out of nowhere and killed the demon with a sword made of fire!!! Don't worry, I'm totally safe. I think I have a tough guardian☺

I don't know why you need to be in Italy, but I know you're part of something big. So keep studying and doing what you're doing. It's important.

Well, I better go. I miss you a lot.

Eden

Micah wasn't sure what he was feeling: shock, anger, worry…

"I was right. She was attacked," he muttered to himself, clicking on the second email, wanting to make sure there wasn't a second attack.

This one was shorter, dated earlier that night.

Hi Micah,

I hope you're doing well! It's really late and I can't sleep. I hope you don't mind me typing away to you! I went out with Andrew again tonight. He's been really nice to me. It's sort of a new thing for me. I know you've had lots of girlfriends, so I probably sound cheesy to you! Sorry! What are best friends for, right?

Now I have to tell you about another thing that happened, but this time it's a good thing! I was sitting in the movie theater tonight with Andrew and, all of a sudden, my eyes go crazy. I take my contacts out and… drumroll please… I can see!

I don't need my glasses or contacts anymore! Isn't that amazing? I'm going to tell my parents or they'll wonder why they don't have to buy saline solution anymore☺

Well, I better go to bed. Write me back when you get a chance, ok?
I really miss you!
Eden

Micah re-read her email.

How interesting… I wonder…

He deliberated a moment, while staring at his laptop. All the words he'd been ready to type before, confessing his true feelings for her, seemed wrong. Eden in a wedding dress gazing into Andrew's eyes was still too fresh.

It makes more sense that I'd be the best man. I'm friends with both of them. Why would Andrew even be there if she broke up with him to be with me? Besides, Andrew is gifted. I have no doubt of that now. And we're going to need him.

Sadness filled his gut as he typed back his reply. Sighing heavily, he clicked send and shut his laptop slowly. His mood wasn't improving.

I'm tired, haven't slept in days, and these visions don't let up.

Feeling justified, he pushed his laptop aside and said, "Sage, I know you can hear me. We need to talk."

He waited. It was the first time he'd actually asked her to come to him. He wasn't sure if it was up to him, or if he even had any authority to ask. Still, he waited.

Sage's red dress filled his view, her body standing at the side of the bed. He glanced up at her face.

He took in a deep breath, and exhaled as he spoke, "I'm not getting you in trouble, am I?"

To his shock, Sage smiled and sat down next to him.

"No, you're not. I can come more freely now. The Captain is very pleased with your progress."

Micah wasn't sure why hearing those words would affect him the way they did. He instantly felt something swell within him, his eyes stinging.

"Besides, I learned my lesson long ago about not showing up when I feel like it," Sage said, her demeanor relaxed. Micah stared back at her.

"Ever hear how the ghost of Anne Boleyn haunts the Tower of London?"

He shook his head.

"Well, I have an uncanny resemblance to the beheaded queen of Henry the Eighth. I was guardian to her daughter, Elizabeth. When the little princess was a young woman, she visited the tower where her mom had died. Feeling for the girl, I appeared, holding her in my arms. One of the gatekeepers saw me and well, that was that."

Micah was wide-eyed. "That's crazy." He was enjoying this open side to Sage. He decided it was as good a time as any to ask. "Who guards Eden?"

Sage cocked her head to the side. "Why do you ask?"

"She was attacked."

"I know."

"You do? Why didn't you tell me?"

She straightened her neck. "Let me show you something."

Micah was no longer sitting on his bed. He was in his backyard, running behind two kids, one boy with thick, black hair, and one girl with long, blonde locks.

He grinned. *It's us; it's our tree fort.*

Then he saw two other people; Sage he recognized, and a man. They were in the middle of a conversation.

"You know, one day this little girl with skinned knees and dirty hands is going to be a beautiful woman," Sage said, as eight-year-old Eden dug in the dirt with a small shovel.

The man glanced at Sage. "I do realize that's what happens to girls when they get older, you know."

"But they aren't Awakeners. It'll be different with her," Sage insisted.

"I'm not worried. I know she's special, but that doesn't change me."

"But that's just it, Gabriel, she *will* change you. That's her gift."

Gabriel? Like Gabriel, the archangel?

"I've been around for a long, long time. I don't think I'm even capable of change anymore," the man named Gabriel stated.

Sage nodded and they both stared at a dirt-covered Eden, who hollered to Micah, "I've found buried treasure! Let's get it in the castle!"

Micah chuckled, watching the boy version of him swoop in, sword drawn, to investigate Eden's findings.

"Cool, look at all the money," Micah gasped, holding up a pile of pennies.

Funny, never thought about where those came from—maybe our moms?

The young Micah and Eden were scrambling up the ladder. Micah peered up from the ground at the tree house where the two kids were hollering gleefully. Then Micah saw it—Eden stepping back, not noticing how close her foot was too the edge. He jumped forward, realizing she was going to fall backwards.

Before he'd made it two feet, Gabriel soared past him with outstretched arms. He pushed her body back, steadying her balance. He remained levitated by the side, watching. *Probably in case she repeats the blunder.*

Micah stared at Eden; her face was flushed, her eyes wide with fear. Young Micah was over in the corner, counting their loot, oblivious to the accident that almost happened.

"One thing's for sure, she keeps you on your toes, Zeus." Sage grinned.

Gabriel grunted. "Never a dull moment with this one."

But Micah saw it, in those deep-set blue eyes; Gabriel loved Eden like she were his own daughter.

Micah's room was back, the vision over.

"Do you understand now? No one is better than Gabriel," Sage said firmly.

Micah nodded, amazed. "So is he *the* Gabriel?"

She laughed softly. "He is much more than just the archangel. Keep studying. You can learn more about him. He trained me, showed me everything there was to being a guardian." She glanced at Micah. "You are the

Seer, and yes, demons want you. But the Awakener, the catalyst for every gift the Captain has to give, now that is a prize the demons drool after. Gabriel's the best. You don't need to worry about your *friend*."

He gaped at her. *Why'd she say friend like that?* "I suppose I shouldn't be surprised you know how I feel about Eden now."

Sage's black eyes studied him. "I hear what you say. I don't know how it or you actually feel." Her eyes turned curious. "I've never lived a mortal life. Human emotions sometimes elude me."

Now Micah was surprised. "Huh, I never thought about that. So will you, you know, be mortal one day?"

Was that yearning in her eyes? "I'm not sure. There may not be time."

Her troubled expression left him uneasy. Deciding to change the subject, he asked, "Why did you call him Zeus?"

Sage's smile returned. "One Seer long ago was awoken, but didn't receive his Interpreter in time. Visions without understanding can be misleading." She gazed directly into his eyes. "This Seer saw the guardians and thought we were some kind of Gods and Goddesses. A lot of mythology stems from that." She shrugged her shoulders. "I like to call him Zeus. Pretty sure that's who they modeled him after."

"Except for the sword of fire," Micah observed.

"It's the Flaming Sword," Sage corrected. "It sets him apart. He's Cherubim; all Cherubim carry flaming swords."

"So how many different types of angels are there? You're Seraphim, Gabriel's Cherubim..."

Sage's eyebrows rose. "There's too many to learn in one night. Another time, you need sleep."

Chapter Twenty-Four

Eden tapped her foot, waiting for her email to upload, not really expecting anything. She used to check it every day, hoping for an email from Micah, but it'd been weeks since she'd last looked. Dating Andrew, she felt she should try to sever feelings for Micah. For her, each day she didn't check was a personal triumph.

She gasped.

He emailed back! Guess my birthday's a lucky day after all!

Stomach in knots, she clicked the mouse. The email was dated two weeks ago exactly.

Hey Eden!

I have so much to tell you, but I'm not really sure how much I should—story of my life, right? First off, I want to say, I glad you're safe. I can't believe you were attacked by a demon. I was afraid it might happen, since I was too. Out in the forest, it was pretty freaky. But I'm fine. You're right. Sage's my guardian. She fought the demon off and appeared to Trent too. Trent's helped me a lot here. And yes, he's done his best to hook me up, but my mind isn't on that now.

You're right. We're in the middle of something big. Bigger than I'd ever imagined possible. I'm getting more and more caught up in it; wish I could explain more now. The whole experience has been an eye opener for me, in more ways than one.

As for Andrew, he's a lucky guy. You deserve the best. I wish we could've stayed closer over the years. I'm glad you're hanging out with my friends. They're pretty good guys most of the time. Just got to watch out for Chase every once in a while, right?

Eden paused. *Does he know about Chase hugging me?* She continued to read:

I'm glad you're happy and I don't think you're cheesy☺ Andrew's a good friend, and like I said, he's lucky to have you.
That's crazy you don't need glasses anymore! I guess sometimes, life hands you a miracle☺ Rome's great, but I'm anxious to get home. I miss you, Eden. You're friendship is everything to me.
Micah

She read it again. *So he's happy for me? He's glad I'm dating Andrew?* She supposed she shouldn't feel disappointed.

What was I expecting? She shut her laptop. *That'd he says he's head over heels for me?*

Stupid, stupid me… like Jessie said… we're just best friends. Why can't I just be satisfied with that?

Jessie glanced around. "Sheesh, nice house."

Caitlyn silently agreed.

Eden was glad her friends were comfortable in Andrew's home. It was Eden's sixteenth birthday, and he threw her a party, inviting half the school, it felt like. Since the McCarthy's townhome would have been busting at the seams, her parents had allowed it to be at Andrew's.

Eden decided the agitation she was feeling was not over Micah's email, but rather the fact that Andrew had yet to kiss her. *I guess we've only been dating a month, that's probably normal,* she told herself as Chase and Willow walked in. Jake waltzed in next, with Megan beside him. Eden whirled around to Andrew.

He held up his hands. "I invited Jake, not Megan."

Great, now I get to have Megan snickering at me at my own birthday party.

She sighed. "That's ok."

Andrew mouthed *sorry* as Jake and Megan came over.

Jake and Andrew greeted each other naturally, with, "What's up, man," while Megan glared at Eden, her mouth set in a frown.

Eden forced a smile. "Hi Megan."

She grimaced. "Happy birthday, Eden."

To Eden's shock, Willow appeared by her side. "Come off it, Meg. Everyone knows you broke Micah's heart, not the other way around. And in no way is it Eden's fault. So if you're going to play mean, just leave. It's her party, not yours."

There were collective gasps by Eden, Caitlyn, and loudest of all, Megan.

Megan's eyes narrowed. "Whatever, Willow."

Chase stepped next to Eden now, pushing his way into the small ring, making room for his large frame. Eden gaped over at him.

Now what's he going to do?

He grinned at Megan. "Oh, Meg, don't be like that. Everyone loves you and you know it. Just let Eden have her night, that's all. Willow just wants you to play nice, no biggie."

Willow stared at Chase. Chase continued to soothe Megan. "What do you say?"

Megan's face slowly relaxed. She glanced at Eden. "Sorry, I'll go if you want me to."

Dumbstruck, she shook her head. "No, you can stay, Megan."

Megan nodded and turned to Jake, who looked anxious to keep his date at the party. They stepped away, and Chase glanced over at Eden.

"Everybody cool?" he asked.

"Yeah, thanks Chase and," Eden searched for Willow, but she was gone, "Willow," she finished.

"Well, that was strange," Andrew stated next to her. "Sorry I didn't rise to your defense like Willow and Chase; they sort of beat me to it." He gave her a crooked grin.

"Yeah, I noticed."

She expected a witty comeback, not for him to lower his head. His lips brushed hers, goose bumps crawling down her skin. He drew her into his arms, his mouth pushing harder on hers. She was lost in the moment, absorbing his taste, smell, and feel. When he pulled back, she toppled into him, her eyes half open.

He chuckled, holding onto her arms.

Her eyes opened fully. His emerald eyes gazed back at her, expectant.

She smiled. "I guess you're forgiven."

Eden lips were still tingling where Andrew's lips had been. The rest of the party was sort of a blur. After eating, Andrew cranked the stereo, and they had an impromptu dance in the living room. Eden didn't care what they did as long as Andrew stayed close; she felt sort of intoxicated by him. Glancing over, she discovered Caitlyn next to them, dancing with a boy Eden had met earlier, but whose name had eluded her. Just as Caitlyn grinned back at her, Caitlyn toppled forward and landed with a thud on the floor.

"Oh my gosh! Are you ok?" Eden asked, dropping down by her.

"Stupid shoes, knew they were too tall," Caitlyn muttered. "Yeah, I'm fine."

The boy she'd been dancing with reached down and helped pull her up. Eden stood up too as Andrew asked, "Are you hurt?"

"No, I just tripped." Caitlyn stepped away from the boy holding her arm and winced.

"Twisted your ankle, didn't you," Andrew stated.

Caitlyn nodded. "I'm such a klutz."

"Come on. Let's go to the kitchen for some ice," Andrew said, as

Eden placed her arm around Caitlyn's shoulders.

The boy took her other arm, and they hobbled from the room, with Caitlyn groaning, "Guys, I'm fine. You're practically carrying me."

Once in the kitchen, the boy helped her sit on one of the stools. Caitlyn smiled at him. "Thanks, Dave."

Finally, a name for him, Eden thought, going to the freezer.

She returned to see Andrew had removed Caitlyn's shoe and was down on his knees with his hands on her ankle. Knowing how Andrew enjoyed learning about medicine, she thought nothing of it. Although, she did notice how Caitlyn's face went from grimace to smiling. He removed his hands and stood up.

"Wow! That really helped. It doesn't hurt anymore," Caitlyn said, flexing her ankle.

Eden held up the ice pack. "Do you need this still?"

Caitlyn shook her head and tentatively stood up, testing her foot on the ground. Her smile widened. "Wow, it doesn't hurt *at all*."

"Good," Andrew said.

Once they were back in the living room, Willow hurried over to Caitlyn. Eden went to join them, but Jessie walked up.

"Can't believe it," she breathed out, grabbing Eden's arm.

"What?"

"Check out Miss Priss." Jessie motioned with her chin. "She's actually being nice."

Eden glanced over, and saw Megan talking to some of her friends. Jessie was right; her face appeared happy, even relaxed.

"Huh," Eden grunted. "That's good."

Jessie's eyes widened; Kevin was coming over. He was in Drama club with Jessie and Eden suspected she had a crush on him, though she'd never admit it.

"Hey Eden, hey Jessie," the freckled, towhead said.

"Hi Kevin," Eden replied, noting how bright his green eyes were. *And he's got a nice smile... Ok, I see the appeal now.*

"Hey Kev," Jessie said, already dismissing him as she walked away.

Jessie, quit running away from boys! Eden wanted to scream.

Kevin hesitated, not sure what to do.

"Go ask her to dance," Eden said. He looked at her, surprised, and then grinned. He was gone as Andrew returned to her side.

A slow song began, and Andrew's arms wrapped around her waist, pulling her to him.

"You must be learning a lot at the hospital," she commented, as they danced.

"I am, actually. Why?"

"You seemed to know what you're doing with Caitlyn."

"Do I detect some jealousy?"

"No." She gazed into his eyes. "Should I be?"

He gave her a lopsided grin. "No way," he murmured, as his lips found hers again.

Chapter Twenty-Five

Micah sat up, gasping, his hands gripping his shirt, and then searching his chest and stomach. There was nothing, no gaping wound or gushing blood.

Just another horrible vision, but it felt so real, the pain unbearable.

The apartment was quiet as he trudged to the kitchen, the terracotta tiles cool on his bare feet. His mouth was cottony, his tongue feeling thick and swollen.

Just need a drink, he consoled himself. He downed three glasses of water before setting his glass down with a clink on the granite counter. Sighing, he debated between sitting at the kitchen table or returning to his room. Lately, his bed felt more like a prison, a deceptive cocoon of bedding, which only trapped him in nightmares night after night.

He longed for a dream of Eden, even if it caused him heartache. It'd been three weeks since he'd emailed Eden. Emailed her good-bye, it'd felt like.

Still, he'd gladly see her now. *I can handle emotional pain… these new dreams are way too physical for my taste. Demons and more demons and now I get to see the prince demon leaders.*

He shuddered. Not wanting to wake anyone, he made his way back to his room. Lying on his back, staring at the white ceiling, he tucked both hands under his neck.

It has to get better, right? I'm doing everything I can. All I do, every day, is search for that temple. I've stopped thinking about what I want. Or, at least I've tried... Eden came to mind. He tried to push her face from him. *She's not for me. There are bigger things than what I want. Like the fire coming,* he reminded himself for the thousandth time.

"Micah," a male voice called in his dark room.

Micah bolted up. "Who's there?" He searched the darkness.

"Don't be afraid, Micah." The voice was rich, full, yet calming at the same time.

"Ok, I'm not afraid, but where are you?" He didn't see anyone.

"I'm with you now. Listen to my voice."

He cocked his head to the side. *There was something so familiar about his voice...*

"I'm listening," he whispered. "Who are you?"

"I am the Captain."

He gasped. "The Captain?"

"Yes, and I am pleased with your service, Micah. You have sacrificed everything, and have been willing to sacrifice even more. I've come to tell you it's time."

"Time? Time for what?" he asked, excited, yet terrified, by the implications.

As if to answer him, Sage appeared. Micah's eyes adjusted to her brightness as she smiled back at him.

"Sage will tell you *all* you need to know," the Captain's voice continued.

Micah gaped at her.

All I need to know... like the...

"Yes, the location of the Enoch's temple," the Captain finished Micah's thoughts.

Chapter Twenty-Six

"Prom's in a few weeks, going with Andrew. I guess that's no big surprise though, since we're dating and all," Eden said to her empty bedroom. She set her hairbrush down. Her hair was silky from all the absentminded brushing.

"So what do you think of my family moving? I'm excited. We're moving back into our old neighborhood, but we won't be on the same street."

Won't be on Micah's street again.

"Can't believe it's April already," she announced, trying to change the subject with herself. Of course, April made her think, *Micah's finally coming home!*

Her homework was done, but she didn't want to leave her bedroom yet. She glanced around, feeling listless.

"Are you here still? Can't you appear again? Just sit with me. I'd love to learn something about you. Like your name."

She waited.

Nothing.

She grabbed her Bible, now a regular fixture on her nightstand. She tried not to force her own actions, hoping her hands would move on their own. The result—the book sat unopened in her lap.

She grunted, "Fine," opening it up to the beginning, in Genesis.

She scanned the first few chapters: the Creation, the story of Adam and Eve and the Garden of Eden, and then, in the third chapter, something caught her eye.

"So he drove out the man; and he placed at the east of the garden of Eden Cherubim, and a flaming sword which turned every way, to keep the way of the tree of life."

"Flaming sword? Like your flaming sword?"

She felt the good feeling.

"So is this you? Are you one of those Cherubim?"

Good feeling.

She grinned. "That's so cool! I can't believe you were in the Garden of Eden." She scanned a few more verses. "So you blocked the way to the Tree of Life, and kept Adam and Eve from eating it. You defended the Garden of Eden, and now you just guard me?"

She glanced around, deciding for some reason to look directly at the empty spot next to her on the bed.

"Why would you be with *me*?" she whispered.

The good feeling engulfed her, and her eyes stung. She wasn't sure what it meant. *Other than he must think I'm worth guarding.*

She grinned at the air, raising one eyebrow.

"Well, one thing's for sure, you angels sure age well."

The good feeling was mingled with something. *Perhaps he's laughing.*

Entering the always-stuffy Biology room the next day, Eden slid into her small, wooden desk. The square classroom felt hotter than usual, the smells of past dissections assaulting her nostrils. She was rifling through her folder, looking for today's homework assignment, when someone touched her arm. She turned, and stared into Damon's chocolate eyes. Dumbfounded, she focused on the pencil held between his black fingernails.

"You dropped this."

"Oh, thanks." She grabbed it and, embarrassed, glanced away. She felt his gaze on her for a brief moment, and then the desk was creaking behind her as he moved into it.

The teacher, Mr. Biggs, began explaining how pumps and valves shuttle ions in and out of cells, and she tried to listen.

She thought she was paying attention until she heard Mr. Biggs repeat, "Eden, can you give me an example in the human body of when myocites beat in unison?"

Her mouth went dry.

Damon mumbled, "The heart."

"The heart," she repeated like a parrot.

"Correct." Mr. Biggs continued with his lecture.

She twisted in her seat to face Damon and mouthed, *Thanks again.*

She supposed the arched eyebrow she got meant, *no problem.* After class ended, she rotated to face him.

"Thanks for saving me."

"No worries." He didn't make eye contact as they both stood.

Enough of this, she decided. *Forget what happened. I'm sick of awkwardness.*

"Hey Damon, do you remember when you used to throw spit wads in my hair?" she asked, and then forced a laugh. *Way to break the ice, Eden.*

He stared at her. "Kind of hoped you forgot about that."

"No way, it was the only attention I ever got from a boy. I think it's funny now."

"It wasn't very nice attention, sorry."

"Don't be, we were kids." She smiled at him, feeling something strange stirring inside.

She was so out of her comfort zone just talking to Damon, she didn't realize what *that* feeling meant until it was too late.

Her mind groaned as her arms reached forward, like a stiff, unbending robot. She had no choice, her body moved on its own accord, hugging him.

She stepped back quickly, noting he did not return the hug. His brown eyes were staring back at her now, his mouth ajar.

He's in shock. Is he breathing?

"Ah, sorry, I like to hug... people," she mumbled. *Of all the people!*

His mouth closed, his black brows relaxing slightly. "Looks like it. See ya."

And he walked out of the classroom.

No one was left, not even the teacher. No one, but her guardian she supposed, could see her collapse into her seat, legs shaking uncontrollably.

He's never missed a day and I should know. I haven't either.

As much as Eden was mortified by Monday's hugging, she was even more embarrassed that Damon missed over a week of school since it. *Does he dislike me that much?*

Wednesday, Damon staggered into the classroom, his face down, his hands shoved into his pockets.

Nervous, yet relieved, she peeked over at him. His face was pale, almost green, and his eyes bloodshot. *Man, he looks miserable.*

"Hey Damon, were you sick?" she asked as he passed.

"Yeah, sure," Damon grunted, not looking at her.

So much for getting rid of awkwardness—I just made it worse.

As class wore on, she heard him muttering under his breath a few times. She tried to understand what he was saying, while sort of feeling bad for eavesdropping, but she couldn't pick out any recognizable words. *Doesn't sound English.*

When class ended, she asked again, "Are you feeling ok?"

He gathered his stuff.

She waited, and then repeated, "Damon, are you still sick?"

He glanced at her as if he seeing her there for the first time. "What? Oh, yeah, I'm fine." He strode from the room.

Micah could see sweat trickling down the boy's neck, the back of his dark gray t-shirt wet. The boy swiped his palms down his jeans. As an unseen passenger in the back, Micah watched the car stop. The boy with black hair jumped from the front seat, already bolting for the house.

"Damon," the woman in the driver's seat called after, "don't make yourself scarce. You father needs help in the yard today."

Damon, Micah assumed, turned, removing the ear buds from his ears.

In his dream, Micah followed the woman as she approached her son. "I know you've been sick, but I think some fresh air would do you good. I need to get all the weeds cleared out of my flowerbeds, and your father's itching to get his garden cleared and ready. You know how he likes to plant too early."

Damon shrugged his shoulders. "Ok," he said, replacing his earpieces.

Micah observed him working for a long time, wondering why he was seeing such an uneventful vision. From what he could tell, there was nothing unusual going on here. Damon had just finished stuffing the last garbage bag full of the weeds.

"Thanks," his mom said, walking over.

"Sure. Is that all?" He hefted the bag onto the other bags.

"Well, your dad's wrestling with that silly stump again. He wants his garden to be a few feet bigger this year. You remember the little stump next to it? He's got it in his head that he can move it all by himself."

Damon looked in the direction of the loud grumbling. "I'll go help him."

"Heaven knows he needs it. I'll get supper on. How does fried chicken and cream corn sound?"

"Good," Damon called as he jogged around the house. Micah followed him, curious.

Approaching, the grumbling became a stream of profanities. Micah grunted. *Guess the stump's winning.*

"Why don't you take a break and let me try, Dad?" Damon offered.

Damon's dad glanced up with sweat was dripping off his nose. "All right. Knock yourself out, kid. I need some lemonade."

The man marched away, still griping under his breath. Damon and Micah studied the stump. It wasn't big, perhaps six inches in diameter. Damon's dad had dug out all around it.

Damon picked up the shovel and dug deeper. After a few minutes, he tossed the shovel aside and, getting down low, grabbed the stump, pulling hard.

"Come on." Damon exerted himself, and then incoherent words were tumbling from his mouth. Damon's eyes widened, perhaps shocked by his own outburst. The words were unfamiliar to Micah, yet the intonation felt powerful.

He wondered if Damon understood what he'd just said.

Damon's mouth dropped open.

Micah saw why. The stump was no longer rooted in its spot. It'd moved three feet over, buried in the earth like it'd been there for years.

Damon straightened up and muttered, "Holy crap."

Then Micah was back in his bedroom, his suitcase sprawled open on his bed, next to his plane tickets.

"Oh man, Trent's going to love this guy," Micah said out loud as he finished shoving his clothes into his bag.

Chapter Twenty-Seven

Friday morning, Eden tugged her dress from her closet. She wanted to look at it one more time before tonight. After Andrew had asked her to go, her mom had taken her shopping. They'd hit several stores before walking into a boutique full of prom dresses in the mall. Eden had immediately fallen in love with her dress. It was sleeveless with a V-neck, and had a crisscross open back. The worker at the store called it a Grecian silhouette, with a high waist hitting directly under her chest, covered in a glittering band. The dress hugged her hips and then flowed out to the floor.

Her mom had gasped when she came out of the dressing room. "It looks like it was made for you."

"Really? You like it? I don't usually get things in red, but I love this," she admitted, doing a pirouette in the mirror.

"You look gorgeous, so grown up," her mom had confirmed.

Now she held the hanger up, the red material silky in her hands.

"I *am* excited to go," she said out loud, maybe to reassure herself. It didn't help knowing Micah was flying back any day now. Her parents weren't sure what day, and she was too embarrassed to call the Hawkins to find out.

At school, there was a definite buzz among the students. Eden felt bad Kevin hadn't mustered enough courage to ask Jessie to go too. By their lockers, she asked Jessie how the play was going in drama, since she had the supporting lead. That got Jessie talking all the way to trig.

Andrew grinned at Eden, not saying a word about their plans. It would only make Jessie feel left out, since she was the only one in their group not going. Willow and Chase, Caitlyn and Dave, and even Jake and Megan were joining them.

Ironically, after her party, Megan was a lot nicer to Eden. Since Eden lingered in the hall a little too long with Andrew after class, she had to hustle into Biology. She wasn't surprised to see Damon already sitting in his chair. He always beat her now.

She hurried to her seat and then, seeing she was still on time, twisted around.

"Are you going to prom?"

He made eye contact "No," and then looked away.

She had decided to continue to be friendly, even if his expression read, *Leave me alone.*

"That's too bad. Are you feeling any better yet?" she probed.

"I'm fine; I'm not sick." He stared back at her.

She sighed inwardly, and flipped around.

He sure isn't making it easy.

Everyone was eating and having a good time at the steak house, until Chase said, "Hey, did you guys hear Micah's back?"

Megan sputtered, covering her mouth with a napkin. Jake patted her back, saying, "Awesome! It's about time he got home."

Eden was glad all eyes were on Megan, not her. Her cheeks felt warm.

Chase agreed. "He texted me about an hour ago, wants to know if we wanted to hang out tonight. He didn't know its prom. I tried to get him to stag it with us, but he didn't want to. He's cool with us coming over later for the after the party-party." Chase grinned. "What do you think?"

Everyone looked around at each other, nodding and saying, "Yeah."

"Is that ok with you?" Andrew asked her.

She swallowed. "Sure."

She caught Caitlyn's hazel eyes gazing at her, an unspoken question in her expression. Eden pretended she didn't notice.

Once dinner had ended, they filed into their cars, heading for the park. The dance was held outdoors this year, in a large park the school had reserved. There was a white canopy set up with white lights lining the entire ceiling and sides. The DJ was on a stage at the front of the tent, and there was some kind of hard flooring down on the ground. It was too packed to even see what it was made of. Eden noticed there was another, smaller tent set up around the dance floor. Peering in, there was one long refreshment table and many small, round tables, where kids were sitting and eating.

After several fast and slow songs, Eden made her excuse. She needed a minute. It felt like her heart was in overdrive and her mind sluggish.

"Mind if I run to the restroom real quick? I need to freshen up. It's sort of hot in here." She felt lame saying it.

"Not at all, I think the bathroom's back there." Andrew pointed at the small building nestled in the trees. She nodded as he said, "Meet you back by the refreshments."

She followed the path to the restrooms, taking long, deep breaths. *It'll be fun seeing Micah again.*

She entered the ladies room with a throng of girls. Impressed, it was much larger than it'd appeared on the outside, Eden searched for an empty sink or mirror. It was packed with girls, reapplying makeup, fixing hair, and pushing up chests in bras. A few girls finished their touch-ups and stepped away, leaving Eden free to stare at herself in the mirror. Though Jessie's makeup abilities were good, she saw the panic in her own eyes.

Why does he do this to me?

Wringing her hands together, she left, and instead of heading back towards the dance, she wandered towards the trees. *Just need a minute to clear my head.*

Hiking her dress up to her shins, she stepped off the path, and further into the dark trees. She was so engrossed in giving herself a lecture on how she needed to let Micah go, she missed the slight push against her chest. Wandering deeper into the forest, she shivered. Her naked skin was exposed to the gusts that were now making the trees sway and bend.

Oblivious to her surroundings, the smell of rotten eggs assaulted her.

She gasped. *Oh my gosh, what have I done?*

Throwing her dress up higher, she spun around, sprinting back. The wind was strong now; her hair lifted off her shoulders, blowing into her face. She compelled her legs to go faster, as she reprimanded herself for being so stupid.

A man's voice commanded, "Eden, run faster!"

Although she had only heard him once before, she knew his voice, and whirled around.

Fire lit up the night as it whipped through the air. Heaping piles of ash surrounded him on the ground. He backed closer to her, his blade between her and the figures approaching. As he continued to lunge forward and slice them down, her eyes began to make out the vastness of their numbers.

Terror shook her; there were hundreds of them, jumping down from trees and climbing out from behind rocks. Feeling too stunned to move, she stared as her guardian sliced through ten more demons within seconds. But more were coming, lots more. Finally registering what she must do, she clutched her dress and bolted. Dashing through the trees, she didn't slow even when she snagged on branches. Her dress was ruined, her bare skin scraped, but none of that mattered now.

She could hear the battle behind her, the shrieks and cries, smelling of rotten flesh and sulfur. Her path was lit by her guardian's sword. He was behind her, holding them back, but not all were destroyed. They were on either side of her now, faster than she was. One to the right reached out just as fire sliced through its arms. Being close, the black forms actually looked semi-human, with long, skinny arms and massive, powerful legs. *Just like Micah said.*

One to her left lunged, and this time there was no fire stopping it. It grabbed her at the waist, knocking her to the ground. But this one didn't gloat over her, as the one in her bedroom had, but instead, it sunk its nasty, long nails deep into her back as it pulled her off the ground, and threw her over its shoulder.

She screeched, not only for the searing pain in her back, but at the insane speed at which it dashed deeper into the trees. Frantically searching for her guardian, she was thrown to the ground. Stumbling back, she saw the demon she'd ridden on lose its legs to the flaming sword. Once she was out of the way, her guardian sliced through its skull.

Her guardian moved to stand over her. She was amazed and horrified at the fluidity and accuracy of his movements; she'd never seen someone so outnumbered fight off so many. She knew it was vital to escape, but was too afraid to leave his side.

The ground shook beneath her.

She scrambled to her feet.

A massive man appeared and unlike the other demons' tight skin stretched over bones, this one had a face with flesh. His hoodless, black robe revealed his bald head and forearms, both blood red with swirling, black patterns on it.

His mouth opened, unnaturally elongated, as he uttered moans and chants.

It had rhythm; every time a deep, drum-like noise sounded in his throat, the demons bowed their heads. In horror, Eden realized, the scurrying black bodies were moving as one and they were all advancing towards her.

Her guardian raised both of his arms above his head, and then lowered them.

A blast of warm air hit her as men appeared, lining both sides of them. She gasped as they drew their swords—every single blade was on fire. She counted twelve standing to her guardian's left and twelve on his right. Their swords were shorter than her guardian's, and didn't burn as brightly, but they were impressive. *They're all Cherubim!*

For a moment, everyone held their ground.

The chanting demon scowled at her guardian and then cackled. It echoed off the trees, surrounding her.

"Is that all?" his gravelly voice asked.

"Oeillet, Prince of Dominions, I would ask you the same thing."

Oeillet growled, spewing black smoke from its mouth. In unison, the demons roared back and charged forward.

Chapter Twenty-Eight

Micah's mind was falling deeper and deeper into the earth, past layers of mud, clay, stone, silt, sediment, his mind delved on. He could feel something was near, something old, ancient, and evil.

He strained against the rough earth, trying to clear his vision. That's when he entered a black crevice. At first, he saw nothing in the inky black, but then, as his eyes adjusted, he made out a face, only a nose and mouth appearing in the shadows. The pale lips moved, white teeth contrasting with blood-red gums.

"Worthless demons, must I do everything for you? You failed in the forest with the Seer."

"But Master, he wasn't alone," a muffled voice whined back.

Micah searched the black space but saw no one else.

"Of course he wasn't alone, you idiot. He has a guardian. I allowed several through; the guardian was outnumbered."

"Yes, my Master, but she's a Seraph. Nothing can withstand her flames."

"Then how did he escape unscathed? Pathetic," the white face growled.

"Yes, Master," the mystery voice graveled.

"And what is your excuse for the girl? One helpless girl who's guardian was gone." The white face contorted into a scowl as he spoke the word *guardian*.

Micah's gut sickened. *One guess who the girl is.*

"I giftwrapped her. Her guardian went to the council our ploy had caused. You had one slice of time, she was alone, and you failed."

There was a grumbling sound. "Master, the demon wasted too much time; her guardian returned before he could secure her."

"Why?" the white face roared.

"She touched it, Master. It affected it, stunned it."

The pale mouth pursed together. "How interesting," he muttered.

Then his lips snarled. "I'll give you one last chance to redeem yourself and then I devote my energy to freeing Azazar; he'll destroy the Seer and all his gifted. And he'll tear the Awakener into bite-size pieces for me."

Micah's fists clenched.

He knew who he was seeing—the Leader of the Watchers, Semjaza.

He is the one orchestrating the demon attacks.

"Send a prince, one with enough ranking to be a worthy opponent for Gabriel. I will open the channel to let thousands, tens of thousands, through. The woods are deep and thick; there will be plenty of places to hide and wait." The lips lifted into a sneer, "Get me the girl; I want her tonight." A crimson tongue licked the pale lips. Micah shuddered.

Eden's guardian stood center with guardians flanking both of his sides. She gaped as angels fought demons; so far, none had broken through the line.

Peeking around her guardian, she shuddered. Oeillet's black eyes stared back at her, as he strolled forward in a leisurely gate.

She ducked behind her guardian, but to her horror, he strode forward as well. She shrunk back, trying to hide behind the other angels. One angel with black hair pushed her behind him. She gratefully used him for protection.

The twenty-four fought like lions, but there seemed to be a never-ending supply of demons. She panicked as she felt claws grab her. The angel with dark hair fought the demon back.

She stared at her guardian, who was running straight for the red-faced demon, his sword whirling in tight circles, killing every demon in his way.

Oeillet sneered, producing a long, golden staff; one end formed the head of a viper.

He hefted it up. "I may be only a Prince of Dominion but you recognize this, don't you?" He snickered. "I have the staff of a Prince of Cherubim!"

"Am I supposed to be impressed by that?" her guardian retorted, as his sword soared into the air. He slammed it down on the demon, but Oeillet blocked the blow with the staff.

It was the first time she'd seen something actually stop the sword of fire. Could he defeat her guardian? *Should I make a run for it?*

Her guardian was undeterred by the staff, as he continued to slash at Oeillet, but the demon dodged and escaped. More arms grabbed her. One began dragging her, but the angel with black hair sliced it down. The longer her guardian fought Oeillet, the more hysterical she became, the terror of the situation overwhelming her.

Then it happened. Claws sunk into her flesh, she flew into the air, and landed on a cold, bony shoulder. The speed at which it carried her away from the angels made her screams useless. Plunging into the dark forest, she knew no one would hear her.

Demons flanked both sides of them, roaring with victory.

Straining to see over her captor's shoulder, she made out a pinpoint of light in the distance. Within seconds, it grew larger and brighter. She craned to see clearer. *Is it him?* The light's diameter stretched further, closing the gap, leaving no doubt. She could smell the charred flesh as he blazed a path with his sword through the demons. *My guardian's coming!*

The demon's body was ice to her skin; she tried shifting her weight to relieve the burning sting. When her torso and legs remained dead weight, she realized she was completely numb, except for her arms. Scared by the loss of sensation, she sent her fingernails deep into the recesses of its skull-like face, hoping to gouge its eyes.

It was a mistake.

The demon howled and snatched her flailing hand, sinking its fangs into her forearm.

Shrieking, she tried to free her arm, but it held it in its mouth, gnawing at her flesh and bones. The pain was too much. The forest went hazy.

Don't pass out!

She tumbled to the ground, the demon finally spitting out her arm. She cried out at the impact of hitting hard earth; it shattered her numbness into thousands of painful splinters.

The demon was decapitated before her, its black head sent hurtling away. She attempted to stand, but her legs refused to obey. Her guardian planted himself over her, fighting demon after demon.

Her head touched the dirt, and she watched in a stupor, counting the demons he killed. Even cradling her wrist against her chest, she was losing too much blood. Her vision was hazy; she focused on counting. Fifty-seven, fifty-eight, fifty-nine...

A piercing pain burst through her heart and lungs.

Eyes bulging, she could only make strangled gasps.

Her guardian slashed at something behind them; at the same time, she felt a pulling, sucking release in pressure. Something had been withdrawn from her back. Now the burning was replaced with an odd, draining sensation, leaving her cold.

She heard the demon's chortling and then her guardian thundered, "Now you die, Oeillet!"

The battle shifted in front of her, and she caught sight of Oeillet's staff, the sharp end covered in blood.

Her stomach lurched. *Is that my blood?*

Her eyes riveted on the weapon that had stabbed her, the viper's fangs menacing. Her guardian reared back and, with both hands, came down hard, splitting the staff in two, the snake head remaining in Oeillet's trembling hand.

The demon's sneer disappeared as her guardian immediately repeated his motion, this time slicing Oeillet from skull to feet, his two halves falling to the ground with a deafening thud.

Barely conscious, she wondered why he hadn't turn to ash like the others. She felt her guardian's arms reach for her, but countless demons piled on top of him. She heard him roar as he fought them off. The angrier her guardian became, the more powerful he seemed to be. Now he was clearing twenty, thirty demons with one slash of his blade of fire.

Her eyes closed again. She tasted something metallic and salty in her mouth.

With her body numb and tired, the thought of falling asleep was welcoming. Detached, she gazed at her guardian, who continued to fight as his twenty-four joined his side. Feeling safe, thinking no other demon would get her, she decided it was a good time to sleep, but the black night suddenly blazed brighter. Heat warmed her body, and she felt a desire to stay awake. Forcing her eyes open, she peered up to see a woman in a red dress standing next to her guardian. Grappling with what was happening, Eden recognized who she was. The woman was on fire.

"Micah sent me," she said, her black eyes staring down at Eden. "We don't have a lot of time; it's more important to get her help. Leave these to me."

Immediately, she felt arms lift her and pull her close. He held her tight against his chest as he ran. The numbness ebbed as his body warmed her, but then the pain returned. The agonizing throbbing in her half-eaten wrist and forearm, paled to the terror of struggling to get in air. It was like inhaling under water, her lungs burned, and her eyes rolled back. Again, the temptation to fall asleep came; it sounded warm and inviting.

"Stay with me, Eden," her guardian commanded.

How ironic he's finally talking to me and I can't talk back.

She nestled her face into him and closed her eyes.

"Eden, I'm getting help! Stay awake!" he shouted at her.

She struggled to open her eyes, but they felt sealed shut.

His lips pressed into her ear. "I'm Gabriel. Eden, my name's Gabriel."

She tried to open her eyes and smile, but couldn't. *Finally, I know what to call you.*

He'd stopped running and was sitting down on the ground, holding her still.

Oh good, he's going to let me sleep.

As she drifted, he pleaded, "Eden, stay with me."

Micah focused his mind on Eden, as he paced his bedroom.

Trent, sitting on the leather recliner, jumped to his feet. "Do you see anything yet? What's happening?"

"Nothing yet. Give me a minute. I have to concentrate," Micah said through gritted teeth.

After telling Sage what he'd seen, Micah had demanded Sage go to them. She'd hesitated and then commanded them to stay put and together. She said Trent's guardian would watch over both of them while she was away, and then she was gone.

He felt desperate to make sure Eden was ok. That she was alive.

He took long, deep breaths, steadying his jumbled thoughts.

Then he saw her, cradled in Gabriel's arms. He was rocking her against his chest, his hands covering her gaping wounds.

Micah cringed at her condition, but remained focused. He didn't want to lose sight of her. *Her skin's so white...*

In his mind, Sage approached. There was smoke flowing from her body. Her black eyes were infuriated; he could see her chest was heaving.

"I failed. I failed her," Gabriel moaned.

"You didn't fail her. It was a calculated ambush. You did everything you could," Sage replied in a low voice.

He shook his head. "Doesn't matter, there's no excuse for this!"

Sage's onyx eyes swept over Eden's body and then she exhaled.

"He's coming."

Micah looked around; he didn't see anyone else.

"Come on, Gabriel. We have to go," Sage urged.

But he didn't move, his arms clutching Eden still.

"Gabe," Sage's voice was soft, as she placed her hand on his shoulder. "She's going to be ok, he's here. But you have to let her go *now*."

Gabriel gazed down at Eden curled up in his arms, her face so still it terrified Micah.

He pressed his lips into her hair and whispered, "Don't leave me, Eden."

Micah watched as he carefully laid her on the ground, and then the two angels disappeared. He moved closer to Eden in his mind, crouching down next to her.

He reached out, hoping to touch her face, but his fingers fell through the space, feeling nothing.

I was too late. She's not going to make it. His throat closed up at the same time he heard a masculine voice yelling her name. Micah turned around, spying someone running in the woods, not far from them.

In that moment, the young man saw Eden. Micah had already guessed who it would be. He was relieved, yet saddened, to know he'd been right.

Andrew was sprinting towards them, falling to his knees once he'd reached Eden's still body.

Micah stepped back, knowing logically he couldn't possibly be in Andrew's way, but wanting to give him space nonetheless. Perhaps it was a symbolic gesture.

I need to move out of the way so she can be with who she's meant to be with. Andrew, who can take care of her, keep her safe. Not me, all I do is put her life in danger.

Andrew was surveying her injuries; Micah peered down. It was like her red dress covered her entire back and chest, instead of her skin completely bathed in her own blood.

Andrew held his ear over her mouth, at the same time checking for a pulse. He straightened, and gingerly examined her hand, which looked barely attached. He pressed his own hands down on bluish skin. The tissues began coming together, bones filling in, and arteries and veins mending slowly.

Micah gaped at it, amazed. He'd suspected this was Andrew's gift, but to see it in action was something else.

Andrew's moves were frantic. He muttered, "Too slow; it's too slow!"

He turned Eden's body slightly, and then fussed over the large hole in her back, shoving his hands over it. A sheen of sweat covered his face. *Healing her is taxing him.*

"Come on, stay with me." He thrust his hands deeper into the wound.

Micah wrung his hands together, and then shoved them through his hair and down his face.

A person brushed past him, female, with light brown hair and a velvet, blue dress. She reached out, touching Andrew's shoulder.

He heard Andrew gasp, but he didn't turn around.

The gaping hole in her back immediately sealed shut, and Eden's chest began rising and falling again. Andrew turned his attention to her hand next, the damaged flesh healing under his fingers. Once her hand was again a normal color, he worked on the cuts covering the rest of her body.

"Amazing," the girl breathed out.

Andrew spun around, apparently forgetting he wasn't alone. *He was totally engrossed in healing Eden. Good man.*

"Caitlyn?" Andrew blurted.

She seemed to hesitate. "I saw you go running off and followed. I'm not sure why, but I thought you might need my help. How'd you do that?"

"I don't know. I heal people by touching them. But you did something too."

Micah stared at Caitlyn.

She shook her head. "No, I just watched. Does Eden know?"

"No." When Caitlyn cocked an eyebrow at him, he added, "Not yet,

I'm going to tell her. Don't say anything."

Caitlyn nodded and Eden coughed.

Andrew turned and pulled her into his arms.

Micah jumped forward as well, wishing he could take her hand in his. *She's ok!*

"Andrew?" Eden breathed out. Her eyes darted back and forth. "What happened?" Her voice was hoarse.

"Kind of hoping you could tell us, but let's get out of here first." Andrew lifted her up.

Micah swallowed. Knowing she was all right now, a different feeling slinked in, replacing the awe he felt over Andrew's gift with sheer envy. *She's cradled in his arms now.* Micah shifted his gaze to the trees.

"I'm ok. I can walk," Eden mumbled.

"What's that?" Caitlyn asked. "Is that fire?"

Micah peered into the distance, where Caitlyn pointed. *Sage's flames.*

He glanced back at Eden as she stuttered, "Please, let's just go."

Then it was all gone. He was back with Trent.

Micah collapsed to his knees, exhausted both physically and mentally.

"She's ok, she's alive. Sage got there in time." He paused. "She was hurt pretty bad, but Andrew healed her."

Trent's eyebrows lifted but, for once, he said nothing.

Chapter Twenty-Nine

The three of them darted away from the light and into the dark woods. Together they made it back to the bathroom, where Willow was pacing.

"There she is!" Willow rushed to Eden, giving Chase a stern look. "I told you Andrew would find her."

Chase's mouth dropped open as he gaped at Eden. "What the—?"

Andrew removed his arm from around her waist, and took off his dress coat. "Here, you're shivering to death," he urged.

"Wait," she slurred, her mind feeling sluggish. "Let me go wash first."

Andrew nodded. Willow and Caitlyn followed her.

Eden was sure they'd be bursting with questions, but neither girl said anything as they wadded up paper towels and got them wet in the sink.

Willow worked on Eden's back, gasping every so often.

"How did you know, Willow? How did you know Andrew would find me?" Eden asked, breaking the silence.

Willow stopped swiping at the blood and stepped in front of Eden.

"I had a feeling you were in trouble, like scary trouble. I told Chase and he just rolled his eyes at me. But I convinced Andrew to go look for you. We checked the bathroom and then," she paused, "I just knew you were in the woods."

Eden didn't miss the way she shuddered when she said *woods*.

She gazed her friends. "Thanks guys. I . . ." Her words choked off.

Willow threw her arm around Eden's side. "I owed you one. You sort of saved me too."

Eden stared at her, confused.

She grinned, and rotated Eden back around. "Come on, you're still a mess." Willow grabbed another paper towel.

Caitlyn rejoined in helping; Eden caught her hazel eyes studying her in the mirror a few times. *First time I've wished Caitlyn wasn't quite so reserved with her thoughts.*

"Caitlyn," Eden probed.

There was a moment of uncertainty and then Caitlyn blurted, "I didn't think the woods had bears… What the heck happened to you, Eden?"

Eden stalled. *Guess I asked for it.*

"I don't know." *Total lie.* "I think I sort of passed out. I don't remember anything after that." *That much is true.* "I woke up with you and Andrew there. Did you see anything?"

Caitlyn shook her head quickly.

Willow's eyes were wide as she gazed at Caitlyn. "There was definitely something sinister in those woods tonight. Maybe not a bear, but Eden's still lucky to be alive."

Caitlyn agreed. "Very lucky. What are you going to tell Jessie?"

Eden bit her lip and scrunched her eyebrows. "Nothing?" She looked to them for understanding. They both nodded.

"Probably best to keep this to ourselves," Willow confirmed.

She was as clean as she was going to get; her red dress masked a lot of the blood.

Coming out, they heard Chase say, "Maybe Willow's right. It's not safe. We should get out of here." He said it chuckling, but Eden saw his eyes dart to the trees behind them.

The sound of sirens cut through the night.

Andrew draped his coat around Eden. "I think the party's about to be busted up because of the fire in the woods."

"Fire?" Chase and Willow asked together.

"Yeah, it's big," Caitlyn replied.

"Let's go," Andrew stated.

As they passed the dance tent, Caitlyn ducked inside. There was a loud announcement from a fireman with a megaphone.

Everyone had to leave. Jake and Megan stepped out of the tent, as there were moans and complaints from students.

"This is crazy," Jake muttered.

Caitlyn and Dave came out of the tent as Chase pulled out his phone.

"Micah just texted; he wants us to come over still. How about it?" Chase asked.

"Heck yeah," Jake exclaimed. "At least the night's not a total bomb." Megan was quiet next to him.

"Not us, I think I'm going to get Eden home, but tell him hey for me," Andrew said.

Thank heavens. I'm in no condition to face Micah and Andrew together tonight, Eden thought.

Caitlyn and Dave decided to head home too, and rode back with them to Andrew's, where Dave's Protegé was parked. No one said much.

Once at the house, Caitlyn and Dave hopped out, telling Eden and Andrew good night. Even after the Protegé pulled away, Andrew continued to let his Bronco idle in driveway. He reached for her hand. She offered it, glad to feel his warmth. She was chilled to the bone.

"Are you ok?" He sounded concerned.

"Yeah, I'm good. Just wish I knew what happened. I went to the bathroom and then," she hesitated, "walked into the trees a bit. Maybe I shouldn't have, but it was such a pretty night. And then, I don't know, I can't remember. I must have fallen down, hit my head or something."

"Maybe you passed out. It happens. And an animal scratched you up pretty good while you were on the ground."

She knew her story sounded lame, unbelievable. He didn't sound like he believed his own solution either. He put his Bronco into reverse and, in silence, drove her home. His fingers squeezed her hand periodically.

It was 11:30 pm. She wasn't sure if anyone would be up; the house was dark and quiet. She unlocked the door and invited him in.

"Why don't you go upstairs and change? Bring me your dress. I'll take our clothes to the dry cleaner tomorrow," he said, sitting down on the couch.

"It won't help. My dress is ripped pretty bad." She ran the shredded material through her fingers.

"I'm sorry."

"It's ok. It's just a dress. I'll go change real quick." She was anxious to get out of the bloodstained clothes. Once in her bedroom, she stripped down, fishing out a white t-shirt and her favorite red boxers. Not wanting to be alone long, she jogged back down to find him waiting for her, his eyes sweeping her up and down.

"You look beautiful," he whispered, as she crawled onto the couch next to him. She'd pulled the clip out of her hair, letting it fall onto her shoulders in curls.

His lips found hers; she responded briefly, but then had to stop. She felt dizzy.

He held her close. His heart thumping against her ear was relaxing.

"Eden," he mumbled into her hair.

"Mmm," she hummed back.

He brushed her hair back, kissing her forehead. "Never mind. Just sleep. You need it."

She tried to respond, but it came out muffled. She wanted to ask what he was going to say, but her body was too drained. She was half-asleep, when she felt him lift her up and carry her to bed.

Chapter Thirty

Rolling over onto her side, Eden peeked through her eyelashes at her hand. *I can't believe it doesn't even hurt.* She rubbed her eyes. Sitting up, she pulled the covers off her legs. She did a quick examination of her body, finding only a few scrapes remaining on the middle of her back.

Staring at her empty bedroom, she dangled her feet over the edge of her bed.

"Gabriel, you here?"

She knew she shouldn't be disappointed that he didn't appear, but she was. *So it's back to the one-sided conversations.* But seeing him last night solidified for her that he was actually there, listening to her now.

"How am I ok?" she asked. "Did you do it?" She felt nothing. "Or maybe someone else helped me?" Remembering the extent of her injuries, she added in a whisper, "Maybe healed me?"

A warm feeling washed over her.

"Someone *healed* me?" she repeated, shocked, and again, the good feeling came.

"Who was it?"

Nothing.

"I'm sorry. I know now how stupid it was to be in the woods alone. I should've been more careful." She paused. "Thanks for saving me. If I'd had any other guardian, I wouldn't be here right now."

She wanted to say more, but there was a knock on her door.

"Come in." She stood up.

Her mom poked her head in the door asking, "Late night?"

Eden peeked at her clock; it read 10:07. *This is becoming a habit.*

"You have a visitor waiting for you downstairs, so get dressed." Her mom disappeared again, shutting the door behind her.

Must be Andrew, she thought as she debated whether to run downstairs as is. *It's not like he didn't see me last night… but Mom wasn't there, and she won't be happy to see me in 'boy's underwear' as she so lovingly calls my PJs.*

She threw jeans on, remembering how after seeing Gabriel the first time, she'd hid when she dressed for almost a month. Finally, she had realized he'd already seen the good, the bad, and the ugly, and she was being silly. So, she found it interesting that after seeing him last night, she felt no need to run and hide now, while she changed. Something about almost dying in his arms, and him pleading with her not to die, made her feel pretty comfortable with him around, no matter what.

She debated on changing her white t-shirt, but decided to leave it since she had slept in her bra anyway. Peering in the bathroom mirror, she saw she'd left her makeup on too. She wiped the black smudges under her eyes away and ran a brush through her hair; it still retained some curls.

Good enough. She jogged down the stairs. It wasn't until she waltzed into the living room that she wondered why her mom had said *visitor* and not Andrew.

Her answer sat on the couch next to Brendon. Instantly, she wished she'd spent more time cleaning up. Micah was joking and laughing with Brendon, like he'd never left. His hair was longer, his body somehow even more muscular than she remembered. She entered the room and he stood; for a split second, they stared at each other.

"I told your mom not to wake you. I know you had a late night," he apologized.

Eden's mom cut in. "He's been here over an hour. I figured you'd had enough sleep." To Micah, she added, "Besides, she would've killed me if I hadn't woken her and you left like you wanted to."

"That's right," Eden confirmed as she smiled. "Welcome home; sorry I didn't come over last night."

"Hey, don't worry about it. I understand." Micah grinned back.

Her heart hammered against her ribs.

Her mom glanced at them, and then Brendon. "Come on, we need to help dad at the house today." Brendon moaned. "It's good to see you again, Micah," her mom said, ignoring her brother. "It sounds like you had an amazing time abroad."

Brendon grudgingly stood up and followed her mom.

"Good to see you too, Mrs. McCarthy. Count on my family to help out with the move next week. See you around, Brendon," Micah called after them.

Eden watched them leave, and then glanced back at Micah.

The door clicked shut and he asked, "Are you ok? I worried about you all night."

Recalling the woman said Micah sent her to help, she wondered how much he already knew.

"I think I'm fine."

Micah's eyes continued to scan her up and down. *If I didn't know he was worried about my health, I'd think this means something else, but I'm not even going to go there.*

"You look good, Eden."

He just means I look well. "So do you." *You look more than good.* There was an uncomfortable lull, and she pointed to the couch. "Do you want to sit down?"

He sat back down in the spot he'd been in, and she chose the chair across from him.

He rested his elbows on his knees. "Willow assured me you were ok, but I had to make sure."

"How did you know?"

"Another vision. Saw you walking into the trees, your guardian fighting countless demons, and then the demon prince stabbing you." He paused, his eyes clouding over. "I know your guardian could've fought them off eventually, but you didn't have a lot of time, so Sage came to help." He stared down at his fingers. "She has a way with demons."

"The woman's Sage then? My guardian's Gabriel."

"He told you his name?"

"Yeah, I think he was trying to keep me awake." She stared at him. "Why do you sound so surprised; you know Sage's name."

"Did he tell you anything else?"

"No, why?"

"Oh, nothing."

"I really hate that answer."

"Sorry." He grinned. "You have a pretty special guardian, Eden. Maybe you'll learn more about him one day."

"Doubt it, took months just to get his name." She debated whether to admit she knew about Gabriel being in the Garden of Eden, but his laugh caught her off guard.

"Don't I know the feeling! The whole time I was in Rome, I felt like I had to unravel a puzzle layered like an onion. I wanted nothing more than a straight answer."

"Did you figure it out though, the puzzle?"

"Yeah, we did."

"Do I get to know any of it?"

"Soon, I promise."

She made a face at him, and he threw his hands up. "You have my word! I'll tell you everything really soon." His grin widened. The effect melted her resolve.

She shrugged her shoulders. "I guess that'll have to do, then." She hesitated. "You said you saw me last night, right, with Gabriel? Then what happened?"

"You don't know?" His blue eyes widened.

She shook her head. "I think, somehow, someone healed me, but I don't know who. Do you?"

He was quiet a moment and then nodded slowly. "Yeah, but I don't think I should be the one telling you."

"But you saw it all?" she persisted.

He gazed at her, his eyes penetrating. "Yes. Did you tell Andrew what happened?"

She sighed. "No, I wanted to last night. He brought me home but we..." She stopped short. "I fell asleep."

He continued to study her. She wanted to look away, but for some reason, she couldn't. *There's something different about him now. He seems older somehow.* Although, logically, she knew he'd only been gone a few months.

"How was Rome?" she asked, changing the subject. She made a point to examine the pillow she'd pulled into her lap.

"Amazing." He leaned back into the couch. "We'll have to go there someday. You'd really love it."

There he goes again, throwing those curve balls at me.

"Let me know when you buy the plane tickets."

He gave her a crooked grin. "Deal."

Her pulse was ringing in her ears, the very thought of going anywhere with Micah made her dizzy.

She peeked up from the pillow to see he was still staring back at her.

She swallowed, mustering the courage to ask something she'd wondered. "So you see things, right?"

"Yeah."

"How does it work?"

He cocked an eyebrow at her.

She fiddled with the ruffle on the pillow. "Do you see whatever you want? Or do just random things pop up?"

"I wish I could control it more, to tell you the truth, but most of the time it just comes to me. Like yesterday, I was thinking about you, and then I'm seeing," slightest hesitation, "you in the woods. Why do you ask?"

He was thinking about me? Ok, focus. "So do you know what's going to happen before it does?"

"Sometimes, yeah, almost like a warning. Why?"

"Um, I guess since you saw me last night, I sort of wondered if maybe you had other visions of me too?" *There, I said it!* "It's stupid to ask."

"No, it's not. It has to be unnerving to know someone is watching you, although maybe that's not a foreign concept to us anymore." He raised his eyebrows as he exhaled. "Yes, I saw you while I was gone. I probably saw you more than anyone else."

Eden felt her face heat. *What did he see?*

He leaned forward, his face earnest. "I discovered a ton in Rome, but the biggest surprise for me was what I learned about myself. It's funny; I thought I was good at making people feel comfortable around me. I thought it meant I was good at communicating. I didn't realize—" Micah stopped as the house phone started ringing.

Engrossed in what he was saying, Eden was annoyed with the interruption. "Ignore it."

Micah continued, "I wasn't one to think too deeply about things before," he made a low chuckle, "that sure changed. Well, I had more time to think things through and... see *things* clearer. I didn't know what I had back here at home. I took," he hesitated, "*things* for granted."

He stared at her.

Ok, I'm lost.

"What do you mean?" she asked.

He sighed. "Man, Trent was right. I totally stink at talking about this stuff. I guess what I'm trying to say is, I—" This time her cell phone buzzed.

She glanced around and spied her purse on an end table. *Curses.* "It's fine, I'll get it later."

"Are you sure? It might be Andrew." He leaned back into the couch.

He's probably right. She dug in her purse and found her phone. It was Andrew. She wasn't sure what to do.

"Go ahead." He nodded her on.

"Hey," she answered, walking into the kitchen. She wasn't sure why she didn't want to talk in front of Micah.

Their conversation was brief and, when she returned to the living room, Micah was standing. The moment of openness was gone, and she was disappointed.

"Is he on his way over?" he asked.

"How did you know, another vision?" she teased.

"No, I just know that's what I'd be doing if you were my girlfriend," he replied, his eyes not leaving hers.

His words did funny things to her insides.

"I better go," he said, walking to the door.

"You don't need to leave. Andrew would love to see you." She followed him, not wanting him to leave yet. *We have so much to talk about still.*

"Did you tell him I was here?" He faced her.

"Well, no," she replied. *Am I trying to hide it from Andrew?*

"Then let's just talk later, ok? Besides, Trent's probably having a fit that I've been gone this long. I swear, he acts like we're married sometimes."

"Trent's here? He didn't go back to Texas?"

"He's moved in with us, going to go to college here. He'll be happy to see you again."

"Oh, I bet. He's probably dying to tease me since last time I jumped into his arms."

"He might. You sort of changed his life with *that* hug." Micah chuckled.

She didn't get the joke, but grinned. "Whatever."

"Speaking of which, can your old friend get a hug good-bye?" He opened his arms to her.

She hesitated long enough for her heart to jump into her throat, and then stepped into his arms. It felt like January again, standing in the tree house. Her pulse was pounding so hard she was afraid he'd feel it through his tight hold. She expected him to let her go, but he didn't.

Is he smelling my hair? She swore she heard him inhale, as she felt his face press against the side of her head.

"I thought I lost you," he whispered into her ear. "I'm glad you're ok."

"Me too," she said into his shoulder.

His hand touched the spot on her back where she'd been stabbed. She wondered if it was a coincidence until he let her go partway, taking her right hand into his. He examined her wrist and arm and then, turning her hand over, he caressed her forearm, right where her injury had been.

Goose bumps covered both of her arms; she hoped he didn't notice.

It was getting hard to remain objective. She wanted desperately to believe it meant something. He snapped her back into reality.

"You should tell Andrew about last night. You'll be surprised with how well he handles the truth."

Just like that, the fairy tale was over. *He's still just my friend, who is not at all bothered by the fact I'm dating one of his friends.*

She pulled her arm away. "Yeah, maybe I will. I feel bad lying to him."

Micah's eyes followed her hand, and then looked up. "You haven't been lying, but I think he deserves the truth."

What does he mean by that? Something crossed over Micah's face; his eyebrows bent low as his blue eyes studied her face. *Did he just glance at my lips?*

"I missed you, Eden." His voice was low, deep.

Her heart ached to say, *I missed you too,* but she swallowed and forced a smile. "Well, you're back now and I'm not going anywhere."

He snapped out of whatever he'd been feeling, his blue eyes dancing again. "True. I had better get out of here. I'll see you next weekend for the move."

"Oh, ok." She felt jolted. "Thanks for coming over, Micah."

He nodded, grinned, and was gone.

She stared out the window as his truck disappeared. She felt weak from the roller coaster ride of emotions. Against her will, she'd hoped for more with him, but ended up confused and upset. To make matters worse, she didn't have time to shrug it off because Andrew's Bronco was pulling in.

One thing Micah had said did make sense to her. *I need to talk to Andrew, no more stalling.*

Chapter Thirty-One

"Good morning, beautiful. How did you sleep?" Andrew asked, coming through the door. He didn't let her answer, because he had her in his arms and was kissing her lips.

"Good. How about you?" She pulled her face back.

He studied her. "Not that great actually. I was worried about you. How do you feel?"

Want the truth?

"I'm fine, really. Don't worry."

Andrew peered around. "Where's everybody?"

"They're over at the house. My dad's finishing installing the new carpet and my mom and Brendon are cleaning."

Andrew glanced at her. "Surprised they didn't make you go."

The moment of truth—did she tell him about Micah's visit?

"I slept in, but I think my mom wants me over there too," she said, hating herself. It wasn't a lie really, but she still felt guilty. "Andrew, can we talk about last night?" she asked, before she lost her nerve.

He gazed at her and then nodded. "I think we should."

She sat down, Andrew sitting next to her. She faced him, rubbing her hands together; they felt cold.

"What I'm going to tell you is going to sound crazy, but you need to hear me out, okay? But first I should probably to tell you what happened in February."

She relayed to him the night in her bedroom when Gabriel had

killed the demon, leaving out how she now talked to Gabriel every day. Afraid
to hear what he would say, she plunged into last night's events. Getting to
the part where Sage appeared, she realized she'd omitted telling him about
seeing her the first time at Micah's. But Andrew seemed engrossed in her
story and didn't ask questions.

She explained how Sage caused the fire in the forest to burn all the
demons. "And that's where I don't know the rest of the story. I remember
being in Gabriel's arms, and then I woke up to you and Caitlyn."

She finally peeked at him, scared to see his reaction, but he was
staring at his hands. She bit her lip, waiting for a response.

Finally, he met her eyes. "When I found you, you were practically
dead." He placed her hands in his. "Your arm looked like an animal bit
through it." He rotated her wrist. "Now it makes sense," he said, more to
himself.

Relieved he believed her, she exhaled the breath she didn't know
she'd been holding. "But if you found me, how did I—?" She stopped, eyes
widening.

Andrew didn't say anything as he stood, pulling her to her feet. He
began lifting her t-shirt up. Still lost on the fact that Andrew was the one to
save her, she didn't resist.

As her shirt started to reach her bra, she pushed down on his hands,
"Andrew, wait."

But he had stopped and was examining her back. He placed his
hand over the few remaining scrapes, and a warm sensation spread over her
skin. Removing his hand, he guided hers to feel her back.

She gasped. The large scab was gone, leaving her skin smooth. "It
was you," she gasped, staring into his emerald eyes.

"I've wanted to tell you for so long, but I was afraid you'd think I was
some kind of freak."

Her eyes welled with tears. "You saved my life. What you do is
beautiful." Overcome with feelings of gratitude, she pressed her mouth on
his.

He returned the kiss, his hands holding her firmly against him. They had kissed before but it had never felt like this. Her head was spinning and she pulled back. He didn't seem to mind as he held her close.

"I love you," he whispered.

The words caused an electric shock to shoot through her. *He loves me?*

She searched her heart, desperate to know if she could say it back.

She needed more time, to sort through her feelings, but she didn't have time. Andrew had laid his heart open bare before her.

"I love you too," she replied automatically. Her heart confirmed it wasn't *un-true*.

A new thought occurred to her, and she pulled back from his arms to face him.

"It was you, wasn't it?"

He stared at her.

"In the theater, why I can see..."

He grinned. "Sorry, I was still learning, didn't have much control over it then."

"My parents took me to the eye doctor like three times! They didn't believe I could suddenly see perfect! I should've known." She playfully swatted his shoulder.

He secured her hand and pulled her close. "You're welcome."

Chapter Thirty-Two

*W*ow, Eden, you're a hot tamale now," Trent announced, waltzing into the living room.

"Hey Trent," she said, noting how Andrew eyed Micah's cousin.

"Hi Micah," she greeted Micah, who followed his cousin through the front door. Eden's parents were already upstairs with Micah's, working on carrying down the bedroom furniture.

"Hey, excited to move back?" Micah asked. She grinned. Then to Andrew, he said, "Hey, what's up, my man?"

Andrew turned his wary eyes off Trent and gave Micah a half-slap, half-handshake. Eden had both dreaded and looked forward to this day. She wasn't sure how it would be being around Andrew and Micah at the same time, but there seemed to be no tension between them.

And why would there be? she reminded herself.

"So Eden, do I get another one of those hugs?" Trent asked.

She braced herself. "Sure."

She hoped to do it discreetly, but Trent grabbed her, saying, "My goodness, it still leaves me feeling all tingly inside."

She stepped away, embarrassed, while Andrew's eyes riveted back to Trent.

"Cut it out, Trent," Micah said. "I don't think Andrew appreciates you having your hands all over his girl."

Eden didn't appreciate it, that was for sure, but Trent was Trent. *What can you do?*

They spent the afternoon loading up the moving truck and other vehicles. Living in a small townhome, they were able to do it all in one day, with only a few trips back and forth.

Driving through Rams Gate was different this time; it wasn't to go to Micah's or Chase's, it was to go home. They turned left on Camelback, the street before Micah's. Three houses down, Andrew pulled his Bronco into the circular driveway. She peered up at her new home, a two-story, colonial, with red brick and dark blue shutters. The large porch was lined with a white, wooden railing. Her mom fell in love with the original wooden floors and the updated kitchen. Eden was excited for the library, somewhere quiet and cozy to read. Brendon only cared about the home theater.

After hours of carrying boxes and furniture from the trucks into different rooms of the house, everyone was exhausted. Eden's dad ordered in pizza and when it arrived, they called it a day. Her dad and Micah's had spent the past hour assembling bedframes and getting mattresses on them. Eden's mom had dug out bedding so they could spend the night in their new home.

Sitting next to Andrew eating, she caught Micah staring at her. She pretended not to notice at first, but when he continued to, she gazed back.

Micah grinned and her heart tumbled in her chest.

"So you heard we have a pool now, right?" he asked.

"Yeah, that's awesome. I'm so jealous," she said, swallowing down her pizza.

"Don't be, just come over."

She peeked at Andrew; he was devouring his pizza. "Thanks, I might have to," she replied, giving Micah a small smile. For some reason, her cheeks warmed. *It's not a date,* she thought, furious with herself. She ducked her face and concentrated on her food.

Soon after eating, everyone left. It was dark and late. Andrew gave her a goodnight kiss on the porch and then drove away. She'd barely reentered the house when she heard a soft knock. Thinking he'd forgotten something, she reopened the door.

She was startled to see Micah in the doorway, holding up a grocery bag. "My mom wanted to give this to you guys."

She peeked inside the bag, finding bagels, different kinds of cream cheeses, and a large bottle of orange juice.

"Your mom's amazing. Tell her thank you." She glanced up, finding his blue eyes gazing at her. "Do you want to come in?" she offered.

"Naw, I better get back. Sage won't be happy I'm out here long." He paused. "I'm glad you guys are back again. Wish it was next door like before, but I guess this is close enough."

"Yeah, it feels like I'm finally home again. Thanks for all the help today. Your family's the best."

Instead of responding, he stepped forward and kissed her cheek. Dumbstruck, she heard him say, "Good night, Eden."

She knew she should respond, but all she could think was how her skin still burned where his lips had been. *Do friends do that? Maybe... They must*, she decided.

Finally the words, "Good night, Micah, I'm glad you're back from Rome," stumbled from her mouth. *Why did I say that? He's been home for a week now...*

He smiled brightly at her and left. She put the food away in the kitchen, or at least where she thought her mom would want it, and walked up the stairs in a strange daze.

I can't believe Micah kissed me... even if it was just my cheek.

Finding her bedroom full of 'Eden' boxes, she was happy for her mom's foresight in packing an overnight bag. She had all her toiletries for the night. She decided since her lamp was still packed, she'd leave her bathroom light on for the night. She'd never wanted to sleep in the dark again, and she was happy her parents never asked about it. *They probably figure I'm just falling asleep reading.*

She pulled her covers up. "Good night, Gabriel." She paused, and then whispered, "Does Micah like me, I mean, as more than a friend?"

She hoped she'd feel a warm feeling but she didn't. Still, for the next few days, she couldn't get the quick peck out her head. She decided if Micah did something like *that* again, she was going to ask him how he felt. She couldn't handle the games anymore, or whatever this was.

What ate her up inside was the fact she had strong feelings for Andrew, but every time Micah was around, she was instantly drawn to him. She had no idea relationships could be so complicated.

On Thursday after school, Eden decided it would be a good time to finish unpacking her bedroom, since Andrew would be volunteering at the hospital. Her mom had the house practically done by now and was getting impatient for Eden to finish. Her furniture was in place, her clothes put away, but she still had two or three boxes to sort through.

Bent over a box, wondering why she kept so much junk in the first place, she heard a knock on her half-open door. She glanced up to see Micah standing in the doorway.

"Hey you," he said, with a crooked smile.

Her chest ached in response. "Doesn't this look like fun?" She sat back on her heels.

"Actually, no. Your mom told me to not let you leave until you finish."

She grunted. "Well, you better come in then; this could take a while."

He grinned and walked in. "Nice room."

"Bigger than my last one," she commented, while he ran his hand along the top of her dresser.

"Yeah." His voice sounded far away.

Studying him, she knew he wasn't thinking about the size of her bedroom. "Where's your other half?"

"You mean Trent? He's registering for fall classes."

It didn't take long for his expression to grow thoughtful again. "How are things for you?" She hesitated. "Are you still seeing visions?"

He glanced at her. "Yes."

She waited, but he didn't say more. "Anything I should know about?" she probed.

"You'll know it all soon enough."

"Oh great, do I do something stupid again?" she asked, hoping to lift the mood in the room.

"Nope, only good things."

"That's so not fair. Why do you get to see what I do before I do it?" she asked, still trying to wrap her head around how that worked.

"Got me. But I never mind seeing you."

His gaze was intense. She turned her attention to the contents of her box. She was having a hard time breathing normally, and needed the distraction.

When she spied what was at the bottom of the box, under the Hawaiian grass skirt she'd hung on to for some odd reason. She laughed. *How fitting*, she thought, pulling out the homemade spyglass and cutlass they'd made together out of paper towel rolls and newspapers.

Micah stared at what was in her hands. He flinched.

Confused by his reaction, she asked, "Remember these? I'm way too sentimental. I can't get rid of this stuff." She laughed, hoping he would join in, but he didn't. "Jessie gets so mad at me for hanging on to any of this," she admitted.

"Why?" he asked immediately.

Her mouth went dry. *Now what do I say? Jessie hates me pining over you?*

He searched her face, and in that moment, she wanted to spill her heart out to him.

She swallowed. "I don't know. I guess she thinks I'm a packrat or something." Her words sounded hollow.

He straightened up. "Hey, I can't stay long, Trent and I have some stuff we have to get done, but I wanted to tell you I'm having a barbeque on Saturday. It's time to bust into the pool. I want you," he paused, "and Andrew to come."

"Ok, cool. Thanks." She was surprised by the abrupt change in the conversation.

"I know you're close to Willow and Caitlyn, mind inviting them too?"

Eden stared at him. "Sure."

"And, there's a Damon in one of your classes, could you invite him for me too? I don't really know how to reach him myself."

This question completely surprised her. *Damon?*

"Um, sure," she said and then she had to ask, "Do you even know him?"

"No. Not yet, but I need to."

She gaped at him. *Need to?*

She was about to ask what this was all about, but her mom came into her bedroom. "Eden, Andrew's on the phone. He said he's been trying your cell phone. Did you lose it again?"

Andrew? Isn't he at the hospital?

"Perfect," Micah replied, "tell him about the party, ok? I better take off. See you later, Eden. Good-bye, Mrs. McCarthy."

"Bye Micah," her mom said, as she handed Eden the cordless phone.

"I will. See ya, Micah," Eden called, as he disappeared through the door.

She told Andrew about the party and he was excited to go. She informed Willow and Caitlyn the next day at school. She hoped Micah wouldn't mind she invited Jessie too. After prom, she could hardly be expected to invite two of her friends in front of Jessie and not include her too. She assumed Micah would invite some of his friends like Chase and Jake. *I wonder if he'll invite Megan.*

Walking into Biology, she had one more invite to give, and she wasn't sure how he'd take it. Their conversations were pretty one-sided, with her coming up with silly questions and statements, trying to have another breakthrough with him, and him regarding her like an annoying fly he wanted to swat away.

Well, Micah said he wants Damon there. So here goes nothing, she thought.

She sat down and turned around, noting how he stared at her like, *Now what do you want?*

"Hey, Damon, have plans tomorrow?" She didn't give him time to answer, but dove in with, "My friend Micah wants you to come to a barbeque pool party at his house."

She waited for the *No thanks,* but Damon was quiet for a moment, and then to her surprise, he asked, "What time is it?"

"Uh, one o'clock. Here, let me write down his address for you." She gave him the address, and he tucked it into his pocket. She flipped back around in her seat.

I hope Micah knows what he's doing.

Chapter Thirty-Three

Eden debated on whether to walk to Micah's house or drive, but then, thinking of the large volumes of trees from her house to his, she grabbed her car keys. Andrew was going to be there late. His dad needed his help moving some stuff out to the garage, but he promised he'd show up as soon as he could.

Jessie and Caitlyn were going to meet there after Jessie's drama club meeting was over, so Eden turned her radio up and rolled down the windows on her Jeep. She was still shocked it was actually hers. When her dad handed her a pair of keys on her birthday, she had gone to the key hook and hung them up, thinking he'd wanted her to put them away for him. He'd laughed, retrieved them, and then steered her outside where a burnt-orange Jeep sat.

Brendon begged her to go off-roading with it, and Andrew told her how hot it was she drove it. She was pretty sure Andrew was referring to the Jeep being hot. He had a soft spot for Broncos and Jeeps.

She pulled into Micah's driveway, seeing no other cars. She would've stressed over being the first one there if it wasn't for the fact the pool was beckoning her.

Pushing her door shut, she heard, "And there's my little mermaid."

She glanced over. Trent stood on the porch.

"Hey, am I the first one here?" She jogged over to him.

"Looks like it. Where's your other half today?"

"He's coming. He's going to be late."

"So what's up with you and Andrew? Is he *the one*?" His emphasis on the last two words was overly dramatic.

When she teased, "Why don't you ask Micah? He's the one with all the visions," she thought he'd laugh, but he didn't.

He gave her a funny look. "Did Micah tell—?" His words were cut off by the front door opening.

Micah's mom appeared startled to see them both there. "Oh, I was looking for Jared. I thought he was out front. Eden, good to see you, hon. Come on in."

She entered, wishing she and Trent could've continued their conversation. She was dying to know what he was about to say, but Trent seemed to take pains to avoid her after that.

Oh Trent, she thought, *you can't leave me hanging like that!* Micah was in the kitchen when they walked into the great room.

"Eden! How about a quick swim before everyone else gets here?" he called out.

"Sure," she said with a grin. Since she'd worn her swimsuit under her clothes, she carried her towel and followed Micah out the sliding glass door. The Hawkins always had a nice, long, wooden deck in the back. She'd been to many barbeques on that deck. She was happy to see it was the same.

Looking down the five steps to the yard, she gasped. "Oh my gosh! That's the nicest pool I've ever seen!"

"My parents went a little crazy on it. Come on."

She followed him down, admiring the long, kidney-shaped pool. There was a small wading area on one end and a diving board on the other. On the backside of the pool was a cluster of huge rocks, with a slide going down the middle of it. There were waterfalls coming off the rocks in all different directions. Water leaving the pool area and shooting around behind the rock formation caught her eyes.

"Where's that lead?" she asked, pointing.

"It's a lazy river, pretty sweet, huh? The current carries you behind the rocks and back out there, by the diving board." He trailed the river's path with his finger.

"Wow." She undid her shorts and yanked them down. She gripped the bottom of her shirt, and then stopped. Micah was yanking his t-shirt off and tossing it on a pool chair. Even though they were obviously getting in the pool, she couldn't shake the feeling she was undressing in front of him. Chiding herself, she slipped her shirt over her head and placed it on the chair next to Micah's. She kicked her flip-flops under the chair and glanced up. Micah's blue eyes stared back at her.

Well, if I wasn't self-conscious before, I am now.

She couldn't help ogling him back. His seventeen-year-old body in a swimming suit was a lot different from when they were kids. *Nothing wrong with noticing he's in good shape... like really good shape.*

Feeling guilty, she peeled her gaze away, and stepped toward the pool. Strong hands picked her up, throwing her into the air. As her body plunged into the water, she thought, *So, he wants to play dirty.* She came up for air to see he was treading water next to her, grinning.

For the next twenty minutes, they were kids again, racing across the pool to see who was fastest (which Micah usually was), trying to out dive one another, out jump each other off the rocks, and eventually drown one another while going around the lazy river. She felt the years melt away and for a time, there were no demons, visions, or barriers.

This is how it always was between us, she rejoiced, and then Micah's hands landed a bit too high while wrapping around her from behind. She froze and his arms recoiled. They both stood up in the water, ceasing wrestling.

"Sorry." He diverted his eyes as her face flamed.

The awkwardness was broken by Micah's mom. "People are arriving. Why don't you two come in for a minute?"

Without a word to each other, they climbed out of the pool and grabbed towels. Jogging up the steps, she was surprised to see Trent sat at one of the deck tables. She didn't have time to ask why he didn't join them, because Caitlyn and Jessie were walking across the deck to her.

"Hey, guys," she said, as they both peered over the railing.

"Holy cow, check out that pool," Jessie exclaimed.

"Pretty sweet, isn't it?" Trent commented, his voice sounding close.

Eden turned to see Trent had moved behind them. He was staring at Jessie. *I hope it was ok I invited her*, she fretted.

"Who are your friends, Eden?" he asked, his eyes not leaving Jessie.

"Caitlyn, Jessie." Eden gestured to both and then added, "This is Micah's cousin, Trent."

"Nice to meet you, Caitlyn," he said, glancing momentarily at her, then his eyes rested on Jessie again, and his tone changed. "And you're an unexpected surprise."

Oh great, maybe this was an exclusive party.

"Jessie, can I just say, there aren't enough redheads in the world." He gave her a crooked smile and an arched eyebrow.

Jessie's eyes narrowed.

So, Trent likes redheads. Too bad he doesn't know Jessie hates flirts.

Willow emerged through the sliding door, and everyone's attention shifted. Eden expected Chase to follow after, but he didn't. Seeing how swiftly Micah moved to Willow's side, Eden had a sinking revelation. After ten minutes of him paying attention to Willow, and Megan and Jake not showing, she was sure she was right. *Micah likes Willow.*

That's why he wanted me to invite her, so it wouldn't be obvious. Maybe prom night when Andrew and I went home, they realized they liked each other. According to what Andrew had told her, Chase was not dealing well with Willow's sudden personality changes.

Then her theory was thrown when Micah then turned his undivided attention to Caitlyn. Eden spent the next twenty minutes working out their love angle. She was relieved when Andrew arrived in time to eat. She needed the distraction. *I'm way too engrossed in watching Micah's every move.*

At a table with Andrew, Jessie, and Caitlyn, she noticed Trent's occasional glance in their direction. Jessie, who was complaining about her drama club projects, was completely oblivious to his attention. Eden appraised Trent. *He seems genuinely interested.* She glanced at her friend, feeling excited, yet nervous, for her. Jessie had yet to experience her first real date. It wasn't that she was unattractive. Sadly, her personality usually got in the way. She had a way of chasing boys off before they'd even had a chance to show her how they felt.

Eden popped the last bite of her hamburger in her mouth, as the sliding glass door opened again. She coughed, trying to swallow down the bun that lodged in her throat.

I can't believe he actually came! Wearing his usual black t-shirt and jeans, Damon stared at everyone gaping at him, and then shifted his eyes to the deck boards.

Willow pranced toward him. "Damon, right?"

He nodded and she smiled. "I'm Willow. You hungry?"

"Sure." His brown eyes flickered at Willow and she marched back to her table next to Eden's, him trudging after. Eden thought it was nice of her to try to make him comfortable. *Poor guy doesn't know anyone here, and for some reason Micah invites him.* She stared at the now-empty table across from her where Trent and Micah had been. *Huh, where'd they go?*

Curiosity took over and, feigning the need for more soda, Eden strode into the house. Searching in the kitchen and living room, she came up empty. Passing by the hall, she heard muffled talking coming from Mr. Hawkins's office. With no one around, she tiptoed closer.

Standing by the door, feeling ridiculous for spying, she waited. Trent's voice pleaded, "Can't I have a little fun? I know she wasn't part of the plan."

"Trent, it's not like that. I'd love for you to do your thing, but we have to stay focused. And she's not helping you out there," Micah answered.

"Ah, Micah, such a love kill," Trent said, but he didn't sound angry.

"I know it sucks. I promise I'll make it up to you one day. Let's just get through this trip."

"About that, you know I'm not thrilled with this whole self-sacrificing plan of yours, right?" Trent muttered, sounding uncharacteristically serious.

"It'll all work out, Trent. Trust me on this."

Her ears were burning and she knew she should walk away, but she couldn't.

"It's not *you* I don't trust—it's all of *them*. How do we know they'll pull their weight, or even know what to do?"

Eden could tell by the way Micah sighed that they'd probably had this discussion several times before.

"Trent, they were born for this; they'll know what to do," he said firmly.

"Ok, well, I'm just letting you know right now, that when we get back from this crazy thing, I'm getting with the redhead. I need a little Trent time, being glued to you is making me lose my game!"

Micah chuckled. "Good luck with *that* redhead."

Eden couldn't agree with him more.

"Speaking of games, you were pretty playful with Eden earlier in the pool."

Her insides dropped, she knew she really shouldn't be listening now, but she had to.

"I know I'm just torturing myself, but it was nice for a moment to forget I'm the Seer," Micah said so quietly, that Eden found herself plastered against the door.

"Who says the Seer has to be miserable?"

"It's not that; we need Andrew," he replied. She gasped and then slapped a hand across her mouth. *Did they hear me? Should I bolt?*

But Micah continued, "I can't do anything to jeopardize him leaving the group. The mission's more important than what I want."

Eden stood up straight. *Did I hear him right? Micah wants me?* Her pulse was rapid, her ears buzzing with adrenaline. She knew she should walk away. What if they came out? She'd be humiliated, but she hung on every word she heard.

When Micah said the next sentence though, her stomach dropped for a different reason, "Besides, I saw her marrying *him*, remember?"

He saw me marrying who? Andrew?

"You don't know that's what that meant, Micah. You didn't—"

"I know, Trent, but, think about it, it makes the most sense," he interrupted.

Trent didn't say anything, and she heard the floorboards crack. She backed away as she heard Micah say, "We better get back to the party. I need you to be on my side for this one."

"I got your back. Don't get your feathers in a ruffle," Trent said, his voice sounding a lot closer.

She panicked and, whirling around, saw the bathroom. She ducked in just as the office door opened. She waited until she heard them walk past, her heart beating wildly at how close she'd been to being caught.

Micah likes me after all! Elated, she stared at reflection in the mirror. She was practically floating, but then slowly, she came back down to reality as she remembered the rest of the conversation.

I marry Andrew?

It wasn't a bad thing really. Andrew was wonderful and she did think she loved him, most of the time. *So why do I feel so devastated?*

She pulled herself from the bathroom, grabbed a soda from the kitchen, and hurried back to the deck. She was relieved everyone, excluding Micah and Damon, were now in the pool. Micah smiled at her as she passed their table. She smiled back, hoping his ability to see things didn't allow him to read minds too.

"Eden, there you are! Come get in," Andrew called out to her.

She hurried toward the pool, dove in, and swam over to Andrew.

"What's wrong? You look upset."

Oh great, am I that transparent? "Nothing." She dipped under and came up, smoothing her hair back off her face.

Apparently, Trent had decided to play chicken in that split second she'd been under.

"Jessie, you're with me," Trent said, giving Jessie a wide grin.

I guess Trent doesn't always obey the Seer's orders. She could see displeasure flashing in Jessie's hazel eyes.

"Come on, Jessie," Trent urged.

Jessie hesitated, and then to Eden's surprise, she sighed. "Fine, but don't complain if we win, Eden."

"That's my girl," Trent laughed. Jessie gave him a sour face. He ignored it and dove under her legs, bringing her up on his shoulders. Eden had barely gotten herself balanced on Andrew when she was sent flying back into the water. Coming up, she saw Jessie giggling triumphantly. Glad to see her friend was having fun, Eden tried again… and again… only to have Jessie knock her off effortlessly.

"Oh, yeah, that's right, Andrew, eat it," Trent crowed. Eden sort of felt bad for Andrew, but was thrilled Jessie was having a good time.

"Enough," Eden cried out, after falling off one too many times. "I'm terrible at this! It's your turn, Caitlyn. I'm going to float around the lazy river."

Caitlyn looked startled as Andrew dove under her legs and pulled her up out of the water. Eden let her body glide away into the current, loving the feel of swimming with the jets. It felt like she'd entered a weightless sphere. Someone bumped her foot, and thinking it'd be Andrew, she flipped around. Instead of blue-green eyes, she saw only light blue. She felt like her heart was being pinched and her stomach did a summersault. *Why's he everywhere I turn lately?*

He swam alongside her, and she didn't push for it to be a race. For some reason, she wasn't in a rush to be shot out into the deep end. She knew she shouldn't do it, but for a moment, she allowed herself to acknowledge the fact that Micah did like her. All those glances in her direction did mean something after all, and now, hearing why he hadn't act on it, she began to understand why many times those stares appeared painful. *He does want me, but he can't be with me. Because a mission? What mission?*

And for the other reason, she thought. *I marry Andrew.*

Eden's body was pushed into the deep end, where the river ended.

Micah swam away, jumped out of the pool, and walked back to Damon on the deck. Treading water, she wondered if he'd jumped in just to swim with her. Searching for Andrew, she found him on the rocks next to

Caitlyn. As she watched, they both jumped high into the air and landed into the water, causing a huge splash and rolling waves. She was glad Andrew's attention was elsewhere. Wondering what happened to Jessie, Eden heard laughing in the lazy river. Relieved Jessie was preoccupied, Eden climbed out of the pool. Normally, she would've worried her friend would see through her with her hawk-like eyes. But for once, Jessie was thinking about Jessie, which was a good thing.

Wrapping a towel around her body, she shuffled toward the house. Micah was still sitting at the deck table with Damon; they both glanced at her.

"Hungry," she said lamely, feeling the need to explain herself. Micah grinned and Damon shifted in his seat. She slipped through the door and, hearing the piano being played, made her way to the living room instead. Her family wasn't musically inclined, so as a child, Eden was always loved when Mrs. Hawkins would sit at the piano and play.

Peering in the room, she was surprised to see it was Willow sitting on the bench, not Micah's mom. *I didn't even know she played.* Since she was still wet, Eden leaned her head against the doorframe. The notes spoke to her, the song beautiful. Micah's parents were sitting on a couch, listening. She'd always admired Willow but now, seeing this hidden talent, she could only stare in awe. She was startled when someone brushed past her.

Her eyes widened; Damon made his way to the unoccupied couch. He glanced once at Willow and then shut his eyes, his face relaxing. His head nodded forward, his shoulders slumping. *Did he just fall asleep?*

She shifted her gaze away and was surprised Micah stood on the other side of the doorway, his eyes focused on Damon. Willow, oblivious to all of them, played, her fingers moving swiftly across the keys, giving Eden the chills. When the song ended, Willow gasped when everyone clapped.

"Oh Willow, that was beautiful," Micah's mom exclaimed.

"We'd love to hear more," his dad added.

Willow glanced at Damon. "Thanks, I don't know too many songs by heart, but that's one of my favorites."

"I have music if you'd like to look through it." Micah's mom went to one of the bookshelves and pulled out stacks of sheet music.

Willow browsed through them and then picked one, placing it on the piano. She began to play, and Eden found it a haunting, but pretty, melody. Damon's eyes were now open, staring at the piano.

Eden glanced back at Micah. This time their eyes met, and she resisted the urge to look away. He cocked an eyebrow at her as her eyes roamed his face. Knowing he liked her added to the tension she felt between them. She glanced at his full lips, wondering how they'd feel. His eyes darted to hers as well, and her heart thumped unruly in her chest.

The moment ended as Micah broke eye contact and stared back into the living room. She wondered why, until she felt warm arms wrap around her waist from behind. She stiffened slightly in surprise.

Andrew kissed her cheek and whispered, "Here you are. You disappeared. You can't do that to me."

She knew Andrew was serious, neither one of them had forgotten prom night. "Sorry, I heard Willow playing. I wanted to listen," she said quietly, trying not to disturb those in the living room.

Andrew nodded. "Nice."

Willow played on while the room was captivated. Damon remained slouched back in the couch, but gazed at Willow now. His head nodded to the rhythm of the music, matching Willow's body movements, both engrossed by the notes.

I must not know enough about music.

Andrew left her side and joined Micah.

She overheard Andrew say, "No way, dude. The Yankees are totally going to take it this year."

Sports. Maybe I should go change. Micah and Andrew both had their shirts on now and, looking into the living room, she saw Willow had changed and Damon, well, he had never went swimming to begin with. Feeling cold, she hurried across the great room and back down to the poolside, where she'd left her clothes. Seeing Caitlyn lounging on a pool chair in the sun, she pulled a chair over and joined her.

"Andrew's looking for you. He went inside to find you." Caitlyn squinted over at her.

"I know. He found me... I needed to dry off more. Man, the sun feels wonderful."

Hearing Jessie's laughter, Eden scanned the pool to see her and Trent shoot out from the lazy river into the deep end.

Caitlyn observed, "I've never seen Jessie like *this* before."

Eden laughed quietly. "I know, me either."

"Do you think he likes her?" Caitlyn whispered.

"Sure hope so, for all of our sakes."

Trent and Jessie disappeared behind the rocks as they rode the river again. Eden leaned her head against the pool chair, closing her eyes.

"Is everything ok?"

"Yeah. Why?" Eden kept her eyes shut.

Caitlyn's voice was quiet. "Jessie told me you and Micah used to be real close." Her voice dropped even lower. "She sort of told me about your crush too."

Eden's eyes popped open.

"You don't have to tell me anything if you don't want to," Caitlyn added. "You just seem stressed out today. Are you ok?"

Great, if Caitlyn noticed, I bet Andrew has too. Then again, he is a guy...

She was half-tempted to tell Caitlyn everything, but this was hardly the time for a private heart to heart; the chance of being overheard was too great.

"I admit it's been," hesitation, "different today, but I'm fine, really."

Caitlyn glanced at Trent and Jessie coming out again and whispered, "Well, I think he likes you."

Eden shot a glance at Caitlyn, her mouth dropping open to protest. "He watches you, Eden. His eyes light up when you enter the room... I know that's cliché, but it's so true."

"Really?" she couldn't help asking.

Caitlyn eyes were sympathetic. "I think it's normal for you to have feelings for Micah. You guys were best friends growing up and now…"

Now he's hot, Eden wanted to finish.

Caitlyn finished, "You're both older, attractive—"

"You're making us sound thirty," Eden cut in, uncomfortable with Caitlyn's continued observations.

Caitlyn cocked her head to the side. "You know what I mean."

Yes, maybe I'm not such a monster. The guilt she felt around Andrew was unbearable.

"Thanks Caitlyn, but I'm pretty sure we're still only friends."

She stood, afraid if she stayed any longer, she'd spill her guts to her friend. *I need more time to figure this stuff out.*

Caitlyn didn't push for more. They made their way into the house. Eden cast one last glance at the pool, getting a glimpse of Trent and Jessie under one of the waterfalls. *At least Jessie's having the time of her life.*

Approaching the living room where everyone had been before, they heard Willow say, "Ok, Micah, I think it's your mom's turn now."

Andrew and Micah were right where she'd left them, standing in the doorway.

Micah smiled at her, sending her heart to her knees, and then turned to his mom. "You're totally right, Willow. Mom, you need to play."

"Oh no, not after hearing you play! You put me to shame!"

But Willow stood from the piano bench, gesturing for Micah's mom to take her place.

"Oh all right, if I must." His mom walked over to the piano.

Willow waltzed to the couch where Damon was and, without hesitation, plopped down right next to him. Damon fidgeted in his seat, his eyes shooting to the floor.

At least he's not giving her the dirty looks he gives me.

Lacey shuffled through the sheet music, and then began playing. Damon's shoulders slumped, his frame not looking so rigid anymore. Willow crossed her legs, her inside foot brushing Damon's leg; he brought the leg up, resting his ankle on his heel.

Ok, I'm totally staring...

Eden shifted her gaze back to the boys across from her; Micah appeared to be just as captivated by Damon and Willow as she was, and Andrew's emerald eyes gave her a quizzical, cocked eyebrow, like, *What are you doing standing so far from me still?*

If that was what that look meant, she wanted to remind him he was the one who stepped away from her in the first place. Instead, she shuffled over to him. He immediately secured her hand in his, and Micah darted into the living room, finding an empty seat next to his dad.

When the song ended, Micah's mom announced it was dessert time.

Mrs. Hawkins had a spread that would make five-star resorts blush. Eden's mouth watered as she tried to decide between mini-cream pies, flaky, cream-filled éclairs, homemade cookies with assorted chips and nuts, and her personal favorite, cheesecake. She opted for the latter. She never could pass it by, whether homemade or made from a box, and Lacey Hawkins's was definitely not from a box.

When she had practically licked her plate clean after her second piece, she spied Andrew going back for his third helping. *Wonder if it'd be bad if I joined him?*

They were sitting in the great room. Most everyone was slowing down on the dessert buffet, other than Andrew, who returned from the kitchen with a mini-chocolate-cream pie on his plate. Micah strolled over to Andrew and they began talking sports again.

Sitting on the couch, with Caitlyn and Willow on either side of her, Eden pulled her legs up and hugged her knees. She hated that she couldn't stop gawking at the guys.

I need to go for a long walk. Walking straightened out inner turmoil for her. Unfortunately, she was too afraid of demons to relax outside now. *Wonder if a treadmill would work?*

It wasn't until Caitlyn asked, "Where's Jessie?" that Eden realized she didn't know where her friend was. *Wow, I'm totally self-absorbed right now.*

Eden peered around the room. *No Trent either. Huh...*

"I think she's on the deck outside," Micah answered.

Caitlyn stood. "I better get going. I'll go get her."

Caitlyn left the room and Willow stood up too. "Yeah, I better go too. Thanks so much for inviting me," she said to Micah.

Micah gave her a nod. Eden waved at her as Andrew collapsed down next to her on the couch.

"Want to go too?" Andrew asked her.

Eden glanced up, meeting Micah's eyes, as he stood across the room.

"Whenever you want," she said, dropping her eyes to her knees.

Caitlyn and Jessie came in from outside, crossing the room. Jessie gave Eden a wink and mouthed, *Talk later.* After saying good-bye, they were gone.

Trent strode into the room after. *He looks pretty pleased with himself.*

Micah regarded Trent. "You know she's only sixteen, right?"

"So, your point is?" Trent asked, as he sprawled himself out on the couch not taken by Eden and Andrew.

"You're eighteen."

"Don't be jealous. Besides, she turns seventeen in three months," Trent countered. Eden was surprised he knew that. *Then again, Jessie can say a lot during an hour of undivided attention.* Eden smiled; she was happy for her friend.

"And just when are you turning nineteen again?" Micah asked.

"Always such a stickler for details," Trent complained, as he put both hands behind his head.

Eden giggled. She stopped when Trent said, "Besides, Micah, you're one to talk," while staring directly at her.

Her throat closed up. *Is he implying Micah's doing the same thing by liking me?*

Andrew, oblivious to Trent's look, saved everyone from the awkward moment when he stood from the couch and pulled her to standing.

"Hey Micah, think we're going to take off, man," he said.

Eden thanked Micah and his parents for the barbeque, and followed Andrew to the front door. In the entryway, she was surprised to see Damon still sitting on the couch. She'd sort of assumed he'd already left, skipping out on dessert.

"I'm glad you came, Damon," she said, not expecting much in return.

He glanced up. "Thanks for inviting me."

Thrilled he even answered her, she said, "No problem."

"Yeah, nice to meet you, man," Andrew said with a wave.

Damon nodded. "You too."

"Hey, I'll see you around, Andrew," Micah's voice came from behind them.

"Yeah, let me know when you want to go play basketball again," Andrew replied as they did the guy handshake thing.

Micah turned next to Eden. "And I hope you know my parents expect you to use the pool."

Eden gazed back into his blue eyes, the shade reminding her of the cool water waiting for her if she did. "Yeah, I'll come over soon."

Micah gave her a crooked smile, his eyes crinkling. "You better."

Chapter Thirty-Four

"You know, Gabriel, it'd be so much easier if you'd just talk to me. You could tell me what I'm supposed to do. I would happily do it." Eden sighed.

But her room remained quiet, as it had all weekend. Andrew had hung out at Eden's house on Sunday and, as Eden watched him play Uno for the fifth time with Brendon, she decided relationships were hairy. On Saturday, she'd felt this crazy excitement over Micah liking her, and she had to admit, that even today, she still was elated over the idea, but then there was Andrew. She stopped. Now, five days later, she was realizing again how wonderful and kind, not to mention good looking, Andrew was. *Why does he want to be with me again?*

"Now what do I do?" She yanked a brush through her hair. She knew she needed to leave soon or she'd be late for school. "You can't give me the silent treatment forever, you know." Setting her brush on her dresser, she added, "Maybe you want me to decide for myself."

The peaceful feeling washed over her. It still amazed her when it happened. Talking to Gabriel was such a habit that when she'd feel his confirmations, she was once again reminded he was real, not just her imaginary friend.

"But that's an interesting point, you know. You want me to decide for myself, but Micah had a vision that I marry Andrew, so it seems like it's already decided. Of course, I wasn't supposed to overhear that part," she admitted.

When she heard or felt nothing, she grabbed her bag. As she came down the stairs, her mom called up, "I hope you're ready to go. You're going to be late."

She kissed her mom's cheek. "I am ready. Bye, Mom."

She thought she was doing a pretty good job hiding her emotional confusion, but Caitlyn's long, appraising stare, made her wonder if she was masking it at all. She was grateful she didn't ask anything, as Andrew sat down next to them.

"Eden, don't feel bad about going over," Caitlyn stated, as if they had been in the middle of a conversation.

"Feel bad about what?" Andrew asked.

Took the words right out of my mouth. She stared at Caitlyn, dumbfounded.

"Don't feel bad about just showing up. Micah made it pretty clear it's an open invitation," Caitlyn continued.

Oh, Eden thought, smiling, *so this is your way of saying resolve your issues.*

"Yeah, you should go swim. Micah won't care. You guys are old friends," Andrew agreed.

Feeling guilty, Eden nodded back at him.

"Why don't you go today while I'm at the hospital?" he offered, poking his soggy piece of cafeteria pizza.

"Ok, maybe I will."

Andrew spied Caitlyn's lunch. "Why does your food always look so good?" he asked innocently.

Caitlyn tore her sandwich in half. "Here." She handed him a piece. "Stop giving me those puppy dog eyes."

Andrew gave her a lopsided grin. "You're the best, Caitlyn, you know that, right?"

"Yeah, yeah," she muttered. But her eyes were smiling.

If Micah thought seeing visions of Eden was bad, he was wrong. Being around her in real life was way worse. Now he could smell her scent, like flowers after a summer storm, and it was about to drive him insane. Then there was her softness of her skin, the way she felt in his arms when they hugged, the tickle of her hair brushing his face... and the accidental grab in the pool. He had to double his efforts to not dwell on *that*; his desires would take over if he did. He'd never felt this way for any girl before. Usually he was in control, or at least didn't care if he wasn't. He left Rome, determined to remain close friends with Eden, sure he could rein in his own feelings. She was happy with Andrew and since not being around her wasn't an option— he sort of needed his Awakener on his team—he figured he would have to control himself.

He shoved one hand through his hair, exhaling. Trent glanced over at him from the passenger seat.

"What?" he asked.

"Nothing. Just frustrated," Micah stated.

Trent stared at him. "It was your idea. I say we just tell them and get this over with."

Micah glanced over. "What?"

"The trip, getting everyone to Illinois without them suspecting a dang thing. What were you talking about?"

"Oh, yeah, that," Micah answered. *I'm not telling Trent I'm about to cave...*

Trent's forehead wrinkled as he frowned at him. "So? Are you going to tell me what's going on?"

Micah mustered forced confidence. "I think we have a good plan. Sage said we can't just blab to everyone what's happening. No one will volunteer to go if they know. We know we have to wait until schools out, so a few more weeks at least. And then we need a reason to all go there. Who knows, maybe we'll win." Micah shrugged.

It was long shot. They'd just entered their names in a drawing to win tickets to Great America in Illinois. It was a random competition they'd stumbled across while out today. Micah had jumped on it, even though the tickets were only good after the middle of July.

Trent gave a low whistle. "Well, if we don't win, we're going sooner. I hate the thought of twiddling my thumbs for two and half months."

Micah nodded. "Agreed. I don't like it either."

Pulling into his driveway, Micah's stomach dropped. Eden's Jeep was parked in the semi-circle. He could feel his resolve melting away, replaced with excitement to see her again. It'd felt like forever since the pool party, though it hadn't even been a week.

I'm so screwed, Micah realized as he slammed his truck door shut.

Climbing up the front porch steps, Trent beat him in, and Micah slowed his step, pausing at the door.

"Sage," he said quietly, "why can't we go sooner? I find out the location of the temple and then we just wait?"

He didn't move, not that he expected her to appear. His answer was purring up his driveway, in a black Honda.

The engine was silenced and the driver's door opened. Micah walked to the edge of the porch as the driver stepped from the vehicle.

Ah, now I get it. Maybe someone else needs a little time to prepare.

Damon's brown eyes stared back at him, obviously hesitating to move forward.

Micah waved him up. "Come on in, Damon. I think it's time we talk, don't you?"

Eden was under water when it rocked back and forth. She shot up, hoping to see Micah, but instead of black hair, it was light brown and poking up in all directions. Trent.

"Finally, it's just you and me, babe." He grinned.

"What? Me come between you and Jessie? I wouldn't dream of it."

Trent chuckled. "Where's Dr. Andrew today?"

"At the hospital—he volunteers twice a week."

"Really? So you're all by yourself then, huh?"

She wondered why Trent was giving her a strange look. "I wanted to swim. Why aren't you with the love of your life?" she probed, wanting to know what Trent's intentions were for her friend. Poor Jessie was infatuated and still waiting to hear from him.

"Good question. Micah's got me on a short leash," Trent said. Wondering if that were true, she hoped he'd mention where Micah was, but he didn't. Since swimming with Trent had not been her plan, she debated on what to do.

"Bet I can do a better cannonball than you, hot shot," he taunted.

She faced him. "Ok, prove it."

Damon scanned the bookshelves lining the walls and said, "There are a lot of books in here."

Micah chuckled. "Yeah, not sure why, since no one in my family reads much. Guess it just looks good." Micah pointed to the two leather chairs. "So, let's sit for a bit. Unless you're here to swim?" Micah already knew he wasn't.

Damon shook his head and sank into one of the seats.

"You aren't getting much sleep, are you?" Micah asked.

Damon appeared startled and then slowly shook his head.

Taking a deep breath in, Micah slowly exhaled. "Ok, Damon, I'm going to tell you a few things. I want you to hear me out. We both know there's something going on with you. Something you haven't told a soul, not even your parents."

Damon shifted in his seat, his eyes widening.

"But I saw it myself. I," Micah gave a small laugh, "have this ability to see things. It can be very handy at times, and other times, it just freaks the heck out of me. Know the feeling?"

Damon's lips flickered into grimace. "Yeah, I do."

"The reason I see things is I'm the Seer for the Captain. He's the one who lets me see what's going to happen and sometimes what has happened." Micah glanced over at Damon. "I saw the stump move."

Damon stiffened, and then slowly his shoulders lowered. "How? How did it move?" he asked, shaking his head.

"I'm still figuring you out truthfully. Tell me about it. What do you feel, see, hear…"

Damon pursed his lips together. "I hear everything, all the time. It never stops."

"What exactly do you hear?"

Damon's brown eyes were electric. "I hear ants commanding their ranks to march, I hear birds chirping about their nests and where to find food, I hear the trees sighing for their buds to grow and blossom. It's like I'm tuned into Mother Nature and I can't turn it off, *ever*."

Micah didn't miss the growl in his last word.

"I'm sure that's exhausting."

"You have no idea."

Micah grunted. "I sort of do, you see, I can't really turn off my visions either."

Damon glanced over at him and grunted back with a nod.

Micah clapped his hands together. "So, I guess the trick is to learn how to control this new ability of yours. 'Cause whether or not you like it, it *is* a gift. And it's pretty incredible."

Another grunt from Damon, but Micah noted how eager his eyes became when he talked about learning to control it.

"You hear things, what else?"

Damon peered around the room, and then spoke a string of fluid words, none of which Micah understood.

Micah was about to ask what he'd said when he noticed his chair was no longer attached to the floor.

Gripping the armrests, he gazed down at the rug a few feet below him. He was floating in the air.

Micah whistled and then said, "Wow. Trent's really going to like *you*."

Eden climbed back on the board. "Ok, let's see you do this."

She glanced up and froze; Micah was walking out on the deck.

She forced herself to wave at him, and then followed through with her dive. Doing a forward flip, she came up, hoping he'd be halfway into the pool, but he was gone.

She was crushed.

"Oh Micah, all work and no play," Trent said.

"Work?"

But Trent deflected her question with, "You need to make Micah play a little more; the kid gets too serious sometimes."

There was no sarcasm in his voice this time. She studied his face, thinking of how Trent had watched them 'play' in the pool on Saturday. Maybe Trent had been happy to see Micah kick back for a minute.

"I don't know, Trent. You seem like you'd be better at teaching him that. You always know how to stay," she paused, "not serious."

But he didn't laugh or smile. He appeared to be debating something, like he was on the verge of confiding in her. She waited, hopeful.

He must have decided against it, because he jumped out of the pool. "I try. What can I say? It's a talent of mine."

He grabbed a towel, and she decided she'd get out as well. Wrapping her towel around her waist, she threw her shirt back on, knowing it would be drenched in seconds by her swimsuit and hair. Following Trent back into the house, she was deflated to see Micah wasn't around.

"Well, I'm getting in the shower and, unless you want to join me, this is good-bye," Trent said, strolling toward the stairs.

"I'll pass. See ya, Trent." She waved.

He disappeared, and she stood for a moment in the empty great room, debating what to do. Should she wait, hoping Micah would show? Feeling silly dripping on the carpet, she grabbed her keys, put her flip-flops on, and shuffled toward the entryway. The office door opened as she passed.

She glanced over as Micah stepped out.

"Glad I didn't miss you. Sorry about earlier, I wanted to jump in with you, but I can't today," he explained, coming closer to her.

Her heart began a series of strange hiccups. "Don't worry about it. Trent kept me company."

"I know. I'm even sorrier about that." He grinned. "I had a friend stop by."

She wanted to ask who, sort of afraid he might say Megan. Then Damon came out of the office.

"Hey Damon," she said, trying to recover from her shock. He was the last person she'd been expecting to see.

"Hey Eden."

The dark circles under Damon's eyes were gone, and Eden realized as he ran his hand through his black hair, that his face had a healthy glow again too. *How'd I miss that before?*

Micah and Damon were both staring at her, and feeling her hair dripping down her back, she knew she was a mess. "Well, I better take off. I'm sure your mom won't appreciate me dripping all over floor." She turned, calling over her shoulder, "See you at school, Damon."

Damon nodded. "See ya."

"I'll walk you out," Micah offered, as he followed her out the front door.

Stepping across the porch, she asked, "So Damon and you are getting close now, huh?"

Micah gave her a quick side-glance. "Yeah, well, we sort have a lot in common."

She glanced over at him. *Like what?*

There was a black Honda in the driveway. "Damon's?" she asked.

"Yeah."

"Do you still hang out with Chase and Jake?"

"Unfortunately, no. Wish I could, but I just have other things I have to get done now."

She gazed at him, wondering what he meant. They were by her Jeep now.

"I like this." Micah placed his hand on the hood.

"Me too, although, I don't do anything fun with it, according to Brendon." She leaned against the front bumper.

He smiled and leaned against the charcoal gray bumper too. "How's Brendon? Feel bad I haven't been over much lately."

"He's good. He has a girlfriend, so he thinks he's the bomb now."

Micah chuckled and, facing her, said softly, "Girls do that to us guys."

Again, her heart squeezed, as she searched his face. Was this the moment she'd been waiting for? Should she tell him how she felt about him?

"I don't know. Having a boy like you, does a lot for a girl too."

Micah's gaze was playful, his smile crooked. "Oh, really?"

"Yes," she barely got out. He was close enough she could feel his breath on her skin, but then something flickered across his eyes, and he glanced away.

"I'm glad Andrew makes you feel good." His words came out stiff.

Her tongue felt glued to the roof of her mouth. "Yeah, he's been great," she answered lamely.

He kicked at the loose gravel, sending a few rocks flying. "That's good."

Silence engulfed them, and she stared at her toes, dimly aware she needed to repaint her peeling polish. Bolstering the courage, she blurted, "You've always made me feel good too." She cringed. *That sounded so corny!*

He frowned, lines creasing across his forehead.

Not understanding why he didn't believe her, she gushed on, "Being best friends made me feel special my whole life, like I mattered. When we moved to Portsmouth, I lost that. You always made me feel like I was your favorite person."

"I know," he gazed into her eyes, "as friends I did. But, I mean, I wish I could've been the one to make you feel special in a different way, tell you how beautiful you are—" he stopped, his face agitated with… what she wasn't sure, almost like he was kicking himself.

She gaped at him and stuttered, "I... uh..."

His lips grew tight. "It doesn't matter either way." His eyes were agonized now. "You and Andrew belong together, and I don't want to mess that up."

She shook her head, "Micah, Andrew and I don't have what you and I—"

He cut her off, whispering, "Eden, I can't."

Can't? He leaned back against the bumper next to her and stared at the ground. She was tempted to grab his chin and make him face her, but she didn't.

"Have you ever wondered how much of life is in our control?" Micah's question caught her off guard.

She gazed at his profile, hoping he'd turn to face her.

"Yes, I have, actually," she sighed, resigning to the shift in conversation.

"Do you think we shape our own destiny? Or do we just play our part like actors in a movie? Just following the script?" He mumbled the last words.

She studied her flip-flops. "I don't know."

She didn't want to admit she'd struggled with this very concept, ever since she'd eavesdropped. When Micah remained quiet, she decided to say something.

"Does this have to do with one of your visions, Micah?"

He faced her. "Yeah."

"Can you tell me about it? Maybe I can help," she offered. *Starting with how you know I marry Andrew?*

He hesitated. "I saw something I'm having a hard time accepting." He looked away.

Undeterred, she pushed, "What was it?"

"It's probably the right thing. I should be ok with it, be stronger."

"Micah—"

He flipped around, bringing his face close to hers again. His warm breath tickled her skin. "Eden, there's so much I want to tell you, but I can't yet. You just have to trust me."

She wanted to argue, but was too distracted by his close proximity. Hoping he'd make his move or at least hold her, she waited, but all he said was, "I should get back to Damon."

Damon? He's worried about Damon? A lump formed in her throat. Panicked her voice might crack, she nodded, glaring at her toes.

"Hey, what do you think of a little road trip?" he asked, his tone sounding forced.

Still trying to grasp what was happening, she gaped back at him. His face inches from hers again.

"I'm thinking Great America, maybe in July."

Great America? Where's that? She thought the words, but her mouth wouldn't move.

"We could go with friends, drive around. It's not far from Chicago, maybe check out the city. What do you think?"

For some reason, it all felt rehearsed. Trying to pacify her throbbing heart, she asked, "You want to drive to Illinois?"

He nodded, his blue eyes sweeping her face.

"Ok," she replied slowly. "That sounds fun."

"Great!" Micah startled her with his sudden enthusiasm. "And don't worry, I've already told Andrew about it and he wants to go too."

She felt her insides drop. "Fabulous," she said woodenly.

He seemed surprised by her response, or at least her tone. "I better get back," he murmured, his blue eyes growing closer, and then he bent over.

Her breath caught as his lips brushed her cheek. He lingered, sending goose bumps all over her. Then his lips were gone, and he pulled her into a hug.

"You'll always be my favorite person, Eden," he whispered, his lips touching her throat just below her ear.

Their bodies were close, his arms securing her against him. She could feel a pounding in her chest, and wasn't entirely sure if was from her heart or his. She was insanely tempted to kiss him, and deal with the consequences later, when they heard the front door open.

Micah released her abruptly, taking an obvious step away. "I'm coming," he called over her shoulder.

She turned around, Trent stood on the porch. She expected a smirk on his face, but his raised eyebrows and wide eyes read surprised or shocked. *I thought he knew Micah liked me.*

"I better get going anyway," she said, turning around. Her flip-flops crunched in the gravel as she rounded the Jeep and reached for her door.

"Come swim again, ok?" Micah said, as she climbed in and shut the door.

She nodded and threw her Jeep into reverse. Trying to control her rapid breathing, she somehow made it into her garage before the tears exploded down her cheeks. She killed the engine, and laid her head against the steering wheel. All the suppressed emotions bubbled out in sobs.

She didn't stop until her nose was stuffed, her eyes puffy, and she had the hiccups.

"Gabriel, I don't understand. Is this how it's supposed to be?"

A peace spread over her body and she knew he was there with her. Maybe even feeling sympathetic for her situation.

Taking a deep breath, she exhaled. "I just can't believe God wants us to be this unhappy."

She felt the warm, comforting feeling again but this time, she could have sworn she heard, "You're right. He doesn't."

Chapter Thirty-Five

The last four weeks of school, Eden engrossed herself with studying. She made a pretense that it was all for good grades, and not that it was to avoid dealing with her growing feelings for Micah. Andrew encouraged her to swim at Micah's often, which made her feel even worse. She was pretty sure she'd freaked him out when she asked about next year's textbooks. He told her she was taking school a little too seriously, and that said a lot coming from him. She stopped by Micah's three or four times, but he never joined her in the pool. She was getting slightly annoyed with the ever-present black Honda in the driveway. *Is Damon over every day now?*

Micah did come over to her house twice during those weeks, but always had Trent glued to him. He talked to Brendon more than her. It didn't take her long to realize he was avoiding being alone with her. On his last visit, Micah asked Eden's parents if she could go on their trip to Chicago. From that conversation, Eden learned Micah had won seven tickets to the amusement park and it was planned for mid-July. The seven invited were Micah, Trent, Damon, Willow, Andrew, Caitlyn, and her, of course.

She didn't think it was a coincidence that it was the same seven he'd invited to his pool party. She knew there was more to this trip then riding roller coasters. In the overheard conversation she'd happened to listen to, Trent talked about a trip they had to get through.

She remembered all too clearly Micah saying Andrew *had* to be there too. The part that replayed over and over was Trent not liking the idea of this being a self-sacrificing thing. Horrified by what all that might mean, she wished she could get him alone to ask about it, but since their talk by the Jeep, he seemed to avoid being within three feet of her.

As the beginning of June finally rolled around and the hot, humid, summer air was making the students crazy, the last day of school finally arrived. With her classes done, and her 4.0 secured, Eden had no choice but to face her feelings.

She cared for Andrew but it wasn't the same as what she felt for Micah. *It's not fair to Andrew. Micah might have seen it in his mind, but it just doesn't feel right. I don't want to pretend anymore.*

As Caitlyn sat across from her at lunch, she decided she'd confide in her. Eden knew Jessie would give her grief, but she had no choice; she didn't have long until Andrew would be entering the cafeteria. She could see Willow was already in line for food. Shortly after Micah's pool party, Chase broke up with Willow. Now she hardly ever saw Jake, Chase, or Megan. Eden found it odd Megan chose to stay with the guys rather than her friend, Willow. It made thinking nice things about Megan, that much harder for Eden. Willow didn't seem to care, choosing to remain close to Eden. Andrew missed being with Chase and Jake, but told Eden he'd rather be with her now. Which, thinking about it now, made Eden feel terrible.

"Caitlyn, I'm a mess," she whispered, sort of hoping Jessie wouldn't overhear, but Jessie turned.

"Why are you a mess?"

Caitlyn asked, "What's going on?"

Eden glanced around. "I'm going to break up with Andrew."

Caitlyn's eyebrows came down as she nodded.

"Am I missing something? Why on earth would you do that?" Jessie exclaimed.

Eden faced her. "I don't feel the same way about him as he does me."

"What? Are you crazy? Oh no, Eden! Don't tell me this has something to do with Micah! Don't waste your time on him," Jessie said, getting ready to give her a lecture.

"Jessie, Micah likes Eden," Caitlyn whispered.

Jessie stopped and stared at Eden. "Really? Are you sure? Did he tell you he does?"

"Well, kind of—"

"Why would you break up with Andrew then?" Jessie asked. "Why not wait until you know for sure Micah likes you. That way, if he doesn't, you still have Andrew."

Both Caitlyn and Eden stared at Jessie. Eden was surprised Caitlyn's pretty eyes could look so indignant.

"Even if Micah doesn't like me at all, Andrew deserves someone who adores him," Eden said firmly.

Caitlyn seemed appeased, as her eyebrows returned to their normal place.

Jessie wouldn't back down. "But, Eden, you aren't thinking this through."

"Trust me, I am, more than you know."

Her mind had repeated Micah's phrase over and over again for the past few weeks. *Besides, I saw her marrying him—remember?* Those words haunted her. *Micah's the Seer for crying out loud.*

Still, Jessie sputtered, "Eden! This's just crazy!"

Caitlyn smiled at Eden. "You should do what you think you should, Eden, and it'll all be ok. Be honest with Andrew, and I just know this will all work out like it's supposed to. You'll see."

Eden sighed. "I wish I had your confidence, but I need to be honest with him either way."

Jessie continued her argument. "I think you're making a mistake, Eden. Not all guys are like Andrew." Eden glanced at her friend. She knew Jessie was taking it hard Trent had yet to call her. After talking, Eden had learned they hadn't kissed that day in the pool, but Trent had tried, according to Jessie. She knew Jessie was right; she may never find another guy that treated her as well as Andrew did.

Willow sat down, her blue eyes flashing at her and then Caitlyn. "So are you going to tell me too?"

There was no point in trying to hide anything from Willow; she seemed to see right through it all. *But what should I say?*

Caitlyn saved Eden. "Eden has relationship problems to fix."

Willow eyed Eden. "But it's not only with Andrew." It wasn't a question, more of a statement.

Eden nodded as Andrew entered the room.

Willow leaned closer to her. "Do whatever Caitlyn said to do and it'll work out."

Confused, Eden peeked at Caitlyn, who appeared just as surprised by Willow's statement as she was. Jessie cleared her throat, in a very obvious manner, as Andrew sat down next to Eden.

He stole a French fry off Eden's tray, asking, "Are you guys looking forward to our trip to Chicago?"

"Yeah, I've never been," Caitlyn responded.

Eden peeked at Jessie, who knew about the trip and was very hurt to be left out. Jessie's lower lip pouted. "Nothing too great about it, just another city."

Willow smiled at Jessie. "When we get back from this, how about a girl's road trip, Jessie? How about Virginia Beach?"

Jessie brightened. "Now we're talking."

Eden wanted to throw her arms around Willow. That had been very thoughtful and, knowing Willow, those weren't mere words either; she'd follow through.

Caitlyn glared at Andrew helping himself to Eden's fries. "Don't you ever eat your own food?"

Andrew reached over grabbed Caitlyn's apple. "No." He took a big bite and returned it.

She gave him the stink eye and bit the apple herself. "Oh, before I forget. Dave wanted to know if you wanted to play basketball on Thursday night, Andrew."

He grinned. "Sure." Then he glanced at Eden. "Do you mind? I know Jake wanted to play too." Eden noticed he didn't mention Chase's name for

Willow's sake, but she didn't think Willow would've cared if he had. She wasn't too torn up about the break up.

"Not at all." *At least he's not totally avoiding his friends because of me.*

"Oh, crud, I've got to get to history early. Mr. Thomas totally screwed up my grade," Caitlyn announced. She pushed her lunch towards Andrew. "You can have it."

Andrew didn't hesitate and grabbed her sandwich. "You're tops, Caitlyn."

Chapter Thirty-Six

No more avoiding it, today's the day. Eden's stomach sickened.

It was Thursday, the last day of school, and Andrew and Eden had taken off at eleven thirty, since it was half day, with kids signing yearbooks. Now, perched on a bar stool, Eden forced her last bite of quesadilla down. Andrew had made them lunch.

He strolled over to her and cupped her face with his hands. "What's wrong? You seem upset lately. I'm not sure if it's something I did, or didn't do."

Oh great, he has noticed. Well, this is it. But she chickened out. "Sorry, school was crazy."

He studied her face. "It feels like more than that," he paused. "Are you worried about being attacked again?"

"Yeah, I guess I am." She felt bad playing that card, but she used it. They discussed what had happened and he insisted again she should tell her parents.

She nodded. "I know I should, and I will."

"Come on. Let's go sit on the couch," he urged. Eden let him lead her into the family room where he sat down, pulling her into his lap. His hands found her face and he began kissing her. She was struggling to respond, but as his soft lips persisted, pressing on hers, she realized something—this would be her last time kissing him. She was overwhelmed with an extreme sense of loss and kissed him back warmly. He kissed her harder, his hand getting tangled in her hair.

She pulled away. *Wait, what am I doing? Not sure how I'm messing with fate, but this needs to stop.*

"Sorry," she mumbled.

"What is it?" he asked, his eyes worried.

"I need tell you something, and I don't know how."

His eyes widened as she scooted out of his arms, sitting next to him instead.

"Gosh, this is hard." She peeked up at him. "You've meant everything to me. You changed me and I'll always care for you," she whispered.

"What are you saying?" His emerald eyes locked on her.

She stared at her lap, twisting her fingers together. "I think we should take a break from each other."

"What? Why?" he blurted, hurt instantly shooting across his face.

"I, I'm not sure I feel the same way about you that you do for me. When you say you love me, it's hard for me to say it back."

"That's ok," he replied earnestly and, with a side-glance, added, "I'm sorry. I shouldn't have pushed it so fast."

Eden saw pain on his face. Immediately, her eyes welled with tears. *This is so hard!* "Andrew I'm so, so sorry. I never wanted to hurt you! You deserve better than me."

He shook his head sharply, his eyes stunned.

"You do!" she insisted, "You deserve a girl that's head over heels for you! I wanted to be that girl, but I'm not. I've been trying to figure out why I've been holding back and it's eating me up inside. I don't want to hurt you." Tears were streaming down her cheeks now.

His eyes shifted to the carpet, while his jaw clenched and unclenched. She was tempted to reach over and brush back the sandy strand of hair falling over one of his eyes. She wished she could kiss him, make him smile again. She had no idea breaking up with him would feel like she was chopping a piece of her heart out. He remained silent, and she was at a loss as to what to say next. She wanted to take it all back, but knew she couldn't.

The tears dripped unheeded off her jaw. "I'm sorry, Andrew. I'll never forget what you've done for me. I just don't think you and I are meant to be."

His eyes jerked towards her, flashing with frustration. "Meant to be? What does *that* even mean?" She was stumbling to find the right words to say, when his face fell in defeat before her. "It's ok. You can't help how you feel. I don't want to force you to love me, or care about me. Please stop crying."

But that just made her cry harder. The chunk being cut from her heart just kept getting bigger and bigger. She wondered if she'd have anything left after this.

"Eden," he said softly. She was sobbing now, her face buried in her hands. "Eden," he repeated. "It's ok. Stop crying."

His hand landed on her back, patting her awkwardly. *He's comforting me!* She felt even worse.

His warm hands wrapped around hers and gently tugged them free from her face. She was forced to gaze into his crushed eyes. "I'm going to be ok. This isn't the first time I've done this. Well, usually I'm the one breaking up with them," he said with a sad laugh. "But hey, now I know how those girls felt."

She stared at him. *How's he so calm?* She tried to regain composure. "Sorry, this is new for me. Here I'm thinking I need to be honest with you," she hiccupped, "so I tell you how I feel, and now I'm aching for you."

Andrew flinched. "Are you sure you want to do this? End us?"

There was a huge part of her that didn't want to say good-bye, but she searched herself, knowing there was something within her that yearned for Micah. She nodded slowly, afraid to speak with the lump lodged in her throat.

He sighed and pulled her into his arms. He hugged her tightly and whispered, "Well, if you change your mind, I'm not going anywhere."

Her body began to shake as she sobbed into his shoulder. When he let her go, she saw she'd left black smudges on his t-shirt. "Oh, sorry, I got mascara on you."

"I don't care." He stood up. She jumped to her feet, trying to wipe her eyes clean. "I have to go to the hospital," he stated. Again, he seemed so calm.

She nodded, pulling her keys out of her pocket.

"Are you ok to drive?" he asked.

Why's he worrying about me? I'm the bad guy here. "Yeah, I'm fine. Andrew, I'm so—"

"It's ok, Eden, really," he cut her off, his tone brisk.

She stared at her mascara-streaked hands, and sniffed. "Ok, well, good-bye."

He hesitated, and then hugged her again. His lips found hers and she gave in, kissing him back fiercely. When he stopped abruptly, she was gasping to catch her breath.

His eyes wrinkled as he gazed back at her, the pain etched in every crease. "Bye, Eden."

Numbly, she managed to find her way back to her Jeep. Cranking the engine, she tried to stem the never-ending tears. It was hopeless. She was reaching for a napkin out of the glove compartment when the garage door opened, and Andrew's Bronco whipped out. She hoped he would glance her way as he peeled out of the driveway, but he never did.

Chapter Thirty-Seven

"So you're saying Enoch spoke the same language as me?" Damon asked, pushing the book he'd been browsing aside. It joined the heaping pile on top of Jared Hawkins's desk.

Spending most of the hot days indoors, Micah had told his parents he was helping Damon study to pass school. He felt bad lying, but needed some excuse for why they poured over books, while the pool remained unused.

Micah planned to tell his parents everything soon. So far, they were ok with things. He wasn't sure if they'd be so amiable if they knew their son's life could be in serious danger.

"Yeah," Micah replied.

"He could command the elements, speak to the earth, and it obeyed?"

"Yep, at least we think so. I read in one account that Enoch felt he was slow of speech before and then, because he was so righteous, God gave him this gift. It says he moved mountains with his words. Your gift's pretty rare, Damon. The Captain doesn't give it to just anyone. We're pretty sure Enoch was the first Seer too."

Damon whistled. "So he had both of our gifts."

Micah drummed his thumb against the book he held. "So it's going to take both of us to get into Enoch's temple and through the nine chambers."

Damon was nodding when he disappeared. Micah recognized the cornfields and knew he was receiving another vision about the underground temple. He felt his pulse quicken. He hoped he could skip over certain parts of this vision. He didn't want to make a scene in front of Damon, grabbing at his chest and crying out in agony. Trent hadn't responded well the last time that had happened.

He was relieved to see his body moving through the chambers instead. *Oh good, we're already inside.* He expected to see himself leading the group through the small opening in the floor but, instead, it was Trent standing in front and explaining things. After a few minutes, Micah realized he wasn't really with his group of friends, but more in the background with the angels, watching. One look at Sage's forlorn face and he shuddered.

He snapped back to his dad's study.

"What?" Trent's voice demanded. Micah's eyes were still shut. "What happened?"

Micah felt a hand on his shoulder and pushed his lids open. He was panting, covered in sweat. Trent stood over him, concern written all over his face.

In the chair next to him, Damon leaned closer and asked, "Vision?" Micah nodded.

"About what, the temple?" Trent asked.

Micah glanced down at his shirt; it clung to his chest with sweat. He nodded again. "Something's changed."

Trent waited for more but Micah wasn't about to admit what he now knew. Trent already wanted to pull the plug on the whole thing. There was a lead weight on his chest; it was a struggle just to get air in. Luckily for him, Micah knew Trent would misread it for vision exhaustion.

But I know the truth. I don't make it into the temple, at least not as a mortal.

Damon didn't stay too much longer, and Micah told Trent he was going to bed early, tired from the day. Trent eyed him walk away but said nothing.

Collapsing on his bed, he groaned loudly, "Sage, what happened?"

He sat up. "Am I going to die now?"

Sage was next to him instantly, her black eyes creased with worry. She placed a hand on his shoulder, her fingers sending a calm rushing through him.

"I don't know. I think it has to do with Eden and Andrew," she said. Her tone was soft, but Micah could tell she was concerned by the way her black eyes clouded over.

"They broke up, didn't they?" he asked, already guessing the answer. *Makes sense—Andrew won't come on the trip and my gaping wounds won't be healed. Hence, I die.*

"Yes," Sage said quietly, as if she was answering his thoughts too.

"Is there nothing I can do? That's that, then?" He was trying to conceal the panic in his voice. He was failing.

Sage's hand was on his shoulder again.

Then he was riding in the back of Andrew's Bronco, radio blasting. It was night, making it hard to see where they were going. Raindrops splattered against the windows, as the tires splashed through puddles. Knowing a summer storm had rolled through that night, Micah assumed he was in the present, seeing something happening now. Andrew slowed at a curb in front of a red brick house Micah didn't recognize. He waited, watching Andrew's moves.

He whipped out his cell phone, shooting off text messages.

Micah leaned over the back seat, pressing his face close to read.

R u awake?

Andrew's phone buzzed back. *Yeah.*

R u making out w/ Dave?

No, he didn't come over after basketball. Why?

Andrew waited a moment and then typed. *Eden broke up w/ me.*

That sucks. R u ok?

Think so. I'm @ ur house. Can u come out?

In PJ's, do u care?

No, get ur butt out here.

Micah sat back. *So, it was Eden who did the breaking up.*

A few minutes later, Caitlyn emerged from the home, and jogged through the drizzle toward them. Andrew leaned across the front seat and opened the door for her. She hopped in, wearing flannel pants and an oversized hoodie.

Now Micah was curious.

"Are you ok?" she asked, folding her arms across her chest, eyeing Andrew.

He blew air out. "Yeah, I'll be ok. I just didn't see it coming. Think I'm still a little shocked."

"I'm sorry, Andrew."

Andrew cleared his throat. "I don't really want to talk about it. I have a question for you."

She gazed back at him and waited.

"The night of prom, when I found Eden on the ground," he hesitated. Micah could see it pained Andrew to talk about it. "I tried to heal her, but it was going too slow and it was really hard, like I was trying to push through something. Then you show up and she starts healing. What did you do?"

"I told you I didn't do anything. You're the one who healed her."

"But I felt something when you touched me. Can you heal too?"

How interesting. Micah was curious as to what Caitlyn's gift was. Up to this point, he'd never had a vision of her other than the time Eden awakened her.

Caitlyn laughed. "Last I checked, no." She placed her left foot on the seat, pulling her pant leg up to reveal a nasty cut and bruise on her shin.

"Ouch," Andrew commented.

"Yeah, did this yesterday. You know me, can't walk straight to save my life. I tripped in our garage and landed on my brother's bike." Caitlyn raised her hand, and then laid it across her shin. After a few seconds, she lifted her hand back up. "So I guess we know for sure now." The cut remained.

Without hesitation, Andrew placed his hand on her leg. After a moment, he removed it and Caitlyn gasped. "Wow! That's really amazing.

Thanks." She ran her hand over her skin.

"No problem. So, what did you do?" he asked again.

"I told you, I didn't do anything." She lowered her leg.

"Ok, tell me exactly what happened that night. Tell me what you did, thought, everything."

Micah was glad Andrew was asking the very questions he wanted answered too.

Caitlyn semi-rolled her eyes at him. "I'll humor you, Andrew, but I hope you're not disappointed when you realize I'm just a regular girl, not some super hero like you. I followed you into the woods, and I saw you with Eden, so I ran up to see what was going on. And that's when I saw all the blood and you putting your hands on her. I wasn't sure what was happening, so I leaned in and realized you were actually healing her. I was pretty shocked. And then you were crying out something like, *Eden, no.* I don't remember exactly, but I realized she might be dying then. I remember thinking, *Eden can't die. She just can't. Andrew can heal her—I know he can.* That's when I grabbed your shoulder. I wanted you to know you weren't alone, but you never turned around until I spoke to you."

So then what happened? Micah wondered. *Why was it when Caitlyn thought he could heal her in time, he did?*

"Sorry to disappoint," she said, when he remained quiet.

"You didn't. I'm just thinking." Andrew stared at his steering wheel. "I wonder if it had to do with what you were thinking." He glanced at her. "I know it sounds crazy," he added, when Caitlyn gave him the full eye roll this time. "But I can heal people. Isn't that crazy too?"

She stopped making faces at him. "I guess you've got a point there. So you're saying that when I think or say something, it happens?"

Seriously? Micah gaped at Caitlyn. *Can she really have that gift? Funny it hasn't even manifested itself. She has no idea she even has it. Then again, it is subtle, even if it's arguably one of the most powerful ones of them all, next to Damon's.*

Andrew nodded. "Maybe. What's something else have you thought lately? Maybe we can do a test."

Caitlyn was quiet for a moment and then she began biting her lower lip, her eyebrows lowering.

"You thought of something, didn't you? What is it? I know you're upset; you're biting your lip."

"I don't think you're going to like it."

"Tell me."

"Ok, don't hate me. I didn't know." She bit her lip again. "Eden told me how she was feeling." When she peeked at him again, he nodded for her to continue. "She was upset because she didn't feel she was being honest with you and stuff. And I," again she gnawed at her lip, "I told her to talk to you. I told her if she did, it'd all work out as it should."

She glanced at him and visibly flinched. Andrew just stared at her.

Micah gasped. *What? It's going to work out as it should? I'm supposed to die...*

Caitlyn, still wide-eyed, watched Andrew.

"I'm not mad at you, so stop staring at me like I'm going to hit you or something. You're creeping me out," Andrew said to her.

Caitlyn's words rushed out, "I didn't tell Eden to break up with you, I swear. I'm sorry if I somehow caused this to happen."

"You didn't. This isn't your fault, Caitlyn. You know, when Eden told me we were done, she kind of alluded to it being the right thing. I was mad because how can the right thing feel so terrible, but now..." He glanced at her. "I don't know. Maybe she's right."

Caitlyn sounded remorseful. "I'm so sorry, Andrew."

She wrapped her hoodie around her body, hugging herself. Andrew sighed, "Caitlyn, stop feeling bad. You know, this has been good for me actually. I feel ok."

Poor dude, lying to make her feel better, Micah thought.

Caitlyn glanced over at him. It was quiet for a moment. "Are you going to go still, to Chicago, I mean?" she asked, breaking the silence.

Took the words right out of my mouth, Caitlyn.

"No, I don't think so."

The words hung in the air, Micah cringing at their implications.

Caitlyn gazed at Andrew and then said, "I should probably go back in. I didn't tell my parents I left, and they might freak when they discover I'm not in my room."

"Yeah, they will. Hey, thanks, Caitlyn." He leaned over to hug her.

Micah didn't miss her hesitation. The hug was quick, and then she grabbed the door handle. Not facing Andrew, she mumbled, "I think you should come still."

"Why?"

She turned around. "I just have this feeling that it'll all work out if you do."

There was tension and then Andrew snorted. "It'll all work out, huh? I think you're trying to use your Jedi mind tricks on me."

Caitlyn's face flushed. "This means I'm crazy, doesn't it?" She wrinkled her nose.

"Welcome to the super hero club," Andrew said sarcastically.

"Awesome, when do I get my cape?"

"I don't know, but I'd love to see you in spandex."

She slugged his shoulder. "If I have to wear it, so do you. So be prepared to look like your underwear's on the outside of your pants."

Andrew laughed loudly. "No way, that only looks good on girls."

Undeterred, Caitlyn continued, "I can see it now—a big D on the front for Doctor Drew, the Healer."

"Oh yeah, you think that's funny, don't you? You'd have a Y then, for Yoda." He paused, "You sort of look like him, you know."

Caitlyn giggled. "Nice, I like it."

Micah folded his arms across his chest, wondering why he still remained in this vision. Not only did he not care to watch two people flirt, he felt like he'd learned what he was supposed to, and he wasn't really in the mood to watch playful banter.

I only have a death sentence hanging over my head.

Then it dawned on him. *They don't even realize they're flirting. They think they're just friends. Man, is it this obvious to everyone else with Eden and me?*

Caitlyn sighed. "I better get back." She opened the door and gave him one last, questioning glance. "So, Chicago?"

He shrugged his shoulders. "Sorry, probably not."

Micah returned to his bed; Sage was gone now. He knew sleep was out of the question. He had too much to sort through. He debated waking Trent but decided against it. Trent would want to drive straight over to Eden's and demand she get back with Andrew.

Micah sat at the edge of his bed. *That's an idea.* As much as he hated it, he had to consider it might work.

He wanted someone to talk to but, for some reason, he didn't call Sage back. This felt like something he had to work through. *Or Caitlyn said it'd all work out, so maybe it's meant to be. Maybe I just have to accept it. It's my fate.* Something tugged at him, something he couldn't quite put his finger on.

Sadness overwhelmed him. He needed to distract himself. Pacing the floor, he let his mind wander. His thoughts lead him to Eden. *Well, she broke up with him, so I guess I know she likes me now. Never could be sure since she seemed to really like Andrew too. Wonder how she feels about all this.*

Now Micah wasn't in his room, but in Eden's. It was dimly lit by a night light in the corner. He could see she was in bed, and he drew closer. Kleenex's sprawled across her floor and littered her bedspread. *She's been crying.* Her eyes were shut, her breathing even. *She's asleep at least.*

Then it was like a layer peeled back and he saw Gabriel, sitting next to her, leaning against the headrest. He was running his hand from the top of her head, down her hair, which covered most of his lap.

Micah cocked his head to the side. There was a low, deep, lulling sound. *He's humming to her.* Micah watched the rise and fall of Eden's chest. She'd obviously spent the night sobbing.

Returning to his bedroom, Micah understood the meaning. *She still cares for Andrew too. And,* he groaned, *I need to convince her to get back with him.*

Chapter Thirty-Eight

icah waited for Eden to come over again, but she didn't. For some reason, he'd assumed she'd pounce on the chance to be with him. He was surprised and relieved by her absence. It sort of gave him hope that maybe she'd worked things out with Andrew after all, as much as it pained him.

It'd been almost two weeks, and Trent's patience was wearing thin.

"Micah, just call her or go see her. You're avoiding it, aren't you?" Trent snapped. His mood had been foul since he'd learned about the break up. He put it together pretty fast that it meant his cousin would die.

Micah glanced up from the Bible in his hands. He spent most of his time reading now.

"I don't care what Eden wants. You tell her what's at stake! She'll do it for you. You know she will. So why haven't you told her? You're stalling."

You're right, I am. As much as he wanted to live, the thought of forcing Eden to be with someone she may not want to be, for him, felt selfish. The more he read and prayed, the more he avoided having *that* talk with her.

He sighed and closed the book. "Trent, Caitlyn said it'd work as it *should.* Maybe it is."

Trent growled. "This is ridiculous. I'm going to tell your parents. You talk to Eden today, or I'm marching upstairs and announcing to your mom what's really happening here."

Micah knew Trent loved him. They were like brothers. *And he doesn't love Eden like I do.*

Micah begun to protest, but they both heard the doorbell ring. Trent was off the couch and to the front door before he'd even stood up.

Micah slowly left the great room, coming into the front entry. His heart dropped. Eden stood in the open doorway. Trent turned around and glared at Micah, his expression obvious.

She seemed unsure what to do since Trent hadn't really invited her in.

"Hey Eden," Micah recovered. "Come on in."

Trent stormed past Micah and muttered, "Well as *fate* has it, she's here. So you better do it." He paused and studied Micah's face, adding, "Don't do anything stupid. Say what needs to be said."

Micah hoped Eden hadn't overheard as he grinned at her. "I haven't seen you in a while."

She nodded, rubbing her arms like she was cold. "Had to finish school and well, summer's been..."

Her words trailed and he offered, "Busy?"

"Yeah." Her voice sounded heavy.

"Want to swim?" he asked.

"I don't have my suit. I just wanted to say hi."

He grinned again. "Good, I'm glad you did. Should we sit outside?"

She smiled. "Sure."

They opted for the deck. Micah cranked the umbrella up for one of the tables, and they sat across from each other.

"So, what've been up to?" he asked, noting how withdrawn her eyes seemed.

She licked her lips. "Not much. How about you?"

"Oh you know, the same—lots of visions."

She arched an eyebrow at him but said nothing.

"What's wrong? You seem upset." He had to say it. *I really don't want to have this talk.*

Her eyes were moist and she looked away. "I guess there's no point in not telling you. Andrew and I broke up."

Ugh, no avoiding it now.

"Really? What happened?"

She glanced at him. "I'm the one who did it."

"Why?"

Her eyes pleaded with him. *She doesn't want to be the one to say it.*

She sighed. "I like him a lot, but when he says he loves me, I can't—"

"Say it back?"

"No."

He hated the fact that he loved hearing her say that. "I'm sorry. When did it happen?"

"A few weeks ago."

"And you're just coming to see me? Man, what are best friends for?"

She stared at him. "I didn't want to interrupt with Damon."

Oh, the Honda in the driveway, of course! She would've come sooner. Some measure of his pride felt better, even though he knew he shouldn't.

"You should have come over anyway!" His grinned and then sobered. "I'm sorry you went through that on your own. Are you ok?"

Pain flickered across her face. "No, I feel awful."

Well, here it goes. Micah forced the words out, hating the taste they left behind. "Really? Maybe you should call him, get back with him."

Eden's expression made his chest ache, her blue eyes confused and dejected. *But the alternative's not an option,* he reminded himself.

He swallowed. The words were like bile coming out. "Are you sure you did the right thing?"

Her gaze shifted to the pool and she whispered, "I don't know anymore."

Micah knew Trent wasn't bluffing about telling his parents *everything*. He knew he needed to sink it in with Eden. *But how?* He hardly thought it fair to her to say, *If you don't take him back, I die, ok?*

Apparently, he'd waited too long to respond, Eden pushed her chair back and stood. Jumping to his feet, he stammered as her eyes swept his face.

"Eden, I'm sorry about you and Andrew. But you need to know that you and I... we can't... we can't ever be," he said at last.

"Why?" she whispered. "I don't understand, Micah. How can you know who I'm supposed to be with? Don't I get a say in it? Doesn't how I feel matter?"

Micah was stumped. *She's right.*

"Yes, you should. You did what you had to. It'll all work out as it should." His words sounded hollow, empty to him.

She stared at him, and then her eyes dropped to the ground. "I'm sorry I didn't do what you wanted me to."

He knew he should say something. He should tell the why behind it all. He knew she'd run back to Andrew; she'd do anything to save him. But he clenched his jaw shut. Forcing someone to live a lie couldn't be what Caitlyn meant.

He glanced over at her downcast eyes.

"I better go," she mumbled.

"Eden wait—" He stepped toward her.

She glanced up, her eyes filled with tears. He reached for her, his heart torn up by her anguish.

"I'm sorry. I just need some time to figure this out." His hand landed on her arm.

Her blue eyes met his. "I don't know why you won't tell me anything. Why I'm in the dark all the time. Don't you trust me anymore?"

He was taken aback. *Is that what she thought?* "No, I do. I... it's just, I thought it was going to work one way and now..."

"I'm sorry," she cut in. "Sorry I messed it all up."

He tried to protest, realizing his words probably made her feel personally responsible, but she slipped through the sliding glass door, escaping him.

He hadn't missed the tears falling from her eyes as she'd left. He sighed heavily, resigning to defeat.

Chapter Thirty-Nine

Eden was surprised when she glanced up from her book to see her mom standing in the doorway.

Eden stretched her legs out, uncurling from the tight ball she'd been in on the recliner. She'd spent the past week living in the library.

Her mom walked in, and Eden already knew what was coming. She'd been here before, back in Portsmouth, when all she did was read, alone, book after book.

"Eden, the sun's shining today. Why don't you go swimming?" her mom asked, fluffing the pillows on the couch next to her.

Eden shoved the faded receipt she'd found on the desk into her book. "I don't feel like it today."

Her mom eyed the book, and Eden slowly shut it.

"You're reading an awful lot, not that I mind it. I just worry it means you're still upset over your break up." Her mom sat down, still holding one of the olive green throw pillows in her hands.

"I'm fine. It's not that."

Her mom glanced over. "What is it then? You seem like your avoiding your friends too."

Eden frowned. That wasn't entirely untrue. Since Jessie didn't hesitate to remind Eden that she was the one who wanted to break up, and that she'd tried to warn her about Micah, she'd been avoiding her more than usual. It was too painful.

"You haven't spent much time with Micah," her mom continued.

Eden cringed. Her mom didn't miss it. "Did something happen with Micah?"

She glanced at her mom and sighed. "I sort of told Micah I liked him, after I broke up with Andrew."

Eden watched her mom's face; she didn't seem surprised.

"And?" her mom asked when she fell silent.

"And he doesn't like me more than a friend." The words caused painful waves to roll through her. Her fingers tightened their grip on her book. She felt desperate to escape her own reality.

"Oh, Eden, I'm so sorry. I really thought he felt differently. It sure seemed that way to Lacey and me. But, maybe it's not you. Lacey told me he's acting strange again. They're really worried about him."

That got Eden's attention. "Really?"

Her mom glanced over. "He's hardly eating anything. It's like he's starving himself. Lacey is beside herself on what to do. I was thinking of having the Hawkins's over for the 4th next week, but maybe we better not." Her mom gave her a sympathetic look.

Not eating again? She hated the dread trickling in.

"No, Mom, invite them. Maybe I can talk to Micah. We're still best friends. I shouldn't be avoiding him."

Eden tossed the cut watermelon into a bowl as the doorbell rang. When Brendon ran to answer it, she debated what to do. Her mom continued to slice tomatoes and pickles for the relish tray. Eden wiped her hands on a towel; her hands were shaking. Taking a deep breath, she retrieved the knife and deliberately sliced into a cantaloupe.

A few moments later, Caleb emerged into the great room with Brendon. Since their kitchen was open to the great room, she watched Caleb set up a video game with Brendon on the big screen TV. Lacey came into the kitchen next. They all said their hellos, and then their moms began discussing the new table saw Eden's mom had bought her dad for his birthday.

Lacey said, "I think Jared wants a new one too. They're out in the garage, looking at it."

Trent strolled into the kitchen, drawing Eden's attention away from her mom's conversation. He plopped on the stool next to hers and began popping chunks of cantaloupe from the bowl into his mouth.

"Where's Micah?" She dropped her voice lower and smiled. "Don't tell me he's still with Damon."

Trent's smile was strained. "No, he's out in the garage with his dad, looking at your dad's tools."

What? No snarky come back?

Studying him closer, she saw dark rings under his eyes. Her bad feeling got worse. *He's not sleeping... Micah's not eating.*

Hearing someone behind her, she stiffened. Trent glanced over his shoulder, and she did too. She almost gasped, but bit her lip instead. Micah's stood behind her, his blue eyes penetrating. She almost overlooked the paleness in his skin since her heart was banging against her rib cage.

She stood and he stepped closer.

He bumped her shoulder with his body. "Hey, stranger."

She nudged him back. "Hey, to you too."

His smile sent a thrill through her.

She glanced away, catching eyes with her mom.

"We got it in here. Why don't you guys go catch up?" her mom offered.

"Ok." Eden felt awkward knowing their moms were watching. She followed Micah and Trent into the great room, trying to remember she had a purpose. *I need to know what's up with Micah.*

"So, is it true?" she asked him as they sat down on a couch together.

He glanced over. "What true?"

"That you're not eating again?" *There, it's out in the open.*

Trent was the one to answer. "He has a name for it, but I say he's just starving himself to death."

She glanced at Trent and then stared at Micah.

He shook his head, grinning. "Always the drama queen."

Trent didn't laugh. He stood up to join Caleb and Brendon playing the video game instead.

"So, why aren't you eating?" she pressed.

He gave her a side-glance. "Don't worry about me. I'm fine."

"Sweet! Did you see that?" Brendon blurted, pointing at the screen.

Micah looked at the TV, but she continued to gaze at his profile. She was debating if she should keep pushing him when her mom came in and said, "Time to eat everyone."

Guess it'll have to wait. Lunch was set up buffet style, Eden's dad bringing in a platter full of hamburgers, hotdogs, and steaks. Micah gestured for her to go first. She shook his head and he gave her a friendly shove forward. She sighed and began scooping potato salad on her plate. His arm brushed hers as he followed her. By the time she'd reached the end of the line, she wondered if all the bumps and brushes were accidents at all. He seemed to be trying to be near her.

She sat at the table, her heart in a tizzy. She was disappointed when he sat across from her. *Guess no more accidental touches.*

But as they ate, while everyone visited and laughed, she caught Micah looking at her, more than once. The first few times she glanced away, afraid he'd see straight through her, but after the third time, she didn't. She searched his face, seeing something new in his blue eyes. *He's worried.* He glanced away this time.

After lunch was over, she carried her plate to the sink. Trent was in the kitchen, rummaging through the cooler full of soda.

Sort of missing his teasing, she tried to nettle him. "Kissed any new girls lately?"

Trent grabbed a can and stood. He cracked it open. "Nope. How about you, now that you're a *free woman?*"

Unsure how to take his comment, she forced a smile. "Trent, you're losing your edge. I didn't think you could go a week without a new girl."

Trent snorted and grimaced. After a long swig, his expression changed as he gazed back at her. "Are you sure you don't want to be with

Andrew?"

Eden was shocked by the pleading in his tone. He waited for response, his forehead wrinkled and his mouth frowning.

"Uh, I'm sure you guys can still be friends without me in the picture," she joked, but it came out flat.

His eyes clouded over and, taking another long drink from his soda can, he walked away, muttering, "It's not the same."

She watched him go and her insides sickened. *What did I do? It seems imperative I be with Andrew.*

Spinning on her heel to leave the room, she walked straight into Micah.

"Whoa, where are you going?" He steadied her with his hands.

She tried to dodge his feet. He was grinning at her when she glanced up. Her heart felt like it was in her throat, her pulse pounding hard. He continued to hold onto her, his hands warm on her cool skin. His blue eyes surveyed her face, taking in everything, including her mouth. She couldn't help but stare at his lips, longing to know how they'd feel.

Caleb entered the room and Micah let go, watching his brother piling his plate with more food.

He cleared his throat. "Leave some for the rest of us."

Caleb peered over. "Micah, you need to learn how to eat. You look like a skinny girl lately."

Micah's muscular build was anything but skinny, but Eden did agree with Caleb on one thing—he needed to eat.

Micah stepped away from her. "Move over—did you leave any bacon?"

She smiled as he built a hamburger to rival Caleb's, stacked high with bacon, avocados, tomatoes, cheese, and condiments. She wasn't sure he'd be able to get his mouth around it, but he did, and she was happy to see him eat all of it.

Everyone was full and mulling around the living room when Micah's dad asked if they'd like to go swimming at their home, and of course, everyone did. Eden ran upstairs to change and was surprised to find the house empty when she returned. *Was I that slow?* Maybe her family planned to change at the Hawkins. She paused by the front door. *Is it safe to walk? It's in the middle of the day...*

She tossed her towel over her shoulder and pulled the front door open. Micah was on the porch swing, waiting for her.

Glancing around, she asked, "Where's Trent?"

"He left with Brendon and Caleb."

"He seems sort of mad at you today."

Micah snorted. "Yeah, but that just means he loves me. Trent's a strange duck."

When he didn't get up, she leaned against the porch railing and waited.

"Eden, I've thought about what you said the other day. I made a mistake in not telling you more all along. It's hard for me to know who to tell what to. But you've always been there for me, believed me from the start. I should've confided in you."

She was happy he was finally opening up. "Micah, you can tell me anything. I want to help carry your burden."

His face appeared relieved at first, and then pained. "Thank you. You don't know what that means to me." His voice sounded husky.

She smiled at him. "What are best friends for?"

He gave her a crooked grin and then took a deep breath, exhaling slowly. "Ok, so you know how I'm the Seer?"

She nodded.

"And how I see things that are going to happen?" Another nod and he continued, "Well, I've seen visions of a huge fire coming. It's going to destroy everything and it's up to me to keep everyone from dying in it."

She stared back at him, her mouth gaping open. "Are you serious?"

Now he nodded.

"That's why you went to Rome, isn't it?" she asked.

"Yeah, my host family taught me about a Prophet named Enoch. He lived before Noah. He was actually his great grandfather. Anyways, Enoch built a special city that was lifted up to Heaven before the flood came. Everyone inside the city was saved from drowning. I've seen a city in my dreams that's like Enoch's city. I need to build it so the people inside will be safe from the fire like they were in the flood. That's what my mission is. That's what I've spent every minute of every day learning and preparing for."

"I had no idea. Micah, you have to save the world."

"Don't I know it," he grunted.

"No wonder you can't eat or sleep."

He hesitated and then said, "I'm fasting, Eden."

"Fasting?"

"Yeah, to help solve a little problem I have."

Oh, you mean the little problem I caused? Her insides sunk. *What did I do?* Then her mind put the pieces together.

She gasped. "Oh my gosh!"

Startled, he glanced at her. "What?"

"Your life's in danger, isn't it? That's why you need Andrew so badly. He can heal people... he healed me." She glanced at him. "You already knew that, didn't you?" She didn't wait for him to respond. "That's why you didn't want me to break up with him, 'cause now he won't come on this trip."

He was quiet, his blue eyes troubled.

"Why didn't you tell me?" she demanded.

"I didn't want you to do something you didn't want to for me."

She gaped at him. "So you'd rather just die? I'd do anything to keep you safe and alive! And I know you'd do the same thing for me. Micah, I love you!"

She clamped her mouth shut as soon as the words flew out. *What did I just say?*

She was terrified to face him now. She couldn't bear to hear him say that they could never be together or whatever other excuse he may have.

She opted for bolting off the porch steps instead. She knew she looked ridiculous, but she ran anyway. It took a minute for Micah to catch up to her.

"Eden, get back here," he called after. He grabbed her arm, bringing her to a halt. Her chest was heaving, both with exertion and fear of what would come next.

"You can't just say that and then run away," he said, breathing hard too.

They faced each other. She threw her hands on her hips. Now it was her turn to be strong.

"I can't believe you didn't tell me. I'm calling Andrew today. I'm going to fix this."

"Eden, wait, don't. How you feel matters. I can't stand the thought of you pretending for me."

She recognized his argument. Wasn't that what she'd said to him only weeks ago? Now it seemed so petty and selfish of her.

"Who cares how I feel! I don't! I'd rather be friends with you than never see you again. Why can't you get that through your head?" Her voice was raising an octave with each sentence.

He grimaced. "You're not going to back down are you?"

"No way." She tugged his hand free and marched back towards the house.

"Where are you going?"

"To get my phone."

Micah was in front of her, grabbing both of her arms, bringing her face inches from his.

She stopped and stared back into his eyes. She could feel her anger ebbing, replaced by intoxicating excitement. His lips were so near.

"Is there nothing I can do to change your mind?" His voice was quiet, his tone pleading.

"No," she mumbled.

He dropped his head and brushed his lips against her jawline, moving from her ear towards her chin, his lips leaving a tingling trail behind them.

"Are you sure?" he asked, his breath warm against her skin.

She closed her eyes, the temptation to forget the whole idea overwhelming. She'd dreamt of this moment, replayed it in her head so many times. Now it was here, and now she was the one to have to say no.

The thought of him injured and helpless flashed through her.

She stepped back. "There's nothing you can do. I'm not going to let you die if I can do something to stop it."

He sighed heavily. "Ok, well, can we at least go swimming together? Can you give me a few more hours before you're *his* again?"

She stared at him, realizing how he felt about it. "You'd rather die to have one day with me?"

He grinned. It reached his eyes, making them crinkle. "Yeah, when you put it like that. You're right. I'd rather not be around while you're with him. It kills me."

She could tell he was teasing, but his words rang true.

"Well, I'm not as noble as you. I'd rather live a lie to keep you safe."

He frowned at her, but she wasn't going to change her mind. *No matter how seducing your lips are.*

"Ok, fine. Just give me the day." He took her hand in his and squeezed it.

She didn't budge when he walked forward. "Just today. I'm calling him tomorrow morning."

"I never knew you could be so stubborn." He grinned at her as she guffawed.

"You'd do the same thing for me." She jabbed a finger into his chest.

He snatched her hand and pressed her fingers against his lips. "You're right, I would."

That took the fight right out of her. She hoped he wouldn't kiss more than her hand, she was pretty she'd cave if he did, but he just chuckled as they walked hand in hand back to his house to swim.

Chapter Forty

Micah couldn't sleep that night and the morning hours dragged. He tried to keep his mind busy with last-minute preparations for the trip the following week, but all he could think of was Eden calling Andrew and what that meant.

I should be happy. Now, maybe I'll live through all this. But he felt miserable, even feeling bad for his friend, Andrew. *We're playing him. This can't be right.*

As the hours ticked by, he realized there had been a plan C to all this after all. He should have told Andrew everything. He was pretty sure his friend would have suffered the trip to save his life.

Trent assured Micah it was the right thing, that now it'd all be fine. After dinner, Micah escaped to his bedroom and paced the floor. The sound of his phone chiming had him flying across the room to grab it off his nightstand.

He had a text from Eden.

I called him, left a VM. Waited all day, but he didn't call me back. Sorry.

Micah texted back. *Not your fault, you tried. He'll call you tomorrow.*

I guess we'll wait and see.

But Friday came and went and Eden texted Micah. *Still nothing.*

It both relieved and terrified him. By Sunday night, Trent wasn't feeling too confident anymore either. Monday, Micah began another fast.

When his phone buzzed around lunchtime, he dreaded reading the message. It was from Eden.

So I know why Andrew hasn't called. He's in Florida visiting his cousins. His phone died over the weekend since he lost his charger. He bought a new one today. I told him I want to talk and he said he'd be back Saturday night.

Micah stared at his phone. They were leaving Thursday for their trip. Andrew wouldn't be back in time.

The letters on his phone blurred. He typed back.

Thank you for trying, Eden. There's nothing we can do now.

There has to be something we can do!

I think we just need to have faith. It'll all be fine. Don't worry.

Micah!

I'm sorry. I better get some stuff done. Talk later?

Ok.

He set his phone down wondering if he should tell his parents. *No, they won't let me leave if I do,* he decided.

"Gabriel, you've got to fix this! I know you can!" she whispered to her empty bedroom after Micah stopped texting her.

She felt nothing, saw nothing. She blinked back the tears. "This is all my fault. I ruined everything."

"No you didn't; you'll see."

Eden whirled around but saw nothing, but she had heard him. She'd heard Gabriel.

"I didn't ruin it?" she asked, tears bursting from her eyes, streaking down her cheeks.

She didn't hear anything else. She waited and then wiped her eyes. *Maybe Andrew will come home early. Or maybe this means Micah won't get hurt at all.* She liked that idea.

Not sure if she'd mess things up more, she avoided going over to

Micah's the next few days. On Wednesday, she shot a text off to Andrew.

Still coming back Saturday?

He replied. *Yep.*

Ok, well, I'll be in Illinois then. I wish you were coming too.

Sorry.

Micah wants you to go still. I could stay home if that's why you aren't coming.

No, don't do that. That's not why.

You sure?

Yes. I'm in Florida, remember?

Oh yeah, guess you're right.

Her phone went silent. *He seems mad. He's not going to take me back. Now that he's not coming back in time, I don't want to do this anymore anyway.*

She glanced at her clock. It was three o'clock. They were leaving tomorrow morning. She hesitated and then selected a different contact in her cell phone.

On the fourth ring, Jessie answered. "Hi Eden."

"Hey, Jessie. How's it going?"

"Good, want to go shopping or something? I'm totally bored."

"Um, yeah. Hey Jessie, I have a favor to ask."

"Yes?"

Eden hesitated. *Maybe I should've done this in person.* She dove in, "Do you want to call Trent to see if he wants to go out tonight?"

There was a gasp in the receiver and then, "What? No way! Why on earth would I want to call *him*?"

This isn't going to work. "Because he's dying to go out with you."

There was silence and then, "Then why are you calling me and not him?"

"He's wanted to," she soothed. "But he and Micah have been preoccupied lately."

"Humph," Jessie grunted. "How do you know?"

"Trust me, I know when Trent's into someone. He really likes you."

It was quiet, a good sign with Jessie. "Has he actually said he likes me?"

Eden was happy she'd eavesdropped because she could honestly say to her friend, "Yes, he told Micah. He thinks you're hot, Jessie. And he wants to take you out once we're back from Chicago. I think they're sort of stressed about going, or something."

"Who stresses about a dumb vacation?" Jessie muttered, but her tone had definitely changed. There was a long sigh. "Oh, all right. I want you to know I'm only doing this for you, because you're my best friend. And maybe part of me wants to tell him off too. What's his number?"

Chapter Forty-One

After twenty minutes of waiting idly, Eden jumped into her Jeep. The wind pushed against her vehicle as she drove to the grocery store. A summer monsoon was on its way. In a few hours, the pewter sky would bring a downpour. She had just parked when her phone rang. She fumbled to answer it.

"So?" she asked, knowing it was Jessie.

"You were right. He wants to go out." Her tone sounded ticked.

Eden tried to ignore it. "I told you he did!"

"So why didn't *he* call *me?* I knew he was just a flirt. I'm only doing this for you. I don't even think I like him anymore actually."

"Thanks, Jessie, I really owe you. What are you going to do?"

"Dinner and a movie. He's getting me in a couple hours."

"Cool." She was thrilled it'd worked and hoped Jessie just sounded more put off than she felt. *She seemed to like Trent at the pool party.*

"So why do you want me to go out with Trent all of sudden? It's not like you haven't listened to me mope over him for the past few months," Jessie stated.

Jessie's right. Why didn't I? I've been completely selfish. "I'm sorry, Jess, I should've done this sooner, but I wasn't sure how he felt." Chagrined with herself, she added, "But I'm sure now and I'm so excited for you!"

There was a pause, and then Jessie said, "Well, I still think Trent's a player but like I said, you're my friend. So I'll suffer through it."

"Thanks, Jessie," she repeated. Redirecting back, she asked, "So what are you going to do until then?" They both had a couple hours to burn.

"Are you kidding? I hope I have enough time to get ready! Do you know how long it takes to flat iron this hair?"

Eden laughed. For all her complaining, she could tell Jessie was excited about the date still. A few minutes later, they hung up.

Mm, what to do for the next few hours? She grabbed some snacks at the store for tomorrow's long ride and opted not to go home, having a better idea. Making her way onto the Turnpike, she headed for the building that used to be her best friend, the library. Fifteen minutes later, she was sitting cross-legged in a chair, tucked behind bookshelves, with a copy of *The Importance of Being Ernest*. She'd read it multiple times, but thought it might keep her mind busy, which it did.

She was shocked when she heard a woman walking by tell her son, "It's almost five o'clock. We need to leave soon."

Really? She pulled out her cell phone. *Time to go.*

Driving back to Micah's, she said repeatedly, "Please don't let Damon be there. Please don't Damon be there."

Approaching Micah's home, she felt a rush of adrenaline. The driveway was empty.

So this is it, she thought, as she pulled her Jeep in. Turning the key, she took a deep breath and tried to remember what her plan was. No words came to mind. Before she could chicken out, she threw the driver's door open. The first few large raindrops hit her face as she hopped up the porch steps and knocked firmly on the door.

Mrs. Hawkins face appeared in the doorway. "Eden, how are you dear?"

"I'm good, thanks."

"Come on in." Eden was about to ask if Micah was home, but she beat her to it. "Micah's up in his room packing. I'm sure he'll be happy to see you. Why don't you go on up?"

Perfect, she thought while she said, "Thanks."

She jogged up the stairs, her heart banging against her rib cage.

Her stomach was rolling with nerves, and her fingers were ice cold. Micah's door was open a crack, and she could hear music coming out. Taking a deep breath, she hit her knuckles against the door, pushing it open further.

"You don't have to knock," Micah called out.

She stepped inside, her eyes adjusting to the dimness, since the light was off. Micah, who'd been sprawled on his bed with his hands behind his head, saw her, and immediately bolted up. His suitcase lay open and empty next to him.

"Hey, Eden." He sounded surprised.

"Hi, Micah. Your mom said to come up."

Panic flickered in his eyes, and his smile looked forced. Stomach sinking to her toes, she asked, "So are you all packed, ready for tomorrow?"

She knew her answer was painfully obvious as his bag was empty, but she couldn't think of anything else to say at the moment.

He gazed at his bag. "No, and no." Glancing back at her, he asked, "How about you?"

"Yeah, I packed a few things. Not much. We aren't going to be gone long."

Wondering why Micah had failed to invite her in, she forced her legs to enter the room. His eyes followed her like she might have the plague. Not prepared for his reaction, she shuffled to the recliner, plopping down before she lost her nerve completely.

Not talking about the elephant in the room's going to be harder than I thought. She didn't want to think about what tomorrow meant. She wasn't entirely sure why she was even here.

She stared at his stereo. "I love this song."

"Yeah, me too." After a moment of listening, he added, "You know, I never noticed before how many songs are about God and life."

"Yeah, especially country." She glanced at him. "Is that what you're thinking about?"

Micah pulled his knees up and rested his elbows on them. "It's never far from my mind." His eyes locked on hers, and she was slightly confused by his expression.

"So speaking of which, any new visions?" she asked, hoping he'd found the solution to their problem.

He gazed back at her. "Nope."

They both fell silent. The awkward pause was interrupted by a clap of thunder and the tapping on the window grew steady. She walked to the window. The rain was finally here; she loved the pounding on the roof, the dampness in the air, and the clean smell it left behind.

The glass felt cool against her palms.

"You just missed Trent. He's going to go out with Jessie tonight."

"Oh really? That's good," she said nonchalantly.

"Trent said you gave Jessie his number."

She leaned her back against the window and faced him. "Trent's so tense lately. I thought it'd be good for him to have a night of fun. Sorry, is that ok?"

Micah strolled toward her. "Yes, it's a great idea actually. He didn't want to go, but I told him he's no good to me here just moping around." Micah gave her a crooked grin.

Her pulse was aware of his close proximity. "Didn't he *want* to go? I thought he liked her." *Poor Jessie! She's going to kill me!*

"No, he does. It's not that."

Uh oh, the elephant's here again. "He just didn't want to leave your side, right?"

Micah nodded, staring out the window, and then he reached by her face. Her breath caught, but he was only unlatching the window behind her. She moved over as he hefted it up a few inches. The drumming of the rain intensified.

She inhaled deeply. "I love rain." She placed her hands on the sill, the drops splattering on her skin.

He placed his hand next to hers and glanced over. "Did you hear from Andrew again?"

Her mouth went dry. "No. As far as I know, he's still not back."

Listening to the rain pelting the glass, she wished she could freeze time. Make this moment with Micah last forever.

She cleared her throat. "So, are we just actors after all? Or do we make our own destiny?"

His blue eyes registered surprise. He smiled, and she was relieved to see it was warm. "What do *you* think?"

"Maybe a little bit of both," she said, noting his interest. "Maybe we make our own decisions. Sometimes good, and sometimes bad, but if we're trying, doing the best we can, maybe our choices land us right into the role that was written for us."

Micah's eyebrows came up as he considered her words.

"Maybe we misread things. Sometimes not everything is what it appears to be," she added.

"So in other words, you're saying maybe I misread my vision?"

She swallowed. *Now that depends on which one we're discussing.* She was about to admit to overhearing his private conversation with Trent, about her marrying Andrew.

"I wish that were it," he admitted. "I really do. But sometimes what we want is just not for us to have. Maybe I need to learn to just accept whatever is supposed to happen, as is."

Feeling panicked by what that implied, she was surprised when a Sunday school lesson came to mind. It was from one of the random churches her family had attended a few months ago.

"If a child asked for some bread, would you give him a stone instead?" she blurted.

Micah stared at her. "Say what?"

"Or if your child asked for fish, would you give him a serpent?"

"I didn't know you quoted the Bible."

"Me either. Not sure why I just thought of that. But, it's still true. If we know how to give good gifts, why wouldn't God know how to give even better ones?"

Micah's eyes danced. "I'm impressed."

"You aren't the only one who knows how to read the Bible." She grinned at him and then asked, "Don't you think God wants you to be happy too?"

"You sort of sound like Trent now." He sighed.

"Well, not everything out of his mouth's completely crazy."

He chuckled and then was quiet. Listening to the rain, she was aware of how close they were now. Facing the window, his arm kept brushing hers, making her stomach flutter with butterflies.

Then the thought of the weekend awaiting sickened her.

"Micah, tell me what you saw. What's going to happen to you in Illinois?"

He turned, bringing them face to face. He hesitated and then said, "I get hurt, pretty bad."

"Can't you avoid it? Since you see how and where, can't you just not go?"

"I have to go. I need to do something that only I can do. Eden, remember my vision?" he asked, when she sputtered in protest. "Everyone's going to die in that fire if I don't complete my mission. This is bigger than me and what I want."

"But you're the Seer! How can you complete your mission if you're dead?"

"Maybe I just have to get you all to that point. Maybe that's all I have to do…"

"What are you talking about?"

He shut his mouth. "I probably shouldn't say more."

Her mouth fell open. Anger was giving way to tears and her reflex to run from the room overcame her. Nothing she could say would change his mind. He seemed bent on carrying through with this.

Tears were rolling down her face as she hustled from the room.

Micah was behind her though, taking her shoulder, and turning her around to face him. "Wait, where are you going now?"

She was embarrassed to cry in front of him. She stared at the carpet, her vision blurring.

"I can't watch you die, Micah," she whispered.

His hand was under her chin, making her look up and face him.

"Caitlyn told you to talk to Andrew, right? That it'd all work out as it should?" he asked.

"How did you—"

"I just know."

He sees way more than I thought. "Yes, she told me that. Why?"

"And you did what you felt in your heart was right?"

"Yes."

"And we tried to fix it ourselves, even though it shouldn't have needed fixing, and it didn't work. You called Andrew and he's not even in town."

She stared at him. "Ok, you've lost me."

Then his eyes stared just past her, his pupils dilating until the black almost overtook the blue. She gaped at him; his breathing was rapid now.

Oh my gosh, he's having a vision.

She waited, each second feeling like an eternity. Slowly, his breathing became even again, and his eyes focused on her.

"Caitlyn was right all along," he exclaimed, a wide grin spreading across his face. "I just needed to have a little faith."

"What? Micah, what did you see?"

Now his face was inches from hers. "Don't worry, it all works out."

"Do you mean you live?" But he didn't answer her, only took a step closer. "Micah—" she began, but his hand wrapped around the base of her neck.

His mouth landed on hers. Shocked, she staggered back, losing her balance, but he grabbed her, holding her against him. Finally registering that this was real, not some daydream, she kissed him back. He responded by kissing her harder, faster. She could understand his hunger—she felt it too. Every part of her body was tingling and numb at the same time. She found her fingers running through his hair, enjoying how silky it felt, while his kisses became frantic. His hands came back up her body and, reaching her neck, he tilted her head back, his lips making their way down her jaw and throat. His warm kisses on her skin left her lightheaded, and she closed her eyes. She had goose bumps everywhere as his lips made their way back to her mouth. Once his mouth was again pressing hard against hers, she realized they were now standing next to the bed. When had they moved?

One of his arms crushed her body against his, while his other hand was tangled in her hair, cradling the back of her head. She knew there was no escaping his strong arms, even if she wanted to. She felt her knees go weak, and she found herself lying down on the bed, Micah next to her. Being so close to him, she could smell his skin and feel how warm his body felt next to her. Somewhere in her mind, she was trying to understand what was happening still, and she was beginning to wonder if lying down was a mistake. She wasn't prepared for the rush of new feelings it brought. She was telling herself to pull away, even though she was afraid she'd be waking from a dream if she did, when he stopped kissing her.

He gazed down at her, resting on his elbow, his eyes searching her face. Lying on her back, aware of his warm arm across her stomach, she smiled up at him. "So you did want to kiss me."

He brushed her lips with his, murmuring, "I'm afraid I won't be able to stop now."

She giggled and threw both her arms around his neck, knocking him off balance and down on her. He quickly propped himself up again with his elbow. Then he was standing up. "We should probably go downstairs."

"What? Why?" she asked, sitting up. *Does he regret it?*

His eyes roamed her face and, instead of answering her, he was knocking her back down with his mouth. She was beginning to understand his reason, when he stopped and practically jumped off the bed. "Yeah, we can't stay in here. Come on."

She wanted to disagree with him, but she knew he was right. She let him pull her up to her feet. As she lumbered toward the door, grasping his hand, she asked, "Can we just talk for a bit?"

He raised an eyebrow at her. "Just talk?"

She smiled, hitching her shoulders up. "Please. I promise to be good."

"Ok, but I'm going to hold you to it, 'cause I can't guarantee anything on my end."

Once they were sitting down on his bench, he pulled her hand into his and began tracing her fingers with his. She watched his hand and then peeked up at his face. "So are you going to tell me what you saw?"

"I live. I see me in the temple now."

"You do! Wait, what temple?"

"Oh, guess I didn't tell you about that."

She waited and he grew quiet. "So?"

"It's Enoch's temple. We need to find something inside of it. I promise I'll tell you more but, right now, I don't want to think about it." She was going to ask why not when he kissed her again, leaving her breathless when he stopped.

Kissing him felt so right. Like she'd found something she'd been missing.

"So this is ok, then? I don't have to be with Andrew now?"

He pulled her into his lap. "Not unless you want to be."

She pressed her head against his chest, listening to the pounding of his heart. "No, I want to be with you."

"Good." He squeezed her around the waist playfully and she squealed at the pressure. "Because I'm not giving you back."

She laughed and then faced him. "So what changed? Why's it all fine now?"

"The miracle came."

"Huh?"

"You have to have faith before the miracle can come. I was doing it backwards, thinking I'd have faith after I'd seen the miracle. That's not how faith works. Once I let myself truly believe it was going to be fine, I saw me in the temple with all of you, including Andrew. He's going to show up tomorrow."

She stared at him and then grinned. "So is *this* part of the miracle too?" *Sure feels like it to me.*

"*You* are my miracle." His lips brushed against hers, sending fire through her veins. He cocked his head to the side. "Or maybe you're my little loaf of bread."

"Ha ha! Very funny. Now you're mocking me. I made a good point, you know."

"Yes," he kissed her lips, "you did. I wasn't making fun, I swear." He winked at her. Then he had that look again, and she loved the rush it gave her to know what it meant. *He wants me.* As his lips found hers, she thought of all the times she'd pictured how this would feel. They paled in comparison.

Micah stopped abruptly. Feeling disoriented, she asked, "What? What's wrong?"

He arched an eyebrow at her. "You aren't keeping your end of the bargain."

"Yes, I am! Besides, I'm not the one starting all the kissing."

"True, but I can't help it. You look too good, so it's really your fault."

"Nice try." She detangled herself from his arms and stood.

"You better not try running away again," he said, as she crossed the room.

"I'm not. You always catch me anyway."

He chuckled behind her.

She pushed the door open all the way. "There, that should help us be good."

"Maybe," he admitted as she turned around. "Now get over here."

She waltzed back and stood planted in front of him. He grabbed her hands and pulled her close, nestling his face into her stomach. She giggled and ran her fingers through his black hair. He tugged down on her arms, but she decided it might be safer to sit next to him instead. He made a funny face at her.

"What? You told me to behave!"

He snorted and lifted her into his lap anyway. "Like you didn't plan this tonight? You sent Trent away on that date on purpose, didn't you?"

She bit her lip. "Maybe."

She pressed her face into his chest, enjoying his scent. Tucked under his chin, she kissed his throat softly. His breathing sped and he turned her neck until her lips met his. His mouth moved with hers. Eventually he stopped, cradling her in his arms. She felt like she was panting, trying to catch her breath.

He grunted. "Poor Trent's been going crazy babysitting me."

"It's been good for him."

"I'm not so sure. You don't know how crabby he can get."

"Well, at least he'll be in a better mood tomorrow."

"Who knows, either way, I don't want to think about Trent right now. I just want to enjoy you."

"Ok, deal." She hesitated and then asked, "When did you know... I mean, when did you realize—?"

"How I felt about you?" he asked, finishing her question.

She nodded.

"I hate to admit it, but it was in Rome. I liked seeing you before I left, but I didn't really think it through, you know. When I started having visions about you and Andrew, I was insanely jealous. It surprised me, but you were with my friend, so what could I do? Besides, I—" he stopped. "Well, you know. I thought you were supposed to be with him. I thought I was ok with it all, but then I see you the morning after prom. Man, I knew I was in trouble then. You walked in and it felt like my heart stopped."

"Really?"

"Yeah. When you told me you broke up, I about kissed you right there, but—"

"I know," she interrupted, not wanting to talk about that.

"I thought I'd done it, you know. Trent's been glued to my side for the past month. Damon's been over almost every day. Then you show up here tonight and I'm going crazy inside..." His words trailed as he kissed her again. There was something in the way he kissed her this time that was different. He wasn't in a hurry. It was gentle, soft, and left her feeling like a puddle in his arms. Dizzy, she leaned her head back, wanting his lips to find her throat again. He did, kissing behind her ear.

Taking her face in his hands, he peered into her eyes. "Eden, we need to go downstairs. As much as I want to stay here with you, I don't really trust myself right now."

She wanted to protest, but she knew he had a point. She followed behind him, clutching his hand, afraid this would all disappear the moment they left his room.

At his door, he stopped. "Before we go downstairs, you have to tell me when you knew."

Her eyes shifted to the floor. "I knew before you, sort of the moment I saw you in the locker hall."

He was thoughtful and then grinned. "You always were the smart one. I really don't deserve you."

She shook her head. "You have that one backwards."

"No, I don't."

She wanted to turn it into a joke, but his eyes were so sincere that all she could feel was the happiness bubbling within her. She pressed her lips on his, closing her eyes, his hand slipped behind her neck, tickling her skin, and her lips parted. He pulled back, his breathing ragged.

His brow was wrinkled.

"What's wrong?"

He took a deep breath. "Wow... nothing... you're just... we need to go downstairs."

She bit her lip, smiling back at him. "Oh. Ok."

They entered the great room where Micah's parents were about to start a movie. Eden sank into the couch, pulling her knees up. She shot a text to her mom, telling her she was at the Hawkins watching a movie. As her mom sent back, *Oh good! Have fun!* Micah sat down next to her. She was wondering if he wanted his parents to know about them, when he grabbed her hand.

So, I guess he's not hiding us. This can't be really happening, can it?

As the movie neared its end, the front door opened and Trent strolled in. She caught the surprise in his face at seeing her there. His eyebrows shot up when he spied their hands clasped together. He plopped next to Micah and slapped Micah's leg hard, saying nothing.

When the movie ended, she overheard Trent whisper, "I can't even leave you alone for one second. So now what?"

"It's all good," Micah replied.

Trent stared at him, his face doubtful.

It was late and she needed to get home. They had a big day tomorrow. She stretched and told Micah's parents good night as they left the room. Trent stared at her; she could see the unasked question in his eyes.

Micah stood up and held his hand out to her. "Are you going to be ok driving home?"

She half-yawned, half-laughed. "It's only a hundred feet away. I think I'll be fine." She took his hand and landed on her feet.

"You shouldn't be out at night by yourself," Micah said.

She wanted to argue, but he did have a point.

"I'll drive you home," he stated matter-of-factly.

"Micah—" Trent began.

Micah cut him off. "I'll be back in a minute."

"Remember what Sage said to us. You think you'll walk back or something? I'll follow you."

As Micah nodded, she thought how ridiculous this conversation would sound to an outsider. She only lived one street over, but they all had a very good reason to be more cautious at night now. Nobody was anxious for another run in with a nasty demon.

When Micah opened the passenger door of her Jeep for her, she realized he wanted to drive. He gave her a boyish grin as they climbed in. "Do you mind? I love Jeeps."

She smiled, noticing Micah's truck following them out of the driveway. Trent could joke about a lot of things, but being attacked was not one of them. They were at Eden's house a minute later.

"Acting like this didn't happen tomorrow is going to be hard for me," he said, touching her lips. "But I think its best we keep this quiet."

She pressed her lips against his finger. "Ok. But just for this trip."

He leaned over and kissed her gently. Somewhere in her mind, she knew Trent could probably figure out what they were doing, since the truck's headlights were shining into the Jeep, but she didn't care enough to stop.

Micah pulled away. "It might be better for Andrew if we waited a little longer than that."

She wanted to protest, but she knew he was right. She didn't want to pour salt into that wound by flaunting her new relationship with Micah. "Ok."

Micah saw her to the front door, where he gave her a warm hug. "See you in the morning. Maybe you can come a little earlier than everyone else."

She smiled. "Maybe I will."

Chapter Forty-Two

Rolling down her windows as she drove, Eden enjoyed the fresh air from the previous night's rain, even if it was a little muggy. She arrived a half hour earlier than what Micah had told everyone else. The sky was blue, not a cloud to be seen.

Micah's dad was the one to open the front door. "Good morning, Eden."

"Good morning, Mr. Hawkins."

"Hey you," Micah called out as he jogged down the stairs. Seeing his huge smile sent relief shooting through her. Braiding her hair into two long plaits earlier that morning, she'd begun to worry he might regret kissing her today. Or worse, had another vision that meant they couldn't be together still. Closing the gap between them, he grabbed her hand, and with a sly smile, led her into his dad's office. Once the door shut behind them, he cupped her face in his hands and pressed his mouth on hers.

Oh good, she rejoiced, as she returned his affection.

He stopped and grinned. "I just had to do that one more time before we leave."

"It's going to be hard ignoring you for the next three days," she admitted.

"Who said anything about ignoring," he teased, and then his blue eyes turned contrite. "Eden, I need to apologize... for yesterday."

Oh no, he does regret it! she thought as she asked, "For what?"

"I kind of went a little crazy with you. I know this is going to sound weird, maybe old fashioned, but I really want to respect you."

"Oh…"

Micah shifted his weight to one leg, his face flushing, as he opened his mouth. He stammered, "What I mean is…" She was sure her face was glowing red as his blue eyes probed. "We can't… I mean, I can't use my gift if I'm not worthy of it.—"

Embarrassed, but trying to make light of it, she forced a laugh. "Micah, I have my limits too. Don't worry, I promise I'll try not to corrupt you."

He looked relieved. "Good, because it's not you I'm worried about." He paused and kissed her lips softly. "You're just way too tempting."

She wanted to come up with a clever comeback, but he was already leading her out the door. Still feeling dizzy from Micah's last kiss, they walked past the living room. When she saw Trent sitting on the couch with his face in his hands, the euphoria quickly left though. *What if Andrew doesn't come? What then?*

Damon was standing next to Micah on the driveway when Willow's Mustang pulled in. It seemed funny to Eden now that Willow drove a bright red convertible. When she'd first met Willow, it fit, but now? She somehow thought Willow might be more comfortable pulling up in a station wagon. She smiled at the thought. They'd already loaded up everyone's luggage in the back of the Excursion. Everyone that was there at least.

She began pacing the porch again. *Andrew has to come. He just has to.* She hoped that by the time Caitlyn showed, Andrew would be here, because she wasn't sure how long Micah would wait for him after that. She peered at Micah. *How's he so calm?*

As Willow joined her, she asked, "Am I the last one?"

"No." Eden wrung her hands together.

Trent came out of the house. "Micah, your dad wants to talk to you, something about Vern."

Micah turned on his heel and headed back into the house, giving

Eden a reassuring smile as he passed. She felt like she was going to throw up. She finally resigned herself to sitting on the porch swing when she heard Andrew's Bronco roar down the driveway.

I can't believe he came! It is a miracle!

She debated whether she should run into the house, or just stay put. *Maybe he came because he thought I didn't.* Both driver and passenger doors opened, and she was surprised to see Caitlyn climb out too. *So, she was right. It did work out, somehow.*

Andrew carried the bags to the back of the Excursion, and Eden heard Trent mutter under his breath as he walked past her, "Thank the good Lord he showed up."

Micah came back out. Seeing Andrew and Caitlyn, he said, "Ok, looks like we're all here. Everyone ready to go?"

She thought he'd react a little more to the fact that Andrew was actually there, but he was already climbing into the driver seat, looking anxious to leave. Micah's parents were standing by his unrolled window, with his dad punching something into the GPS. She didn't think they appeared too concerned that their son was taking a bunch of teenagers three states away, or was it four? She didn't even know.

She hung back, not sure where she should sit. She had hoped Andrew would at least glance her way so she could say hi. She hadn't seen him for over a month. Watching him climb into the back of Excursion, she realized how much she'd missed him. Damon followed Andrew, and when Trent jumped into the front seat, she saw it'd be the girls in the middle seat. Glancing up, she caught eyes with Micah in the rearview mirror.

This is going to be one long, weird day.

When Micah made their first stop four hours later, they were in Pennsylvania. She enjoyed driving through DC, but the rest of the drive had been uneventful, with everyone listening to their own music. She stretched her legs out, her knees stiff and sore. They were at some local "hole in the wall". She didn't care what they sold as long as it was edible; she was starving. She nibbled at her French fries, while carrying her tray over to the two tables they were occupying. At one sat Micah, Trent, and Damon, and at the other, Andrew and Caitlyn. Since she wasn't about to cozy up to Damon, she had no choice but to take the seat across from Andrew. Willow slid in behind her, leaving her feeling trapped.

This is ridiculous! We can't avoid each other forever. She peeked over at Andrew; his eyes were glued on his food. She waited, hoping he'd look up, but he didn't. Defeated, she followed suit and ate in silence. Willow and Caitlyn tried to make the situation less awkward by talking to Andrew nonstop, while she shoveled fry after fry into her mouth. Eyes down, she ate every bite of her greasy hamburger, just to have something to do.

When Micah asked if everyone was good to go, she was desperate to push Willow out of the way to escape. Instead, she waited as Willow gracefully slid out. Seeing Micah already heading for the parking lot, she smiled. He was determined to get there. But then again, could she blame him? Thirteen hours of straight driving was a long day.

Once the black Excursion was backing out of the parking space, Micah called back, "Hey, before you all put your earpieces in, I have a question for you." No one said anything, and he continued, "Would anyone be opposed to a slight change of plans?"

Again, no response.

"I know we're planning on touring Chicago on Saturday, but my dad made a request of me. Well, he sort of gave me an ultimatum. He said since you're taking my car and my gas, you can do a favor for me. He wants me to check on our land while we're there."

"You own land?" Andrew asked from the back. Eden could tell he was leaning forward to be heard. She felt his fingers pull her hairs as he gripped the seat.

"Yeah, well, my grandfather does, or did I should say. My great grandfather was a farmer out in Dekalb County. My grandpa grew up there as a boy and when he was old enough, he took over the family farm. About the time my dad was born though, they moved to Virginia. They didn't sell the farm but leased it out to other farmers. My grandpa couldn't part with it. My dad usually takes a trip out every year to check on it. He wants me to this year since we're out here."

"You said *did*. Did your grandpa pass away?" Willow asked.

"Yeah, in March. So now my dad and my uncle technically own it."

Feeling bad, Eden said, "I'm sorry, Micah. I didn't know."

"It's ok. I was in Rome. My grandfather was a great man. He lived a happy, long life."

Everyone murmured their condolences and Caitlyn asked, "Was it your grandpa too, Trent?"

"No, our moms are sisters," Trent answered.

Damon answered Micah's question first. It startled Eden because he'd been so quiet, but then again, when was Damon not quiet?

His voice came from the backseat. "Fine by me."

"Me too," Caitlyn agreed.

"Yeah, I don't care either way," Andrew said at the same time as Willow's, "I'd love to see the cornfields."

Staring at the back of Micah's head, she thought, *This little detour wouldn't have to do with that temple, would it?*

Chapter Forty-Three

inner was even worse for Eden than lunch. Andrew was avoiding her as much as possible, even when it was painfully obvious, and Caitlyn and Willow were still making it their mission to talk his ear off. And Micah, well, even if she wanted to go near him, always had Trent on one side and Damon on the other.

How ironic, Eden mulled, *at the beginning of the week, I felt bad for Damon, thinking he'd be the odd duck out, but I am.* Then she reminded herself, *I'd rather see Andrew happy than me.* They got back on I-80 West, somewhere in the middle of Ohio. With not much to see but flat countryside, she leaned her head against the window, hoping to fall asleep. When Caitlyn jostled her arm what felt like moments later, she was startled to see tall skyscrapers spanning her window.

"Sorry," Caitlyn apologized. "I didn't want you to miss Chicago!"

Eden rubbed her eyelids and stared out her window. *We're here? How's it possible? I swear I only slept five minutes.* But it was Chicago, brightly lit against the darkening sky. Not knowing what any of the buildings' names were, she was impressed with the height and busyness of it all.

"Wish I could say we're there, but we've got another forty-five miles to go," Micah announced.

Eden kept her face plastered to the window until the buildings began to fade. Soon, it was countryside again. Trying to stay awake, she read street signs passing by: Skokie Highway, Belvidere Road, and then Route 21. Six Flags sign suddenly loomed in the window, and she could spot roller coasters poking through the trees. Excited, she craned her neck to see better, but it didn't take long for the last metal loops of a ride to disappear. A few minutes later, the Excursion veered left into a small parking lot. *Best Western has never looked so good*, she thought.

They'd reserved two rooms: boys' and girls'. After unloading their bags, the girls meandered into the boys' room, though Eden wanted nothing more than to take a hot shower and forget about the long, torturous ride. Andrew was sitting on the edge of the bed closest the door, surfing the TV channels. She strode past, avoiding eye contact, making a beeline for the lone chair across the room. Caitlyn plopped down next to Andrew, and began chiding him for skipping every chick flick. On the bed closest to Eden, Damon lounged, leaning against the headboard with his ear buds shoved in.

Her eyes shifted to Trent and Micah, who were in the corner of the room behind her. Micah appeared to be rifling through his small bag, searching for something, while Trent stood over him like some kind of bodyguard. She wanted to say as much to Trent, when she overheard him mutter, "I'll be glad when this is all over."

She felt a flutter of nerves when Micah spied her gaze. His warm smile dissipated her jitters, replacing it with a longing to be near him again. Watching his blue eyes dance was the highlight of her entire, horrible day. She grinned, hoping he'd move closer. He straightened up and ambled towards her, his eyes remaining locked on her face. Her breath caught in her throat, the tiny pinches of adrenaline bursting through her body, until he brushed past her and reaching the sliding door, wordlessly stepping out on to the small deck.

Does he want me to follow him? She didn't have time to respond, because Trent, *the bodyguard,* was already out the door before she'd even stood up. *Why's he so glued to him? It's not like he's got to keep him from kissing me again. Micah's hardly looked at me the entire day.*

Frustrated, Eden glanced back at the room, noticing Willow was now perched next to Damon, eyeing him. Intrigued, Eden temporarily forgot her irritation as she tried not to gawk.

"What are you listening to?" Willow asked, trying to peek over Damon's shoulder at his music player.

He shifted his iPod to his hand furthest from Willow. "Nothing."

"Nothing? Then why don't you take these off?" Willow teased, snatching one of the ear buds. Before he could stop her, she had it tucked in her ear. Her eyelids half closed over her sapphire eyes while she listened, oblivious to Damon's uncomfortable plight. Curious as to what type of music Damon could be so embarrassed about, Eden was surprised when she handed the earpiece back to Damon, saying, "I love Rachmaninoff too. Good choice."

Damon stuffed the earpiece back into his ear, saying nothing. Eden was stunned. *Classical music? He sure doesn't look the type, but then again, neither does Willow.*

Even with Damon's silence, Willow appeared comfortable remaining next to him. Caitlyn finally won out and Sleepless in Seattle remained on the TV. When Willow moved to lie on her stomach, propping her head up with her wrists to watch, Damon stuffed his iPod in his pocket and stood. Awkwardly, he tried to skirt around Eden's legs, which she pulled in immediately, and then he disappeared through the sliding door.

Eden tried to pay attention to the movie, but for some reason, found it sort of depressing. When Caitlyn flopped onto her stomach as well, Eden finally let her eyes dart in Andrew's direction.

Her insides dropped.

He stared back at her with bent eyebrows and downturned lips.

She attempted a smile, pretty sure it came out a strangled mess.

Unprepared for the coolness in his blue-green eyes, she shuffled from the room, having to pass painfully in front of him. Once inside the girls' room, she slid down the door, sinking to the floor until her knees hit her forehead. She groaned. *I shouldn't have come. Micah's needs Andrew here, not me.*

Micah had hoped Eden would've followed him out. He couldn't believe how much he wanted to hold her. He could tell she was in pain and he was about to sock Andrew. Although, he conceded, Andrew was probably acting cold and distant in order not to break down in front of them all.

Micah could see Andrew's pain. *He still loves her.* Standing on the deck, Micah was disappointed when Trent and Damon were the ones to join him, not Eden. Still, he appreciated their loyalty.

Damon eyed him. "So, do I know everything I need to?"

Trent glanced at Micah and then stared at the railing.

Micah nodded. "Yes, you're ready Damon."

No need to tell him more, he'll just try to stop me.

They stayed outside for a few minutes longer. Trent seemed to be stalling.

"No worries, the guardians are ready. Sage said everything's all set," Micah said, trying to reassure him.

Trent nodded, his lips still frowning. "Why don't we just skip the amusement park tomorrow and get this over with? Then I'll enjoy the rest of this trip."

Damon nodded. "I agree."

Micah shrugged. "I think everyone will get suspicious. Let's just keep with the plan."

Trent huffed and opened the sliding glass door.

Andrew's voice carried to the deck. "You think that's funny, do you?"

There was a shriek of laughter. Curious, Micah followed Trent. Andrew had Caitlyn locked in his hold, tickling her mercilessly on the bed.

She was trying to free herself, but he had her pinned good. She wailed, "Andrew, s-s-t-t-o-o-p! I'm going to p-e-e-e my p-a-a-n-t-s!"

"Nice try, but I don't believe you." In all their noise, they hadn't noticed they had an audience.

She was laughing hard enough that tears were rolling down her cheeks now. She kicked him away, gaining a little leverage. Andrew's body flew off the bed, but he had secured both of her wrists, and pulled her down with him. They landed with a thud on the floor, Caitlyn's fall buffered by his body.

Micah looked around the room. No one else was there. Eden and Willow were gone.

"Well, well, what have we here?" Trent quipped.

Caitlyn looked over at them and gasped. Andrew let her hands go, and she hustled from the room, shutting the door behind her without a backward glance.

Andrew rose to his feet, his face somewhat embarrassed. "She was trying to make me laugh."

"Looks like the other way around to me," Trent commented.

Andrew shrugged. "Dave just broke up with her. I was trying to cheer her up."

Micah grinned. "Mission accomplished, Andrew." *I have a hunch Caitlyn influenced you to come along, in more ways than one.*

Chapter Forty-Four

Eden carefully closed the door, trying not to wake anyone. Thinking of the free breakfast waiting for her downstairs, she spun around to find herself face to face with Andrew. After crying herself to sleep once the other girls were out, she'd made up her mind she'd have to talk to Andrew. *But I didn't think it'd be at 6:30 in the morning! My eyes are still puffy!*

"Eden," he said, when she turned to go. She stopped. "Can we talk?"

Relieved his voice didn't sound angry, she nodded.

"How about over breakfast?" he offered.

"Sure."

She piled her plate with fruit, a yogurt, two pieces of bacon, and, trying to decide between a poppy seed or blueberry muffin, grabbed both.

He was already sitting at one of the small tables. She sat across from him, noting he'd gone with only cold cereal. He glanced at her plate. "That's one thing I always loved about you. You weren't afraid to eat."

Trying to reply while chewing the cantaloupe she had just popped into her mouth, she slurred, "Thanks, I think."

She was glad to see there was no sadness behind his smile. "So, yesterday wasn't very much fun for either of us," he said right off.

"No, it wasn't." *Thanks to you ignoring me all day.*

"I don't want it to be like that between us. I hate seeing you upset. You should be having fun." He stirred his cereal around without taking a bite.

"Don't worry about me." She paused. "I'm actually surprised you came. What happened to Florida?"

He gave her a lopsided grin. "Caitlyn wouldn't let up with it. Kept telling me I *had* to come. And well, my dad came home early to deal with an emergency at work, so I figured, why not?"

Thank you, Caitlyn! "Well, I'm glad you did. Hope you're not regretting it."

"No, I'm good. Maybe you were right. Maybe we're supposed to be just friends, I don't know. What I do know is we can't keep ignoring each other. I don't want you to feel bad anymore. I'm doing fine."

She searched his face, his eyes. "I would love to be friends again, but I understand if you need more time. The timing of this," she gestured to the room, "wasn't the best for either of us." Without thinking, she added quietly, "I've missed you."

Seeing something cross his eyes, she inwardly berated herself. *What am I doing giving him hope?* She knew it was partly true, though. How could she expect to spend every day with someone for almost five months and then suddenly never talk to him again? Although, what she missed and what he missed were probably two very different things.

His expression was hard to read, his emerald eyes conflicted. "I've missed you too," he admitted finally, and then he forced a smile. "So truce then?"

She was both saddened and relieved. "Yes, please."

The truce over breakfast seemed to filter through the day. The day at the amusement park was fun. Being an odd numbered group, they rotated partners. Everyone rode with everyone. Though partnering with Damon and Andrew was extremely awkward for her, she loved when it was Micah's turn. The other highlight was seeing Willow tug on Damon's hand. His expression made her giggle. He wasn't annoyed, more like stunned. He would lumber after her while Willow practically bounced on her toes.

Trent was quiet most of the day, almost somber at times. She knew he was worried about Micah.

Hours of twisting, dipping, cork screwing, going upside down, backwards and sideways, left Eden's head throbbing. They all stopped for a drink break. As she drained the water bottle in three long swigs, Andrew walked up, holding a pile of churros, which he handed out. There was enough for everyone, but after Andrew took a few bites, he offered his to Caitlyn. She shook her head no.

That's odd. They always share food, which is kind of weird now that I think about it, Eden mused as she pressed her fingers into her temples.

Strong hands rubbed her shoulders from behind. "Have a headache?" Micah asked.

"Yes, my head is killing me."

She glanced at Andrew, nervous he'd be able to see through their charade, but he was staring at Caitlyn. Willow studied Andrew and then Caitlyn.

What's that's all about?

A few hours later, they called it a day. Eden wasn't the only one with a headache and sore feet. Surprisingly, the one who didn't want to leave was Micah. *He's like a child, prolonging his bedtime.* She grinned and then realized why he might be prolonging the day. Tomorrow loomed ominous to her.

Once back at the motel, Micah wanted everyone to pile up and watch a movie together. Willow settled next to Damon, leaning against the headboard on one bed, with Caitlyn lying across the foot of the bed on her stomach. Andrew plopped down in front of Caitlyn, sitting cross-legged on the floor. Eden didn't care what anyone thought, she sandwiched herself between Trent and Micah on the other bed. Trent got up, opting for the lone chair at the table. Halfway covered by blankets, she was in heaven when she felt Micah's hand slide over to her, securing her fingers in his.

As they watched Will Smith kill aliens in Independence Day, Andrew leaned his head back towards Caitlyn and murmured, "Come sit by me."

Caitlyn clambered down next to him and Eden wondered why her face looked anything but happy about it.

Chapter Forty-Five

"It'll take a little less than two hours to get there," Micah announced as they filed back into the Excursion. The same seating arrangement applied. Trent's worried glances in Micah's direction added to her apprehension. *Today's the day. Whatever Micah saw, it happens today.*

After an hour of zigzagging through the countryside, Eden was caught up with staring out her window. According to the rearview mirror compass, they were heading southwest. She'd never seen so much farmland in her life. Both sides of the road were lined with fields, most of them corn, as they drove mile after mile. There were farms interspersed throughout, and then they began to see more houses and buildings as they entered a city.

"This is Sycamore, probably the closest city to Clare," Micah said.

"Clare?" Willow asked.

"Yeah, it's a small farming town with nothing but a post office. That's where our land is," he called back.

Passing grocery stores, a few city buildings, and parks, Eden thought it was a nice-looking city. She loved the huge trees everywhere. *Wonder if there are sycamores and that's why it's called Sycamore.* Within minutes, they left civilization and were once again submerged in cornfields. It was hypnotizing to watch the stalks go flying by as Eden checked the minutes between farmhouses. Micah decelerated as he came to an intersection, heading right on Clare Road. A short way up the road, they came to another intersection and Eden saw the small, dilapidated post office on the corner. She wondered if it was even still operational. At this, Micah turned right again. Again, she stared at the corn, but this time Micah drove slower and it didn't make her dizzy.

He made a right and then an immediate left. Another mile down the road, he pulled off onto an almost invisible driveway. Eden felt her pulse quicken as the Excursion bounced down the long, dirt driveway. She could see a farmhouse ahead, painted a dusty red, with a large wraparound porch and a steep, shingled roof.

Micah parked and then twisted around to face them. "If you want to sit tight, I'll be right back."

Eden gaped back at him. *Isn't this why we came here?*

"I have to make sure there's no problem with the land, irrigation, and make sure they've got my dad and uncle's info since my grandpa passed. They should, my dad's been here before." He smiled broadly. "After we leave here, I want to stop by Vern's farm. I think you'll really like it."

With that, he jumped out and slammed the door. There was some confused chatter as Eden stared at Trent, who remained planted in his seat. Ten minutes later, Micah came jogging back toward them. He opened the door. "Ok, we're all set."

They were all gawking at Micah now. They'd been under the impression they were going to walk around the Hawkins' land, not some other farmer's. Micah glanced at Trent and Eden barely caught the words, "Are you ready for this?"

She frowned as Trent shifted in his seat. Micah flipped the Excursion around and soon they were bumping back out the driveway.

"So, who's Vern?" Willow asked once they were on the main road again.

Micah's eyes were in the rearview mirror, peering back at them. "He was my Grandpa Hawkins best friend growing up. His farm neighbors ours. My dad wanted us to stop by and see him, since my grandpa passed away this year."

Andrew asked, "Have you met him before?"

"My dad brought me with him when I was about five, I think. I just remember Vern saying, 'You call me Grandpa Vern and you can eat as much ice cream as you want.'" Micah paused. "My dad told me later that Vern never got married or had his own family, so every year when he'd go back, Vern asked how his favorite grandson was doing."

"How sweet," Willow murmured.

Eden smiled. "No wonder you want to go back and visit. He'll be happy to see you."

Micah nodded. "I know. He's a neat man. My grandpa has told me lots of stories about their time together as kids. They were adventurous, like we were." Micah gave her a wink in the mirror.

After a few minutes, Micah again made a right down a gravel driveway. This time, Eden could see the large, white farmhouse from the road. It was set back, maybe an acre, with grass in the front yard, and huge, tall trees everywhere. As they continued down the drive, Eden discovered a long zip line strung between two trees. *Didn't he say Vern never had children?*

Getting closer, Eden saw the house was two stories with a small front porch, and black shutters. As they pulled to the side of the home, she spotted three large barns and two silos behind the farmhouse. This time, they all got out. She gazed at the large garden on the other side of the driveway. She realized it was probably Vern's own personal garden. She could see rows of corn, beans, tomatoes, and melons.

Micah was the first up the four steps, giving the dark red door a firm knock. As they waited, Damon and Willow brought up the rear of the group. Willow's eyes darted around, squinting, her lips pursed. Damon's back was to them, and when he moved, Eden noticed he was mumbling under his breath. The front door opened.

"Grandpa Vern!" Micah's voice boomed. Eden wasn't sure if he was just excited, or saying it loud enough for Vern to hear. She saw a hearing aid in one of Vern's ears.

Vern stood much shorter than Micah, wearing a thin-looking, white, button-up shirt, gray, well-worn slacks, and blue suspenders. His white hair barely covered his head as it was combed neatly to the side. His eyes appeared blue-gray from where Eden stood. He had the grandpa ears that were slightly large and hairy. His face was worn but clean-shaven. She noted the glasses case and glasses in his front pocket, and realized there was a calculator behind that, making the pocket bulge out.

His wrinkled face broke into a smile as he squinted up at Micah. "Is that Jared Hawkins's boy?"

Micah stooped down and hugged Vern, saying, "Sure is!" Micah straightened. "These are some of my friends. We came to visit you."

Vern's smile widened. "Wonderful, come on in."

They followed Micah through the door, single file. As Eden crossed into the home, she saw they stood in a family room with wood floors. There were curtains hanging on the windows, and fading flower wallpaper on the walls. There were two small couches and one rocking chair in the corner. Micah walked around, examining the room.

Vern gestured to the couches and everyone sat down. "Ok, Micah, now who do we have here?"

Micah smiled and introduced them all. Eden didn't think he'd remember all their names but he went down the line asking each of them where they were from, and what their parents did. Vern smiled at them and said, "Lots of catching up, but how about some lunch first?"

Once Vern had shown them where the kitchen was, Willow smiled at him. "Why don't you let us girls make you lunch for a change. Go sit down and relax. We've got this."

Vern tried to object but Micah called from the dining room, "Is that Grandpa Hawkins in this picture with you?" Vern shuffled away.

Willow finished washing her hands. "I absolutely love him."

Caitlyn joined Willow at the sink to wash her hands. Eden handed them the towel to dry and began pulling bread out of the bag, saying, "I feel sort of bad about eating all his food. We could've stopped at the grocery store in Sycamore if Micah had given us a heads up first."

Willow dried her hands. "Yeah, but to tell you the truth, I have a feeling it makes Vern happy to feed us. I don't think he has a lot of visitors."

Eden peered around the large kitchen, most of the dishes looked like they hadn't been touched in a long time. There was a hand towel laid out on the counter next to the sink with one bowl, plate, cup, fork, and spoon.

"Doesn't this house feel a little big for one farmer?" Caitlyn asked.

Willow and Eden agreed as they made turkey sandwiches for everyone. After chopping up a few cucumbers and strawberries, probably from Vern's garden, they carried the food into the dining room.

Vern waited until everyone was seated at the antique, wooden table and then lowered himself into the chair at the head of the table. Holding his hands out to Micah and Trent, who were on his left and right, he said, "Dear kind Lord, thank you for this day, and thank you for these friends who've come to see me."

Everyone quickly took hands and bowed their heads. After his prayer ended, Andrew said, "Micah said you grew up with his grandpa."

"That I did, Joseph was a good friend."

"Your family's been here a long time then?" Willow asked, glancing around the room. Eden sort of wondered what she was looking at. She seemed to be staring at the walls.

Vern's blue-gray eyes took on a faraway gaze. "Yes, starting with my eighth great grandpa, Charles, in England. The story goes he started having dreams of this land with fields flowing like honey. He was poor, single, with nothing but his hands to labor. He heard of the great migration to America, where land was plentiful, and knew it was for him. He arrived in Massachusetts and worked as a laborer, trying to save up money. He kept having a dream of this land; it called to him. But he married, had kids, and their kids had kids. He never left Massachusetts. But he passed the story along to his grandkids, so when my fifth great grandfather, Dr. John Brown, came along, he wanted to find this land. With his family, they journeyed into the wild frontier. And it was wild back then. Many Indian tribes were not friendly with settlers, and vice versa. But by some miracle, they made it here."

"Here? You mean here, here?" Andrew asked.

"Yep, the original homestead's back behind the barns. I can show it to you if you'd like. Lucky for them, the Dakota Sioux tribe was friendly enough. When they realized he was a doctor, they were suspicious but, eventually, Dr. Brown's medicines helped heal one of the chief's sons. It was a big deal because they didn't trust white men or their medicine. The Dakota's helped the Brown's become successful corn farmers, and they entrusted my ancestors with this land."

Vern paused and Micah said, "My grandpa told me the land's special."

Pain flashed across Vern's blue-gray eyes. "Yes, it is. My family has stayed here since. My third great grandfather, Albert, built this farmhouse. These walls have seen many families, children, grandchildren, and even great grandchildren, run through these halls, but now it's just me left."

So that explains it. She could almost feel the ghosts in these very rooms. Thinking of Gabriel near, she knew she probably wasn't far off with her feeling.

Willow's eyes swept the room. "Your family's still here with you. You can feel the love in this home."

Vern sighed. "I suppose you may be right."

"She is," Micah confirmed. "Grandpa Vern, my grandpa told me a story when I was a kid. He told me about the well."

Vern's head snapped up.

Micah's eyes were locked on Vern's face. "We've come to fix it."

Vern cleared his throat several times and then asked, "You know how?"

"Yes." Micah eyes never left the old man's face.

There was a strange tension in the room. No one interrupted to ask questions.

"With your permission, I'd like to go see it now."

Vern's eyebrows dug into his forehead and then he nodded.

Micah grinned and stood. "Perfect. We'll be back soon."

When they all began to rise from their seats, Vern's eyes widened. "They're all going with you?"

"I need their help to fix it." Vern started to protest, but stopped as Micah placed his hand on Vern's shoulder. "Don't worry, Grandpa Vern, it's going to be fine. Just stay here and rest."

This was the first time she'd heard Micah even mention a well. *But I have a hunch it has to do with that temple.*

Vern followed behind them as they walked out the front door, Micah taking the lead.

Being the last one out, Eden stopped when she felt Vern's hand on her arm. "You kids be careful. Not many people go to see the well. It's changed a lot over the years." He paused. "I can't say for sure what it'll be like for you today."

She tried to smile but her insides were panicking. She waved good-bye and caught up with the rest of her group. They'd crossed the green lawn to the left, and had begun trudging through the lush cornstalks towering over their heads. She marveled Micah knew where to go. Once inside the corn, it was impossible to keep a sense of direction. It all looked the same to her.

I guess Micah's visions are pretty detail oriented, she thought, trying to ignore Trent's *self-sacrificing* words bouncing around in her mind.

Chapter Forty-Six

Eden plodded behind Damon at the back of the line. She would have passed him but she found his behavior fascinating. Damon ran his hands along the corn leaves, speaking in hushed tones. He stopped and examined a cornhusk, and she slowed her pace. His mouth moved again. *He must just talk to himself.*

The crop was dense. She could only see Damon; the rest of the group was swallowed up by the stalks. She was content to stroll behind him though. When he smiled at the corn, she was shocked to see his eyes crease, his expression soften. *He must really like corn.*

A few feet later, he frowned and stopped to study the leaves again. That's when she noticed the stalks were bowing. *Wonder if Vern knows his crops aren't getting enough water out here.* The leaves had brown on the edges. *Or maybe there's a beetle or worm eating the crop.*

She stepped closer to Damon. "What's wrong?"

He glanced at her. "They're weeping."

She stared at him.

He straightened up and moved on.

Weeping? She regarded the crop. *It's shriveling up. I suppose it looks sad.*

Damon was almost out of sight by the time she scurried after him. Her feet slipped a little as the ground began to slope downhill. It was gradual at first, and then the grade became steep and arduous. She clutched at the cornstalks to keep from falling.

What the heck? Aren't cornfields flat? I'm scaling a cliff here.

When it finally leveled off, she breathed a sigh of relief. Peeling her eyes from her shoes, she gasped. The corn was now parched and dead. Damon touched a leaf and it turned to powder in his fingertips.

Damon scowled and she took a step back. *I'm never going to understand him. Why's he so mad about dying corn?*

She rounded him carefully, and hurried to catch up with the others. Willow's long, black hair became visible through the withered stalks. She increased her pace, reaching Willow just as she halted.

Running into her backside, Eden mumbled, "Sorry Willow."

Willow didn't turn around though, just stared straight ahead. Eden peered around and saw why. In the middle of the dead stalks, stood a stone wall, perhaps eight feet high. She couldn't tell where it began or ended because the corn hugged it tightly in both directions. Everyone was congregating around it, with Micah running his hands along the stones. Trent was close to Micah, gazing at the ground, kicking at the dirt with his shoe. His body language didn't bode well with Eden.

The wall appeared ancient; the stones crafted to fit together. She stepped back and stared. The builder of the wall had used different colored stones, and studying it, she saw a pattern emerging. The faded, red stones were positioned to create large, horizontal ovals, which repeated over and over. She was amazed someone would've taken the time to add such embellishments.

Revulsion in her eyes, Willow backed away, whispering, "Micah, what is this—?"

Micah cut her off. "It's ok. I know what you sense, but we can't run away. It's time to take a stand."

Willow stared at Micah, shifting her weight between her feet, looking like a doe ready to bolt.

Eden was surprised that is was Damon who spoke next. "Willow, Micah needs us."

Willow's eyes searched Damon's face, and then she nodded her head. "Ok."

"What is this place, really?" Andrew asked, "Last I checked, cornfields didn't have old stone walls in them, or crazy hills either."

Micah glanced around at them. "What I'm going to ask of each of you might seem strange, but I need you to trust me. There's an opening in this wall," he gestured to the right, "down there. Inside here, there's a well." No one said anything and Micah continued, "This well's extremely important. It's been here for a long time. It always had water in it, until recently. For seventy years now, it's been dry, and because of it, the land around it died. You probably noticed the corn." Eden thought it funny Micah thought seventy years was recent. *How old is this place?*

"I need to fix the well, and I need all of you to do it. I know you have questions and I promise when we're done, I'll explain everything. But I can't yet. I just ask that you trust me." Micah's tone was pleading.

Trent came to life. "Micah needs our help. Let's get this done."

She noticed Andrew and Caitlyn whispering to each other. After Caitlyn nodded, Andrew said, "All right, not sure what you want me to do, but I'll help."

Willow's voice was strained. "I trust you, Micah. And I trust that you know what you're doing."

Damon had already shown his allegiance to Micah, and Eden realized everyone's eyes were now on her. She gazed back at Micah. "I don't know anything about wells, but I'm with you, Micah. You know that."

He gave her a reassuring smile, his eyes lingering a moment, before turning to go. Aware her heart was galloping in her chest now, she watched the procession follow after with Damon and Trent first, and Andrew and Caitlyn stepping in next. Willow hesitated and then jogged after, leaving Eden once again in the back of the pack.

Alone, she whispered, "Gabriel, what's going on? Feels like we're walking into some kind of trap."

"It'll be ok, Eden. I'm with you."

She jumped; his voice had been so clear. Spinning around, she gasped.

Gabriel stood behind her, smoke radiating from his sheathed sword.

"You're here! Wait, why? You only come when I'm in danger, like serious trouble…"

"It's good to see you too." His tone didn't sound tense.

Maybe not everything's as bad as I think.

"Don't get me wrong, I'd love for you to come more often," she said quickly.

He steered her shoulders around, pushing her forward. "You need to stay with the group." Then he was gone.

She sprinted after Willow, panicking that she could no longer see her. As she followed along the wall in the direction they'd left, she soon collided with the group. They'd stopped in front of a tall archway, the opening covered in dry, dangling vines.

Micah voice was firm. "It's important we stay together."

He moved to go through, but Trent shoved him out of the way, taking the lead. Eden knew Trent was trying to protect his cousin. The sick feeling came back as Micah and Damon disappeared through the tangled vines.

Andrew peered at Caitlyn. "What do you think?"

Caitlyn chewed on her lower lip. "It's ok. We should do what Micah said."

Andrew glanced at Eden. *He's probably remembering what I looked like prom night.* Everyone could feel something wasn't right. Willow's behavior acted like a warning beacon. She wanted to nod at him, but she wasn't exactly sure what they'd find on the other side of this wall.

Caitlyn plunged through the vines. Andrew hesitated and then trudged after her. Willow, however, didn't budge.

Remembering Gabriel's instruction, she linked arms with Willow. "We'll be fine. Let's stay together, okay?"

Willow sighed and then nodded. Once through the scratchy vines, Eden saw they were in a large, enclosed area with the stone wall encircling them. The area looked to be about the size of a football field. The ground was barren, devoid of cornstalks, grass, or even weeds.

Damon dropped to one knee and ran his hand through the soil. "It's totally dry, almost sandy," he commented.

Only Eden heard him. Everyone else stared at the well, sitting dead center. It appeared to be just an ordinary well, as far as she could tell. Crafted from the same stones the wall was, she admired the oval pattern running around its circumference. There was no cover, and she wondered if perhaps the original one had weathered away.

Willow glanced at Micah. "Are you sure about this?"

Micah's voice was calm. "It's ok, Willow. Just trust me."

Damon stood up, retaining some of the dirt in his hand as he moved to stand next to Micah.

"So, that's the well, huh? How do we fix it?" Andrew asked.

Eden thought he sounded tense. *Like he's thinking, let's fix this thing and get out of here.*

"Good question. Now, everyone listen. I need you to stay together. You're going to see frightening things." He glanced at Eden and her skin crawled with goose bumps. "However, if you stay close, you'll be safe."

I really don't like the sound of this.

Andrew stepped toward her, closing the gap. Grasping her arm, he pulled her close. "Something's not right here. Do you know what's going on?"

She shook her head no, and glanced at Micah.

Andrew followed her gaze. "What do you mean, we'll see frightening stuff?" he asked, but Micah was looking at Damon.

"Damon, it's time."

Andrew released Eden's arm, his grip a little too tight for her comfort. He strode over to Micah and then halted when Damon spoke.

Eden strained to understand. It was definitely unlike any language she'd ever heard before. The words flowed, the rhythm and tones pleasant to hear. What caught her off guard was the way they made her feel physically. It filled her with a strange longing, like trying to remember a forgotten dream.

A biting gust of wind smacked her face and, being too close to Willow, she was buried by both of their locks. She stepped a foot away and secured her own hair in her hand. The wind was howling, the sky producing black clouds right before her eyes. She gasped at the size of the thunderheads rolling in. Within seconds, the afternoon sun was blocked, leaving them in a gray shadow.

Trent was next to her. "What just happened?" she asked.

But his eyes were fastened on the stone well, like he was waiting. She glanced at Micah on the other side of him. His eyes were locked on the same thing.

This can't be good.

Then she heard it.

One long shriek, followed by another and another, until it became a chorus of wails, screeches, and chortling laughter.

Everyone whirled around in circles, trying to find the source of the awful sounds. It was hard to tell the origin because it reverberated off the stones surrounding them.

Willow, Andrew, and Caitlyn pulled away from the group, making a run for the exit. Eden was tempted to join, but her feet felt stuck to the ground where she stood.

When the screaming halted, leaving them in an eerie silence, Micah's voice boomed, "Stop! It's not safe over there!"

Willow doubled back. "We're surrounded, aren't we?"

Andrew marched back to Micah, Caitlyn on his heels. "Why would you trap us like this?" he demanded.

Damon stepped between Micah and Andrew, pushing on Andrew's chest. "Back down. We have to trust Micah. Our lives depend on it."

Andrew's eyes flashed. "Our *lives?*"

Caitlyn placed a hand on his arm. "It's ok," she soothed. "We're all going to be fine."

Andrew glanced at Caitlyn, his jaw muscles bulging. Grunting, he moved a few feet away from Micah, turning his back to him.

Everyone was scared. She could see it in their faces, except perhaps Micah and Damon. Damon's brown eyes were enraged, but it wasn't like Andrew's. He appeared ready to attack whatever came their way. Micah's mouth was set in a grim line, his eyes narrowing.

More than anything, she wanted to call out to Gabriel, to beg him to appear. Then she realized, *None of my friends know they have guardians too.*

She was going to say something to try to calm everyone, but the shrieking began again and, instinctively, they huddled closer. The sound was suffocating, coming at them from all angles. A subtle chill was infusing the warm air. The tip of her nose felt cold. The smell of dirt was replaced with an acrid, sulfur stench.

I know what's coming.

Andrew and Trent both swore under their breath when she saw it.

Long, black claws reached over the side of the well, a bony hand protruded, followed by another hand, and then two leathery arms. An ugly, black head popped up, its red eyes glittering back at them.

It was the first time Eden had seen one so clearly. The other two experiences had been at night, in blackness. Now she could make out details, though she wished she couldn't. Its disintegrating flesh nauseated her, reminding her of all the crime shows she'd watched where the victim was little more than bones and rotten flesh. Only this flesh was moving, its mouth sneering.

"Stay together!" Micah commanded.

The demon crawled over the side of the well, resting on its hands and feet, like a caged animal ready to attack. The wailing rang in her ears. *There's more coming, lots more.*

Caitlyn gasped and Willow clutched at Eden's arm. More claws reached over the side of the well. Demon after demon climbed out, gnashing their sharp teeth and shrieking. But they stood their ground, not advancing.

"Behind us," Andrew called out.

Eden turned to see what she had feared, demons climbing down the wall, the stones covered in black movement. Trying to escape the approaching army, her friends pressed their backs against each other. She knew she should feel the panic she saw in Willow's eyes. Micah grabbed her hand and she glanced over.

He still stared at the well. He didn't appear to be fazed by the demons now scaling the walls around them. It sent a chill through her. *He's still waiting for the enemy to appear.*

"What are they?" Caitlyn whispered, as the black bodies rapidly filled the dirt, clawing and hissing at them.

"Demons," Trent answered.

"*Demons?*" multiple voices cried out.

"They're going to destroy us," Willow moaned.

"We're not alone. It's going to be ok; there are others with us," Micah reassured.

"Others?" Willow's eyes widened and then she mumbled, "That must be what I'm feeling."

Micah pulled Eden behind him at the same time Damon stepped in front of Willow. Andrew followed suit with Caitlyn, and the three girls were encased by the guys. Though it was a brave move, Eden knew it was futile. None of them were armed. They had nothing to defend themselves with. The demons would tear through them in seconds. She unconsciously rubbed her wrist.

Row after row, the demons lined up, the space separating them getting smaller, until it was only a few yards. Their snarls were terrifying. One reared its head back and howled, sending spit flying towards them. It splattered against Micah's legs.

Eden felt and heard a deep drumming come from the well. Like a car stereo with its bass pumped up, it made the ground vibrate with each beat.

This is feeling way too much like prom.

She was halfway expecting another red-faced demon to pop out of the ground, when the demons lunged forward.

One lunged for Micah, its yellow teeth biting the air.

She screamed, "Gabriel!" at the same time the demon burst into flame and ash before her eyes. The flaming sword decimated it. *Gabriel's here!* As was Sage and others.

Their tight circle was surrounded by angels now. Her friends stumbled back, gawking at their guardians. As the angels destroyed the advancing army, Eden knew her friends were realizing they were here to help them. They were the good guys.

Eden's first impression of Willow's guardian was Egyptian princess; the woman's black hair was swept up in a knot. She was adorned with a golden tiara and matching armbands. Her silky, cream dress hugged her body, moving with her lunges. The jewels on her necklace flashed as she struck demons with golden daggers. Eden was in awe at the poise she did it with. Her moves were graceful, even in battle.

Damon's guardian was hard to miss. He towered over the rest of them by several inches. With short, black hair and a solid build, he swung his long arms out, sending multiple demons flying with his double-sided battle-axe. When he turned, Eden stared at his eyes. The shade of blue so light, it was almost a milky white.

In front of Trent, a heavier set man stood. She hardly could tell where his beard ended and his face began. All she could see was thick, red hair, leaving only a small opening for his features. *Muscle builder meet lumberjack.* His meaty arms shot out, crushing demons with a hammer and spiky mace.

If they were not in the middle of a precarious battle, she would have laughed at Trent's bewildered expression. *He knows he has a guardian. Why's he staring at his like that?*

Moving swiftly down the line, she took in the young man standing in front of Andrew. His brown hair hit his shoulders in waves and his clothes were similar to Gabriel's, with short sleeves revealing tan arms. Instead of wielding a sword, he sent arrows shooting out. His agility fascinated her. He stashed his bow and pulled out a wide, metal sword.

At the last guardian, she did a double take. Fighting for Caitlyn was a girl who could've been plucked straight out of high school. She looked to be seventeen, wearing a t-shirt and jeans. Her blonde hair was pulled into a high ponytail, with a long braid whipping around her back as she moved. Then, seeing what was in her hands, Eden knew no teenager could fight like that. Double-ended spear blades graced her hands like Japanese fans. Only these weren't the kind with calligraphy; they cheese grated the demon's faces with each move the girl made.

Hot air slapped Eden's body. She peered around Micah, who still stood guard over her. Their tight circle was enclosed by an even larger span of angels wielding flaming swords. *There's definitely more than twenty-four. Gabriel doesn't want to take any chances this time.*

Chapter Forty-Seven

*W*hen Gabriel called down the Cherubim, Micah knew it was time. His friends were safe now. Gabriel would call down angels until every demon was destroyed. The plan was for no one to get hurt, at least none of his friends. Micah glanced at Eden, relieved to see she appeared calm, considering their surroundings. *But this isn't her first experience with demons.*

He glanced at the others and saw they were terrified, but pacified by the army defending them. *Hopefully, they'll forgive me one day for all this.*

He reached for Eden's hand again. She smiled and his heart ached knowing what she was about to see would probably give her nightmares the rest of her life. He gave her hand a squeeze and let it drop. *I don't want to see her face for the rest of this.*

He stepped forward, raising his hand out towards the guardians, who immediately parted. As he made his way through them, he felt Trent step next to him on his right.

Micah pushed Trent's shoulder, shaking his head, but Trent just shoved him back saying, "Are you crazy? You aren't doing this alone."

Micah expected as much, but it still pained him to think of something happening to his cousin. When Micah felt someone on his left side, he already knew it'd be Damon. Though he hadn't asked this of him, he knew what Damon's choice would be. Micah nodded at him and Damon's head came up, a gesture that said, *Come on, let's do this.*

As the Cherubim opened a hole in their tight line for them to pass through, Micah heard Eden's voice. "Micah, promise me you'll be careful!"

He hesitated and then turned. Not knowing what else to say, he mouthed three words. Her eyes widened and he twisted around, needing Trent and Damon's strength to give him the courage to take the next fateful step.

As his feet hit the dirt, leaving the Cherubim behind, Micah saw Sage go into attack mode. Not being lit on fire, she danced around them, slicing demons with her pronged weapons. He'd first seen the bright red handles hanging from her belt when they were in Rome. With all the planning, Sage had realized she wouldn't always be able to rely on fire to protect him. Though Micah had seen the weapons on her, this was the first time he saw them in action. He knew he shouldn't be surprised that she mastered the martial art form perfectly. After all, she was an angel. Damon and Trent's guardians defended their right and left sides with their powerful arms striking hard into the demon pack. Micah both felt and heard Damon's words as they continued to step forward, his eyes never leaving their destination, the well.

Damon threw a handful of dirt from his hand. Instead of falling to the ground, the granules were sent flying like shrapnel from a grenade, instantly killing any demon near them.

Trent gasped. "Holy freak!"

Damon's words continued to ring out, now in a booming voice that carried. The impact shook Micah's chest. The wind whipped around, circling them with growing force. Within seconds, the dry ground gave and they were submerged in the vortex of a dirt tornado. Cornstalks shot past like whips, decapitating demons as they sliced through the air. The demons were blasted back by the force of the wind. One managed to get in the vortex, only to have a cob of corn shatter its skull.

"That's what I'm talking about!" Trent shouted at Damon.

Being in the eye of the storm Damon's words had created, Micah's feet prodded forward, each step bringing him closer to his destiny. The guardians continued to defend them: Brutus smashing skulls with his mace, Seth annihilating them with his battle-axe, and Sage spearing them with her pronged weapon through the gut. As the well loomed closer, he knew it was time to make their stand. Trent and Damon flanked him tightly and Sage crouched in front of him, weapons held out.

Damon shouted one word and the swirling tunnel they'd traveled in subsided. Stalks, dirt, leaves, and rocks continued to shoot around them as deadly missiles.

Ok, this is it.

Micah raised his arms into the air. "Astaroth, Prince of Thrones, in the name of the Captain, I summon you!"

The ground rocked back and forth, like it was trying to spew out the prince. A rolling laughter made the other demons' shrill cries pale in comparison. The strength of the cackle vibrated Micah's body.

Then above the well, Astaroth hovered, his dark red robes spreading out like heavy, velvet tapestry. His albino skin was deeply wrinkled and sagging, and his bald head showed deep fissures and cracks. Yellow eyes blinked and squinted back at them. Micah wondered how long it had been since the prince had seen the light of day, although, with Damon's storm clouds thundering overhead, it wasn't exactly bright out.

He gazed around, disorientated. Then, spying Micah, he hissed, "Who are you to summon me?"

Micah stood straighter. "I'm the Seer."

Astaroth threw his head back and cackled, revealing sharp, yellow fangs. "What? You are nothing more than a *foolish boy*!"

"If that's all I am, why don't you come get me? Or maybe you're afraid I speak the truth," Micah responded. Trent stiffened next to him.

Astaroth's eyes narrowed as he spat, "I would never leave this for a boy. My pawns will deal with you." He began to descend, as if he were dismissing Micah.

"Astaroth, I'm not done with you!" The authority in Micah's voice caused the demon to stop. He snarled as he flew up into the air, still hovering above the stone well.

His yellow eyes took in Trent and Damon. With lips lifting high away from his teeth, showing how unnaturally long they were, he growled, "How dare you boy! You have no power over me!"

Micah smiled. "You're right, I don't. But the Captain does and I serve the Captain. I *am* His Seer!"

At Micah's last words, Astaroth let out a howling cry, black smoke spewing from his lips. The black pillar shot out and then split into several offshoots. As each column of smoke touched the ground, a hooded figure appeared. Micah counted thirteen. Their black shrouds showed deep shadows where faces should be.

He knew enough of demonic orders to know these wouldn't be as well trained as the ones attacking his friends, who relied on sheer number. These thirteen towered over the common demons, having more than sharp claws and teeth to contend with. They held powers; they had dominion. They were the Elites.

Sage stood in front of Micah; he could feel the sudden heat she was releasing.

"Whoa Sage, not yet," he said quickly. She wasn't happy about the Elite guard either. They were a formidable opponent. Damon and Trent's guardians doubled back, almost standing on top of them.

Astaroth's lips sneered. "You challenge me? I see no robes of power on you. I see nothing but common angels defending you. And now you will wish you never summoned me, your worst nightmare."

"A lot of words, Astaroth, but no action. I think you're afraid," Micah said calmly.

Astaroth growled angrily, causing the earth to hum with vibrations. In response, the thirteen Elites' arms came up in unison, crossing in front of their chest, revealing bony, white hands and forearms.

Micah was slammed to the ground, an invisible force knocking him to his back, Trent and Damon crashing down next to him. As they clambered back to their feet, Sage and the other guardians advanced on the Elites, weapons drawn. Tasting something metallic in his mouth, he saw blood trickling down Damon and Trent's lips. The Elites' action was like a punch in the face.

Micah straightened up as Astaroth snickered. "It has been a long time since I've had something to entertain myself with. You mortals make such great sport. Too bad you die so easily."

In a fluid movement, the Elite each swung their right hand out, their hand in tight fists. This time, Micah and Trent tumbled through the air like ragdolls doing cartwheels. When Micah skidded to a stop, Damon was already next to him, pulling him to his feet.

He was apologetic. "I'm still learning how to counter their attacks. Sorry, this time I'll get you too."

Damon's coming into his own. "I'm good. Protect Trent. Don't interfere with me."

Damon's brown eyes narrowed, but nodded. Trent stumbled towards them, his forehead revealing a deep gash. When Micah's vision blurred by something dripping down, he realized he had a similar cut. Damon was unscathed.

"What are they, Gabriel?" Eden clutched at his arm. "Oh gosh, Micah's hurt!"

"A little busy right now." Gabriel shirked her hand, killing several demons with one lunge.

"Gabriel, what the heck are they?"

"Eden," Gabriel's sword swung wide, taking out five more. "Now's hardly the time for a lesson in demonic order."

"Well, when's a good time? You only come when I'm in mortal danger!"

He glanced back at her.

"How can I learn about demons from yes and no warm fuzzies?" *I sound completely nuts,* she realized. But some part of her felt like, *If I know what they are and what they can do, I won't fear the outcome so bad.*

Gabriel grunted. "Of all the times." He shoved her behind him while his flame burst through a demon launching at her. "Please, stay put. I can't defend you if you're jumping all over me!"

She pressed herself against his backside. "Sorry!"

"I swear I'll ask why we can't sit and have tea together at the next guardian council if we survive this, but you're not making it easy on me." Gabriel smashed a demon with the hilt of his sword, and took out four more with the flame.

Maybe if he can joke, things aren't as bad as they seem.

"They're fine," he yelled back to her, as if reading her thoughts. "The hooded are the Elite guard. Demon princes don't like to get their hands dirty by fighting their own battles. Astaroth's a Prince of Thrones. Technically, both Sage and I outrank him. Happy?"

He pulled her close to kill a demon on her right side.

"No! Sage isn't doing anything against the Elite's attacks!" When Gabriel said nothing, she pushed past him. He grabbed her waist and put her behind him again. "Eden, stay back!" he ordered, and then mumbled, "You're making me fight one handed!"

Micah faced Astaroth, who shrugged. "Enough with the play time. I'm tired and bore easily. You have no powers to even defend yourselves. It's pitiful really. Not very challenging, and no longer entertaining. My Elite will deal with you."

Astaroth descended toward the mouth of the well, but Micah stepped forward. "I'm not done with you. Now stay put!"

The demon stopped short. He glared at Micah, his scowl revealing confusion and uncertainty. Then he roared out, "Destroy him!"

The Elites' arms rose above their hoods, their wrists bent, with their white fingers fanned out like claws. The effect was immediate; Micah felt sharp hooks tear into his stomach, ripping his insides out. Glancing down was like watching a gory horror film, his shirt rapidly turning crimson from his own blood.

Chapter Forty-Eight

Hearing Micah's cry, Eden twisted around Gabriel in time to see Micah double over, his shirt blood soaked.

"Gabriel!" she shrieked. "Micah's hurt bad! Help him!"

Smashing two demons' skulls together, Gabriel yelled back, "I'm not leaving you."

"He needs *you!*"

Her guardian faced her, his eyes conflicted.

"Please," she begged, tears forming.

He sighed heavily. "You're right. They need help. Elite's need fire to be destroyed and Sage can't show her flames yet. I'll go." He turned to the angel at his right. Eden recognized him as the angel with black hair from prom night. "Aaron, keep her safe. Don't let anything even *touch* her. You're in charge now."

Aaron nodded, taking Gabriel's spot. Spinning his wrists, Gabriel's sword became a blur of fire as he flew towards them. The hooded Elites noted his approach.

"Get him out of here," Gabriel commanded Trent's guardian. Micah watched Trent fight against him, but the burly, bearded angel easily dragged him away.

Good, Trent doesn't need to be here.

The Elite guard took a wary step back towards the well, Astaroth's eyes sizing Gabriel up. "So this boy does have more than mere angels protecting him after all. I recognize you, but I do not fear you, Gabriel."

Astaroth flicked two fingers out. Following orders, the Elite arms shot out, with three fingers on each hand pointing at Gabriel.

Damon's arm wrapped around Micah's waist, supporting him. At the same time, foreign-sounding words flew from his mouth.

Micah felt nothing. The Elite's attack must have been thwarted, whatever it might have been.

"No," Micah mumbled to Damon.

"Whatever, man. I'm not leaving," Damon spat back. "And I'm not letting you get hit by their stupid attacks anymore. I can stop them."

Gabriel glanced at Damon and muttered, "That's the man I used to know."

Micah stared at Damon. *Wonder if he's figured it out yet...* Micah felt the ground beneath him sway. Heat was radiating off Sage. *I don't have a lot of time left. She's desperate to ignite.*

Gabriel must have felt it too. "Your desires are your weakness." Gabriel rose into the air, until he was eye level with the old demon.

"Fool!" Astaroth snarled as he soared higher.

Gabriel grinned and continued to ascend. Micah knew he was trying to nettle the demon, to push his pride far enough to break him free from the well.

If only that's all it took.

But the demon's yellow eyes narrowed and he dropped back down over the well's mouth. He sneered. "You think I would leave this for *you*? You think too highly of yourself, Gabriel."

Gabriel remained levitated but moved near Micah and Damon. "No, but I'm pretty sure you would for *him*. You know he speaks the truth and you know what his soul would mean, the glory he'd bring you."

Astaroth's lips curled up, desire dripping in his eyes. Gabriel slapped Damon's shoulder. "I think it's time for the Elites to know their place."

Damon grimaced. "With pleasure."

The words rushed out, the force and power of them felt even by Micah. The Elite crossed their arms over their face to defend themselves, but the impact was apparent. Hoods snapped back, the shrouded figures stumbling to regain footing. They retaliated swiftly with left hands shooting forward, palms facing out.

Damon's words shielded them again.

Micah felt his chin hitting his chest, and his knees go weak. *It's happening too fast. I'm losing too much blood.* Damon's arm was the only thing holding him up now.

"He doesn't have much time left," Sage observed, lacing her arm under Micah's other shoulder. He felt a rush of warmth and strength shoot through him.

"Enough Astaroth, you know you can't win. Now it's time to bow to the Captain!" Gabriel roared, raising his right hand.

Immediately, all thirteen hooded figures collapsed to their knees, their white hands clutching their hoods, as if trying to block out Gabriel's demand. Gabriel held his sword out, the bright flame sending them into shrieking wails.

Green vines shot up from the ground, wrapping around the Elites' robes like pythons. Astaroth squinted at Damon, his eyes studying him. *Yeah, you're realizing he's not just a kid, aren't you?*

Gabriel took advantage of Damon's vines trapping their extremities. He flew toward the Elite, sword drawn. As his flames burst through the first hooded demon, sending an albino head flying free, Astaroth snarled. Gabriel worked down the line, decapitating them. When he was halfway through, Micah heard a whistle and a snap just past his ear.

He forced his head up off his chest.

Astaroth had unfurled his whip. Micah shuddered, memories exploding in his head. *That's the whip I saw.*

Gabriel dodged it and Astaroth's yellow fangs gnashed at the air. His attempts to stop Gabriel's killing spree were thwarted by Damon's words, which intercepted the weapon, sending it far off target when it landed.

As the head of the last Elite soared past Micah, Gabriel muttered, "So much for your Elite guard."

Astaroth's robes fanned out as his wrath mounted. He slashed at them with his whip repeatedly and Damon continued to stop it, but barely. Astaroth was already calculating his counter attack.

When the tangled ends of the whip landed just inches in front of Micah, its nine tails hooking and clawing at the dirt, Micah grimaced. He pushed the words out, "Go, it's time." The effort it took to speak pained him.

Sage and Damon both stared at him.

"No way," Damon barked back.

"Damon." Micah grasped at Damon's shirt, his fingers too weak to even gather the shirt together in his hand. "This has to be. You have to leave me, now."

Damon shook his head. "There has to be another way. If you had told me more—"

"Now you know why I left some parts out." He tried to grin but gasped for air instead. "Our friends need you for what comes next. Save them."

Damon hesitated, eyes raging.

A blood-curdling cry shot through the air from behind. Damon twisted around. "They broke through, demons have Willow." He cringed.

"Go," Micah urged.

Damon sized Micah up and then glared at Sage. "Don't you let him die. This *plan* of yours was flawed. And you all knew it."

He's figured it out, our ruse. But how else could it have worked?

Damon swore under his breath and gently detangled himself from Micah, and then he was gone. Micah was too weak to turn and see the chaos behind them. Sage's hot body was pressed against him, his skin burning where she touched him.

She fumed. "Gabriel, hurry! Get them all out here, now!"

Gabriel was gone, shooting through the air like a bullet.

Well, this is it. Micah mentally braced himself for it. He'd seen it so many times, but it hardly prepared him for actually living it.

As the whip again snapped in the air, the impact almost popping his ears, Micah knew it would be the last time Astaroth missed. The nine tails landed in the dirt, being once again thwarted by Damon's last command before leaving Micah's side to rescue Willow. Watching the cat o' nine tails, covered in sharp glass, rocks, and metal claws, scrape at the ground, sent terror rippling through him.

It was worse than any nightmare she'd ever had. All of her friends shrieking in horror as, one by one, demons snatched them away. Aaron was true to his word. She was fine, but no one else was.

She saw Damon running back. *No! Don't leave Micah!*

But she saw he was darting after the demon that tore Willow from the angels.

She tried to make sense of it all. The demons had broken through the line. Guardians were desperately chasing after her friends.

Gabriel's voice rang out, "Get her out of here!" She peered around Aaron to see Gabriel was there and meant her.

"Wait, no! What about Micah?" Eden screamed at him, but he was already gone to help rescue the others.

Aaron scooped her up into his arms like she was weightless. She pushed against him, struggling. A demon leapt on top of them, and he had to release her to fight it back. It was the moment she needed. She sprinted away, numb to the danger surrounding her, twisting and pulling free of the claws that grabbed at her.

Chapter Forty-Nine

*M*icah heard Gabriel roar, "Guardians retreat!"

At the same time, Sage taunted, "Astaroth, why don't you come claim your prize?"

As Astaroth reared back again, determined to do just what Sage jeered at him, Micah remembered someone else who'd suffered at the end of such a whip. His last coherent thought was a prayer to Him for strength. He was half-aware of Sage squeezing his body against hers; he felt one last burst of strength course through his veins.

He squared his shoulders, facing Astaroth, whose whip was already cresting in the air. "Just think of your master's reward if you capture me. Your power and glory will be endless. You'd be more than just Prince of Thrones; you'd be Prince of Seraphim."

Astaroth's greedy eyes stared Micah down as he bellowed, "So I shall be!"

Micah stepped forward, leaving Sage's arms behind, knowing where the cat o' nine tails would land. Sage gasped as the tails seared through his skin, burrowing into his shredded flesh, some tails hooking in and others tearing free.

Eden felt the impact, like it had been her own body struck. She heard the crack and the deafening sound of contact made. She staggered as she ran, blinded by tears. She swiped the back of her arm against her eyes, clearing her vision. Kicking back the nails that bit through her pants, she scrambled forward, ignoring the demon pursuing her.

She gaped at Micah's body, his frame limp and lifeless, as he crashed to the ground.

He's going to die! Where's Andrew?

"What now?" Sage called out. "Will you stay there forever and miss your opportunity? You know your master will reward you. What are you waiting for?" Sage stood over Micah's body, which was so still it terrified Eden. She took hold of the end of the whip, its tails still wrapped around Micah.

Why isn't she freeing him already? It's killing him!

Astaroth reeled in his whip, trying to retrieve 'his prize'.

Sage's grip brought him up short. "Come and get him, or stay where you are."

Eden's view was blocked by Gabriel's chest as she collided with his body.

"Where do you think you're going?" Gabriel shouted.

Let him be mad! I don't care! How can he leave Micah behind to die?

"Micah needs you—" she began, but he pulled her into his arms and shot off the ground.

She punched at his chest. "Gabriel, go back! Don't leave him!"

But she knew she'd never get free as they soared towards the exit. Below them, Caitlyn and Trent were ushered out by their guardians. Andrew came into view. He was fighting against his guardian, trying to free himself too.

"Wait, I can heal him!" he yelled, but the angel didn't seem to care.

"Eden, tell him!" Andrew shouted up at her. The opening in the wall loomed closer.

"He can! He heals people. Let him help Micah," she begged.

But the angel with the bow and arrow only hefted Andrew up by his arms and forced him through the opening.

Damon appeared, carrying an unconscious Willow in his arms. Eden could see her clothes were ripped and there was way too much red covering her. If she weren't worrying about Micah's eminent death, she would have panicked over her friend more. As it was, she yelled to Damon, "Help him! You can help him!"

Damon's brown eyes stared up at her and then he plunged through, stowing Willow.

Realizing this might be the last time she'd ever see Micah, Eden strained to look over Gabriel's shoulder.

She wasn't seeing the collapsed young man wrapped in a barbed whip; she saw the boy with a mess of black hair and big blue eyes helping her into the tree fort. *He always wanted to be a brave knight. I didn't get to say good-bye!*

The vines scratched her back, as Sage's voice rang out, "Then stay, and never progress!"

Astaroth's red robes clapped behind him as he lunged for Micah's body, leaving the well behind.

Sage consumed herself with flames and comprehension dawned on Eden. *It was a trap.* Sage would level the prince, and all remaining demons, with her searing, white flames.

The stone wall and cornfields whirled below them as she sobbed uncontrollably into Gabriel's chest. He landed and held her tight against him as he ran. She caught glimpses of her other friends doing the same thing, as they weaved through the cornstalks.

Micah was the bait, her mind repeated, as the earth shifted and they were suddenly tumbling down a steep hill, which came out of nowhere.

Lightning catapulted across the sky, and the ground rumbled with cracking thunder. Seconds later, they were submerged in a downpour unlike any Eden had ever seen. Visibility was limited to only a few feet in front of them.

"Gabriel, wait," Eden shouted up to him.

"What?" He craned his neck down.

She pressed her lips into his ear. "We've got to go back! This rain may have saved Micah!"

Gabriel stopped running, his arms still cradling her. She knew he was reluctant to let her go until he decided it was safe to return.

At that moment, Damon's body surged past them, sprinting full speed back uphill the way they'd come. He was swallowed up by the sheets of water. Then Andrew nearly collided with them, shooting past.

Oh good, Andrew!

She peered up at Gabriel, waiting.

When Trent ran past them next, he set her on the ground.

"Ok, but you'll go faster if I carry you. This hill's pretty steep and slippery."

"I'm not going to argue with you there." She was confused as to why there was a hill to climb in the first place. *Didn't we go downhill before?*

Willow and Caitlyn came into view, grasping cornstalks to keep from falling backwards. It seemed all the guardians were letting them go back now. Eden could see the rain had washed the blood off Willow's skin. Eden couldn't detect any serious injuries.

"Are you ok?" Eden hollered.

"I'm fine. What happened?" Willow yelled back, trying to be heard over the rain.

Eden glanced in the direction of the well. She was anxious to get back.

"It's ok, I'll fill her in. Go to Micah," Caitlyn shouted.

"Thanks."

Gabriel scooped her up and took off. She ducked her face into his chest. The rain was painful at the speed they were moving. They reached the opening at the same time as Damon, Andrew, and Trent. Being airborne, they flew over the wall. Damon glanced at the sky and shouted out something. Immediately, the rain ebbed, slowing to a drizzle.

Damon sent the rain! Maybe he saved Micah! Gabriel landed, releasing her. She ran forward, the once-barren dirt now a muddy quagmire.

Sage was on the ground near the well, Micah's head was in her lap.

Her fingers were gingerly freeing the barbed whip from his flesh. Relieved his body didn't look burned, she sickened at the amount of blood staining the pool of water Sage and Micah sat in.

He looks so pale... his lips are blue!

Damon and Andrew dropped to Micah's side. Andrew wasted no time thrusting his hands on Micah's chest. Damon gasped.

"It's ok, he's helping," she said, touching Damon's shoulder as she knelt beside him.

The gashes are closing! She gazed at Andrew, still amazed by what he could do. Then Andrew put his ear over Micah's mouth.

"What is it?" Damon demanded.

Andrew ignored him, burying his hands in Micah's abdomen. Eden panicked at seeing the open wounds, torn flesh and strips of fabric tangling in a bloody mess.

"You can save him, right?" Damon pushed as Andrew again checked for a pulse.

"I don't know," he shouted back, his hands and arms now bathed in Micah's blood. Abruptly, Andrew's face shot up, peering around. "Caitlyn!"

Sage broke her silence. "Alaina, bring Caitlyn now!"

The young, blonde girl immediately appeared, holding a bewildered Caitlyn by the arm. Caitlyn's eyes swept the scene. She dropped down by Andrew, reassuring, "Micah's not supposed to die now. His mission isn't over. You can save him."

Andrew nodded and the gaping wounds sealed together in rapid succession. After minutes that felt like hours, Micah's chest rose and fell. There were collective gasps from the audience. After another deep breath in, Micah began coughing. Sage helped him sit up. Eden couldn't help it; she grabbed his hand, pressing it against her wet cheek.

Micah turned and focused on her face. He gave her a weak smile. "It's ok. It's over now."

A lump had taken over her throat and she could only nod, afraid she'd sob if she tried to talk. Micah lowered their clasped hands and gave her fingers a squeeze. Somewhere in her brain, she knew she shouldn't act so obvious. Andrew was sitting next to her, watching. But at the moment, she didn't care. *Micah's ok!*

Damon rose to his feet and moved closer to Willow, who stood behind Caitlyn. "Sorry I left you so fast. Are you sure you're all right?" he asked, looking her over.

A strand of wet hair stuck to Willow's lips as she smiled back at him. He hesitated, and then brushed it back. Her smile deepened. "Yes, I'm fine. Thank you for saving me."

Damon gave Willow a somewhat awkward smile before glancing away. Micah was climbing to his feet; Damon leapt to his aid.

"Thanks, I'm good," Micah said, gripping Damon's hand. "How'd you do it?"

Damon shrugged. "Looked like you could use a waterfall."

Micah chuckled. "Glad you're on my side, Damon." Then his face sobered as he walked past them. Eden turned and saw why. Trent was on his knees, his complexion drained of color. He swiped at his eyes with his forearm and took a deep breath.

"Never again, Micah, never ask this of me again!"

Micah nodded. "I know and I won't." Micah grabbed his hand, pulling him to his feet. They both thumped each other's backs.

Trent muttered, "Good, 'cause Aunt Lacey still believes I'm a good influence. How could I ever explain myself if you died on my watch?"

Micah grinned as they stepped apart. "Welcome back, Trent."

Trent sighed over-dramatically. "Don't think I'll ever recover from this one. You owe me big time, Micah." He rubbed his hands together. "But now that it's over, let's get to the good stuff."

Micah peered around at all of them; they were all drenched, covered in mud, and in some cases, blood. "Yeah, I think we could all use some good stuff right about now."

Chapter Fifty

Good stuff? I'm still trying to get my knees to stop shaking. Micah glanced in her direction and winked. Now her body felt weak for another reason and she had to resist the urge to run into his arms and smother him with kisses. Trent joking again was a good sign. *Maybe the worst is over.*

Her jeans felt stiff and cold as she plodded through the mud. Moving closer to the well, she slipped. Throwing her arms out, she smacked Andrew across the chest.

"Oh sorry," she breathed out, unaware he had been so close.

"I think I'll live," he answered. He squinted at her. "Are you hurt at all from before?" His blue-green eyes swept her body up and down.

Embarrassed, she said, "No, I'm good. How about you?"

"I'm fine." He straightened up. "Just checking if you needed anything… you know, healed. Glad you're ok." He quickened his pace as he stepped away.

Not sure how to take his concern, she looked up to see Willow was now kneeling next to the well, running her hands along the stones. *So now that it's demon-free, she's captivated by it.*

"I owe you all an explanation," Micah stated.

"Yeah, a big one," Andrew muttered.

Micah glanced at him. "You're right. You have every right to hate me. Let me explain things and then maybe you'll all forgive me for today."

There were a few murmurs.

"To start, this well's no ordinary well."

"You think?" Caitlyn whispered to Eden. Eden smiled back at her.

"It's been here for thousands of years and marks a very sacred location. For a long time, the demons have set up camp here. You all saw the freaky demon with the robes?" There were nods from everyone. "That was Astaroth, a prince in the demon world." Micah glanced around and said, "To fix the well, we had to rid it of *all* the demons. Tell you what, I'll tell you more once we get inside."

Inside what? Surely not the well...

There were murmurs of confusion. "Oh," Micah blurted, "and since we purged this place, it's special again. You know, sacred. So we all need to take our shoes off."

"Say what?" Andrew asked. Eden stifled a laugh. It was a strange request.

"I know it sounds funny, but it's holy ground again. So let's follow Willow's good example." Micah pointed at Willow's feet. Sure enough, they were bare.

Eden complied and everyone tossed their shoes aside. A few of them wore socks still. *Well, wherever we're going, we're going to get it muddy.* But seeing Damon's clean socks ahead of her, she thought, *Maybe this land is special. His feet aren't mud pies.*

Trent dropped down next to Willow, who moved over to give him space. "What does this mean?" Willow asked, pointing to a stone that had some kind of hieroglyphics on it.

"Well of Enoch," Trent answered.

"Who's that?" Andrew asked.

Micah didn't answer, but instead threw his leg over the side of the well. *What's he doing?*

"Like I said, I have a lot to tell you, but first, we all need to go down there." He pointed at the bottom of the well.

"Are you serious?" Willow asked, standing up.

Trent grabbed Micah's arm and Eden hoped he would talk some sense into him. Instead, he griped, "Why do you get to go first?"

Micah grinned. Grabbing the side of the well with both hands, he tossed his other leg over. *What, is he going to just fall to the bottom?* He didn't sink. He seemed to be standing on something.

"There's a ladder built into the stones on the inside. Don't worry; your guardians won't let you fall." Then Micah's stepped down. Trent swung his leg over and followed. Eden caught eyes with Caitlyn.

"This day just keeps getting stranger and stranger," Caitlyn said, shrugging her shoulders. Damon was next, but seeing Willow behind him, he took her arm and helped her over the edge.

"Thanks," she murmured. "I'm not great with heights."

Damon followed her. When Andrew disappeared, and it was only Caitlyn and her left, Eden realized Gabriel was gone.

After Caitlyn scaled down, Eden whispered, "Where did you go? Do you still have to hide from me?"

He appeared. "No, but it's easier for me to keep you from falling if I'm in my own spectrum. You don't have the best balance, Eden." Then he was gone.

She teetered, with one leg over the edge.

"You better be holding on tight then," she said through gritted teeth. *Couldn't he just carry me down?*

The well was dark, and the stones, though they protruded, didn't have the best handholds. She was still drenched from all the rain. Relieved, she felt her feet finally touch the ground. The area was much larger than the well's girth.

"Eden, over here," Caitlyn hollered.

"Ok," she called back, and then whispered, "You can come back now, Gabriel."

Gabriel's bright form lit up the area. He took her arm and guided her to the small hole in the wall the others must have gone through. He gestured for her to lead. Crawling through, she fought the sensation of claustrophobia, thankful it was only a few yards long. Climbing out, she searched behind for Gabriel. She felt his hands hoist her up.

She smiled up at him and said, "Cheater."

He cocked an eyebrow at her. She peered around the small cavern they were in now. It was perhaps ten by ten, with earth making the ceiling, walls, and floor. She inhaled. It smelled like a summer garden. Then she noticed everyone staring at her. *Did I take too long?*

"Good, we're all here," Micah said, glancing at her. *Guess I did.*

Since Sage and Gabriel were the only guardians left, their warm, yellow light cast deep shadows off everyone else. *Wonder if the other guardians are watching.*

As if reading her mind, Micah clapped his hands together. "Ok, first things first. Introductions. Guardians, can you join us?"

Instantly, the already-crowded space got tighter as the guardians appeared, brightening the room. Her friends gaped at the angels.

"So I think it's safe to say we all believe in demons and angels now, right? Ok, so these wonderful angels are your guardians. They've been assigned to protect and guide you for your entire life. They know you pretty well. So let's have you meet them." Micah gestured to Sage. "This is Sage. She's my guardian."

The man with the red beard, standing behind Trent, boomed in a deep voice, "My name's Brutus."

Trent shot a glance at Sage, "By redhead, I didn't mean Captain Red Beard." Sage pressed a finger over her lips, hiding a smile.

The guardian with the milky blue eyes, towering over Damon, said, "I'm Seth." Damon studied Seth's face and then nodded slowly.

"Daniel," the man with the bow and arrow said. Andrew struck out a hand. "Nice to meet you, man." Daniel appeared surprised and then slowly took the proffered hand, giving it a firm shake.

"Caitlyn, I'm Alaina," the girl with the long braid said softly.

Caitlyn smiled back. "You look like you're my age."

Alaina's smile twitched slightly, the smallest glimmer of sadness sweeping her baby blue eyes. "I am your age."

Caitlyn cocked her head sideways, obviously wanting to ask more, but the woman with the gold tiara was saying, "I'm Esther."

Willow's face beamed. "You're who've I've been feeling! It makes so much sense now!"

Esther inclined her head forward with a regal nod. "Yes, it has been me you have felt."

"Eden knows who I am," Gabriel cut in.

Micah glanced at Gabriel and then said, "Ok, great. Any questions?"

"I have one for Sage," Trent grumbled. "What part of hot didn't you understand? Because I was picturing someone with a few more curves and a lot less flannel, if you know what I mean." Trent glanced at Brutus. "No offense."

Brutus appeared nonplussed. Eden was startled to hear Sage's laughter roll through the room; it was a beautiful sound. Micah joined her, chuckling. "Any other questions?"

"Micah, she didn't answer me," Trent pointed out.

"Any others?" Micah repeated, ignoring him.

"Well, yeah," Andrew butted in. "I sort of get clearing the demons out of here, sort of, and that these angels are here to protect us. But why us? And why are we standing in the bottom of a well?"

"Great, good questions," Micah said, not really answering them.

"And, don't forget to tell us who Enoch was," Willow piped in.

"Yes, perfect. Any others?" When no one said anything, he said, "Let's start with the why you're all here. I bet you've all noticed you aren't exactly normal, right?"

Eden peered at her friends. *That's definitely true of Andrew and Damon, but what about the rest of them?* No one said anything as they glanced at each other.

"You're gifted. The Captain handpicked you, giving you power and abilities far beyond your own. You have jobs to do. Some of you did your part already. Others of you may still be figuring yourselves out, and that's ok. The Bible talks of gifts of the spirit; prophecy, healings, faith, the gift of tongues, and more."

That's what I read in the Bible! Gifts of the spirit.

Micah continued, "The Captain named me His Seer. There've been many Seers over time. It means I receive information from the Captain through dreams and visions. The visions let me know what I need to do, and what's going to happen in the future."

"Trent's," Micah pointed at his cousin, "my Interpreter. He can understand pretty much every language and helps me decipher what my dreams and visions mean. He keeps me," he paused, "sane."

Trent gave Micah a smug look.

"Damon's gifts are extremely rare, only given a few times before. I think we all witnessed how powerful it is. He has the gift of tongues. That doesn't just mean he can speak Spanish or Italian. He knows an ancient, powerful language, the pure language of Adam. Yes, the Adam and Eve, Adam. He can speak to animals, bugs, plants, pretty much anything, and they understand one another. As we saw today, he can also command the earth."

Damon shifted under everyone's gaze. All the times she'd thought he was talking to himself, he'd actually been conversing.

"Andrew can heal with just the touch of his hands. Anything can heal, unless the Captain doesn't want it healed." Micah shot a glance at Andrew. "You can do a lot of good with your gift."

Micah turned next to Willow. "Willow has the gift of discernment. It not only warns her of danger, but helps her sense her surroundings and see what's really happening. Willow, as you learn how to use it, you'll find it does even more."

Willow grinned, her blue eyes dancing.

"Caitlyn." Micah's gaze rested on her. "Your gift is… well, amazing. You have the gift of pure faith. The Captain trusts this to hardly anyone, truthfully. It's pretty limitless in what you can do. And Caitlyn," Micah's tone softened, "don't worry, you've done everything perfectly so far."

Caitlyn's downturned lips flickered into a small smile. *Wonder if she doubted herself before?*

Eden knew she was next. She honestly thought Micah would have to make something up, because as far as she could tell, she hadn't done anything miraculous lately. She waited for Micah to say her name, but he didn't.

Instead, he said, "The Captain picked you, but you can still choose to go your own way. It's up to you if you want to be a part of this. I will tell you this—He knows each of you personally, and you're all very special to Him."

Eden knew Micah was saying something important, but all she could think was how stupid she felt at the moment. Many of her friends were still staring at her, obviously wondering what her gift was. *Did he bring me along simply because he likes me?* She'd always thought there was nothing special about her, but being in a room full of gifted people, when she was not, really nailed it in. *Don't cry, don't cry...*

"What about Eden?" Willow asked. Eden's face flushed. "I know what I see in her. What's her gift?"

Micah locked eyes with Eden, and she resisted the urge to duck her head. *He's probably searching for something nice to say.*

"She's the reason we're all here today," Micah replied. She inhaled sharply. *Say what?* "And the best part is—she has no idea why."

You got that right.

"Our gifts don't just come naturally. They need someone to turn them on. They need an Awakener."

All eyes were on her now, but she had no idea what Micah was talking about.

"Eden," Micah's voice was velvet. "You're the Awakener, the final and last Awakener."

Huh? Final and last what? She glanced at Gabriel, who nodded back at her.

Micah continued, "Though I speak with the tongues of men and of angels, and have not charity, I am becoming as sounding brass ... and though I have the gift of prophecy, and understand all mysteries, ... and though I have all faith, so that I could remove mountains, and have not charity, I am nothing."

I read those exact verses!

"And now abideth faith, hope, charity, . . . but the greatest of these is charity," he finished.

She stared at him, lost.

"Your true gift's Charity, the pure love that never fails. Because you have pure love, you're the Awakener. Your touch awakens others to their true potential. The beautiful and ironic thing is, your gift's the greatest, but you'd never know it unless I told you, because yours is love. You awaken in others what they didn't know was possible, with no glory for yourself."

She resisted the urge to push up her glasses, something she hadn't done in a long time.

"Micah, I didn't touch—" She stopped. *All those hugs!* She laughed aloud as she gaped at Gabriel. "It *was* you."

Gabriel grinned. "I may have helped you a little with that."

"When the time was right, you only had to embrace us," Micah explained.

She took in her friends faces, each one of them holding a piece of her heart with them. She swallowed down the lump forming. She needed to change the subject or she'd break down and blubber. "I had no idea. I just thought I was making a fool out of myself."

There was some laughter. Damon stifled a grin.

Micah chuckled and then said, "I better keep explaining things."

"Yeah, I'd like to know why we were sitting ducks up there." Andrew's tone was hard.

"Andrew." Caitlyn placed a hand on his arm.

"It's ok. You're right, Andrew. I need apologize to all of you. I couldn't warn you beforehand. You see, we needed all the demons to come out, not just Astaroth, to really clean the place out. Unfortunately, I was great leverage for Astaroth, but the other demons—"

"We were live bait, in other words," Andrew finished.

"Because you're gifted, you attract demons like crazy," Micah said quietly. "The plan was for you all to stay behind the angel barrier and be fine, albeit terrified."

Andrew stared at Micah. "I can see why you didn't tell us. There's no way I would have come. But then again, if I knew you needed me to heal you..." Andrew sighed. "Ok, but next time, a little warning."

Trent snorted. "Next time?"

"You have my word, Andrew. Next question, who's Enoch? Let's start with something familiar. Everyone's heard of Noah's ark, right?" There were murmurs of yes. "I'm going to tell you the story behind that story. Around 3400 BC, there was a prophet, named Enoch. He kept a record known as the Book of Enoch, which Trent and I studied from in Rome. Where we stand, all this land was Enoch's. Being a master builder, Enoch knew the secrets to building, and he created a city like no other. When he was 365 years old, he and his entire city were lifted up to heaven—no one ever tasting death."

Micah glanced around. "So why is that all important to know? Because Enoch's great grandson was Noah. And like the story you heard when you were a kid, with Noah's Ark, there was a flood. Enoch's city was saved from the flood, because they were lifted up, gone before it even came. The only thing left behind of Enoch's city, was his underground temple." Micah pointed at the ground. "This well marks the entrance to his temple."

Chapter Fifty-One

"Wait, we're in the underground temple now?" Willow asked with wide eyes.

"Yes." Micah grinned.

Eden peered around. *Doesn't look like a temple to me. Then again, it's old. Maybe this was beautiful once.*

Micah continued, "The temple's a series of vaults, or chambers, stacked on top of each other. There are nine layers. We're standing on top of one now. There's something of great worth in the ninth chamber, something we need to take with us."

Eden's curiosity was piqued as Trent suggested, "Micah, why don't we tell the story as we go?"

As far as she could tell, there were no doors out of there. It appeared completely enclosed.

"Ok with everyone?" Micah asked. They agreed. He strolled to the far end of the room and dropped to one knee. "Right about here, I think. All right, Damon, it's all yours."

Damon muttered something under his breath and the dirt split, forming two piles to either side of a large, square stone. Smooth and flat, it appeared to be a hatch.

Trent tugged at the corner of it.

"It's sealed shut, remember?" Micah said.

Trent glanced up at Damon. "Well, what are you waiting for?"

Damon mumbled something and the stone lifted, hovered, and

then lowered to the ground. She leaned forward to get a better look at the square recess it'd left behind. Cool air made the hair on her arms stand up, and she wrapped her arms around herself. *The smell totally reminds me of seventh grade art; there must be dried-out clay or something.*

Micah gestured to Trent. "After you this time."

Trent practically threw himself down the hole. After he had disappeared, Micah descended, saying, "The steps are steep. You might want to go down backwards." Eden noted Micah faced forward, as did Damon, Caitlyn, and Andrew. As Willow bounced on her toes, waiting for her turn, she decided his words of caution were meant for her. She found it interesting that each guardian disappeared as their charge descended, leaving only Willow's guardian Esther and Gabriel.

Willow's voice was giddy. "Isn't this exciting?"

Eden grinned and then watched Esther disappear into thin air; Willow on her way down.

She turned to Gabriel. "Does this mean you're watching me, making sure I don't fall?"

"I think you'll manage. See you down there." And he was gone.

Eden stared at the space he'd left behind. "Haha, very funny," she muttered. Still, as she stepped through the opening, she secretly hoped he was with her. Since everyone else had gone down normally, she did too, but when her feet slipped down two steps, she flipped around and crawled. Reaching the bottom, she was relieved the only one staring at her was Gabriel. Everyone else stood by the two huge pillars in the middle of the room. The room was made of the same stones they'd seen on the well.

"Micah, it's just like we thought! The brick and marble pillars marking the entrance to the temple," Trent gasped.

The pillars stood about five feet apart with the ceiling, forming a beautiful stone arch between them. Glancing up, Eden wondered why the ceiling didn't come crashing down on them; it looked heavy.

Micah's arm brushed hers. "Enoch built the arch above us. He was a master of arches." The light cast by their guardians reflected off Micah's blue eyes. "He built pretty much the whole temple, his son Methuselah did some too." He paused. "I still can't believe we're actually in here, seeing this."

"It's better than anything we ever imagined as kids."

He gave her a crooked grin. "Yeah, you're right."

"Micah, the columns have inscriptions," Trent interrupted, poking his head between them.

"Really?" Micah followed Trent back to the middle of the room. Damon was staring at the pillars, one of his hands resting on the brick column.

Caitlyn stepped next to Eden. "Why are they made out of different material?"

Eden shrugged.

Micah answered, "What we're seeing today, scholars have speculated over for 5000 years. Like I said, Enoch knew the flood was coming, so he built these vaults, wanting to keep sacred things safe. He knew the temple would have to survive water and fire. These columns symbolize that. They're the indestructible columns—one made of brick so that it wouldn't sink in water, and one the other made of marble, so it wouldn't burn in the fire."

"What fire?" Andrew butted in.

Micah opened his mouth but Trent said, "The brick one talks about the seven sciences of mankind."

What's that? But Trent straightened up and moved to the marble pillar.

"Ah-ha, here we go. This says a short distance away a priceless treasure will be found in the subterranean vaults!" Trent jumped to his feet. "Let's go!"

"Ok." Micah moved a few feet over, pointed to the ground, and grinned at Damon. "A little harder, it's stone."

Damon snorted back at him.

The steps were wider this time, and she easily made her way down. Entering the even larger room, made of the same rounds stones, she saw that, again, there were two pillars in the middle of the room—this time they were made of metal.

Andrew was examining them. "Are they brass?"

"Too old to be brass, they're bronze," Micah answered, his eyes connecting with Eden. She stepped closer to him, passing Damon leaning against the wall, in the shadows. Damon's lips were pressed together in a tight line. It was either a scowl or a look of concentration. Either way, she knew better than to bother him.

Happy to be near Micah again, she gazed at the pillars. Where the other ones had no embellishments, these two looked almost like fiery palm trees. The pillars were smooth and round with metal flames coming out the tops, and a band around the base of the flames. Metal palm leaves spread down and away from the flames, almost like the fire was built on leaves instead of logs.

Micah glanced at Trent. "Do you think these are the original columns Solomon modeled his after?"

Trent rubbed his hands together. "Maybe."

Confused, Eden tugged on Micah's arm. "What are you talking about?"

Micah leaned closer. "In King Solomon's Temple, there were two bronze pillars marking the entrance. And in his temple, the pillars had names written on them."

"Holy Toledo," Trent exclaimed. "It says Boaz and this one says, drumroll please, Jachin."

"Is that supposed to mean something to us?" Andrew asked.

"Boaz and Jachin are from the Old Testament," Micah explained, "and they're the same names Solomon put on his temple. So since these were built long before, we can assume that maybe this is what Solomon modeled his after."

Trent straightened up. "The word Boaz means *strength* and Jachin means *word establish*."

"So, in the strength of this temple, the word will be established," Willow commented more than asked.

Micah smiled. "I think you may be right."

Trent slapped his hands together. "Hot dang, it doesn't get any cooler than this!"

"I thought the real treasure was in vault nine," Caitlyn said evenly.

Trent pretended to stab his heart. "Such a killjoy."

Caitlyn stared at Trent and Micah agreed, "You're right. This isn't what we're after. Let's keep moving. Ready, Damon?"

Damon was standing on the next hidden hatch. *Wonder if that was a coincidence.*

"Methuselah built this chamber," Micah said as they passed through the third chamber, which was made of faded, red bricks. When Damon was again on top of where the next hatch was, Eden decided, *He knows where the hatches are.*

The fourth chamber was also made of brick, the room larger, the ceiling ten or eleven feet high. There were four brick columns nestled in the corners of the square room. Between each pillar, the ceiling once again formed arches. In the middle of the room sat a square table with a large, golden triangle resting on the top.

"It's an altar," Micah said, running his hand along the top of the table. "And this," Micah pointed at the gold triangle, "is the small, golden delta."

"Delta?" Andrew asked.

"A delta's a triangle made out of pure gold. Enoch had two made, one small and one large. He inscribed on them some of the hidden treasures of Heaven."

Trent's mouth gaped open, speechless, his eyes scanning the delta up and down.

The triangle didn't look small to Eden. It was two dimensional, about four feet high and six inches thick. *How much is this worth if it's made of solid gold?*

Caitlyn pointed and asked Trent, "What do all the markings mean?"

The engravings reminded Eden of a homemade board game with linked square spaces making a swirling path along the delta. She could almost see kids rolling a dice and moving their game pieces along the spaces.

She saw there were symbols at the 'start' and the 'end'.

Trent's eyebrows gathered together. "Interesting," he muttered.

"Care to share?" Andrew asked, folding his arms across his chest.

"It's fascinating really—" Trent began.

Micah cut him off, "Some things aren't for us right now. Besides, we need to keep moving."

Trent sighed heavily. "You're probably right. But promise me we'll come back."

Micah gestured to Damon. "Ready?"

Again, Damon stepped to the side and removed the barrier of bricks. This time the stairs were decent sized and made of smooth, gray stone.

Stepping off the last step, she saw the walls, floor, and ceiling were all that same light gray stone. It felt granular to the touch. There were five bronze columns resting in each corner and, counting the walls, she realized the room was shaped in a pentagon. In the largest corner of the room sat another stone altar.

The five ornate columns had metal vines running down them, shaped to look like ivy. She saw the leaves ran along the arches between the columns as well. It felt like she'd walked into a Roman temple, the altar also draped in metal ivy.

"The room's made from granite. And the vines are copper; that's why they aged green," Micah commented next to her.

"It's beautiful," she exhaled.

"Like you," he whispered, giving her a wink.

She smiled, feeling a warmness creep across her face. For a moment, she almost forgot they weren't the only two in the room.

Then Trent yelled, "Yo Micah, you ready or what?"

Snapped back to reality, she stepped to where Damon had already opened the passageway. Chamber six, also made of granite, had six bronze columns and six walls, making it a perfect hexagon. The vines were replaced by engravings in the granite walls and ceiling depicting stars; she counted twelve star constellations. More fascinating to her were the stone tables lining the walls, containing artifacts: gray vases in every shape and size, hand-sculpted pottery, and odd-shaped metal pieces, some long and smooth, and others round and ragged.

"No touching," Micah warned Trent, whose fingers were inching toward one of the metal pieces that looked like a spear. She adored this new side to Trent. *All guys are still little boys dying for a treasure hunt.*

Damon lifted the square piece of granite to open the hidden hatch. Marching down to the next level, Eden realized the guardians were no longer with them. Entering the seventh chamber, she was saddened to see only Sage. *Where'd Gabriel go?*

Still, her warm light was enough to brighten the space. Eden saw the room was made of different stone and, examining it closer, she discovered fossils embedded in it. She could make out seashells and small, ancient sea creatures. She skirted the room, counting columns. When she reached the seventh pillar, she noticed the room was a heptagon now. In front of her was granite altar, with a single bowl on top. It was shallow but wide, made from earthy brown clay. She was curious to know what it had been used for in the past.

Glancing around, Eden saw Damon leaning against one of the walls, in the shadows.

Willow stepped in front of him and asked, "So, are you going to tell me what's wrong?"

Damon stared back at her. "No hiding things from you, I guess."

"Nope."

His eyes dropped to his feet. "Nothing's wrong. I'm just taking it all in."

Willow's lips opened, but Caitlyn said, "Look, there are moons now too."

Distracted, Eden gazed up. The star motif now showed all phases of the moon from full to new. She sought out Trent. Surely, the stars and moons meant something. He was examining one of the pillars.

She squatted by him. "What do you see?"

Andrew overheard and stepped closer. Eden could feel him lean over her.

Trent glanced at Eden and then with a, "humph," stood and strode towards Micah.

"Maybe it's time we start telling the rest of the story, Micah," he announced, grabbing everyone's attention. Eden stood and nearly knocked Andrew backwards.

"Sorry," he muttered, backing up. She stammered, "Its ok…" but he was already retreating, not looking her way. Sighing, she plodded over to Micah and Trent.

"Yeah, I think you're right. I think we're far enough into the temple. We should be safe," Micah agreed.

Oh great, Eden thought, catching the eyes of the others.

"Let me rephrase that," he said quickly, seeing the reaction. "We shouldn't be overheard now."

She stared back at him thinking, *Who in the world could overhear us down here?* They were farther underground then she cared to think about. She didn't want to start hyperventilating.

Chapter Fifty-Two

Micah cleared his throat. "Let me begin by telling you a little more about angels. Not all angels are guardians. There are different hierarchies, or ranks, within angels, with different powers. In the highest ranking, or first hierarchy, of angels there are Seraphim, Cherubim and Thrones. These angels have specific jobs to do for the Captain and are granted power and knowledge to do it. Sage is Seraphim. They're the closest angels to God. Eden's guardian is Cherubim. He's actually the leader of the Cherubim. He called down the angels with the flaming swords earlier to protect us." Eden glanced around, wishing Gabriel were visible.

"Demons have an order too. Astaroth was a Prince of Thrones. I don't want to spend too much time there, other than to point out that the Devil isn't that creative, and uses the same titles for his leaders, or princes. So that gives you a little understanding of the position Astaroth held. He was one of the more powerful demons. The other black demons you saw are what they call their pawns, minions, or just plain demons. They aren't that lethal." Micah paused, hearing the sounds of disagreement. "Unless there are a lot of them, like there were today. If there's no end to their supply, even the most powerful of angels can fail. You all saw the hooded demons, right? Those were Astaroth's Elite guard. Only princes of the first hierarchy have them. Anyways, enough on that, let's get back to angels. So, we have the first level with Seraphim, Cherubim, and Thrones. Then there's a second and third level; most of your guardians are angels from the third level. Some are ranked higher, like Sage and Gabriel."

"What's a Throne?" Andrew asked. "You talked about Seraphim and Cherubim, but not Thrones."

"To tell you the truth, Andrew, I'm not one-hundred percent sure exactly who or what they are. In the Book of Enoch, he referred to them as the 'many eyed-ones'. They're portrayed as wheels conjoined, covered in eyes, in the Bible. Their primary purpose is to carry the Captain's chariot. They see everything and they move the Captain's plan forward. I'm not sure how exactly."

"Wheels with eyes... sorry I asked," Andrew mumbled.

Micah chuckled. "Well, it may be figurative. Cherubim are said to be part man, ox, lion, and eagle. Looking at Eden's guardian, I can picture how his feet are like an ox, totally immovable, his body's a lion, fierce in battle, and his eyes are eagles, missing nothing."

"That's really cool," Willow said, rubbing her hands up and down her arms. Eden wondered if she was cold or just got goose bumps.

"I want to tell you about another group of angels. They're angels from the second hierarchy. They're the Watchers." For some reason, now Eden's body was covered in goose bumps too. "The Watchers are a group of angels given heavenly knowledge and power. During Enoch's dad's time, a group of these Watchers decided they wanted to be with mortal women. Angels are forbidden from having," he hesitated, "human relationships with mortals, let's just say. The Watchers knew they'd be cast out of heaven forever, if they did, but Semjaza convinced them to swear an oath to each other that they'd go down together and do whatever they wanted. So Semjaza, and two hundred other Watchers, made the pact, and came to earth, marrying mortal women and having children.

"Now this isn't like in the books where an angel falls from heaven for a hot girl. These angels knew they were banned from Heaven, and they wanted man to be miserable like they were. They used their power for evil. They taught mortals forbidden arts of enchantments and divination, sorcery and astrology, and one of the leaders, Azazel, taught them the art of war. He showed them how to forge weapons: swords, knives, breastplates, and shields.

"The angel's offspring grew to be giants that consumed everything. When the food and wildlife was gone, the giants began hunting down men, eating their flesh and drinking their blood." Micah paused, peering at the group. "This is what Enoch was born into. When he was old enough, he went into hiding to stay safe, from not only the giants, but also the fallen Watchers. Enoch was lifted up to speak with holy angels a lot. As you can probably guess, people were praying pretty hard to be spared from the monsters. Well, another group of angels heard their cries. They're known as the Holies. They're angels from the first hierarchy. They're basically next in command after the Captain. In this room, on these pillars, are the names of the seven Holies." Micah turned to Trent. "Want to read them now?"

"Yeah." Trent pointed to the granite column in the point of the heptagon. "This one says Michael; he's over the best part of mankind and over chaos."

Chaos? Eden didn't have time to ask what that meant, for Trent was moving to the next pillar. "Raphael, over the spirits of men." Trent moved swiftly to the next. "Raguel, who takes vengeance on the world of luminaries. Remiel, the holy angel who's set over those who rise. Saraqael, over spirits who sin in the spirit."

They were looping back around the room as Andrew muttered under his breath, "Are we supposed to remember any of this?"

Caitlyn shrugged. "Let's hope there's not a pop quiz when he's done."

Andrew laughed quietly as Trent continued, "Uriel, the holy angel who was set over the earth and Tartarus."

"Tartarus?" Damon cut in.

"The lowest level of Hell. The place prepared for the vilest and most evil of sinners," Micah answered, peering at Damon. Eden was pretty sure Damon's brow was permanently bent down by now.

I wonder if he'll have a new wrinkle between his eyes when we leave this place, she mused.

Trent interrupted her thoughts. "And finally, the last one's Gabriel." She did a one-eighty, facing Trent. *Gabriel? My Gabriel?* "He's over Paradise, the serpents, and the Cherubim," he finished.

She felt a subtle, warm breeze behind her and turned to see Gabriel's blue gray eyes gazing back at her.

"You're one of the Holies?" she gasped.

He nodded once.

"I had no idea—all this time. Why didn't you tell me? Oh wait, I mean, you don't have to tell me anything if you don't want to—"

"Eden," Gabriel interrupted. "Calm down. It wasn't necessary for you to know about me, who I am. Personally, I would've told you from the beginning. It's not that important."

"Not important? You're one of the Holies! Your name's on a pillar!"

Gabriel's lips twitched.

"What?" she asked. "Why do you look like you're about to laugh at me?"

"You're right. My name *is* on a pillar." Gabriel's tone was bemused.

Having his name on an ancient pillar's probably the last thing Gabriel cares about. With a suck in of air, she covered her mouth with her hand. Memories flooded in. All the times she called him weird nicknames, trying to nettle him into saying his name. The times she complained to him about schoolwork, or a thousand other stupid, little things, and all the nights she cried to him about Micah not liking her. Her cheeks burned with shame.

I even called him a cheater for not climbing through the tunnel with me! She was mortified. She glanced at him, meeting his steady gaze.

"What's wrong?" he asked, his faint accent sounding more pronounced for some reason.

She shook her head, aware her friends were gawking now, all except for Willow, who only had eyes for Damon.

Gabriel stepped closer. "I'm sorry I laughed."

Taken back by his apology, she sputtered, "No, it's not that at all. I'm the one that's sorry. I've treated you like my own personal diary for the past year. I'm so embarrassed."

Gabriel's shoulders relaxed. "Oh that. Don't worry, Eden. I wouldn't have had it any other way."

"Really?"

He grinned. "Guarding you has been some of my most enjoyable and *entertaining* years. You shouldn't be ashamed of who you are."

Her heart squeezed. "Thank you."

His smile reached his eyes. It didn't help her pathetic attempt to control her emotions; her eyes welled. Not wanting to make a scene, she took a deep breath.

Trent cut in, "Don't want to interrupt anything here, but are we ready to move on? I don't know about you, but I'm dying to get to vault nine."

Micah glanced at Eden and she nodded back at him. "I'm good. Sorry."

Damon went to work revealing the next hatch. When Gabriel took a step forward, Eden grabbed his arm. "Do you have to leave again?"

He turned and gazed down at her. "I'll stay for the rest. Now catch up."

Chapter Fifty-Three

Chamber eight had the same fossils in it, and Eden overheard Andrew tell Caitlyn he thought it was limestone. There were eight granite pillars this time, and though they were embellished with carvings along the tops of stars, moons, and suns, there were no inscriptions for Trent to read. Again, there was an altar in the center of the room, and this time the ceiling was decorated with a large sun, as well as the moons and stars. The room was interesting, but she was anxious to get into vault nine.

Micah didn't walk to either side of the room though, but leaned against the altar. Soon everyone congregated, waiting for direction. "This is where my vision ends. I don't know where the entrance is," Micah announced.

"You saw the other openings in visions?" Willow asked.

"Yeah," Micah said. "I saw everything, even what happened by the well, although some of that was a bit sketchy."

More like terrifying, Eden thought as Trent grunted.

"Great," Andrew muttered.

Micah glanced around. "I'm open to ideas."

"Do you know the way?" Willow asked Damon. His eyes clouded over, almost like he was trying to remember something. He shook his head. "But you knew the other ones, didn't you?" Willow probed. He nodded slowly.

"Maybe there's a hidden message somewhere," Trent offered. He began scouring the walls and pillars. Andrew joined in.

Gabriel shifted his weight, catching Eden's eye. "Do you know?" she asked.

Gabriel and Sage exchanged looks and he said, "This one's for you to figure out."

She wished she could think of a convincing argument, but knew better than to question two high-ranking angels. Damon's lips began twitching. *He's probably asking whatever will listen for help.*

"But you've seen inside the ninth vault though, right?" Willow asked Micah, tapping her index finger against her lips.

"I've seen parts of it. I know we get into it. I'm just not sure how. Its sealed shut." Micah still leaned against the altar, crossing his ankles.

"But all the vaults were sealed," Damon stated.

"Yeah, but this one has a different kind of seal. It's not meant to be found by just anyone."

"You aren't just anyone. You're the Seer," Damon countered.

Willow peered at Damon, her face puzzled, and then she hopped on her toes. "But *he* isn't supposed to find the opening. *We are.*"

Micah smiled. "Good, Willow. You're using your gift. Trust your instincts."

Willow missed the admiration on Damon's face because she was already stepping away, but Eden caught it. With head down, Willow slowly moved five or six feet and then stopped. She peered up at the ceiling, and Eden's eyes followed. They were standing directly under the large, swirling sun motif.

Willow tapped her foot on the ground. "The opening's here."

Damon dropped to one knee and touched the spot she'd indicated. Eden wondered why he wasn't already saying his 'magic' words.

After pushing the dirt around with his finger, he said, "There are markings here."

Trent bent down and Eden scooted closer to get a better look. Symbols were engraved in the limestone, kind of like cursive writing.

"It's Arabic for faith," Trent stated, peering at Caitlyn.

All eyes turned to Caitlyn. "What? I don't know how to open it," she replied.

"But do you believe you can open it?" Willow asked, giving Caitlyn an encouraging smile.

Caitlyn's hazel eyes shifted from Willow to Micah. "I don't know."

"Give her a minute," Micah said, stepping away from the group. Damon and Trent followed after.

"It's ok, Caitlyn. This is new to all of us," Eden said.

"I don't know what I'm supposed to do. Do I just think 'open up'?"

"Can't hurt to try," Eden laughed back.

Willow leaned over. "It's ok if you have doubts, even with your gift of faith. Listen to your gut, not your head."

Caitlyn glanced at Andrew, who had remained next to her. He bumped into her with his arm and shoulder. "You can do it, Yoda."

Caitlyn sighed and closed her eyes. Nothing happened at first, but then the ground moved under their feet, not violently, more like an elevator coming to a stop. The marking cracked in half as two stone tabs opened like shutters, revealing a square opening to below. A cool gust of air came out, smelling like a spice cabinet.

"Excellent, Caitlyn." Micah squeezed her arm as he passed. Then glancing over his shoulder, he called, "Gabriel, Damon, we'll follow you in this time."

Surprised, Eden watched Gabriel defer to Damon to lead out.

"Interesting," Willow mumbled. Eden glanced at her and she grinned. "There's so much to take in! It's been like a feast, hasn't it?"

Feast? Not exactly the word I would've chosen, Eden thought as she became aware of her grumbling stomach. *How long have we been down here?*

She scurried after Gabriel, descending the white stairs. The echo of pounding footsteps reverberated behind her. Entering the final vault, she gasped at the size of the massive room made completely of marble. Elaborate carvings and engravings covered the nine marble pillars spanning the room. She glanced up to see the ceiling was an actual mural, no longer just symbols of the sun, moon, and stars. It was an ancient fresco, depicting planets and galaxies.

She spun around, trying to take it all in, when she discovered a tall altar in the corner with another golden delta on top. The triangle reached to the ceiling, its sharp point touching a yellow, swirling planet in the mural. Trent was standing in front of the altar, gazing up at the enormous delta. Micah and Damon were next to Trent, examining stacked stones on another altar. Noticing Caitlyn and Willow perusing the marble shelves lining the walls, Eden decided to join them.

"Look at this one." Willow pointed to an emerald the size of a baseball.

"Wow." Caitlyn leaned in. "Wonder how much its worth."

The shelves were packed with artifacts ranging from pottery, vases, knives, beads, pieces of metal, gold, rare stones, and crystals. Admiring the spread of jewels, it dawned on Eden they were sparkling. Not one piece in this collection was dusty. In fact, as she peered around the room, everything appeared clean. *How can that be?*

Moving down the wall, the shelves no longer contained beads or gems, but were stuffed as high as the ceiling with rolled parchment. *Trent's going to love this*, she thought, just as Trent's face appeared next to her.

"Looks like papyrus. And they thought the Dead Sea Scrolls were a find. Check this out!"

"The dead what?" she asked, glancing at him.

But Trent's attention was redirected to Micah, who was approaching.

"Just one scroll. Just a peek," Trent begged, clasping his hands together as if praying.

"This isn't what we came for. We got what we need," Micah replied, giving Trent's shoulder a friendly slap.

"You did?" Eden asked as Trent grumbled. She was shocked it'd happened so fast.

"Yeah, we did."

She glanced at the two altars, where everyone else was gathered. "Is it the big, gold triangle?"

"Well, sort of. Come on, I have to finish telling the story," Micah replied, taking her arm. Feeling his warm body, she realized how chilled her damp clothes had made her.

She peered at what everyone was gawking at. On the alter sat stone tablets, rectangular in shape, perhaps an inch or two thick each, stacked to form three columns about two feet high. One stack was wrapped in a gold band.

Andrew's blue-green eyes spied her arm laced through Micah's. When a frown tugged at his lips, she stepped apart from Micah, saying, "Why don't you finish the story?"

Not missing a beat, Micah began, "Where did I leave off? Oh yeah, the Holies. So, the Holies hear the cries of the mortals, as I said, and they go to God for a solution. God gives four of the seven Holies specific jobs to do. Uriel was to tell Noah about the flood coming and instruct him. I guess we can assume he was showing him how to build the ark." He paused, raising an eyebrow at Gabriel.

Gabriel nodded and Micah continued, "Two of the Holies, Raphael and Michael, were given the task of rounding up the Watchers and burying them in the earth. Azazel, the one who taught the art of war, was bound and thrown deep into the desert, where rocks covered him. Semjaza and all the others were thrown into the valleys of the earth. And Gabriel had to destroy the giants."

"How'd you do it?" Andrew asked, staring at Gabriel with wide eyes. Eden was pretty sure her mouth was hanging open.

"The flood," Gabriel said simply.

"That makes sense," Willow commented. "While the ark floated safely on top of the water, the giants drowned." There were a few murmurs of agreement.

"So back to Enoch, before the Watchers were thrown into the dark pits, they pleaded with Enoch to intervene for them. They called him the Scribe, since he could write. Since they were fallen angels, and not allowed in God's presence, they wanted Enoch to write a petition, asking God for forgiveness. Enoch wrote it and had a vision of where God dwells. He describes it on this golden delta. Enoch used the deltas as a symbol of God, sort of like Moses and the burning bush."

"What does it say?" Andrew asked, pointing to the hieroglyphics etched into the gold.

Trent tapped his thumb against his lips as he read. "Looks like Enoch's words. It says, 'I looked and saw therein a lofty throne: its appearance was as crystal, and the wheels thereof as the shining sun, and there was the vision of Cherubim. And from underneath the throne came streams of flaming fire so that I could not look thereon. And the Great Glory sat thereon, and His raiment shone more brightly than the sun and was whiter than any snow. None of the angels could enter and could behold His face by reason of the magnificence and glory and no flesh could behold Him. The flaming fire was round about Him.'"

Trent paused. "Should I keep going?"

Micah glanced at Gabriel and Sage, who both nodded.

"Let's see here. So, Enoch approaches God's throne and basically falls on his face, trembling. Ok, here we are… 'And the Lord called me with His own mouth and said to me, 'Come hither, Enoch, and hear my word.' And one of the Holy ones came to me and waked me, and he made me rise up and approach the door: and I bowed my face downwards … and I heard His voice: 'Fear not, Enoch, thou righteous man and scribe of righteousness: approach hither and hear my voice. And go, say to the Watchers of heaven, who have sent thee to intercede for them: 'You should intercede for men, and not men for you.'"

Trent stopped. "You know, that's a great line. Angels should plead for mortals, not mortals for angels."

"So what happens next?" Willow asked.

Trent squinted at the delta. "There's a name written here—"

"No!" Micah blurted. "Not that!"

Trent stared back at Micah.

"Why? Whose name is it?" Andrew asked.

"It's God's true name, one of the many things buried in here to keep it hidden from the world." Micah pointed at the delta. "It's written on this."

"Trent knows it. What about him?" Andrew asked.

Micah peered at Trent. "Unfortunately, that's going to be your burden to carry. You can't help what you can see as Interpreter, even if it's not meant to be seen."

Trent threw his hands on his hips.

Micah soothed, "Just remember not to reveal it to anyone or say it out loud, and you won't have to face something far worse than I did today."

Trent harrumphed. "Next time, a little warning would be nice! Don't let me be reading things guaranteed to shorten my life span!"

"You'll be fine, Trent."

"I'll have you know, I have plans for my future, Micah, and they involve Eden's redheaded friend back home."

Oh good, Trent does like Jessie after all.

"Ok, I'll warn you next time, happy?" Micah asked.

Trent shrugged. "It's all good."

I think mentioning Jessie just lifted his mood, or at least distracted him, Eden mused.

"So to answer your earlier question, Willow," Micah replied, "after Enoch saw God, he was told to tell the Watchers their petition wouldn't be granted at that time. They have to remain buried until judgment day."

"Wait a minute. Are you saying they're actually in the earth still?" Andrew blurted.

"Yeah," Micah hesitated, "although somehow their influence is still felt. Semjaza, the leader, is the one sending the demons after Eden and me. We can probably assume he'll want all of you too."

There were several gasps.

"Your guardians don't rest; they watch over you night and day. You don't need to worry," Micah added. His eyes met Eden's.

"The demon in my bedroom," she mumbled. "All those demons at prom." Andrew stiffened. "Semjaza sent those after *me*?"

Micah hesitated and then said, "Yes."

Gabriel moved closer to Eden. "Semjaza is still bound; he's not free."

Eden nodded but it still terrified her to know an ancient fallen angel had a personal vendetta to kill her.

Micah placed a hand on the top of the stack of stones. "This is what we came to get today. The angel Uriel gave these tablets to Enoch."

Trent hefted the first stone off the stack, holding it up for everyone to see. It was the first thing allowed to be touched, let alone picked up. Eden immediately recognized the oval symbol on it, with writing underneath.

"It says City of Enoch," Trent announced. "These stones are the blueprints for Enoch's city."

"Andrew, you asked about the fire earlier. Well, I kept having visions of a fire." Micah explained to them all about the fire and the city he saw, finishing with, "We have to build these cities, and these plans will help us do it."

"Us? Last I checked none of us are architects or builders," Andrew cut in.

"We don't need to be," Micah answered.

"What does the oval mean?" Eden blurted. "I keep seeing it everywhere. On the well, the stone wall, the chambers of the temple, and now on these tablets."

"It was Enoch's favorite symbol—it means Eternal. Everything has a way of coming back around again. Take for example what we're about to do now. Enoch lived over five thousand years ago, and he used these plans to build a city, saving people from the flood. And now we'll use these same plans to save people from the fire." Micah stared at Damon and Gabriel. "There are other ways things are coming full circle."

Willow glanced at Damon and nodded.

"Ok, we got what we came for. It's time to leave the temple," Micah said. The room brightened as all the guardians became present again.

Trent handed out stacks of stone tablets to everyone one by one. As Eden stepped up for her share, Micah smiled, saying, "I can get the last part, don't worry about it."

"But what about those?" she asked, pointing at the remaining stack.

"The ones with the gold wrapper stay," Micah explained. "They're the sealed portion, not for us, yet."

"Oh," she replied, not sure what sealed portion meant, and painfully aware she was the only one not carrying anything. *Does he think I'm that big of a klutz?*

She wondered how they'd ever scale the well wall back up while carrying heavy stones, when she saw Damon walk to the wall with a gigantic sun motif on it. He carefully set his tablets down on a nearby shelf, running his hands along the wall.

He spoke, and the rays surrounding the perfect circle cracked like the stone was being pushed through a cookie cutter. The entire sun sank back behind the wall, revealing a five-foot opening.

"Nice," Trent said as he followed Damon.

Micah explained, "Enoch built another way out."

As each of them passed through, their guardians walked directly behind them. Before Eden exited, she glanced back to make sure Gabriel was with her. She was surprised to see him lagging, staring at the room.

"Gabriel?"

He faced her.

"What's wrong?" There was definite pain in his eyes.

He glanced around again. "This used to be a familiar place to me many years ago. Now, it is just memories from another time."

She was touched by his openness but, as quickly as it came, it was gone. He turned her around and pushed her forward. "Got to keep up, Eden. Don't want to miss anything, do you?"

She sighed and scurried through, stepping into a tunnel made of clay and brick. She knew they'd descended a long ways going into the temple, but after ten minutes of uphill hiking, she was felt there was no end in sight. Being the only one not bearing a heavy load, she caught up to Willow and Caitlyn quickly. Sweat was beading on their foreheads. After insisting, they lightened some of their loads into her arms. A few minutes later, Eden regretted it. Her arms burned.

She was ready to complain to Gabriel, holy or not, when she realized the tunnel was leveling off a little. A few feet more and she saw a bright opening at the end.

"Finally," she grunted. Gabriel chuckled behind her. "By the way, why couldn't the angels carry these things out?"

She felt a gentle push from behind, and was surprised by the sudden weightlessness she felt.

"We're not allowed to remove anything from the temple. Micah was instructed to remove the tablets."

"Oh," she replied, enjoying how light her body felt, with her feet still on the ground.

"I may not be able to carry the tablets, but I can help carry you out," Gabriel said, close to her ear. "Besides, you're taking forever."

"I'd think you'd be much more patient, considering how long you've been around."

He snorted and then his hands were no longer pushing her, her body growing heavy again. Thankfully, they'd reached the end. She squinted, trying to see anything, but it was too bright.

Gabriel steered her by the elbow. "Careful Eden, you're going to drop them!"

Her eyes rebelled against the brightness. Through tears, she made out her surroundings. They had emerged out on a small, grassy knoll. Seeing the stone hefted to the side, she assumed Damon had cleared the way for them.

Everyone was together, holding their stones, blinking in the sunlit cornfields. Then, without a word, Willow turned on her heel and disappeared into the cornhusks.

Chapter Fifty-Four

"here's she going?" Damon asked.

"Why don't we follow and see?" Micah suggested.

Can't we set these down first? Eden scampered behind Caitlyn's guardian, Alaina, her arms throbbing. *So unnerving how much she looks like a regular teenager.* Again, they were scaling a hill and sweat began rolling down Eden's back. Breathing hard, Eden watched the corn give way to the stone wall again. She glanced around. *Where did all the dead corn go?*

The archway loomed just ahead of them. Where shriveled vines had been, green ivy draped the opening. Leaves tickled Eden's face as she passed under.

She gasped. The once-desert ground was covered in a soft, rolling grass. The stone wall was now draped with bright green vines and leaves. Kneeling next to the well was Vern, his face buried in his hands.

Spying the two neat stacks of tablets to the left, Eden was anxious to relieve her arms.

"Careful, not too fast," Gabriel warned, as she lay the tablets down.

After making sure they were secure, she sprinted over, catching Grandpa Vern saying, "I don't understand. How did you do it? This well's been dry for over seventy years."

Eden peered over the side of the well and was astonished to see there was indeed water in it. *No wonder we couldn't come back the way we'd gone.*

"It's all done. The land will be fertile again," Micah answered.

Willow knelt beside Vern.

"I've always blamed myself," Vern said quietly. "I thought, because I broke the rules, the well dried up, and the land was cursed. I've spent my life hoping I could mend my wrong."

"This was never your fault. When you showed my grandfather it, you were just kids. That's not what caused the curse. The Captain would never hold a child accountable for something like that."

Vern peered up at Micah. "Then what happened?"

"Your father was greedy. He told other farmers about the water from the well, how it guaranteed a huge harvest every year. He hated being a farmer and kept trying to sell the land, but when others believed his wild tales of magical water, he decided to sell the water itself. He came out to pump the well one morning and found it dry. This water is not for sale."

Vern's eyes widened. "That explains his unhappiness for all those years. As a child, I'd always believed he'd blamed me, that maybe he'd figured out what I'd done."

Eden's heart ached for the old man. What kind of burden would that have been like? *That's why he never married or had his own family. He blamed himself.*

Eden felt something stir within her. She knew what she was feeling now. Glancing at Gabriel, who stared back at her expectantly, she held out a hand and said, "I got this one."

Gabriel smiled and then nodded.

Eden dropped down next to Vern. Putting her arm around his bony shoulders, she squeezed gently. Vern glanced up at her and gave her a small smile.

"Grandpa Vern, the Captain wants you to know you're special to Him. He wants you to let go of your guilt and shame; they were never yours to carry. And he wants to call you to His work." Micah said the words and Eden felt a warm rush flow from her arms. *Funny, I never noticed it before. Guess I was too busy being embarrassed.*

Vern attempted to stand. Willow and Eden helped him up easily.

"Now, what's this about work? I'm an old man. I don't know how much I have left in me." Vern stopped, peering around, "Wait, there's a lot more of you now."

"Yeah, there is. I'll introduce you to everyone, but I think there's someone wanting to speak with you first." Micah gestured behind them.

Eden turned with Vern to discover a man looking to be in his mid-thirties, with wavy, dark brown, shoulder-length hair, and a neatly trimmed beard. Bright hazel eyes peered out from under bushy eyebrows. He wore a white, tailored dress shirt and light brown pants ending at his knees, with tan stockings and black loafers. His dress reminded Eden of Benjamin Franklin or Thomas Jefferson. He was definitely not from this time period.

"Vern," the man said in a rich, English accent.

"Yes? Do I know you?" Vern replied.

"I suppose we have not been properly introduced in this life. My name's Charles Brown. I'm your eighth great grandfather. And I am your guardian. You are fulfilling my vision. This is what I saw so long ago."

Vern's mouth gaped open.

"This young man, Micah, is the Seer for your time. He has come to do much more than just reclaim the well. Listen to him, for he is the Captain's mouthpiece. I will be here for you, to assist in your new calling."

Vern stared at Charles and then Micah.

Micah introduced the rest of the guardians and told Vern about their spiritual gifts. He told Vern about the temple, and what the tablets contained. Eden didn't mind rehearing it all; it was so strange and new. Although, she noticed Micah didn't go into the story of the Watchers.

Vern listened until Micah stopped, and then asked, "I think I understand, but I'm not sure what work I'm supposed to do. As I said before, I'm too old to be building a city."

Micah smiled brightly. "You've got more in you than you think. The well isn't to be hidden anymore. It's to be seen by all. With your permission, on your land, we'll build the first city. For a city on a hill cannot be hid."

"From the Sermon on the Mount," Vern replied, his face thoughtful.

"Yes, of course you can build here. This land was entrusted to my family and my ancestors," Vern added, glancing at Charles, who nodded in agreement.

"It will be the Captain's city, built around the well Enoch built for Him. The well's special because it contains the waters of everlasting life," Micah explained.

"Everlasting life? Like the fountain of youth kind of stuff?" Andrew stepped closer and peered over the side at the water.

"Slow down there, tiger," Trent cut in. "Not just anyone can run up and drink it."

"Trent's right, the Captain says who does and doesn't drink this, or even touches it," Micah added, at which Andrew jumped back a step.

"Everlasting life, incredible," Vern whispered, scratching his thumbnail across his chin. "I'm happy to give my land to you. Is that the work you spoke of, Micah?"

"It's part of it. The Captain needs an architect to oversee the city's construction. You're His Architect."

"Architect? But I'm just a farmer."

"And I'm just teenager. The Captain calls who He wants and needs. Besides, you're more than just a farmer to Him."

"Micah's right, you know. I see greatness in you. You're humble and willing. The Captain couldn't ask for a better person to do this," Willow confirmed.

Caitlyn nodded her head. "Sometimes we're asked to do things that seem beyond our own abilities. And they are. We have to rely on the Captain, and then anything is possible."

Couldn't have said it better.

Vern threw his hands up and smiled. "Ok, I'll do what I can. But I really don't know the first thing about building."

"We have the blueprints. Trent will translate them for us," Micah said.

"But having the plans and knowing what to do with them are two different things," Vern clarified.

"Don't worry. Eden took care of that," Micah answered. "She gave you a gift when she hugged you."

"Really? What is it?" Vern asked.

Wish I knew. I just do the hugging.

Micah grinned at Eden and then said to Vern, "The gift of knowledge."

Comprehension dawned on Vern's face, and his lips split into a wide grin. "That will do it, yes, that will," he said happily, clasping his hands together.

"Andrew's going to give you something else to help too," Micah added.

Andrew jumped and then strode over Vern, laying his hand on the old man's arm. Vern's smile faded while he concentrated on what Andrew was doing, but when he removed his hand, the smile rapidly returned.

"Better?" Micah asked, gripping Vern's shoulder.

"Oh, hold on." There was a piercing, high-pitch sound, as Vern fished his hearing aid out of his ear and tucked it into his pocket. "Much better. Andrew, that's amazing. I can hear everything again. I can even hear the corn growing. Oh, how I've missed that sound."

Micah squeezed Vern's shoulders.

"I just have one question. Where in the world did this hill come from? All of sudden, I've got a mountain in my cornfields."

Trent slapped Damon on the back. "You've got him to thank for that."

Vern stared at Damon, who shifted under his gaze. "Now people can see the city better. Sorry if I ruined your crops."

"Incredible," Vern whispered. "The well's always been in a bowl. From the road, you couldn't tell what's hidden out here. But I guess it's time for the world to see it now."

Chapter Fifty-Five

*W*anting to soak it all in before they left, Eden found her feet slipping away from the group. The grass was soft and cool between her toes, the sun was bathing her back with its warm rays, and the gentle breeze sent the ivy on the surrounding walls dancing. It felt magical. Stooping down, she let her hand glide through the blades of grass, when something caught her eye. There was something growing. Cocking her head to one side, she was overcome with a desire to touch what appeared to be a small sapling. Just as her fingers extended, her body hurdled back, flying through the air, and landing with a thud.

"Do not touch it, Eden!" Gabriel's voice roared with such authority it scared her. Gasping for air, she grappled with what just happened. She gaped at Gabriel standing over her, sword drawn, spitting flames.

Where's the danger? She searched Gabriel's stone-hard face, trying to understand. He didn't flinch, only held his sword like he was ready to strike. *Wait, he thinks I'm the threat!* She scrambled to her feet as someone pulled her up from behind.

"Are you ok?" Micah held onto her arm, looking her over.

"Yeah, I'm fine." She glanced back at Gabriel. "What did I do?"

Gabriel's face softened, but his stance remained rigid as he hovered over the small tree. "Eden, I can't permit you to touch this tree. For this tree, no mortal's permitted to touch until the great judgment, when He shall take vengeance on all and bring everything to its consummation forever. It shall then be given to the righteous and holy to eat."

"Just like it says in the Book of Enoch. How interesting," Micah commented next to Eden.

How interesting? Eden gaped at Micah. *Gabriel's talking crazy and I'm shaking head to toe!*

What frightened her even more was how powerful a being Gabriel truly was. She had grown accustomed to their easy relationship; she sort of forgot who he really was.

With wobbly legs, she shuffled away.

"Eden, wait," Gabriel called.

She hesitated and then peeked over her shoulder. Gabriel lowered both of his arms and a line of Cherubim immediately surrounded him, their flaming swords drawn and ready. Without a word, the angels encircled the sapling. Gabriel examined them and then sheathed his sword. His eyes met Eden's as he walked towards her.

"Eden, I'm sorry. I know that seemed a bit rough, but I had to keep you from touching this tree," he explained once he was close.

She nodded, staring at her toes. Somewhere in her mind, she wondered where she'd tossed her shoes earlier.

Micah touched her arm. "You need to understand… this is Gabriel's first command from the Captain. He's to protect the Tree of Life."

"I know. I read it in the Bible," she whispered.

Micah's eyes widened. "That little tree's the same tree that was in the Garden of Eden. It'll grow and the Cherubim will stand guard, protecting it until the day the Captain returns."

She supposed that should make it all fine, but for some reason, she couldn't tear her eyes from the ground. In her peripheral, she saw Gabriel shift his weight between his feet, his hands balled up at his sides.

Trent called out, "What happened?"

It didn't take long for everyone to gather around. Micah told them. She was embarrassed more than anything else. With the Cherubim glaring them down, eventually they all backed away, leaving only Gabriel and her left. Perhaps Micah sensed she needed a minute alone with her guardian.

"You understand, right?" Gabriel asked. His tone sounded worried.

"I wouldn't have tried to touch it if I'd known."

Gabriel exhaled. "It's my fault. I should've been looking for it. I wasn't expecting the tree to appear so quickly. You had no way of knowing what you were doing." He paused and then his tone became lighter. "Just because I'm an angel doesn't mean I'm perfect. We mess up too sometimes."

She peeked over at him. There was small smile on his lips.

"Sometimes?" she teased.

He grunted.

"I'm fine, really. You just scared me a little."

"You aren't afraid of me now?" He cocked an eyebrow at her.

"Should I be?"

"Maybe, but I don't want you to be."

Why I ever deserved him as my guardian, I'll never know. She threw her arms around him before she could second-guess herself. He stiffened, and then slowly, she felt his warm arms wrap around her.

Chapter Fifty-Six

The drive back home was very different from the one out. Eden glanced back to see almost everyone was asleep now as they drove. Trent had climbed into the back and passed out hours ago. If he wasn't snoring, he was muttering under his breath. *Probably the first real sleep he's had in weeks.*

Andrew, next to him in the back, would periodically shove Trent over when he toppled in his direction.

Willow had insisted on Damon sitting next to her on the middle seat. Eden peeked over her shoulder. Damon stared at the window, with Willow curled up next to him. *Ironic that Damon's unnerved by Willow, considering how powerful he is. But I doubt he's ever had a girlfriend as gorgeous as she is. Maybe if Willow were a tree, he'd be more comfortable.* Eden grinned and turned back around, happy to be riding alongside Micah in the front. She ached to hold his hand, but with bucket seats, it'd be too visible for Andrew.

She glanced at Micah. *Now I know why he seemed so old when he got back from Rome. After these past few days, I don't feel sixteen anymore.*

Micah peeked over at her.

"Just checking for gray hair," she admitted.

"Huh?"

"Remember in that movie the Ten Commandments, when Moses comes down from the mountain and suddenly has gray hair?"

Micah slowly nodded, staring at her.

"I just had to make sure we're still teenagers."

Micah chuckled.

"It's going to be weird being home and going our separate ways. I feel so connected to everyone now," she said quietly.

He nodded.

"I overhead you telling Vern you're coming back soon."

"Yeah, I'm going to talk to my parents. See if I can fly back Thursday." Before leaving Vern's home, Micah had encouraged everyone to go home and tell their parents everything. She was still mulling over how to begin *that* conversation.

"I'm hoping my parents will come too. We'll stay the weekend so Trent can have some time translating and Damon can start clearing the land. He's better than any backhoe, that's for sure," Micah added, with a glance into the rearview mirror. Damon was asleep.

"Yeah, he is," she agreed. "So, you get a break for the next few days then?"

Micah snorted. "Sort of, I've been told by Trent I'm not to bother him until we leave. I think he needs a little down time."

"I've been hearing his plans from the back. Sounds like they all involve Jessie. Hope she's ready for him." She grinned at Micah. "How about you? Do you get a little *down time* too?"

"I sure hope so. I think I need it as bad as Trent right now."

The visions were coming rapidly now. After a long night of dreams, Micah was anxious to talk to Trent, but he'd gone out shortly after they'd arrived home. And if Micah knew Trent, he'd been out late. He decided it was best to let his cousin sleep. Eden came over around ten o'clock and he was glad for the distraction. When Trent did emerge around noon, he was already dressed to go out.

He saw Eden sitting on the couch next to Micah. Giving them both a salute, he said, "Off to fill my canteen a little more. It's going to be another long weekend, you know."

Micah laughed at him, completely understanding his need. He felt desperate to enjoy every minute with Eden. They started in the pool, but after seeing Eden in her swimming suit, he decided she needed to have more clothing on. Even on the couch, they couldn't stop kissing each other once Micah's parents went out shopping for a few hours. Eventually, they ended up on the porch swing, Eden leaning her head against his shoulder as they gently swayed back and forth.

It was almost dusk, and the sun was finally leaving, giving them some relief from the humid heat. Micah was glad for the mosquito-repelling candles his mom had placed all over the porch, knowing they'd be eaten alive without them.

As the fuzzy light faded, and the crickets began to chirp, Eden asked, "So, did you mean it?"

"Mm...?"

"Those three words you said—did you mean them?"

Micah knew exactly what she was referring to, but teased, "Now that's not fair, because as I recall, you didn't say them back."

Her head popped up. "Well, as I recall, I'm the one who said them first. And you didn't say it back then either."

"That's because you were too busy running away then." Seeing her anxious eyes peering back at him, he said, "Yes, Eden. I meant it. I love you."

He pressed his lips on hers, each kiss feeling like the first kiss all over again. Each time left him wanting more. When he stopped, she leaned her head against his chest.

"I'll miss you while you're gone. Promise you'll be safe. No more fighting demons, right?"

Micah kissed the top of her head, mumbling into her hair, "I'll be fine. We just have to get things going and I'll be back. We'll be going to Vern's a lot, but you don't have to worry about those trips."

As soon as he said it, he wished he hadn't. Her head came up. "What trips do I need to be worried about then?"

"None, sorry, that came out wrong."

"Micah, you're a terrible liar."

He sighed. "I'm seeing things and I'm not sure what it all means yet. I promise I'll tell you once I know. Ok?"

"That answer again?"

He smiled at her. "Guess I sound like a broken record. Sorry your boyfriend's half crazy."

She grinned back at him. "I like the sound of that." When he laughed, she added, "Boyfriend... not you being crazy."

"Sure." He chuckled.

She swatted his shoulder and he pinned her arms. *Her smell's driving me crazy.* He kissed her again, loving how soft and warm her lips felt.

She pulled back, her eyes troubled. "Have you seen more about that angel, Semjaza?"

He grunted. *Guess she catches on fast.* "A little."

She stiffened.

"Don't worry about it. Gabriel will pull down half of heaven to protect you. You know that right? And I'm not done with what I need to do." He paused, kissed her again, and said, "Let's not let fallen angels, or demons, ruin this moment."

She sighed. "Ok."

Pushing his feet against the ground, Micah kept the swing rocking gently. He was running his hand through her hair, when he began to see the dry, brown landscape again. It was somewhere he had never been before. There were no trees, just brown land as far as the eye could see. The desert plants were sparse as he walked amongst the sagebrush and tumbleweeds. Just ahead, he could see a large rock formation. There were other lone rocks dispersed around, but this one called to him; he found his feet plodding closer.

He was nearly to the rock, feeling a surge of adrenaline, when Eden's voice cut through the scenery, causing it to disappear.

"Micah?"

He pulled himself back to be present. It was a strange sensation, almost like waking from a too-vivid dream. "Yeah?" he replied, blinking, trying to regain full consciousness.

She wrapped her arms around his neck, pulling his lips to hers. All lingering thoughts of the desert were gone now. He kissed her back, enjoying how silky her skin felt, when she stopped and whispered, "I love you too."

He loved the way those words made him feel. They spent another hour talking and kissing and, though he didn't want the moment to end, he knew he needed to get Eden home soon. He needed uninterrupted time; the visions were begging for his undivided attention. Reluctantly, he drove her home, walked her in, chatted a few minutes with her family, and then hugged her good-bye one last time.

Driving home, his mind continued its journey towards the lone rock formation. His need to get close to it was overwhelming. In his mind, Damon was next to him now. He felt the strength Damon brought to him and he knew what needed to be done. Suddenly, Gabriel was marching alongside them. Panicked, Micah searched for Eden. Gabriel never left her, but he didn't see her anywhere. Good. She didn't need to be here for this, but Gabriel did.

In his vision, Micah turned toward Damon, asking, "Ready for this?"

Damon smiled. "Looking forward to it."

Sitting up in bed, Eden tried to get lost in a book, but it was useless. She tossed it aside. "Gabriel, are you still here? I guess I know you are. Why am I so nervous?"

She waited but it remained silent.

"Can you help me sleep?" she asked. This time she felt something. The sweet, peaceful, calm she'd come to recognize as Gabriel's touch.

Sighing, she laid down. "Thank you." Then, to her surprise, Gabriel was sitting next to her on the bed.

She glanced over. "There you are."

Startled, he jumped back. Eyes wide, he gasped, "You can see me?"

"Yeah," she replied, baffled.

Gabriel ran his hands through his hair, leaving the curls standing on end. She wanted to laugh at seeing him so disheveled, but then noticed his troubled expression.

"You didn't mean to appear to me?" she asked, sitting up.

"No. I didn't cross over." He stared back at Eden.

"But I can see you," she said, stating the obvious.

"I suppose the barrier's getting thin for you. You've always believed I'm there. Perhaps, your faith's allowing you to see more."

When he remained thoughtful, she asked, "Isn't that a good thing? Why do you look upset?"

Gabriel folded his arms, his feet planted shoulder-width apart. "Yeah, it's fine. Don't worry."

"Your body language isn't backing up your words, Gabriel. You look like a drill sergeant right now," she said, tugging her blanket around her.

He gazed at her and then peered down at his stance. Unraveling his arms, he sat at the foot of her bed, giving her a quick smile, "Sorry, I'm not use to you seeing me. This will change things slightly." His smile faltered, leaving his expression hard to read.

Still, she grinned. "Now you know how I feel. Does this mean I get to see you all the time now? I would love that!"

He grunted. "I don't know, but you must remember, I'm not crossing over right now. That means no one else sees me. You can't be walking around talking to me, or they'll think you have lost your mind."

She giggled loudly, at which he gave her a funny look. She'd already been talking to him like he was her imaginary friend. This didn't change anything for her, only made it so much better.

"Ok, deal." But even as she said it, she could no longer see him. "Where did you go?"

She felt the warm peace settle on her. Apparently, he was still there, just not visible again.

"Well, now that I can't see you, can you come be by me again? I sleep so much better when you're near." The peaceful feeling washed over her as she lay back down. She turned to where he would be sitting and whispered, "Good night, Gabriel."

It felt like five minutes later when someone jostled her arm, and then her shoulder. Opening her eyes, she saw Gabriel's face.

"Eden, get up."

"I'm up, aren't I?" she asked, rubbing her eyes. Sometimes it was hard for her to tell if she was still dreaming or not.

"I think so. Why don't you sit up and see."

Reluctantly, she obeyed. Stretching her arms above her head, she asked, "What time is it? Why are you waking me?"

"Micah's leaving in a few minutes. I thought you might like to say good-bye to him again. I know you had a hard time going to sleep."

Eden stared at him. "Thank you, Gabriel," she said, throwing her covers aside. Gathering her clothes, she faced him. "Am I seeing you on my own, or are you here? You know, on this side of the barrier?" She hoped he'd understand. *It's one thing to dress when he's invisible, but now?*

"Unfortunately, you're seeing me. This is going to get interesting. I'll leave the room and wait for you in the hall."

She got ready quickly. Pulling her door open, she was happy to see he was still there waiting. It felt strange to have Gabriel right behind her as she jogged down the stairs. *Does he always walk? I thought he flew.*

Coming into the kitchen, she found her mom loading the dishwasher. Being eight o'clock, her dad had already left for work and Brendon was still sleeping.

"Good morning, hon. Have fun with Micah last night?"

"Yeah, do you mind if I go over and say good-bye? I think he's leaving in a half an hour," she asked, while trying not to gawk at Gabriel standing between them. It was sort of distracting. Her mom had no idea an angel was standing right next to her.

"Sure. When you get back, you'll have to tell me all about your trip. I've hardly seen you these past few days. You and Micah are inseparable now." Her mom's smile spoke volumes. Eden knew both of her parents had been happy when she'd told them she was dating Micah now.

"Ok, I will," she replied as she hurried out the front door.

Once on the porch, she turned to Gabriel. "I want to walk over."

He shrugged. The air felt wonderful on her skin and, taking deep breaths in, she felt like her body was finally waking up. Having Gabriel beside her, seeing his large, threatening frame, made her feel safe.

"I like this," she said, glancing over at him. "Do you usually walk with me?"

He raised an eyebrow. "What?"

"Well, I guess I thought you floated or something."

He smiled. "I sort of do both. It's different when I'm on my side of the barrier. I thought it'd feel more natural for you if I walk though, since you can see me."

She nodded, amazed she was conversing with him so freely. A subtle breeze sent the leaves bouncing on the trees. Eden instinctively hugged herself.

"Don't worry; it's safe. I don't sense anything."

She nodded and then gasped. "Oh no, does this mean I'll see demons more often too, since the barrier is thin for me?" She didn't like *that* idea.

"No, I don't think so. I'm the only one you're seeing, right?"

"Yes, but who else would I've seen?"

"Your mom's guardian was in the kitchen. Did you see her?"

"No." Curious, she asked, "Who is she?"

Gabriel shook his head. "Not sure if I should tell you or not. I don't know how it could be harmful." He seemed to be talking more to himself. "But let me see what the Captain's instructions are regarding this first."

This new world was fascinating to Eden. She had thousands of questions she wanted to ask him, but they were approaching Micah's house now. Seeing the Excursion parked in the driveway, she quickened her pace. They would be leaving soon.

When Micah opened the front door for her, she wondered if he would see Gabriel too. But peering around, she could no longer see Gabriel.

"Good morning, sunshine," Micah said to her.

"Good morning. Surprised I'm here?" she asked, following him in.

"No, I knew you'd come."

"Saw it in vision?" she teased.

"Yeah, I did, actually."

"Really? What else did you see?"

He grabbed her hand and squeezed it. "Lots of things. Tell you all about it when I get back."

They were entering the kitchen now, where his mom and dad were talking quietly. Seeing Eden, Micah's mom said, "Hi Eden. Glad you came over."

"Wanted to tell Micah good-bye," she replied, feeling silly for some reason.

"Eden-Eden-bo-beeden!" Trent hollered, entering the room. "Are you coming with us?"

"I wish, but no." She turned to Micah, "Tell Grandpa Vern hello for me, ok?"

"I will," Micah said with a wink. She smiled and then caught Micah's mom staring at them. She wondered what Micah's parents thought of all this.

Lacey turned to Micah's dad, saying, "Jared, you better get your stuff loaded up. Don't want to miss your flight."

Doesn't sound like his mom's going, Eden thought.

As the group filed to the front entry, Eden hung back to walk next to Micah.

"So, what do they think?" she asked quietly, nodding her head toward his parents.

He sighed. "They're taking it surprisingly well. . . It's a lot to swallow, you know."

Eden nodded when Micah glanced over. "You're going to tell your mom and dad too right?" he asked.

Cringing, she replied, "Yeah," as the doorbell rang. It was Damon.

He was greeted by everyone as they exited the house, carrying their bags. Watching Trent hand the luggage to Jared, she mulled over Micah's question. She was dreading sitting down with her parents and rolling out with, 'Hey Mom, Dad, I'm the Awakener. Yeah, I know that sounds funny, but I see angels and demons, and give people spiritual gifts by touching them.' *That sounds so ridiculous; they'll never believe me!*

She jumped when someone touched her arm, breaking her reverie. Thinking it'd be Micah, she was surprised to gaze into Damon's chocolate-brown eyes.

"I never got to tell you thank you," he said so quietly, she had to strain to hear.

"Thank me? For what?" she whispered back, for some reason.

"For my gift," Damon replied. He climbed into the Excursion before she could think of a response. *That was unexpected.*

Peering around, Eden saw Micah's dad hugging his mom, and she realized they were about to leave. But where did Micah go?

"Trent, where's Micah?"

"In the house, powdering his nose," Trent replied as he climbed into the Excursion.

Eden quickly reentered the house, where she found Micah jogging down the stairs. She smiled up at him. He reached the bottom step and closed the gap between them, pulling her into his arms.

"Man, I'm going to miss you," he said between quick kisses.

"Don't worry. I'll be here when you get back."

"I know." He smiled and then his expression changed, turning intense.

"Micah, what is it?"

"Will you stand by my side for what comes next?"

Eden felt a rush of nerves, not sure what he meant. "Of course. I don't want to be anywhere else than by your side."

A look of relief shot across his face, leaving him looking suddenly very young and boyish. It was as if the mantle he had been carrying, had been lifted, leaving him vulnerable.

"Good. I need you, Eden," he said softly.

She melted into his arms as he hugged her tightly. "I need you too," she whispered back.

"See you in a few days," he said, slowly letting her go. *Are his eyes wet?*

"Ok. Be safe," she called, as they crossed the porch. She hugged herself as he jogged away, climbing into the Excursion. Micah's mom waved good-bye to Eden and then got in the driver's seat. She was going to drive them to the airport. As the Excursion rolled away, Micah waved from the window, and then with a right turn at the end of the driveway, they were gone, swallowed up in the trees.

Already feeling a lonely void, Eden strolled back home.

"He's coming back, Eden, and in one piece."

She gasped and turned to see Gabriel smiling back at her. She grinned, "Thanks. I think I could get use to this."

"What?"

"Walking, talking, together. It's so much better—don't you think?"

Gabriel grunted.

"Come on, you have to admit it's nice. I'm sure you're so tired of just listening to me all the time."

Gabriel glanced at her, giving her a crooked smile. "It wasn't that bad before."

"I guess it was probably easier for you when I couldn't see you. You didn't have to talk back. You could just ignore me and my ramblings," she said, wondering how he could stand being by her all the time. *Maybe I drive him crazy...*

Gabriel laughed. "I love your ramblings, Eden. Ramble away."

She halted and stared at him. "Really? I don't bore you to death?"

"You're refreshing to guard."

"Refreshing? That might be a stretch, Gabriel."

He chuckled louder this time, and then reached over and tousled the hair on the top of her head.

"Let's get you home. I'm under strict orders to keep you safe."

"Orders from Micah?" She kicked a pebble flying across the road.

"No." His hand rested on the sheath of his Flaming Sword. "From the Captain."

Acknowledgements

I wish I could personally thank and acknowledge all the friends and family who helped make this possible with their encouraging words and advice!

A thank you to my good friend Gail, who showed me that even a mom of three, small children, could find time to write a book. She awoke a sleeping giant in me, reminding me of my childhood passion. Thank you friend!

To my parents for loving me and believing in my story! Dad, you taught me faith and hard work; Mom you taught me hope and perseverance. I love you both!

A thank you to my husband, Josh. Without you, this story wouldn't be what it is! I love our 'hashing' times where I can pick your brain and find strokes of genius! I consider you my best friend, my writing partner, and the love of my life!

Wattpad friends, you know who you are! I couldn't have done this without you! Your enthusiasm for my writing gave me new life at a time when I wanted to give up.

Lastly, and most importantly to me; I thank my God and my 'Captain'. Thank you for every miracle in my life!

About the Author

Born in Dekalb, Illinois, Amanda Strong has called Utah, Arizona, Hawaii, Virginia and now New Mexico home. Amanda has been spinning tales since she was a child. Her family still remembers finding young Amanda with her bright pink glasses, hiding in random corners of the house while scribbling away in one of her many spiral-bound notebooks. You could say that some things never change since Amanda is still writing today. Amanda began her writing career when she uploaded The Awakener, her first full-length novel, on Wattpad where it received over 430,000 reads in four weeks. She was blown away and humbled by the reader support and feedback she received. Because of The Awakener's success as a non-published book, she was asked to talk on 1400 KSTAR about her story.

In September 2013 Amanda Strong signed with Clean Teen Publishing for publication of The Awakener. The Awakener is the first book in an all-new young adult paranormal romance series called: The Watchers of Men.

When Amanda isn't writing, you can find her chasing her three rambunctious children around the house and spending time with her wonderful and supportive husband. On some occasions you can still find Amanda with her not-so-pink glasses, hiding in a corner reading her favorite young adult fantasy novels or working out only to blow her diet by eating ice cream.

Clean Teen Publishing